Dr. Excitement's Elixir of Longevity

by
WILLIAM RYAN

Dr. Excitement's Elixir of Longevity

DONALD I. FINE, INC.
New York

Copyright © 1986 by William Ryan
All rights reserved, including the right of reproduction in whole or in part in any form. Published in the United States of America by Donald I. Fine, Inc. and in Canada by General Publishing Company Limited.

Library of Congress Catalogue Card Number: 86-81475
ISBN: 0-917657-99-3
Manufactured in the United States of America
10 9 8 7 6 5 4 3 2 1

This book is printed on acid free paper. The paper in this book meets the guidelines for permanence and durability of the Committee on
Production Guidelines for Book Longevity of the Council on Library Resources.

For Alan Hodgkinson

"Lieutenant!
This corpse will not stop burning!"
-Galway Kinnell
The Book of Nightmares

"To break the rules is to break the spell."
-Christopher Lasch
The Culture of Narcissism

Credit is given
to John Richards and Mike Beamon with respect
for pieces of their lives and thoughts
and thanks to Annie
for her love and support

1

I REMEMBER THE DOTS OF THE DIGITAL CLOCK SCRAMBLING and forming into 6:00 as though one moment is followed by another—I remember the first bird. So this is where I begin—one thrush singing nervously in Paterson, the arrogant dots of the clock.

I knew the alarm would hum her awake at 6:30.

It had been a long night—a dull ringing in hollows of the dark house, distant sirens and occasional cars hissing on the wet street—a hushed background for the busy noise of my brain.

The shivering that had entered me at 4:00 was getting confused with a scary tittering as the darkness began to leave by the window. Mr. Excitement was on the edge.

It still seemed odd to me that a person could sleep as soundly as she did.

My eyes were stinging—wide and dilated. They hung heavily above the dull radiance of her slender body.

It was hot—oppressively humid—yet she slept, the sheet clinging to her moist skin, the last moonlight clustered in droplets in the down above her lips, the heated coils of inner-city Jersey steaming relentlessly.

When I heard the bird, its song thin and tentative in the early dawn, I turned my eyes from the woman's face to the window where the morning moon shone, the image of her face still lingering, burning in my unblinking eyes, illuminated and pale in the gray dawning out of blackness.

I could hear my brain advancing in measured bleeps, a computer calculating sidereal time, amplifying the repetitive anxious music composed from the mathematics of tracking the movements of stars. It was marking seconds on the way to nothing, dispatched toward nothing, a plodding rhythm synchronized with a slapdashing of sharp fragments in the skull. Shrapnel of thoughts I couldn't contain were loose in the precision workings.

The mechanization, the computer analogy repulses me now, yet then it was almost poetic as the numbers of the clock dissolved and reformed and the galaxy moiled in pandemonium. But I turn over these details now because they do repulse me, as I begin stalking through the jungle toward the burning corpse.

I remember seeing the seven of the 6:17 rearrange into an eight as I peered from behind my static eyes, holed up inside my motionless body, breathing with her breathing, confusing past and present in my faulty electronics, repeating every thought over and over until my lips and tongue worked silently to exorcise the echolalia.

Mr. Excitement wasn't in the habit of giving a fuck about very much, but that morning he was worrying, laboring at tracking the fragments of possible explanations, though he didn't want anything to do with explanations. He was worrying about such things as daylight—about the way it approached under the predominance of the green numbers. He was anticipating an appearance in a well-lit courtroom, wasted on a year of opium, fucked-up in the brain, imagining everything that could go wrong when prodded from his dark jungle into the light.

I had too much to hide and way too many lies to cover. I was confusing my crimes with the crimes of the world.

I never prepared a defense—I just worried, opiated and confused. A lawyer had appeared as if by magic to prepare the defense. I only spoke to him once. His buddy was wired for sound beneath the inconspicuous clothing of the CIA. I told them everything I knew about why I had assault charges against me: I beat the snot out of four assholes is what I told them. Self-defense.

They told me not to worry. I had the sense remaining to know the outcome of the hearing would be taken care of, but the thought of appearing there in the courtroom, in the daylight and owning up to . . . To what? True identity, at least. Blown cover, for sure. That had me worried. It was like a toothache that came back after the anesthetic wore off.

I didn't want to think about any of it—recent or long past. I didn't want to explain anything. Too much opium. A bad attitude. A bad toothache climbing out of the numbness throb by throb. It was a dilemma just thinking about being who my birth certificate says I am, and the thought of coming up with explanations . . . The whole deal is fucked, thought Mr. Excitement, and perhaps it's time to disappear again. It was too hot. I was a hair trigger away—a naked man discovered in the ancient jungle hills.

Outwardly, though, except for the shivering, except for the tittering, I was cool and controlled—a professional, breathing with her breathing, bone dry in the close heat.

The clock read 6:20. I held the bottle of George Dickel up to the window. It was half full. I knew from the full moon that I'd broken the seal a month earlier. I'd kept this woman in my steamy B movie for a long time, while I lived on thin air and profane berries, secure in the upper canopy of the opium forest, where explanations were not only impossible but unnecessary. Mr. Excitement was not one for reflection. Reflecting was a quality of shiny objects and some other kind of beast. My kind of beast did not reflect. I was dark and dull and avoided light, applying what I'd carried like a host organism back from the U Minh, the Forest of Darkness.

What the hell, I was an honor student. A professional. That's what I was thinking then, the digital numbers green and crisp in the graying dawn, the annoying music repeating in my brain. An honor student, I thought, smiling wearily, watching the dots form 6:25. I was programmed for it—that's what I mouthed silently to her as I shivered in the heat.

What can I say? What can they expect of me in this heat? What B-movie hero ever explained his tricks or answered for his behavior? Mr.

Excitement was full of questions. He was damned if he did care and damned if he didn't. The dots formed 6:26.

She was a great-looking woman. Lived alone. Senior secretary for a law firm. Her skin was ivory by moonlight—the only light I'd ever seen her in. Her face would waver, then lose its individuality as I stared, eventually becoming a round luminescent form rising and falling with a tidal motion. I can still smell it—the scent of her bedroom. Her scent. The heat containing it and infusing the air with the fragrance.

My own scent had a nervous, hot electric smell that morning, and the cask of the dark, which mellowed me, was leaving again as the whiskey tried to fine-tune the opium to a steady even modulation.

I stood and drew the blinds closed, returning them to the way they were when I'd arrived. I returned the Dickel to the cabinet in the kitchen, urinated a small puddle into my cupped hand, poured it in a fine line across the kitchen floor by the back door and was about to leave when the door opened and a man entered and switched on the light over the kitchen counter.

He saw me at once and was startled. I couldn't quite believe I'd been caught. I felt indignant at first, imposed upon. Now I would even have to speak. How would I communicate with this man? The traffic sounds encroached: car horns, sirens, the drone of internal combustion—then the name on my birth certificate—intrusions in my wilderness. My stance widened and my nape bristled. I glanced quickly behind me.

The man braced himself against the kitchen counter.

"What are you doing in my house?" I asked.

His eyes darted around the kitchen in the dawn light. Still startled, he was about to apologize when he realized he was in the right house.

"I'm just kidding," I said, "but be quiet—she's sleeping."

"Who are you?" He stuttered slightly, reaching for the door to close it.

"Friend of Ellen," I whispered. "I was just leaving. Who are you?"

"I'm Ellen's brother."

"Sh-sh-sh," I hushed him with my finger to my lips. "She's told me a lot about you. I have to get going."

"Why don't you wait here a minute?" he said, stepping in front of the door. He called into the dusky rooms. "Ellen. Ellen, it's me, Donald. Are you awake?"

"Donald," I said, "I really have to be going now."

He called again, staying between me and the door. I took a step toward him, prepared to go through him to the door, but I stopped. We stood there silently for a moment, then he called again, louder this time, violating once again the sanctity of the dawn.

I heard her behind me and turned to face her. She was like an image walking out of a film or a dream—animated, almost real. I wanted to watch her move and hear her speak.

"What's going on?" she said in the hoarse voice of a deep sleeper. "Donald," she said, approaching him and kissing him on the cheek. "What's going on? I wasn't expecting you guys till tomorrow."

"He's not with me," Donald said.

"What are you talking about?" She rubbed her eyes.

"He says he's a friend of yours. He was in the house when I got here. I've never seen him before in my life."

She looked at me, her mouth dropping open. I smiled, nodded—always the gentleman.

"In this house?" She looked back at Donald.

"He was standing right there when I opened the door!" Donald said.

She pulled her robe tighter—the green robe that hung on the back of the bedroom door. She looked back and forth from Donald to me, growing uneasier by the second. Expressions I'd never seen on her kept reaching into her face. "How did he get in?" she said, now turning to me, staying calm, the voice I'd never heard, frail and fluttering. "What are you doing here?"

"I don't know what I'm doing here," I said, "or I'm not at liberty to discuss it—one or the other." I knew immediately that I shouldn't have said it. I knew I shouldn't say anything. "I should leave now," I said.

"Are you a burglar or what?" Her voice had that urban tough edge to it—a kind of challenge unstated in every sentence—a voice that had grown up in Paterson. She was holding tightly to her composure.

Donald was stiff as a board in front of the door.

"No," I said, "I'm not a burglar. It's just a hobby of mine. Don't be alarmed. I didn't come to hurt you or steal. I was passing by, that's all. No problem. I'm sorry. I like you and I wouldn't hurt you. You wouldn't understand. I won't be back. This is not as bad as you're imagining. I'm not as crazy as I seem." I wanted her to understand. "I bet you won't even miss me," I said, smiling, but it was no time for the charm. "What you don't know won't hurt you."

"What the hell is going on here!" The pitch of her voice was climbing, tightening, just when I was trusting her toughness to bear us through.

She looked to Donald for some explanation, her face filling with what was coming from me. I slowed my heart, altered the broadcast signal, breathed deeply.

"Are you some kind of lunatic?" Donald said to me.

"How many times have you been here before?" Ellen asked.

"You'd better have some explanations," Donald said.

With the heart slowed, the shoulders and eyebrows dropped and relaxed, the *chi* energy flowed. Fists tightened—I loosened them. I reached for a blank, an absence aloof and beyond us there as we stood uneasily on the linoleum.

"I've been here several times," I said. "I don't count." I wanted to explain. "Maybe we could have some tea."

Donald's face contorted slightly in a look of anguish. "What do you mean by several? How many?"

It seemed like a ridiculous question. "Maybe thirty or forty. Does that make you feel better? Can we have some tea and talk this over. Maybe a cookie. I'll try to explain." What was I going to explain? "I don't mean to be rude." I felt a small spasm like I was going to cry like a child.

"Rude!" Her fists rose then jerked downward. "Rude! What in the holy goddamned . . . While I'm at work?"

"Only once while you were at work. The rest of the times while you were sleeping."

"Oh my God! Jesus God!" She walked a few steps, returned to her place by the refrigerator, dropped her eyebrows and peered at me. "I can't believe this! I can't . . ."

"Take it easy, Ellen. It's not gonna happen again," Donald said. His shoulders were hunching from tension and his stance widened. I could smell the aggression mustering in him.

I didn't like where the aggression was leading us. I could feel Ellen's heart throbbing painfully fast in my brain. They both looked at me, not knowing what to do next.

"Well, thanks for having me," I said. "I'll be going now. Sleep well. And don't worry—I won't be back. I promise." I took a step toward the door, toward Donald.

"You're not going anywhere until the police get here," Donald said.

He took my arm and pulled me toward the table. Handing the phone to Ellen, he said, "Call the police emergency number," his voice an octave too high from fear.

"It would be best if I just left," I said, trying to sound reasonable and convincing in the midst of what had become utterly absurd to me. "I've really got to be going. Ordinarily I'd love to stay for the police, but I really can't this morning." I spoke sternly then, as a warning, allowing the man to tighten his grip on my arm. "It would be best to let me go and pretend I was never here, because you don't know how to deal with me, believe me, Donald." My eyes widened to allow more light—shoulders set, center of gravity located, a coiling mechanism cranking tighter.

I think it was because he didn't know what else to do. It was a difficult situation for him. He was a big fellow. Big brother. He swung at me, trying to hit me on the chin, trying to protect his sister. I went for his solar plexus. He went down like a sack of beans, unable to get air into his lungs. Ellen shuddered and backed against the refrigerator.

I tugged my gloves on, opened the door. Donald was grunting loudly for air. As I nodded to her I saw my face the way it must have looked to her—expressionless, reptilian, without a clue. I closed the door softly behind me.

I waited in the shadows for the cops to come. I couldn't help myself.

I crept to the window and listened to Donald's description of me. When he told the cops I stood about six-two, I called through the window screen, "Five-eight and a half," and disappeared. I could never have passed for a Vietnamese at six-two.

Sunrise chasing me again. Slightest hint of breeze on my sweaty forehead. A ration of adrenalin coursing the veins. I was more cautious than I had to be as I headed for downtown Paterson to become invisible in the morning bustle. Two cruisers were dispatched to the neighborhood. I took over an hour to travel a distance I could have covered in ten minutes. I knew where both cruisers were before I moved a muscle. A small pocket mirror was all I needed. I'd rigged it to the extendable stem of a portable radio antenna. It was a handy tool for observing the world from behind corners. At times I waited when I could have gone, allowing the cops to widen their circle by a few blocks to contain me within their perimeter so I could play the game of escape again. I liked cops for their diligence. Great competitors.

As the sun edged up to first-story level, still unseen behind the haze, I entered the fringe of downtown through a Puerto Rican neighborhood. Cars were stacking up at the red lights, people gathering at bus-stops. I paused before crossing the Wayne Ave bridge to gaze down at the Passaic River flowing beneath me. It was there, under the bridge, that the river seemed to hesitate in clusters of small eddies, anticipating the Great Falls.

Forget it, I thought. Fuck it, I urged myself. No explanations necessary. Dismiss it. I'm not at liberty to discuss it. Isn't that the stock response? Staring into the eddies, the falls roaring, I repeated aloud, "I'm not at liberty . . ." Then mouthing the words silently, the music repeating in my brain, "Discuss it, discuss it, discuss it . . ."

How could I care? I was too young then—stupid, agile, clever, covetous of powers—I did what I was told. It was easier that way. Having been kidnapped without explanations, or so it seems to me now, it was easier to do what I was told. And it gave me the opportunity to experiment with the powers of youth, with thresholds, human potential, cunning, with the development of extrasensory techniques through the guidance of experts. It gave me the freedom to think of abject irresponsibility as the land of the free. It was the freedom of a graceless state. No matter what was done, it was bound to be a mistake—a tragedy. It took many mistakes to cover up the original. I was good at it. An honor student.

I walked down to a small green where the Passaic took an abrupt turn and fell a few hundred feet into a swill of tires, boards, soapsuds, cardboard, plastic bottles and foaming brown vortices of itself, all sucking down and eastward to dump in the Atlantic at Newark Bay.

Standing in the middle of the steel footbridge over the falls, I panned the Paterson cityscape of factories and smokestacks layered against the populated hills behind. Two hundred years of industrial strata had grown out from the source at the fall of the river, where the water then continued eastward, hemorrhaging poisons into its mouth.

After a heavy rain a brutish din would rise at the bend where the river fell, and the dogs in surrounding neighborhoods would howl through the night. Those nights were special, giving me the cover to move even more silently in the dark, distracting the ears and noses of dogs from my passage.

The mugginess increased as the sun came full into the sky behind the haze. I could see the courthouse through the veil of smog; a sickly yellow light bathed the east roof. I ached to be inside my house, as I usually was by the time the day's brightness began. Out in the sun the mechanical forced march of the brain was confusing past and present, four men with four ghosts.

Honor student, I repeated. I had it down to a science. I didn't know who they were—the faces, the ghosts. I didn't care who they were. Why care now? They were just photos in a dossier. I couldn't care. I was an honor student. Clever. Drawn to it. Made for it. Groomed for it. A romantic notion. One of the select few. The *hashshāshīn*. Eyes that could see in the dark. Footsteps that vanished into dark water. Stoned to the dead-silent core of the brain. Traveling by the dark of the moon. Emerging from the cool unconsciousness of a rice paddy, bursting from a pile of dung to snuff a single select flame from the heavens. Were we not gods with green faces, patient as stone in the shadows? This was a religious mission foretold in agatized runes and carbon-dated tablets and books of the dead—a mission to leave terror coiled where we'd been, to leave the enemy's tracks where we'd walked, to eat the heart of the enemy to become the enemy, to turn terror against terror, to turn people against themselves, to win their hearts and minds and undermine their defenses against themselves. And this jungle—it was the original jungle, and when it got dark it was original darkness. Nothing else mattered.

A stream of cars flowed down McBride Ave and up past Falls View hot dog stand, along the same route Lafayette and Washington paraded after the Revolution. I remembered reading that the frog general and Honest George were brought to view a freak during their visit to the industrial heart of the new nation—some poor fucker with a head as big as his body. Confined to a basket, he was a must-see for luminaries visiting Paterson. The same buildings that were then soon to become silk mills still stand beside the falls, shadowing the bronze icon of Alexander Hamilton that foppishly regards the tumultuous swill below. And there I went, in the wake of such history, through the jungle and down McBride Ave toward the diner.

A Puerto Rican in his low-rider glided over the Wayne Ave bridge, kicked in the four-barrel and the '55 bellowed up the hill with its pipes wide open, leaving a burst of pigeons silhouetted in the glaring heat. It was there, at the intersection of McBride and Wayne, hearing the '55 fade into the city static, that Mr. Excitement delayed his breakfast to begin writing. On the pad he carried in his pocket, which had been left blank until then, he began hacking away, turning over rocks, undoing the jungle toward the burning corpse. He remembered dropping a cement block on a box turtle when he was a kid—he wrote it all down.

For years after I crushed that turtle I'd worried that I might be killed that way in return, as though I knew such things did return, and through that initial writing I came to terms with at least one fact—during my work as an assassin-kidnapper in Nam I tried to be as painless as possible. For whatever it's worth, as pathetic as it may be, I have that much to believe.

I was clean, deft. It was better that way. I was good at the sport—a good sportsman. Blink the eyes and you missed it. I made it look easy. I think it was only the belief that I'd minimized the pain that allowed me to begin telling the tale.

Of course, the pain fell mostly on the survivors, and the pain that returned to me is the pain of a survivor. And I suppose some of them —the ghosts—had to be mistakes. Mistakes at the top. Some of everything usually is. Mistakes passed down the chain of command for me to execute at the end of that chain. That was the rumor even then. Secret deaths. Secret slant-eyed *friendly* deaths. Small deaths. Numbered deaths. Secret orders from the head secret honcho. Make it look like Charlie did it. No sweat. Mistakes were indistinguishable from missions accomplished. Mistakes were figured in. Nothing that was not another mistake.

Some of the ghosts were on both sides—canceled by their own scams, by their profiteering. And some of it was just tidying up, plugging leaks, laying bait, floating decoys, covering the asses of operatives—ritualistic sacrifices to intelligence.

These small deaths had nothing to do with the hearing and the four men I'd worked over in front of the VFW bar—only in my imagination, where it doesn't matter what is truth and what isn't. The imagination embodies a truth of its own, even in this confusion. There is truth in the confusion I brought home from the war, Mr. Excitement insists. And the ghosts? Well, I'll not be the one to tell them they are imaginary.

It wasn't until after the hearing that I first started thinking of myself as a survivor, and I think that's why this tale begins where it does—with the hours approaching the hearing. After the hearing I made a deliberate decision to go on, and I quit the opium. It was like a fall from grace and I didn't like it—somehow it seemed easier when death came toward me like a blessing . . . like a birthright.

Now, having fled from Paterson to Newark, as I try to record what I can, halting and doubting, these words seem almost sacred. It is important to make it to the end of the sentence, as though the written word might somehow protect me, keep the ghosts at bay or of the helpful sort, cast spells and build immunities, ward off the poisons and pathogens that once took hold in my throat, dig up the runic shards buried in my stomach to say it all at once with one primordial phoneme.

And this hearing—it was nothing—a comedy—not worth dredging up what I'd buried in my stomach. But that's what I did, until my stomach was gnawed from the inside out.

As I approached the diner that morning in Paterson and saw the cars in the lot and the heads lined up at the counter, I knew it was the daylight that was dangerous. I knew it was the daylight that stirred the dormant roots in my stomach until they began their heliotropic restlessness. Suppose the fat man from the poker game waddled past me? Suppose I ran into Marie, my first patient? What kind of explanation would I need then? Suppose John Oswald, the mayor of Angleton, happened to be in the courthouse on business? I wasn't prepared to deal with any of it, crashing off the opium in broad daylight, the sun violating my eyeballs. Suppose the prosecutor turned out to be a ghost? It was certainly possible, any of it.

And after getting caught at Ellen's I knew I should leave Paterson as I'd left Hollywood and Montclair and Angleton. I knew I should crawl off to assess the damage, which I feared was substantial.

I moved to Newark, where I am now. To nothing. To begin from there. With nothing.

And as I begin this tale I turn over the details, repulsing myself if I have to with what might scramble from beneath as I crawl toward the corpse that won't stop burning.

2

I REMEMBER I HAD COFFEE AND A BOWL OF BEAN SOUP. The men at the counter were combed and shaved, but they seemed tired, already sweating at the temples. Cigarette smoke rose around them and into the hood over the grill. A yellow strip studded with flies hanging over the coffee urn. Hot roast pork special on the blackboard—gravy, mashed potatoes, vegetable, soup or salad. For some reason, on the wall, prints of ink drawings of American Indians.

"Never see you here in the morning," Nate said, refilling my cup. He wiped his forehead on his greasy forearm.

"Court this morning," I said, leaving the coffee and passing through the opening in the counter into the kitchen, as I'd done many times at night to drink water from the tap.

Old Eddy had his bony arms up to the elbows in hot dishwater. Steam and ammonia rose from the silverware bucket. With a wet hand he took a felt-tip pen from his shirt pocket and wrote "A.C." in a square of the steam-curled calendar as I poured a glass of water from the tap. I drank four glasses before he spoke.

"Some son-of-a-bitch puked at the counter last night during bar rush," he said, "and when I come on it looks like goddamn Emilio went over it twice with a dry mop. Stunk like shit. The son-of-a-bitch!"

I poured another glass. A man chopping onions at the far end. A mud of odors—ammonia, onions, coffee, bean soup, bacon frying. The odor of Paterson water under my nose.

"What are you saving coffee grinds for?" I asked.

"Worm farm," Eddy grumbled.

"Where do you fish?"

"I fish all over."

"Salt water, too?"

"Any damn water. That spic ain't worth a shit. I don't know why Nate don't—"

"You don't use worms in salt water, do you?" I asked.

"I sure as hell do. I use 'em any damn where I please."

"No shit?"

"No shit, buddy."

"Bluefish'll bite on worms?"

"Blues'll eat turds," he snapped over his shoulder. "That's where the charters and commercials go, you know—where they dump the shit off Sandy Hook."

"You fish the river?" I asked, pouring another glass of water.

"What river?" He pulled the tap around to his side of the sink.

"Passaic."

"Passaic! Fuck no." He shook his head, lips tight to his teeth. "Nigger fish—that's all's in there. Nigger fish and turds." He wiped his face with the towel around his neck. "Never seen you in here in the daytime."

"Gotta go to court this morning," I said, reaching in front of him to pour the tenth glass.

"You like that Passaic River water, do you?" he said.

The Passaic is a dark river from its backwater origin in the Great Peace Meadows, a network of swamps and pools that surround long stretches of highway. The river disappears, returning to its underground nature in several places along its course, sliding under concrete and forced into canals and pipes and emerging again with the fouled blood of an earth-flesh saturated with oil and synthetics.

From Paterson it labors southward to Delawanna and Nutley and into the Newark area. Toiling under the burden of debris, it bends south again, under the General Pulaski Skyway and into Newark Bay, passing a waste dump that stores, among other poisons, dioxin, a by-product of the manufacturing of agent orange.

I paid Nate for the soup and coffee, then walked up Spruce Street and through a parking lot to an overlook. There I sat at the feet of the statue of Alexander Hamilton, near where Hamilton himself must have been when he foresaw the industrial potential in converting the energy of the falls into electricity and prophesied the great banks beating at the heart of America. A great pool of soapsuds breathed and undulated at the bottom of the Great Falls. I've always thought of the falls, the gaping expanse, the rugged walls of the gorge, as a kind of window to a world far removed from the bustling of the surrounding city. It defies the steel and concrete that covers the earth all around it. There is a wilderness in the falling of the water. The unutilized space goes unaffected by the mere death of cities.

I didn't want to remember who I was, the sun spreading behind the haze, drawing the hearing closer—I wanted to be empty of name. Tires and boards like insects trapped against the cliff below. Soapsuds heaving. To speak for the name on the birth certificate and justify his behavior would be impossible. I considered leaving immediately—stopping for some clothes and money and disappearing once again. But the fact of my revealed identity held me there—a fly banging at a window—two hours before the hearing, the brightness wearing me down. I walked to the vicinity of the courthouse, entered a darkened tavern and sat in the corner with a George Dickel.

The barkeep was still cleaning and preparing the bar for the day. Two Italian men at a table with shots and coffees, playing a game with painted wooden picture cards. Cigarette smoke curling into dim bars of light coming through a tiny window in the door. Crumpled pack of Winstons and an empty peanut bag on my table. The glass was empty in less than a minute. I got up to get another and stayed at the bar, half standing and half sitting on the stool. The heart clamoring in its cage. The brain blinking, counting, repeating. The whiskey oiling it all, the dangerous mechanics. The opium beginning to hurt as it left me there.

I remember placing my hand on the Bible like a child might touch a dead rabbit and waiting until the bailiff was through with whatever mumbo jumbo he canted before I said yes and sat down. I said the appropriate things. Seventeen deranged monkeys were spitting and pissing all over each other, running up the walls inside me, and I was cool on the outside. I played the tapes. It wasn't as difficult as it was full of discomfort. I was sick and dizzy, willfully containing the shivering. I missed a lot of the proceedings—some of it I remember well.

In the beginning the D.A. put this meathead on the stand. He was the mouthier of the four, as I remember the incident at the VFW bar. The D.A. had his witness describe the particulars of the fight. The witness's three buddies, looking comical and pathetic, sat in the first row of seats behind the D.A. One was out in the aisle in a wheelchair.

"We had words," the meathead said. He was no orator. "We got into an argument, me and three of my friends and the defendant. And the next thing you know we're throwin' hands, and the defendant there, he just picks us apart like he's eatin' barbecue ribs—kickin' and headbuttin' and doin' all this stuff with his hands."

"What kind of stuff?" the D.A. asked.

"Kind of paralyzing us. He just grabs you somewhere and you just go limp, and you can't defend yourself. Then he'd let us have it good and hard."

"Can you tell us the details?" the D.A. asked. "What exactly did he do to you and your friends?"

"Well, me, he broke this arm and tore ligaments in my right knee and hit me several times in the face and head, causing a broken nose, a hurt jawbone here in the joint, a wrenched neck, a split lip, a tooth got knocked out and bruises and cuts. I was a mess. I was like chewed up and spit out. The guy didn't know when to quit."

I remembered my elbow flattening his nose. He lost his will to fight when he started swallowing his own blood. He was lucky. I wanted the guy with the bottle.

"How about the others?" the D.A. asked.

"One guy lost an eye and got a broken jaw that still ain't right—and broken ribs that almost punctured a lung."

The fucker with the bottle.

"And another guy, Howard there, he got his knee kicked in like mine, torn ligaments there, plus cuts and bruises on the face and a fractured bone here in his face. And Paul—there's something wrong with his back now. He got some vertebrae broke, but there's something else wrong with his back, according to the doc."

An accident.

"They don't really know if he'll walk right again. And he also got a broken collarbone and a dislocated shoulder."

"Were you able to retaliate with blows of your own?" the D.A. asked.

"Not really. Not much. It all happened so fast we couldn't do much."

It was kind of funny—the big crybaby whimpering like that—but my head was aching. I stared at the witness, half smiling, dazed, still crashing off the O.

When my lawyer, a government stooge named Clarke, cross-examined the meathead, he tried to get the guy to admit to throwing the first punch, but his efforts seemed halfhearted, and nothing clear came of it.

At some point I got up from my TV chair in the hinterland and walked into the movie. The bailiff shoved the Bible at me as though it meant something. The D.A. looked uneasy. This was an unconventional move in a preliminary hearing. I think the rancid smell of the bait was reaching the D.A.'s nose.

I told them I had no time to consider what might be fair and equal response. A man was coming at me with a bottle, I said. I pulled the trigger on a series of routine attacks designed to incapacitate the aggressor. I gave back what was coming at me. The men broke easily. They were brittle, fat, stiff. They had no business fighting. I had no choice. Blah blah. When I *could* speak, I said nothing. I said what I was supposed to say. One drop would have started a flood. I acted sane under the portals of justice, speaking with only my tongue.

"My client was under attack," Clarke said. "His life was being threatened by four rather large men, all soldiers trained in hand-to-hand combat themselves at one time."

Clarke was square-shouldered, trim and poised. He looked like he was modeling the three-piece suit he wore and sounded like he'd been hand-picked for the timbre of his voice, a deep voice that filled the room with authority.

"He responded reflexively to this attack," Clarke continued, pacing his lines, "in the only way he knew how, to protect himself from harm. The State's witness said in his statement that it happened so fast that he couldn't defend himself. This testimony might help us imagine what was an automatic and reflexive response to the possibility of bodily harm. It's true my client is highly trained in hand-to-hand combat. It's true that in the course of his duty to his country in a time of war he was called on repeatedly to use this training. He *is* experienced. And it's true that these same reflexes were triggered when he was threatened by four men. Your Honor, to deprive the defendant of his right to use these skills is to deprive him of his legal right to defend himself, especially when considering he was outnumbered four to one. He was simply reacting in a way that he has been trained to react in a life-threatening situation. And that's why I'm convinced enough that this is a case of self-defense to go on record with testimony from the defendant." Clarke simplified it all for us and sat down.

"I understand that you were a Navy SEAL," the D.A. said in his cross-examination, "and I understand that the SEALs are a highly trained, specialized outfit, but I have a hard time understanding that any soldier is trained or encouraged to become a machine with no judgment, if you will—an entirely reflexive animal that doesn't maintain some composure, some degree of control over himself to apply judgment and discretion in any given situation. In fact, it's my understanding that the more highly skilled a soldier is, the more he can be expected to stay cool in the face of danger." He walked closer to me. "Would you agree that a soldier is generally trained to be a controlled fighter able to respond to varying combat situations accordingly—according to their individual distinctions and varying degrees of severity?"

"I don't know," I said. I meant it. I wanted to be honest with the guy. I wanted to encourage him. "Maybe that is *generally* true, but I don't know. I never figured out what a soldier is trained to do with distinctions and varying degrees. And my training was far beyond the general, beyond A.I.T., beyond the SEALs. I was trained individually for a specific purpose."

I knew what the next question would be before it was asked. I looked at Clarke and sensed his anticipation. I wanted to say to the D.A., let's go have a drink, and I'll try to explain.

"And what kind of training are you talking about," the D.A. asked, "that would make you see only black and white?"

Before the D.A. finished his question my boy Clarke was on his feet. I snorted a blast of air at him and shook my head. The guy was born slippery. He was on the ball. There we were—precisely at the point in the proceedings where he'd planned to be when, a month earlier, he'd made a motion in advance for a protective order, accompanied by an affidavit from the Secretary of the Navy. He put his hands in his pockets, showing a flat stomach beneath the vest of his three-piece and waited for the D.A. to finish his question—the question Clarke had been waiting for. Clarke rocked on his heels, smug, square-jawed—the slick summer suit, the D.C. address, the briefcase with three combination locks, the gold Cross pen atop a neat stack of typed notes. The D.A. was intimidated by him, I think, and was about to find out the breadth of what he was up against.

"Your Honor," Clarke said, "my client is not at liberty to discuss his training beyond the standard Advanced Infantry Training a Navy SEAL receives."

The ghosts booed. The one in flames started running in circles in the back of the courtroom.

Clarke told the magistrate it was a matter of privileged information —executive privilege or State secret or some bullshit. I'm sitting there, not at liberty to discuss my own self, my own bullshit, and it pissed me off. When I *couldn't* speak, I wanted to tell all. I had that opium crash edge and the headache that goes with it. I concentrated to stop the shivering—I fought to maintain my professional cool, fighting an urge to blow the cool in a spray of tears and spit of anger or even deteriorate into childish blubbering.

"I dispatched people, sir," I said under my breath.

Clarke shot a look at me.

The ghosts cheered, but I clamped my mouth shut.

"I sent them off to their ancestors," I said to myself. I thought it through for a moment, as well as I could with the anxious music repeating in my brain, and I wanted to stand up and calmly plead guilty. "Just as the spirit was leaving them," I wanted to say, "just as the spirit was ready for its reunion with the ancestors, I removed the liver from the corpse—just following orders, sir—and the spirit spun around and returned to earth like a kite in a downdraft. The party was over for that spirit—no liver, no reunion. It squatted there on its haunches, looking at me, a ghost with nowhere to go. I can produce one or more of these ghosts for the court—the one with no face or the one on fire or the one holding his intestines or the one in two parts. I'll just need a little time, some darkness, my glass pipe. . . . But these ghosts are confused, sir— I should warn you, Your Honor. As men, they were working for us, and they knew, as it was happening, that it was no VC who dispatched them. They looked into your eyes and they knew."

Clarke had asked me a question that I hadn't heard. They were all waiting for my reply. I started pumping spurts of adrenalin like an IV drip of meth. I chewed my mouth and tongue. My eyes were stinging and my brain was worn out from repetition and my mouth was dry from dealing silently with the brain's nonsense. I wanted to get up and leave, go home and sleep it off. "Who cares?" I said under my breath. "Fuck it."

"What did you say?" the magistrate asked.

I clamped my mouth shut and looked at him. With my eyes I tried to say, "I kidnapped people, sir. I brought them back to S-2s and other Intell creeps. I took great care to not damage the goods. I had long conversations with them in broken Vietnamese, broken English, broken French. I helped them with tenses, which they found confusing. I turned them over to the creeps and the creeps kicked them out of choppers to make their buddies talk, and their buddies were eventually kicked out too, whether or not they talked. And when I wasn't in the jungle I drank and kicked ass. I kicked the snot out of officers and Marines. I stole whiskey from officers and I didn't give a shit if they knew it or not. I did what I wanted. I'd earned that much. And nobody said shit about it. How could they bench their star quarterback? Who else could connect on the long one? Who would travel by night in the jungle? Who could convince the villagers that the VC had just offed Mr. Tran? And slowly, Your Honor, by the end of my second tour, as I learned more of the language, as I spent more time in the jungle, as I spent more hours crouched in the tree line watching hamlet life, I started thinking in Vietnamese. And I won't say what happened then. I'm not at liberty to discuss it any further."

Clarke put his hand on my shoulder. He looked at me menacingly as the D.A. stood and walked toward the bench hurriedly.

I wanted to jump up and grab Clarke by the balls and drag him around the room, growling and screaming. But I remained the professional. "Sorry, sir," I said. "I missed the question."

The ghosts laughed, even the one with no face.

Clarke turned and walked away.

"I assume, then," the D.A. said, "that the defense will also assert that the duties and assignments for which the defendant received this classified training cannot be discussed."

"That's correct, sir," Clarke said.

"Then how are we to determine," the D.A. said, "if the defendant's response was reflexive or not if we don't know the nature of his special training?" The D.A. had a disgusted look on his face suddenly. It was as though he glimpsed the outcome.

The magistrate leaned back in his chair.

One of the four men seated behind the D.A.'s chair—the meathead's one-eyed friend—groaned and wagged his head.

The D.A. tapped the point of his pencil into his palm.

Clarke sat down, twisted the Cross pen shut and put it in his jacket pocket.

I sat on the stand like a can of worms.

"The defendant is evidently so skilled at hand-to-hand combat," the D.A. began, "that he could have stopped the fight without the excessive unnecessary violence that left men seriously impaired. He chose not to respond with commensurate retaliatory force, but with brutality beyond what was needed to defend himself. The severity of the injuries to these four men is clear evidence that the State has a responsibility to recognize the defendant's acts as assault."

The magistrate called the lawyers to the bench.

It had not been an ordinary preliminary hearing for assault charges. Clarke had explained to me that it wouldn't be, but I hadn't listened very carefully. Evidently there had only been five or six similar claims of privilege in two hundred years. Beginning to filter through my confused brain was the distinct feeling that Mr. Excitement was definitely not supposed to make the talk-show circuit with his autobiography. What was the big fucking deal? Without all of Clarke's slick maneuvering, what could they do, send me up for assault for doing what I'd been authorized to do—after what I'd been decorated for doing?

No, it had not been an ordinary preliminary hearing from the onset. I guess the D.A. ordinarily wouldn't have even attempted to bring the case to trial—it was a sure loss, considering the witness for my self-defense claim was on hold in Clifton. And in an ordinary preliminary hearing I wouldn't have been on the stand at all.

I was on the stand by design. Clarke told the court he was willing to go on record with my testimony for the sake of expedience, whether or not it would be used for or against me if the case went to trial—he knew it wouldn't. He asserted that he was sure it was a simple case of self-defense and was sure the court would be convinced after hearing my testimony. That was bullshit. Actually he'd planned for the D.A.'s cross-examination of me to proceed exactly as it did so he would have the opportunity to make a claim of privilege. This, he knew, would get him in closed quarters with the magistrate. Then he wouldn't have to prove self-defense or get into sticky areas with the brutality of the beatings. He wouldn't have to prove anything. It was the quickest out —minimum information spent—that was the primary concern.

I began to wonder at what lengths the government had gone to investigate the D.A. and his motives, what kind of axe the D.A. had to grind and what he'd hoped to open up through bringing the assault charge to trial. And I began to wonder about the nature of my crime —not the fight at the VFW bar, I understood that, but the other crime, the one the D.A. might have brought to light. What crime was this? Had John Oswald's influence finally caught up to me? Was this crime one of the ten thousand I'd committed but barely noticed? Or was this D.A. a witch hunter? The magistrate leaned forward, folded his hands and spoke to the lawyers. "We'll have an *in camera* hearing at this time," he said. "The bailiff will show the counsel and the defendant to my chambers." He stood and left by a door behind the bench.

What now? I thought. I wanted to go home and draw the blinds. What the fuck was an *in camera* hearing? I will refuse to be videotaped. They *will* let professionals refuse to be videotaped . . . won't they?

"No," Clarke told me, "it's just a Latin term. This is what we want."

Could I want what *he* wanted? I felt kind of sorry for the D.A. It was all about to end, and the D.A. had taken it on despite high odds against him—a witness who had seen one of the four jerks throw the first punch. Maybe his liberal humanitarian fur was ruffled by the brutality of the fight, and when the intimidating D.C. lawyer showed up, the D.A. felt obliged to give it a go. Maybe that's all it was. Or maybe he had something else on me . . . But what?

Somewhere in my heart I wanted the D.A. to get us into trial. I had no explanations, and that fact alone seemed significant. I needed to explain myself. It was remaining the cool professional that was the hard part—it might have been easier to shiver and quake and blubber and try to explain officially, right there, on record, the facts as I remembered them. What kind of privilege was it that left me there replaying the tape loops in my brain?

We met for the *in camera* hearing. We were supposed to tell the magistrate what it was I couldn't make public in the courtroom. Clarke unlocked his briefcase and took out a stack of letters, all marked CLASSIFIED, all bearing the seal of the government and the signature of high government officials. He had classified documents of official orders I'd received, complete with maps. I was amazed. All the letters referred to me personally.

Clarke handed the magistrate a letter. "This is a follow-up to the affidavit signed by the Secretary of the Navy that I sent you on twelve July," Clarke said. "You'll find the materials the Secretary refers to in order here." He put the stack of documents on the desk. "Also, there's a gentleman in the courtroom who is authorized to address the situation at this time if that's necessary. The defendant was one of his babies."

"One of his babies?" I asked.

Clarke just looked at me, said nothing, then turned back to the magistrate.

It wasn't necessary to bring in my slippery father figure, though the D.A. became more adamant after he read the letters.

"We can't simply dismiss this!" the D.A. complained. "There's a question of excessive brutality here—there is obvious disparity in the nature of this man's response, even if it was self-defense. This man is out of control by his own admission, supposedly because of some mysterious training that was administered over ten years ago! The government, even the CIA, has a responsibility to the American people! The courts can't bow to the names of influential people in its pursuit of justice!"

In his last pitch the D.A. said, "Can I impress you with the notion that there are reasons beyond assault charges that this case should go to trial?"

As it turned out the magistrate wasn't impressed, but the D.A. had my attention. The magistrate browsed the documents. Clarke stood by comfortably. What could those reasons be, I thought, and in the tension that hung there I conjured a number of the possibilities.

The D.A. must know about the break and entries, I thought. Have I been this deluded, this screwed up on the O, to think I was executing with precision and secrecy acts which were common knowledge in the D.A.'s office? Or was it the opium? Mrs. Horney must have called the cops after finding the mutilated poppy buds. The CIA had turned on me and had passed falsified incriminating evidence through the appropriate channels to the local authorities to get me off the streets before I became a public embarrassment to the Company. Or was it the smashed box turtle, surely one of my most wicked crimes? I mean, how far into the jungle should I go, how far into what I no longer allow myself to know? Maybe I've been working for the CIA all along without knowing it, I considered, mumbling some nervous eruption that turned the three heads toward me. "Is that possible?" I asked aloud. "Did they implant a programming device during the surgery?" They all looked at me but said nothing. The D.A. grunted and his face twitched like he needed a few Valiums. Then there was that meeting with the ex-CIA agent now working million-dollar deals with shady Arabs. I *did* turn down that offer, I assured myself—I hadn't even considered it. Still, the meeting had depressed me severely. I'd stayed in an opium dream for days afterward. Was there a tape of that meeting in the D.A.'s file? Was my entire ugly soul on tape somewhere? Or maybe Fatso, the poker ace, is fatter than I figured. Maybe he has the D.A. in his pocket. I shouldn't have fucked with that game or his brakes or his wife. And I shouldn't have been so openly suspicious or so friendly with Leroy at Oswald's party. Oswald must have thought we knew each other. Maybe Leroy and I *do* know each other, even though I still don't know who he is. I shouldn't have told so many lies—it's impossible to sort them out, and if given the chance, if the D.A. could get me into trial, I thought it might be remedial to tell the truth. But that wasn't about to happen, and in the end it came down to what I didn't say, as I knew it would. The words were taken away from me.

The next day I prepared to move out of Paterson. It was time to climb out of the sleeper on the Opium Express. Either I had to pick up the pace and step into some big league play, which I had the means to do, or I had to get out of the game. At the level I was playing I was growing too lax and careless. It not only embarrassed me to be caught at Ellen's, I also didn't like causing fear in her. It had seemed like the perfect relationship until then.

I considered the possibility that I'd been caught because I'd impaired myself with the constant use of O, though I didn't really believe that. I felt sure my nocturnal activities could have continued indefinitely without facing any consequences. I think I wanted to get caught, and that's why I got caught, like I wanted the hearing to go to trial. My behavior, the places I entered at night—it was all becoming too routine, and that, ultimately, would have become a great danger. I needed to break the patterns before they consumed me.

As I made preparations to leave I couldn't stop thinking about the VC journal and the clues it seemed to hold, clues to a puzzle I could never understand. Maybe they were clues to identifying this crime—maybe it was the nature of the crime that I couldn't understand. I had some things to investigate, and it wasn't going to be in Paterson where the name on my birth certificate was tailing me and my best girl didn't want me hanging around anymore.

I ran an ad in the paper to rent the house I was renting from Mrs. Horney, giving only the number at a nearby phone booth. The ad said to call between three and four, so each day for ten days I took calls and showed the house, mostly to students from the colleges in Montclair and Paterson. It was an easy scam. Students are the most naive people on earth.

Because fall semester was approaching, and because I underpriced the market, before long I'd rented the place to seven separate parties, collected a month's rent and damage deposit from each and told them they could move in on the first of the month.

I found out through Social Services that the monthly food stamps were mailed on the twenty-seventh, so on that day I followed the mailman around the low rent districts of Bloomfield and picked up the stamps from mailboxes. I carried an armful of sale brochures that I stole from a local discount department store so in case I ran into any suspicious sorts I could say I was delivering them. Still I had to limit myself to houses and tenements where no one was around. It wasn't the best way to pick up pocket change—it was too much like work—and it kept reinforcing my apprehension over the petty level of operation. I abandoned it after a few hours.

I did manage to collect 855 dollars in stamps, which I sold the next day for half price in the slums and barrios of Newark.

I packed what I needed from my place in Paterson and went back to Newark. There, along a canal that diverted water from the Passaic River, I found a neighborhood that was partially boarded up. It was quiet there, and rents were cheap. I rented a one-room with a small kitchen above a dry cleaners and disappeared.

3

I'VE MANAGED TO STAY OUT OF TROUBLE IN NEWARK. I STAY inside a lot, writing what I can, lying in black and white, turning over the rocks—Monkey at his window, trying to recall, among everything else, high school Typing 1.

It's not very exciting for Mr. Excitement around here—no villains, no heroes, no apparent danger out there, no femme fatale, nothing weird happening, no good plot stuff for a detective novel, just old Willie Sykes, Jim Kelly's dive, the sounds of intermittent hammering. It's quiet here for a big city. It's dying quietly. Recuperation is easier in this kind of obscurity. Dying cities make me feel good. I like living in the cavity from where the heart was torn. The hammering of nails is an odd sound around here. But just *this* will do for now—the way it is out the window there.

On the southwest corner there's a pale yellow two-story building. For three days now some guy has been hammering in there, and there's a new pile of old junk against the wall along the alley. I'll check it out tonight for salvageables, round objects, things with holes in them that are good for connecting to other things. From here I can see a headboard from an old bed, a snarl of conduit or wire or tubing, two tires, cardboard boxes full of stuff, a paint can, a dirty metal shelf—just now a brown and black mutt is sniffing the boxes.

Beyond that building is what was once a small hotel—it's boarded up. The garbage cans at the mouth of the alley have "Becky's" painted on them in crude block letters. The mutt runs by with something white in its mouth.

I'm developing new methods in my search for clues. Rather than collecting information and spying on people, as I did compulsively in Paterson, I collect objects now, objects that might attract clues. I'm like the Mohawk brave who, instead of stalking, sat and waited for a deer to pass under his perch. This isn't inactive hunting—like the Indian I do things to improve my chances.

I wrap objects in foil or twine or wire or colored cloth, objects I find in the streets and empty lots and railroad yards. I attach objects to other objects—clips to keys, washers to springs, screw eyes to rubber balls, bits of metal to bits of chain, belt buckles to beef bones, sinkers to padlocks to brass dog licenses, then I attach these assemblages to other assemblages and hang them on doorframes, store them in drawers or boxes, submerge them in oil or water, stick them in potatoes, arrange them on the sill or fire escape or dresser, tack them to the walls, keep them under the bed or in the turtle shell, bury them in the garden or in various corners of the neighborhood, toss them into the Passaic. I spread the junk on the round white table, the bolts, metal collars, bars with holes in them, tabs of copper, tubes, hooks, patterns cut from sheet metal, caps, points, channels, clamps, fittings, handles, knobs, braces, grommets, rivets, brackets, couplings, hinges, slugs, beads, bones, eyelets, trinkets, bells; and with twisted wire, key rings, epoxy, cord or fishing gizmos, I attach them, one to another, until they are something.

I made a cockroach trap—it didn't work, of course. I made a thing to ward off cockroaches. I made a thing to make cockroaches extinct, flirting with the urban ecosystem. I made a thing that is an offering to cockroaches. I made a thing to receive messages, to guard the door, to heal sore throats, to help the potted weeds grow. I made a thing to bring into my dreams with me, to look at in my hand in the dream, to give me the power to act in the dream and to guide the nature of that act, to let me look at myself in the dream as I'm acting. I made a thing to watch over the entrance where my body in the dream emerges into the sleeping body and the sleeping body submerges into the dream. Yesterday I made a thing which is my heart—it's on the round white table next to the box of junk. Now I'm working on a thing to help me just remain normal, keep to myself, stay inconspicuous and not do anything weird. It's been a couple of years since I did anything weird, so I figure I need such a thing about now. And I think it's about time to add a few appendages to the thing that has kept the ghosts away.

It's been two years since I was caught at Ellen's, almost four years since I discovered the poppies growing along Mrs. Horney's sidewalk. It must be ten years since I lived in Hollywood after returning from Nam. I wonder if I've survived.

They were yellow poppies, but judging from the shape of the leaf, which was identical to the illegal white poppy, I had a strong suspicion that they might be close enough. Sweet O.

The intense yellow was what caught my eye as I passed old Mrs. Horney's place one spring day. Yellow poppies are rare in the States. I never saw any others in all Paterson.

One night during my habitual nocturnal prowl I made several slits with a razor blade all around the buds, just the way the mama-san had shown me.

When the sap began to ooze I collected it and patiently went through the whole number with rice paper. Then I put it to the test, and o-o-o-o-o-o, mama, that faint whistle way off in the skull—that distant train, the tiny light, bigger and bigger. The sun fluttered on the leaves—that special light when the clouds break after a rain. The hiss of a car passing on the wet street intrigued me. A Beethoven concerto for two flutes on the scratchy radio. The green more deeply green in the yard back by the alley. The drops clinging to the porch eaves contained curved replicas of the whole world, at least. A small breeze tossed the blank page of my journal away, and what was left seemed even more significant. I thought of Li Po floating his poems downriver, waking from a nap to wonder how many blossoms had fallen. I thought of Po Chu-I destroying his five vital organs, according to Basho, and of Basho becoming absurd ahead of his time on rice wine, anticipating the efficiency of the Hatuskari Limited Express. Ancient China was lush. A drop of dew could lie for months waiting patiently to be observed closely and from afar by an antisocial oversensitive drunk somehow capable of seeing in it no less than this curved replica of the world towering to peaks above his famous grass hat. Without a doubt—sweet O. And a decent grade at that. Mrs. Horney's sidewalk lined with the damned things. Where is my grass hat? I thought. Today I will do nothing.

I collected the sap at night and stayed stoned for over a year from that single cache growing two doors away.

While in-country a guy I knew in Navy Intell showed me a journal that was taken off a dead VC. That journal was the reason I eventually looked up the mama-san who knew about opium. I never knew anything about flowers or plants before I photocopied that journal.

* * *

I was on four days R & R in Saigon between assignments, did some LSD for recreation. All the residual fear and tension from a month in VC turf gushed up my backbone and drove me off the streets and up to the hotel room. When I closed my eyes I was still in the dense foliage of the Jungle of Darkness, still up to my knees in sucking mud and snake-infested water in the Mekong Delta, still expecting an AK-47 to open up from thirty feet away. The whole Phoenix Program had me spooked. I was beginning to think, and that was bad. Mumbling dangerous questions to the mirror.

Now, looking back—nine years since James Robinson's suicide in L.A., almost eleven years since debriefing—I'm sure I was deranged, with or without drugs, during the last year I spent in-country.

At the time I thought I was going along mostly unaffected, weathering the strain better than most. That's what I was trained to think—to maintain the delusion that I was above and beyond trauma. Wasn't I one of the select few? We were above thinking, feeling.

Now I realize it was as if key molecules in my body had been removed and replaced with a government-issue transplant, and it was only a matter of time before my body would begin to reject them. But what then—live without these critical molecules? I guess that's what James Robinson tried, and he has become one of the ghosts. Now it seems as though he was never alive. I had a better time with his corpse than I ever did with him. At least what I brought back is not a heroin habit.

The VC journal was nothing more than a catalog of vegetation in the region and some letters written to a woman, but there in the hotel window, suffering waves of paranoia intensified by the acid, squalor breeding in my brain as it was in the streets below, the journal took on a kind of magical quality like some oracle—the Southeast Asian Book of the Dead—speaking to me from the blood-enriched soil of the forest. I felt like I was reading a man's journal the way a shaman would read the entrails of an animal, divining the traces of an ancient psychic map. Maybe from this old knowledge I could construct a bridge across the abyss of lost molecules.

The descriptions of plants were extremely detailed and included the Latin names for genus, species and family for hundreds of plants that the man identified in both high and low terrain. I was able to lose myself in the detail, using entries as clues to a puzzle. I became obsessed with this imaginary puzzle and convinced that the journal was a cryptogram that if cracked could provide some knowledge vital to my sudden need to understand what I was doing in Vietnam, why I'd become increasingly more uncomfortable with daylight and why I felt more like a VC than a GI.

It's true I'd been trained to look, move and think like a VC; the covert operations depended on that. It was dangerous ground—thinking like a VC, looking down on Tu Do Street with a head full of L-S-Crazy. The VC whose journal I was reading had switched sides. Intell had determined that he'd deserted the ARVN from I Corps to join the National Liberation Front—the VC.

Evidently this was not uncommon, and it worked both ways. Typically, in the Vietnamese culture, what's right and wrong can easily vary according to the situation at hand—a response to a present condition rather than to ideologies. VC had shown up in ARVN ranks, apparently not as infiltrators but as soldiers, then later were found dead in black pajamas. Some men were known to have switched sides four and five times. Translate that to English.

I began thinking that I should have stayed in the States after my tour, as difficult and alien as it seemed during my brief Christmas visit, because the second stint, from the onset, was filled with uncertainty and oscillation.

I could call in F-4s to tidy up and B-52s to dump an arc light that shook the ground for ten miles around—a hundred thousand dollars worth of ordnance at my beck and call. I was responsible for lives, million-dollar choppers, crucial political hush-hush, but in Jersey during Christmas visit I couldn't bring my own popcorn into a fucking movie theater—not without shuffling to the end of the line, jumping through a hoop, eating shit and liking it, putting the bag where the jerk-off couldn't see it and filing back in while he got off on his petty authority. And I couldn't believe that the world was continuing with business as usual. I couldn't stop thinking about Juan because he was from Jersey, too. On Thanksgiving we'd watched our buddy's head pop into the air. Business as usual. Popcorn laws. People enraged because the bus was late. I couldn't wait to get back in-country.

The VC must have been a university botany student before he was siphoned off to the war. The letters, which were sometimes written in

French, seemed to be to his wife. Every word was translated and entered into an official Intell document—descriptions of plants and love letters.

I began to dabble in the study of botany when I had some free time near a base library, and one day in Da Nang I picked up a small notebook and began my own catalog of plants I identified. I rapidly became compulsive about it. I was in need of a diversion.

I felt like I knew the VC who wrote the journal, like I could hear his voice in the words. I could picture him squatting over a tiny fungus while the Big Boys pounded the mountains, while incoming mortar rounds walked closer. I felt like I wanted to complete his catalog of vegetation.

He seemed so different from the psychological profiles depicted by CIA and Provincial Reconnaissance Unit briefing teams. It wasn't just the letters to his wife that fascinated me with their tenderness and their perceptions—simple perceptions that, at the time, seemed so profound —but even the plant catalog was mysterious, dark and imaginative, elucidating ideas and emotions through description. Just simple sentences—an Intell translator had knocked them out between coffee breaks—but they held me to them as though they bubbled up from some primordial wellspring. Using what I knew of the language and an English–Vietnamese dictionary, I began to translate some of the entries back into Vietnamese.

I still remember his entry on the rosary pea (*abrus precatorius*): *In this twisted, creeping, woody vine is the communion of the sacred and the profane. The scarlet seeds, blemished and adorned with black spots and laden with poison like the breasts of a she-demon, become prayer beads when plucked and strung by a monk or a peasant."*

At times he wrote of himself as though he were a billion-year-old star or a snarl of vines on the forest floor, vines that had the feelings and thoughts of a man.

He was on his back resting in a meadow at night. He imagined himself floating in the middle of a sea. *"Above me one star is, like me, floating,"* he wrote, *"and we are gone, the star and I, and you are gone, my love."*

Since the VC were forbidden to keep journals for security reasons, all this had to be written on the sly. I liked the image I had of him writing in the dark, defiant and intense.

His descriptions of plants were detailed down to the grains of pollen lodged among the appendages of the pistil, and the descriptions sometimes extended outward, leaping to an associative relationship with people, ideas or emotions. In the fall of ivy he saw his mother's mother. In the various green hues he saw her duties and moods. He saw her holding a fish with her fingers in the gills, going with a group of children to a lake where water had killed a valley of trees.

I became so involved with this man and his meticulous work that I was planning to go back to university as a botany student when I got out, but that never happened.

I had to discard the journal before CIA debriefing and the Navy exit interview, so I can't go back and inspect it now for what it was that affected me, but I know that while in-country it did serve as a sufficient tool, or at least a distraction, that to this day I think saved my sanity, though I'm sure many people would disagree. And without that background in plants I would never have given Mrs. Horney's poppies a second glance.

Opium, it seems to me, is a malleable drug that can be used to different ends. I've known people who can't get out of their chair once they've smoked or eaten O, who settle for dreams, observing the way one dream moves so easily into the next. I can't sit still for a minute—or at least I couldn't then. I originally started prowling at night because once I'd smoked I had to get out of the house, and once out of the house I had to be probing and collecting, trying doors and mapping back-street avenues of escape.

While in Paterson I lived only six or seven blocks from the Passaic Falls. Mrs. Horney was a great gardener. Her husband had died just a few months before I moved there. Her daughter visited her often, and she kept busy with a large vegetable and flower garden behind her house. Sometimes, just before dawn, on my way back home I'd come down the back alley, enter her garden from the rear and pull a row of weeds before sunrise, before closing my door to the brightness.

I'd fled from a bad scene in Angleton, changed my identity again and rented Mrs. Horney's place—her husband's brother's old place. She was the perfect landlady because she asked no questions.

Around midnight each night I smoked some O, and by one I was prowling in the alleys and back yards, crawling through fields, climbing fire escapes or frozen in a squat in some tangle of weeds for hours at a time, watching the way the night behaved, refreshing my body and mind with nocturnal knowledge.

Opium puts most people into a nod where they oscillate between dream and a foggy notion of the waking world, and I did use it that way too, at times—usually during the day. At night my adrenalin cut through the drug to calculate the angles to determine the degrees of the shift in perception caused by the O, and I would pull on the dark clothes, blacken my face, drink the ten glasses of water and pocket a few small tools and the extendable mirror, my mind and body fallow for more seeds of a nocturnal language with which to describe the world.

I was eating a high-protein diet at the time, like some Muscle Beach health freak. Lots of grains and beans and vegetables—reserving the use of meat as a catalytic chemical agent that I would add or subtract, increase or decrease as need be. Mostly I stayed away from meat in order to burn quickly at a hot temperature and to maintain the veil that kept me less perceptible to dogs in the dark. With a belly full of meat my body radiated a signal that I found generally unwieldy on the subtler levels of obscuration.

I rarely left the house during the day, so by nightfall, like a dog bred for work, I had to get out and move around despite the narcotic effect of the O. I worked the raw energy down through systems until it was refined and controlled, then opened the pin valves of stillness of heart and patience and annealed my concentration until it had the density of a steel girder.

I would sometimes initiate the night's work by traveling the river where it slowed down and widened to about eighty meters, walking up to my chin in water thick with chemicals, soapsuds and sludge, moving unseen from neighborhood to neighborhood. I could disappear completely into the river if I had to. No cop in the city would look for me there.

River travel is strangely peaceful. The head seems to float on the current, enveloped in the darkness and guiding, like a periscopic device, the submerged part of the body. The eyes can see in the dark, using diminished light reflected off the water and amplifying it like a Navy Starlight Scope. The ears track bats overhead and gauge the yaw of the body. The nose tests the air, sensing the wind shift at the bend in the river. The mouth, as though it housed a gyro high in its domed roof, senses the shifts in the river bottom. The overhead branches pass the stars like progress over a grid, and I move like a sluggish fish, a granddaddy catfish negotiating the slimy rocks, paint buckets, refrigerators—the ten thousand pieces of refuse rusting away at the bottom—calculating by dead reckoning my position in the hollow of water.

I'd often imagine that submerged museum of junk and sort through the items as I walked—artifacts in ancient repose, plated with rust and umber and nested in luxuriant slime—vestiges of some age I'd forgotten. If I imagined vividly enough I could maybe recall that age—maybe I could summon up a piece of the puzzle and fit it to another piece. A child's shoe—Buster Brown, scuffed—and below it, cigarette burns on a plank floor. A Louisville Slugger 32-ounce. An American Flyer, customized. A pint of Twister, peppermint wine, empty. A Mexican switchblade, broken. A rubber tree, chained to a Michelin radial. Two poems by Li Po. A French dictionary. Uncle Ho's diploma. Four layers of Catholic priests. Four layers of Buddhist monks.

I practiced similar meditations while traveling the irrigation canals in the dead of night in Nam. Under the water, dynasties had come and gone. I wanted to remember. Strata of golden urns descended beneath me. My brain was a world, a planet, and the forgotten age had been there, inside the skull, the mythical age that had never really existed, existing in the vessel of my body. This kept my mind in a mode where I could open wider my awareness of the immediate surroundings, hear and smell small events in the paddies. This was a safe wave to radiate in VC turf—it wasn't easily detected.

In Paterson, with the help of the O, my senses became even keener than they had already become from the nocturnal activities in Nam. O slowed the world to a halt, and I was able to focus my concentration on minute events. This heightened awareness improved my vision, as though knowing what to look for allowed it to be seen more easily. I could crouch for hours waiting for a house light to go out or a dog to fall asleep. I rubbed myself with leaves, dirt, dew. Cats couldn't detect my presence. I could get within a few feet of a person, with just a window screen between us, without causing the slightest suspicion. If a cop passed—even if he aimed the car spotlight in my direction—I would not be noticed. I could become a tree stump or a shrub or any nondescript inanimate form in the dark of a yard—a heap of trash in an alley, a lawnmower with a tarp thrown over it, a shadow cast by a streetlight, a blank, a hole, nothing.

I was skirting a rooftop one night and dropped to the first level of a fire escape when a spotlight from a cop car panned toward me from the street below, following the window level of the third-story apartments. Contact. Cheap thrill up the backbone. I needed that shot of adrenalin.

By the time the beam of light reached me I had become a shadow on the brick wall, my arms pressed together above my head, head held back, filling the gap between my arms, my eyes focused on a bright star. Check-out time. The room was empty. I ignored the light and emptied myself of concern, feeling the star filling me back up with dispassion and precision control. When the light passed I smiled, the cool brick against my cheek, the star winking, the cop probably relieved that he didn't have to get out of the car. But the game was on. I dropped to the ground and paralleled the cop car, staying behind the building.

I pocketed some rocks from beneath the shrubbery and ducked between the building and a dumpster. The cop car pulled into the parking lot, driving slowly. It seemed routine enough. The driver was slumped slightly. His partner aimed the spotlight here and there in the crannies of the building. When the spotlight went off I hurled three rocks at it, slipped around the corner and ran into the shadow of a big tree in the open yard between two buildings.

The car rounded the corner. Doors opened and closed. I pulled the tee shirt up over my head and stretched the bottom over my knees and knelt on the ground facing the cops. I was in the open, about forty meters from them, between the tree and a bench, a brick barbecue ten meters behind me, a wire trash can near the barbecue. My wool watch cap filled the neck hole of the tee shirt. Through the knit of the shirt I saw them searching the shrubbery with flashlights. I dropped my head and closed my eyes. I remember thinking about the tree near me as I disappeared. I pictured the root system and felt roots of my own spreading downward from the knees.

If you look at something long enough it will look back at you. Ignore it if you want to be ignored—ignore it with eye and mind, with the entire body, bone and muscle and nerve. Turn the head away so the eyes do not attract, so the face does not reflect light, and refuse to acknowledge cops, dogs, women walking half asleep toward the bathroom in the dark of the night. Shut it down. Be a dead man. Slip over the edge of vulnerability into asylum in the invisible. That was the game—to slip out of the game, past the rules, past the cops, past the sentinels of substantive existence. Who would follow?

This simple meditation had been rediscovered and misused—synthesized in government-subsidized think tanks, developed with university research grants, tested with rhesus monkeys, written up in clipped military jargon, issued to Special Forces officers and passed on to operatives as a jungle savvy.

It was an easy technique to use in Paterson because I had so little concern to begin with. I never had a fear of being seen, so I was never seen, and the fear of being among the unseen had been uncommonly diminished. Fear was something else, something that had plumbed me much deeper. The thought of a cop seeing me stealing under a window did not alarm me. I knew I couldn't be caught. I knew I would emerge whole, hear the drone of the world and be separated and visible again.

If by freak chance I was cornered, I knew I would never be taken— not by the baddest or biggest or best-trained, not by ten men, not by gun or club or the meanest dog.

It was a graceful transition from opium to the darkness of alleys and backyards at night. I used a glass pipe and heated the underside of the bowl until the O began to smoke and the smoke began to fill the stem. Drawing easily then, I'd watch the smoke run up the stem. Sometimes I ate the O, but I liked the instant rush of smoke, and I liked the ritual of smoke—the transformation of the tarry earthen substance into pearly smoke through the union of fire.

After the first lungful I'd begin the first of the ten glasses of water I'd drink before leaving the house, and as a consequence I developed the habit of urinating in select places on my route each night.

When I'd inhaled enough O, I took the dark clothes from the drawer. Before I put the clothes on, while naked, I stretched and loosened all my joints. I always stood at the window then and watched the darkness of the sideyard, slowing my heartbeat, breathing deeply and clearing my mind of clutter before I blackened my face, neck and hands.

Then, through the window, I could always conjure the same vision and see it as though it was really there in the dark yard between the lilac bush and the Rose of Sharon. I'd see a Buddhist monk in a saffron yellow robe seated in petals of blue flame. I'd watch until the monk fell forward, then go into the yard and sit where the monk had been. I'd spend ten or fifteen minutes preparing myself, then begin the nightly prowl by crawling, sometimes on my belly, into the shrubbery and out to the rear alley.

Just four blocks from my house a main drainage line intersected with four smaller pipes beneath a drain grill across the street from Minardi's bakery. I could bend over low and pass through stretches of absolute darkness to three other intersection rooms, rooms where pipes emptied into a concrete well studded with steel ladders. These rain pipes stayed dry when the weather was dry. The main pipes all led to the river. I could travel for miles underground. Rats, generally, were not too much of a problem, and they were half the size of the rats in Nam. It was easy enough to travel unnoticed above the ground, so I used the pipe network only now and then, exploring them only to map avenues of escape and when I had the urge to be under the city in the dark.

Most of the houses I entered were vacant during my visits. The inhabitants worked nights or frequented the beds of others. But there were a few houses I entered repeatedly while people were sleeping in them. Through trial and error I found the sound sleepers, people like Ellen, who would not stir as I moved around their beds or went through their desk drawers. I spent enough hours beside some women that I began to feel like I could crawl into bed with them without alarming them. I felt like I knew them, though they had never seen me. When I visited Ellen I didn't black my face—our relationship had grown too comfortable for that.

In the homes of the well-to-do I collected information. I copied down the names of drugs on prescription vials, the payees on check stubs, addresses from card files and letterheads. I noted credit card numbers, the dates of appointments entered in calendar books, the information on birth certificates and any scrap of data I came across.

I kept a file on each house and accumulated more data with each entry. Periodically I spread all the data from a specific house on a table and tried to make connections between bits of information, playing a detective game, trying to figure a section of the unknown. Bits of information would lead me to comparing the files of two houses, establishing common ground between people and speculating on directions for further information.

At times I ventured out to see these people, hear them talk, talk to them, observe them. I sat behind them on buses, at tables close to them in cafés and bars while they met for their appointments.

I found out about a rendezvous between a man and a woman who'd had an affair that had ended a year earlier. I decided to observe the scene and studied photos of the man so I could recognize him in the restaurant where they were to meet. I put together a sketchy dossier on her from her letters, which the man kept locked in a file cabinet. She was from big money—suburban development money from the west coast.

I waited in the bar of the restaurant. He arrived first and sat a few stools away from me. I bought him a drink; we chatted; he bought a round. The woman was more than fashionably late, so he was a bit anxious and drinking on an empty stomach. An hour passed. Several drinks. Cautiously, by talking about my fabricated debts first, I was able to fill in minor gaps in my information concerning his large outstanding debts to an apparently fraudulent company in Bakersfield, California. I also found out the name of his lawyer, and a week later I began a file on him.

I was curious about this meeting because I knew it had been a year since they'd last seen each other. The affair had ended in emotional and financial snarls. It was she who'd invited him to dinner, and she had been the one who'd called off the affair a year earlier.

He looked around to the door every time someone came in.

"Where is that bitch?" he said, a bit greased from the scotch.

"Joanne?" I asked.

"Damn her!" He took a drag on his smoke, then swung his head to me. "How do you know her name?" He studied my face.

"You mentioned it earlier."

"I did?"

"When you were telling me about how your wife found out through the waiter at the country club." Actually his wife had found out from his secretary, who had subsequently moved to an apartment on East 64th in Manhattan. I'd found that letter locked in his wife's file.

"I told you her name?" he asked.

"Joanne," I said.

"I'll be"—he hit the bar with his fist—"fucked! I must be drunk. Jee-sus Christ!"

"Hey, pal, I don't even know your wife," I said, "and I don't give a rat's ass what you do on the side, or with who. I'm just sitting here at this bar, that's all, and you tell me about this tomato Joanne who almost fucked you to death, and . . ."

"I swore I'd never make a dumb mistake again." He turned to me with that studious look again. "Are you working for my wife?"

"Gimme a fucking break! I don't work for anybody." Mr. Excitement was insulted.

"I'm sorry," he said. "I don't know who to trust. It's not losing my wife that worries me. I could deal with that."

"Fuck it," I said. I lit one of his smokes and ignored him.

He and the woman were intense but quiet during their dinner, talking constantly. When they were finished he went back to the bar and she left. I went to her house.

The house was supposed to be well protected with bullshit electronic devices. All the lights were off except for upstairs. I inspected the place for future access, then sat in the shrubs and smoked another of the guy's smokes. On the way through the back yard when I was leaving I tested the glass slider out of habit, and it moved. Lots of expensive burglar proofing but not the presence of mind to lock the door.

I slipped inside, moved to a dark corner and listened. She was in the shower upstairs. There was a TV on. When the shower stopped I heard a man's voice. I went up and stopped at the head of the stairs.

"The guy's an asshole," the woman said.

"Fuck him then," the man replied.

"But I need to be careful," she said.

"Fuck him carefully."

"It's not that simple."

"Fuck him." He turned the channel selector several times.

"I don't trust him," she said. "I can't believe he's that dumb. I can't be sure I'm not getting sucked in."

"What reason does he have to suspect you? Suck you into what?"

"Into showing my cards," she said.

"But from what you told me before he doesn't even know he's in the game. Burn the fucker! You said he's an asshole!"

"He *is* an asshole."

I thought of her sparkling eyes and her laughter as she touched wine glasses with the man over dinner just an hour earlier.

"Then burn his ass," the man said, turning the channels again.

I heard her leafing through papers. The man went to the adjoining bathroom and turned the shower on. I crawled to the door of the bedroom, spread the telescopic stem of my pocket mirror and found her in it. She was sitting against the headboard in pajama bottoms, still studying the papers.

"It's all right here," she called toward the bathroom. "I could have his ass."

"Have it," the man yelled over the sound of the shower.

She crawled across the bed for a smoke, fell to her stomach on the bed, dropped the papers to the floor and lit the smoke. I slipped into a dark room off the upstairs hall.

When the lights went out and they started making love I returned to the doorway and watched them run through their repertoire in the dim light of the bright moon in the window.

When they were asleep I went downstairs and looked through the drawers of her desk and through her strongbox, which, like the glass slider, was left unlocked.

It was the notes I took there that initially led me to Ellen's house, where I was eventually caught. The notes led me to a highly paid corporate tax lawyer. Ellen was his gal Friday, trusted personal secretary and senior administrator in a large office. I discovered that she often took home important and confidential documents to catch up on work to be done. I started going to Ellen's to read the documents, interested in running across information connected to whatever was going on between this man and woman I'd watched in the restaurant.

I did, eventually, when the woman played her hand, come across such information. I planned some strategies to meddle in the affair, but I became disinterested, distracted by Ellen, and stopped my research and data collecting. Once it became obvious that I could influence the outcome of the litigations my interest shifted to Ellen. Besides, the man and the woman were both slimeballs in my opinion—let dog eat dog.

I sat at Ellen's bedside while she slept, night after night. I didn't know why. Much of the time I didn't even enjoy it. It became tedious, yet I kept returning. Often I sat there trying to figure out why I was there, feeling like Cro-Magnon Man blundering through his first intellections. In some ways it was horrifying. I'd sit there stripped bare of rationalizations to explain this offensive habit.

Sometimes—it was usually around four o'clock—she got up to use the bathroom and get a drink of water. One night, rather than step into the shadows in the drapes, as I usually did, I just rolled under the bed from where I was sitting on the floor. She came back and got into bed and moments later sat up quickly. I was sure she could hear me breathing. I held my breath. I listened as hard as I've ever listened, listened with my entire body for the rhythm of her breathing, and when I felt the rhythm I expired as she did and my next inspiration came with hers, and I think she must have credited it all to her imagination then—she fell back to sleep. But for a long time I lay there like that, breathing with her breaths, counting heartbeats per breath, enduring the metallic claptrap of my brain until suddenly the brain cleared—no mechanistic repetition, a clear horizon all the way to where it curved—a void that was at the same time teeming and fertile. I wanted to hold on to that moment of tranquility, avoid the first thought and maintain the opening, the opportunity, but, of course, the thought came, and much to my surprise it seemed to present me with a reason—a reason undeniable in its natural source—to be at peace with myself.

I returned on other nights hoping to experience that opening again. I also returned simply because I could return. It fascinated me that I had regular access to her bedside, that I could be so close to her without having to talk or be somebody. It was easier to develop a habit than find another sound sleeper whom I liked as well. It became a matter of relying on the familiar. I had to do something at night. Theft didn't interest me. It wasn't like Mr. Excitement could stay home and watch TV. And, as I've said, I think I got caught there because I wanted to get caught to end the routine. Routines threaten my security.

Though it was obvious to me that the women I visited the most were the prettiest, I never touched them, though I could have easily, and though I fall in lust as easily as the next guy, my lust would always give way to a stronger desire. I would be overcome by a kind of longing—not for their bodies . . . or, yes, it was for their bodies . . . but not to fall on them or even to have them willingly accept me, but a longing for the peacefulness of their sleeping, the peacefulness of what I can describe inadequately as the energy or electrical charge or polarity of their molecules—something like that—the energy of the lunar blood responsive to the pull of the moon.

This, of course, would seem a shoddy justification to anyone on the receiving end of these invasions of privacy and latent violence, but I felt that if I could wrap my body in Ellen's I would be somehow grounded, that the electricity that raced ceaselessly around in the overloaded circuits of my nervous system would instantly rush into the earth and complete its frenetic search.

The whole time I was preoccupied with Ellen, I was working with information I'd collected on other people. Eventually I'd made enough connections that I had the capability to seriously manipulate the lives of several people. These games kept me entertained for a while, but I had enough information on some people and enough access to their homes and offices that the game had to move up a league or become boring. I contemplated some big-league hardball, planning to ruin businesses, break up marriages, steal fortunes, frame people, bring justice to wrongdoers and compensation to victims—or simply create havoc in ordered lives. Some of the plots were sketchy, but some would have worked flawlessly.

Ultimately, when it came to enacting these plans, they were always secondary to one primary obsessive drive, which had less to do with manipulating individual lives or petty business deals than it had to do with the ability, kept in reserve, to orchestrate a large-scale, intricately interconnected scenario, a spectacular pageant of events of a more panoramic nature.

I had enough on Ludlow Chemical, for example, to possibly lure the Environmental Conservation Agency into an unnecessary cover-up. In the files of a plant in West Paterson I'd come across some poisoned bait —some of their own medicine.

It seems an environmental action group called Earthrite had notified the State ECA that barrels in a Ludlow storage facility were leaking into the Passaic. The barrels contained dioxin, a highly toxic carcinogen, so I pursued my snooping with a special interest because the dioxin accumulated through the production of agent orange, the herbicide used to defoliate Vietnam.

Under the pressure of Earthrite and one of the local newspapers the ECA ordered Ludlow to clean up the hazard. Ludlow has a safer storage facility nearby, but this site was filled with barrels of DDT, which could no longer be sold legally in the States. Paperwork from Columbia, Costa Rica, Honduras, Guatemala, El Salvador and other countries of Central and South America indicated that Ludlow had been exporting the DDT to fruit and coffee growers, thereby gradually making space available for the dioxin in the safer storage site.

When the ECA checked up on Ludlow and found a steady if slow movement of dioxin from the hazardous site to the safer one, they agreed to allow Ludlow to proceed at the same rate of dealing with the problem. Though the ECA must have known what was happening to the DDT, they officially did not ask—this was not part of the investigation and not mentioned in the Earthrite complaint.

Though there is nothing illegal about selling DDT to foreign countries, the ECA could have been embarrassed by its choice to ignore the fact that the companies that purchased the DDT dealt almost exclusively in exports to the States: the DDT-contaminated produce was—and still is—coming directly back to U.S. kitchens, juice and jelly manufacturers, coffee importers, etc.

But more incriminating to the ECA was the evidence I found in a locked file that linked a State ECA official to a cover-up of a large dioxin spill that even Earthrite had no knowledge of. Evidently the State ECA official neglected to inform his federal superiors of the spill and was content to ignore the hazards at Ludlow entirely until Earthrite started pulling on his coat sleeve.

Ludlow probably kept this record of their dealings with the State ECA official to protect themselves and to, if necessary, double-cross the ECA official by proving Ludlow had notified him, as required by law, concerning the spill when it occurred.

Then I read an article in the paper about a company that manufactures metal table pedestals. They were buying their stock metal from a Mexican company because it was cheaper. The Mexican company—because it was cheaper—was melting down illegally purchased x-ray machines to produce their stock metal. The final products of this cost-efficient liaison were table pedestals loaded with radioactive cobalt, and the pedestals, of course, were distributed all over hell. I mean, if you can get cancer from your kitchen table, where could I begin with my little game of puzzles?

So in Paterson I collected information that I did nothing with—there was nothing to be done. If I couldn't unburn the corpse, reunite the atom with itself, give the grafted and the cloned molecules back their sacred individuality, implode some near star for dramatic emphasis, then I didn't want any of it.

At the time I would rather consider the Buddhist monk who, in conjuring flames in a faraway place, invoked a powerful and holy fallout that still covers the world. Who would follow that act? Mr. Excitement?

No, it was no battle against the enemies of the people that I was engaged in then. I was indiscriminate in who and what I exploited—it was all haphazard. The game against Ludlow Chem started because I had fairly easy access to their files—the place was nearby. I saw no purpose in distinguishing between fragments of a fallen world.

Eventually the fragments of information annoyed me—the separate files I kept seemed to represent illusionary distinctions between people I was investigating and somehow, beyond the details, which I became too cranky and woozy to tolerate, was one undivided, indiscrete, incorporated mess. Yet all the bits of information represented unfinished business, and that nagged me too, so I buried it all in a few boxes.

After that came an obsession to remove all information in all its forms. I got rid of the radio; I wouldn't read the paper; I stopped eavesdropping on people in the diner; I emptied the house of books. . . . Eventually even words, encoded with their information, became objectionable.

Word fasts are like food fasts—after a few days a haughtiness sets in, a superiority over people who eat, over people who speak. Hunger, which enslaves lesser people, is conquered—language becomes a crude way of communicating, an unnecessary crudeness.

I refused to count the days because that would have been beneath the magnitude of the act, but I'm sure months passed without a word escaping my mouth. I greeted Mrs. Horney in the garden without speaking. I bought groceries and ordered coffee at the diner without a syllable.

I thought about what word I would use to break the fast, then that, too, became an indulgence to overcome. I tried to forget the words used to describe objects as I saw them and concepts as they occurred to me, thinking without words, seeing without words. Every time a word entered my mind I drove it out.

One night I sat up in bed while sleeping and screamed, waking myself, recalling no frightening dream, just the feeling of scrambling back into existence from outside of it.

A few more days of fasting followed when, one morning at dawn, as I came through the hedge into the back yard from the alley, I encountered Mrs. Horney in her garden and said, "Good morning." "It's a lovely morning," she replied, and I stopped dead in my tracks. The morning swelled up around me in a yellow light, in a green rustling of leaves, in a delirious racket of birdsong. An electricity rose in my backbone and broke open in the back of my skull. My entire substance—flesh, blood, sap, water, salt, gray matter, electricity, thoughts, nerve impulses—all rushed out of my navel as though through a pinhole open to a vacuum, and as the last stuff of me squealed out and I reached to grab the tail end, I felt the dew on my hands. Mrs. Horney was crouched over me saying something, her hands rubbing mine.

That night after I sat in the flames of the Buddhist monk, I crawled on my belly to the alley, staying on the narrow edge of weeds beside the hedgerow, and crawled on my belly all the way to McBride Ave. At the mouth of the alley, tucked between a forsythia bush and a stone wall, I listened and smelled, pressing my cheek to the cool dirt. I spread my hands and tried to grip the roundness of the earth.

I made my way to the entrance of the rain sewer across from Minardi's bakery and slipped beneath the grate. This was where I wanted to be. It was the imaginative tunnel that children descend beneath the blankets of their beds to explore passageways that unfold before them. I followed the main pipe all the way to the sluice. There, by moonlight, I climbed down the concrete, down the rock cliff and into the Passaic.

4

TODAY HAS BEEN A FAIR DAY FOR GATHERING FOOD—A decent day's work. Newark feels like home today. My body's a bit weary from the trip to the shore, and it feels good. I feel my shoulders from swimming and my legs from so much walking. I'm well fed and well into a new pint of homemade cherry liquor. There's a dull glow on my arms and face.

I've been able to sort some things through since I've been in Newark. Just getting away from those poppies helped a lot. The ground may be shaky beneath me, and I don't know where I'm going, but I'm getting along.

The sun is deep yellow, almost orange now behind the buildings, making even this beat-up section of Newark seem almost charmed. I sit and sip the liquor and continue this journal. I've only scratched the surface—just raised the rock slightly. There were long years before the hearing in Paterson with nothing to hold on to, no reason not to rip people off, no reason not to schlep a man's wife off to bed. There were not many reasons to go on. Except James Robinson, a combat vet I knew in L.A., decided against going on, and that made no sense to me either. I think I carried on just to devour myself—to get down to nothing, where there must be a germ of sense.

I try to recall L.A. and what followed—what led to my condition in Paterson—to see what crawls out. But for now I seem to be occupied with Newark—Monkey at his window, the sun going down, the bass throb of the jukebox from the open door of Kelly's Tavern.

Five minutes ago I cried suddenly—I don't know why. It's among a number of odd moments that have passed recently. My arms, then my throat and face heated up—a glow from the sunburn I thought. I looked around the room, and the room, as though it were capable of human emotion, seemed unbearably sad—the lamps, the soiled chairs, the human sediment, the silt and odor of living, the yellowed Enos Slaughter baseball card stuck in the frame of the mirror, the constructions I'd made of rusted junk, each with its own pathetic reason for being. I looked it all over, then I laughed, then cried. A heavy sigh, an audible pout, a spasm, then a few dumb tears. Sad red leaning on the sunset now. Sad old fart changing his oil down the block.

Without any conscientious effort on my part, this way of life is beginning to make sense, and this sense is revealing itself to me through the things I do everyday, which seem to be singular and true reflections of what I *want* to be doing. There is no progression involved, no steps to accomplish, no sense of going anywhere. There is the cure of the ease of doing. There is the choosing of what things to do. There is the intuition of value in that choosing. Nothing more concrete—nothing more articulate. No mechanical clout of brainpower imposing gauges to calculate productivity and efficiency.

The things I do are mundane compared to the way I used to live, but they are a rich resource. When I first arrived in Newark, shaken from withdrawal from the O and the stress of the final days in Paterson and the years of weirdness before, I was determined to get enough of my life together to prevent another hurried getaway. I thought I'd try a job so I wouldn't have to worry about food and rent—the levels of self-deception are many. A job wasn't in the cards—fortunately.

I had to take a lie detector test at my first interview—security guard. I couldn't help myself. I told the machine fantastic lies, blowing out a thick smoke screen of nonsensical untruths and truths to escape behind. The readout was going wild, and the technician was trying to draw the interview to a hasty close when I persisted.

"I love lie detector tests," I told him, "and I want to answer that last question, so you just wait a minute—sit back down before I break your bones." I found myself committed to bedlam and resigned to unemployment. "This is a wonderful experience for me—plugged into the machine like this," I said. "I want to do well and learn something from this opportunity."

He sat on the edge of the chair warily, putting various pens in his pocket.

"Yes, I've stolen from every company I've ever worked for," I said. "I try to steal something every day—it makes me feel good. Once I stole a Cadoo Coupe De Ville and the salesman and took them both on a test drive. I stole him for the entire working day. I told him I'd kill him with his matching pen and pencil set unless he enjoyed himself. We drank beer, watched a Little League game, visited his mother in Kearny. I bought him lunch. I bought a Tom Waits tape for the cassette, a pint of George Dickel Tennessee sippin' whiskey, a couple of Marsh-Wheeling cigars, and we cruised all day in the Cadoo with the air conditioner on and the windows open. Then I walked away—disappeared into Willowbrook Mall. I'm creative and energetic. I'd be an asset to this company. You should recommend me to the white people here. I have a high sense of loyalty. I'd work overtime. I'd work my life away. I'd die a thousand deaths. I'd eat shit and like it."

I think I realized when he plugged me into the machine that a job would make it tougher to survive. James Robinson was trying to do his job well. I'm not recommending anything. I happened to slip through the net. I'm not sure it's working.

Judging from today, it's working. I hitched back from the shore with two albacore, a bunch of blue claw crabs, some apples and some mint. As usual I had to wait for a truck driven by someone who knew that cars won't stop for a hitcher with a load. I sat up on the wheel well in the back of the pickup all the way. Wind in my face. Feeling pretty cocky. Don't know about those tears.

Most folks who charter a boat down the shore for a day don't eat albacore because the flesh is so bloody, so it's easy to pick them up for free at the docks when the charters come in. All they need is a good soak in salt water. Then I just throw them in the oven with butter, parsley and lemon. The meat flakes off in chunks. It's a mild fish when baked —good hot or cold or in salad or sauce.

The crabs are free for the grabbing. They're not as abundant as they used to be, but if time is not a problem, which it isn't for me, just dragging a fish head along the shallow coves near the marina will lure plenty of good-sized blue claws into the range of a net.

Lots of fruits and vegetables can be gathered at the shore too. I usually wait for the cover of night for the vegetables, but apples, peaches and pears, when in season, can be had any time of the day. I know of several orchards that are still surrounded by woods or some type of cover.

There are lots of ways to get food in the city as well. In fact, in some ways, it's easier in the city, but I enjoy the fresh fish, and apples are best as they come off the tree, and since I'm never in a hurry I usually take time for a long swim in the ocean.

I prefer to live in the city though. It's easier to be anonymous here, and it's easier, in general, for a man who doesn't talk much and won't work a job. And if I really want to I can get fresh fish in the city by fishing the Passaic. People say it's poison and any fish that can live in it is poison. I know the river's sluggish with chemical waste, but I've never gotten sick from eating the carp and catfish, and I don't think I ever will. And the carp, because no one fishes the river anymore, are fat and plentiful.

There's a small patch of earth along the factory wall behind the dry cleaners. I plant herbs and vegetables there. Tomatoes and peppers do well because the wall holds the heat of the sun and shelters the plants.

Experimenting with recipes has become a satisfying way to pass the time. I use mostly inexpensive foods and foods I can gather for free, although, as the mood strikes, I'll throw together a fairly extravagant dish—maybe paella with fresh shellfish and sausage made at Pat's Italian Meats. I usually invite Willie Sykes for these feasts.

I cook a lot of dried beans, rice, soups and stews. Last week I made a great pesto. Basil plants love that spot along the factory wall. I was surprised to find pine nuts at the Italian markets. I can spend an entire day cooking.

Though I don't speak much anymore I still manage to have a few acquaintances in the neighborhood. As far as most people are concerned, I don't speak at all, unless someone buys me a drink—then I'll talk some, but even then I mostly listen and nod. At times people get me drunk to make me talk. This has only served to encourage my silence, since a free drink is by far the best drink, and there's only one thing better than cheap whiskey, and that's good whiskey, and good whiskey is at its prime when it's paid for by some fish on the hook of silence. "What'll ya have?" they ask. "Anything on the top shelf," I say.

Then, typically, after an initial warm-up of sports talk, which I know very little about, they want to know about me—how I make a living, where I come from, why I'm living in Newark, what sports I played in high school . . . Sometimes I tell fantastic lies, and sometimes I tell the truth, and they never know the difference. "I wasted a small-time politician in a fight over his wife," I tell them, "and I'm hiding from the law." They say, "Why would you tell us that if it was true? Suppose we turn you in?" "Of course," I say, "you're right. Then I'd have to waste you too." "How do you make a living?" they ask. "I'm a retired assassin and kidnapper on a government pension," I tell them. "When are you going to tell us the truth?" they ask. "Soon," I say, "soon."

There's a college nearby, and I can eat lunch there every day if I want to. I walk around the cafeteria until I find a tray with a portion of food left on it. I eat what I want of it and move to another table and do the same. Often from there I go to the college library. Lately I've been reading pharmacology texts and collections of old writings about the uses of herbs. On a good day I can read eight hundred pages. I read all of *Ulysses* while I was sitting on the can. The janitor came in and asked me to leave at closing time. My heart was going like mad and I said yes I will Yes. We talked for a long time while he mopped. "Tell me you didn't really climb into this guy James Robinson's coffin in front of his whole family," he said, leaning on his mop, looking me in the eyes. "Well," I said, "I never really closed the lid." What the fuck—James got a kick out of it. We giggled like children in there. "Fuckin' awright!" James said. "Don't let them open the lid."

In my one-room I have heat, a small kitchen and a bathtub with hot water. I made real art for the walls and put the salt in an eyecup that was left in the medicine cabinet. I sanded the rust off a discarded cast iron Dutch oven and seasoned it with olive oil. No need to paint—I wouldn't touch the walls—the plaster has aged like meerschaum. The cracks are perfect, especially where the plaster has fallen and the lath is exposed. I'll never want more than this. I can get by on ninety dollars a month, sometimes less. The rent is only seventy dollars a month because the place is run-down and in a run-down neighborhood, and Newark, generally, is run-down. I furnished the place with junk I found in the trash and banged together. It's very chic. And I don't mind the neighborhood at all. It's actually a decent place to live.

The cop on the beat can go into Kelly's Tavern down the street and have a few shots and nobody cares. There's not much traffic because there's not much reason to be here. The tavern gets by on the warehouse men, a handful of regulars and their wives and girlfriends, Johnny from Nutley who drives over because he likes the place, the Wonder Bread driver, six or seven Saturday-nighters from Bingo at the Catholic church, Miguel and a few of his *compañeros,* a few younger women who stop over after the wire factory closes . . . It's a good joint.

I was reading a novel about down-and-out club fighters, and the liquor store on the corner was mentioned. A few welfare hotels and apartment buildings are scattered throughout the vicinity—white and black and hispanic and all the combinations—people from the state mental institution, unwed mothers, women who need to change men quickly so they can collect half of the rent each month, alcoholics on pensions . . . Some people just grew up in the buildings and never moved.

There's no murder or serious theft here. Last month a vegetable truck vendor was had for a crate of rutabagas. A man was stabbed in the thigh with a fork last year. A man was charged with biting off his girlfriend's eyebrow after she stopped him from hitting another woman. And last year it came out in the newspaper that a man around the corner tried to trade in his baby boy for a used Corvette. The car dealer and his wife couldn't have children, but after deliberation they turned down the offer because they realized they would eventually have to tell the boy he was traded for a car. Decent folks around here. I wound up with a few of the rutabagas myself. Willie Sykes had a hand in the plunder.

The trees here are old ones that tore up the sidewalks long ago. The vacant lots will be vacant forever. The streets and sidewalks are free of Coke cans and McDonald's bags. There's no fast food in the neighborhood, no upward mobility—nobody's buying up. It's a great neighborhood to walk in if you don't have anywhere to go.

I sometimes manage to earn the rent by buying and selling used inexpensive but useful items or trading for something I know a buyer for. I listen at the bar for what people are needing and I read the classifieds and bulletin boards.

If the month goes by and I haven't earned the rent, I can take it from a meager but, to me, substantial savings I accumulated years ago. I haven't touched this money since six months ago when I bought a used typewriter from an office supplier downtown. I can usually pick up odd jobs from Jim Kelly, who owns Kelly's Tavern, or from the woman who runs the dry cleaners downstairs or through several opportunities that present themselves during the course of a month.

The jukebox at Kelly's is mostly jazz—Dizzy, Louis, Ella, Benny, two sides of Sidney Bechet, some Glenn Miller tunes. There are even a few Billie Holiday songs and a Lil Green record. Some old Sinatra, too, and Clarence "King Pleasure" Beeks doing "Symphony Sid" and "Little Red Top." It's an interesting collection for a shot and beer joint. Jim Kelly was a swinger in his youth, a cool cat—loves the old jazz—I've heard the stories. There's a color TV above the bar, too, so if I'm in the mood for a ball game I can sit there all day without drinking or talking.

Lately I've been carrying cases of beer up from the cellar for Jim Kelly in exchange for a few shots. I like to leave after the whiskey to enjoy the alcohol in my blood out in the weather—out in the street where I can watch people in their comings and goings.

I often run into Willie Sykes in the street. He likes to sit on the stoop of the Blue Eagle News Stand and unwrap his egg sandwich from the Essex Diner. I usually roll a smoke from his can of Prince Albert while he spreads catsup on one half of the hardroll and mayonnaise on the other. He then opens his container of coffee and gets comfortable. Between halves he always rolls a smoke and smokes it before eating the second half. Willie knows how to savor an egg sandwich.

During the winter, out on the stoop there, it's his chance to complain about getting "murdered in Dallas" every season. He hates Tom Landry and swears it comes back on him because he loses no matter which way he bets.

But now, in the summer, he doesn't play the numbers. "Baseball," he said yesterday, "I don't bet on baseball. It's a sacrilege. Football is good for nothing but betting. It's like basketball—back and forth and back and forth—ten-foot shines running back and forth like trained seals. But baseball is an art, and you don't bet on art unless you're a barbarian like Bernie—he bets on baseball. He'd bet on the date of his mother's death —if he had a mother."

Bernie is Willie's buddy. They retired the same year. Their wives died a year apart. Now they're going through their second adolescence together.

So Willie rattled on about the Newark Bears yesterday, and that got him onto "the old days" and the fighters from Newark and his 880 record at Barringer High. Willie was here when people fished the Passaic, when there were great rock fights between the Irish and Italian neighborhoods.

"In the old days," Willie said with a mouthful of egg sandwich, "well, I knew a woman, a friend of my mother, who got cheated by a shopkeeper down neck. He was a tailor, and I don't remember exactly what happened, but he cheated her out of some bucks. He wouldn't give her the money, no matter how loud she complained, you see. So she storms off down to the cop on the corner. There was this big Irish cop who was always around that corner a lot. She tells him what happened, and he says, 'I'll take care of this,' and the two of them walk back up the block to the tailor shop. The cop goes in and asks the guy—he was this Jew tailor, you know, I forgot to add that—he asks him if he owes the woman some money. So the woman is yelling just like a guinea woman can yell —you know, you've heard them—and the tailor is yelling back. So this big Irish cop—he was a big fella, too—he just picks this Jew tailor up and turns him upside down and starts shaking the money out of his pockets, which is not easy to do with a Jew, as you know. The cop tells the guinea woman to take what's hers, and she probably took a little more for an offering to St. Anthony or a bag of chickpeas or something, and he puts the tailor back on his feet, tells him to watch his bloody ass and goes back to his corner. That's the way it worked in the old days. Things don't work that way anymore, as you know."

"How did he know the tailor cheated the woman?" I asked.

"A good cop just knew these things in the old days. I wouldn't trust them now. Nothing against the Jews, you understand, could have been anybody—happened to be a Jew tailor—that's the way I heard it. I had a good friend when I was in my twenties named Chi-chi Bob. Jewish fella, tough as nails, good fighter. Had these big ears sticking out." Willie pulled his ears out and laughed. "Chi-chi Bob. Had this tight, kinky black hair just like a . . . black fella. Whenever there was a substitution at Laurel Gardens—you know, when a fighter canceled—Chi-chi Bob would fight. He'd get in the ring with anything from a featherweight to a middleweight. Give them a good scrap, too—always. Chi-chi Bob.

"They had some big bouts at Laurel Gardens, you know—some of the big ones." He took a bite of the egg sandwich and spoke through it. "I seen a painting in a book by a fella named Thomas Eakins. It was a fighter sitting in his corner. It was in Laurel Gardens." He took a sip of coffee. "It was a fifteen-foot ring, you know—a small ring, so there was no running. You had to stand and fight.

"My father's brother lived up in Canada," he continued. "He had this string of fighters for a while—real palookas, most of them. He used to call them his 'meal tickets' all the time. He came into Newark with them, looking for some bouts. I was fighting at the time, and he asked me about a place to train, and I was training at Joe Grouch's, so I sent him over to Joe Grouch's. Joe Grouch had a barber shop, and behind the barber's was a gym—right down next to Louie Ting-a-ling's. You know Louie Ting-a-ling's?"

"No."

"This Italian hot-dog joint. You get the Italian pocket bread stuffed with all that garbage—sausage or hot dog and potatoes, peppers, onions —all stuffed in the pocket there. Right next door was Joe Grouch's, which was where Tony Galento trained. It was Tony Galento's lucky gym. Even after he was in the money he still trained at Joe Grouch's before a fight. Galento, you know—he fought bigtime. Fought Joe Louis, Max Baer . . . So my uncle goes down there with his meal tickets, and whatta ya think? Two-ton Tony Galento himself walks in. So before you know it, Galento is looking my uncle's heavyweight up and down." Willie stuck out his lower lip and moved his head up and down. "First thing you know they're in the ring sparring. They get into a clinch in the corner, and they're leaning against the corner post, and just like that —whoosh—the whole deal comes down, post and all, and over they go —baboom!" Willie threw his head back and laughed. "They're both laying there on the floor, rolling around like a couple of hogs." He laughed again. "And, ah, you know—that's the story."

"Did Two-ton Tony ever fight Chi-chi Bob?" I asked.

"Nah, nah—Chi-chi Bob was a middle, tops. Galento was bigtime." He put half of the sandwich down on the paper and took out the can of Prince Albert, filled a rolling paper and handed me the can.

"Newark must have been something in the old days," I said.

"Oh, jeez . . . " He shook his head and rolled up the smoke. "People used to come from all around. Lots of dance halls and all that—the Colonial Ballroom . . . That was a jitterbug joint. Everybody'd be out on the floor like this." He stuck his head forward with his mouth open, an intentionally stupid-looking expression on his face, and rocked to and fro from the waist. "With their mouths open—like this." He opened his mouth and rocked again, then laughed. "I was making twenty-one bucks a month in the Army—just before I went overseas. And Maggie had her two-dollar allowance—she gave the rest to her mother. We weren't big spenders, but we had a good time. Maggie would walk miles to work to save her bus fare for the weekends. We'd get two glasses of beer and nurse them all night. Shit-poor, I'll tell ya." He wagged his head again and lit the smoke. "Chi-chi Bob," he said with a tone of finality, his lips closed on the smoke. Then, "Look there." He pointed to a crack in the sidewalk. "Wildlife. Newark wildlife." He gently touched the small bug. "Potato bug we call them. What do you call them?"

"Potato bug," I said.

"I've heard them called different things. We call them potato bugs because they eat your beets and rutabagas, not because they look like potatoes. You're looking at Newark wildlife in its natural habitat. Pigeons, starlings, carp, potato bugs . . . What else?"

"You mean potato bugs don't eat potatoes?" I asked. "Just beets and rutabagas?"

"They'd eat potatoes, too, if I planted potatoes, but I don't have room. I had rutabaga greens one year sticking up like they had goddamned basketball rutabagas under them—regular bushes, they were. I wait till prime picking time and grab one of them greens and yank and almost fell over backward. Came right up with nothing on the end. Damned potato bugs ate the whole row—right up to the greens. Left just enough where the rutabagas stuck out of the dirt to make me think I had basketballs down there. Not a damned blessed thing—not a damned blessed thing down there but fat potato bugs."

"You can't use a little poison down there?" I asked.

"Nah, nah. My garden's too small for that. Getting smaller all the time, too, because I get lazier every spring. But poison comes back on you. Nah, nah. It's the only piece of earth I got. My grandmother used to say there isn't any difference between a potato bug and a wart—one's just a kind of dormant form of the other. She was crazy though. Old Grandma O'Neill. She said if you piss on the wart—you know, wipe your own urine on it—then kill a potato bug, the wart would fall off."

"Did it work?"

"Never had no warts. I had one—right here on this knuckle—had it for years. Never tried the potato bug remedy. It just fell off one day right in front of the main post office downtown."

Willie is the only person I talk to around here. I like to tell him long lies with a straight face. Sometimes he believes me and sometimes he doesn't, and sometimes, after listening intently for several minutes, he throws his head back and curses me and calls me a "lyin' bastard" and gets up, turns around and sits back down. Though I know he's curious about my past, he never asks.

Just as he lodged the last bite of egg sandwich in the side of his mouth and held it there while he sipped his coffee, I told him that I'd spent five years on a farm team trying to make the Chicago Cubs lineup.

"Then my wife left me," I said, "because it became evident that I wasn't going to become a big-leaguer."

Willie almost choked trying to get his words out. "You played in the Chicago organization?" he asked, drooling a little coffee down his chin. He wiped his mouth, lowered his eyebrows. "You never told me that."

"Well," I said, "when my wife left I quit. Then times got hard. I fell into some bad company and some bad habits. I didn't know how to do anything but play third base."

"The hot corner," Willie said, scrutinizing me.

"No shit."

"Clete Boyer—that was a third baseman," he said.

"I couldn't find a job I could keep. I was running with the wrong crowd. We started knocking over gas stations and 7 Elevens. Got hooked on the adrenalin rush—a replacement for the excitement of playing ball in my case. These other guys, they were combat vets from Nam. Couldn't adjust to not being shot at or flying a million dollars worth of chopper. They were a little shocked to find out they were nothing when they got back—nobodies—kids grown old inside. They craved some excitement, some contact, plus they were used to handling weapons and they weren't scared of getting shot at. I swear sometimes I think they wanted to get caught so they could have a fire fight with the cops. They were generally pissed-off too, from taking a lot of shit about being over there. Then I met a woman who had expensive tastes. I had to step up the gas station business to keep up with her. She was the overemotional type, crisis oriented—'Honey, get my purse, I'm gonna kill myself.' Eventually I got shot and busted and did some time in Rahway."

Willie was eyeing me suspiciously, about to call me a lyin' bastard when I pulled my shirt up and showed him the scar from the wound.

"No shit," he said, as though the scar authenticated the rest of the story.

But Willie was no dummy.

"How'd you do in the minors?" he asked.

".317 lifetime at the plate, and I was a better fielder than I was a hitter."

"Not bad at all. I never knew you played serious ball. Wait till I tell Bernie. He told me he thought you were an athlete. You're not very big for the pros though. Maybe that's why you didn't make it. Gotta have some beef. You from Chicago?"

"No. Just had a tryout there."

He offered to buy me a drink, so we walked down the block to Kelly's.

"Two drafts," Willie said to Jim Kelly, "and two shots." He took his Prince Albert out, filled a paper and pushed the can toward me.

Kelly put the drinks in front of us. "What are you boys up to today?" he said.

"Braggin'," Willie said, lighting his smoke. "Braggin' and lyin'." He raised his beer. "To the Cubs," he said.

I raised my glass.

"Get yourself a drink, Kelly," Willie said.

"For the Cubs?" Kelly asked. "I thought you didn't bet on baseball."

"I didn't win no money. I'm drinking to art."

Kelly poured himself a beer. Willie pushed a dollar to the back of the bar.

"To art," Kelly said.

"The Cubs, art, braggin' and lyin'," Willie said, his glass in the air. He turned to me.

"Braggin' and lyin'," I said, and we drank.

"I met Tony Kubek," Willie said, "and I don't mean by chasing him down at the stadium for an autograph. I had lunch with him."

"The Tony Kubek story," Kelly said, moving to the register.

"A friend of mine from work knew him," Willie said.

"Great ball player," I said.

"You bet your ass. My friend invited me over to lunch when Kubek was visiting. Salami and cheese and tomato sandwiches. And whatta ya think? Ballantine, of course. We made the three ring sign and drank a case." Willie laughed, then his eyes dropped, remembering. "It was off season. I was a Yankee fanatic at the time. Hell of a deal. Great guy, Kubek. Great time.

"Then I got involved with the Mets," he continued. "Wished I never had. But I've always liked the Cubs. I always thought they should've moved them to Brooklyn when the Bums left. What does Chicago know about baseball? Brooklyn fans could make winners out of even the Cubs."

"I think you're right, Willie," I said.

"Hell yes. Lotta energy comes from those grandstands when they're full, as you know. The right fans can make a club click. I've seen it happen."

After a brief pause Willie said, "You know, you should come over for chicken wings Tuesday. Bernie and I are cooking up a mess of wings. We do it about once a month. Wings, potato salad, beans, sliced tomatoes, a case of beer."

"Tuesday, huh?" I hesitated.

"Yeah. Whatta ya got big plans for Tuesday? Come on over."

"Okay," I said. "Sounds great. I'll make the potato salad. How's that?"

"Nah, nah. I just pick it up at the deli."

"I can make better potato salad than that."

"Don't bother, really. Deli's good."

"I don't mind making it."

"It's good at the deli. We like it."

"I bet you use canned beans, too."

"What other kind of beans is there?"

"There's dried beans."

"Too hard. Break my teeth." He chuckled.

"Cooked with lots of garlic and onions and pork," I said.

"Why bother?"

"Because it's much better and much cheaper. You'd probably have money the last week of the month if you cooked your own beans and potato salad."

"Who needs money the last week of the month when the first of the month is only a week away?"

"You could save on the chicken wings too, if you buy whole chickens and save up the wings in the freezer."

"What is this, Helpful Hints from What's-her-name? Then what do I do with the backs and necks, dear? Stuff my throw pillows?"

"Backs and necks are good for the stock pot."

"What stock pot?"

"The one you don't have. Soup, man—stock for soup. That's the secret of good soup. One of them, anyway. Much better than Campbell's, and it's much cheaper. You could drink more beer—even buy a pack of humps once in a while."

"Better than Campbell's? I don't know."

"Would I lie to you?"

"You fucking would. Sounds like a lot of trouble."

"I forgot, Willie. Your schedule is pretty tight these days. I lost my head. You have to sit on the stoop of the Blue Eagle and tell lies. You have to—"

"I don't know how to make soup stock. Campbell's does. When my TV goes on the blink I don't go in with a claw hammer—I take it to the man who knows."

"Soup is easy, and it doesn't take a lot of time, and whatever time you put in you get back because your own soup makes you live longer. You buy a whole chicken and cut it up into breasts, thighs and wings. Throw the wings in the freezer . . ."

"I'm not listening, and there's no such thing as living longer than you're gonna live, and I'm not interested in what's cheaper. I especially like to lose money mysteriously, and I don't—"

"Throw the wings in the freezer until you have enough to feed Bernie," I said loudly to interrupt him. "The breasts and thighs are good for baking or whatever you do."

"I eat them raw."

"The rest—the back, neck, legs—throw them in a pot of cold water with a couple of carrots, an onion, some celery, a bay leaf and whatever leftovers you have hanging around."

"Like Campbell's cream of tomato?"

"Ends of broccoli, old lettuce—any damned thing except starchy stuff. No potatoes—makes it too gluey. Then simmer it for a few hours—just forget about it."

"I'm trying."

"Go get an egg sandwich, then come back later and strain it. Save the chicken for chicken salad. Put the stock in the fridge overnight, and in the morning all the fat will be on the top. Take it off. Pour the stock in a pot and make soup—any kind you want—any kind Campbell's can make."

"Whatta you got against Campbell's?"

"It's not as good as homemade."

"Sounds like a lot of work."

"It's not."

"Sounds like it is."

"It's not."

"I don't know you very well," Willie said, "but I trust you."

"Try it—I'm tellin' ya."

"I'm not talking about your damned soup. And I don't go around saying this to everybody on the street."

I flagged Kelly for another round. Willie pushed the can of Prince Albert toward me.

"How can you trust me when I lie to you?" I asked.

"Ah, bullshit. Lying has nothing to do with it. Talking is lying. Now don't get me wrong—I mean, I'm not a queer or anything, and I don't want to borrow money. Bernie and me and Joe Duffy and Dave from the wire factory, we were talking, and we all agreed."

"That's amazing."

"It is, but we were thinking that you'd be the right man to talk to. Like I said, I don't know much about you, and they know a lot less. You're not exactly a talkative guy. I don't know what you know and what you don't know, or what's a lie and what isn't, but I know, somehow, that you are the man to talk to. I trust you."

"I'm not your man, Willie, no matter what you're going to spring on me here. I'm not your man." I pulled a Zig-Zag from the pack and opened the can of tobacco.

Willie held up his palms to me. "Lemme just pull on your coat sleeve here for a minute. No harm in listening. You see, this guy Miles—his name is Miles—a colored fella. Lives over by Jeanie's place. The market, you know."

"Yeah, I know Jeanie's. Don't know Miles."

"Well, Miles got himself a job—a decent job, I mean, a job he likes—and it's perfect, you see, because it's only two blocks away, and Miles is in a wheelchair. He got shot up in Vietnam, and he doesn't have a car and can't afford one, especially with all the special rigging he'd need.

"He was okay when he got out of the Marines," Willie continued, "at least he thought he was. I guess something happened to his leg a few years later. All these civilian doctors say it was because of an operation he had while he was in the service, when the doc patched him up after he was shot. Eventually they had to take the leg off, but this is all years after he's back, you see, so the government won't pay for a thing. They won't even increase his disability money."

He pulled another rolling paper from the package. "He's had it to court and appealed the decision and the whole ten yards, and the government just refuses to take responsibility. So he's got no car. He's got no money. In debt up to his ass. And he finally lands this job playing piano in the bar over at The Embers. Fancy place, right? Kind of place you can't afford to eat in. The pay is good. The guy can play like a pro. And The Embers is only two blocks away, as the crow flies, but—"

"—The canal's in the way," I said.

"The damned river canal's between him and the job, and the closest bridge is what?—six, seven blocks, with that damned hill in the way. And to top it off, the fucking shine bus driver—can you believe this?—the shine bus driver won't stop for him because it's a big fucking deal to drag the damned wheelchair on board. It puts him off schedule, he says, and Miles is a shine too—brothers, right?

"So we called the city, and supposedly the driver was told to stop, but he doesn't. So we called again, and this is after Miles called five times, but it's no good—the bastard just drives by like Miles isn't even there, and the city won't do a thing about it except tell us they ordered the driver to stop. Can you believe this? None of us have cars, right, except Dave and Joe, and they both work, and the wives need the car and this shit and that shit, and that's no good anyway—we can't be haulin' him to work everyday. You see what I'm saying? We gotta do something.

Miles is about to give it up. We gotta do something in writing or something—some legal shit—and we're all lucky we can write our names, and since I know you're probably writing more than just your name over and over on that typewriter . . . "

"Come on, Willie. You guys aren't stupid. Get a lawyer."

"That's the last resort. Nobody can afford a lawyer."

"Get a free lawyer. Miles would probably qualify for free legal services. Hell, go to the ACLU. Maybe they'd—"

"See, that's the kind of stuff we need you for. But look—I think there's a way without all that, and the courts would take time, and Miles doesn't have time. He'll lose the job. The job is more important than winning a court battle with a bus driver. We thought you could help. Not just with the writing. Maybe you could point us in the right direction. Maybe you could think of something that would work quickly."

"What makes you think I could do that?"

"I don't know."

"Drag the driver off the bus and stomp his ass."

"That won't solve the problem. We think maybe this guy has something against Miles personally, but Miles says he never saw him before."

"I can't do it. You boys get something on paper, and I'll take a look at it, but I'm not dealing with no city council or legal system or any other pack of dogs. I can't do it. I'm invisible, and I want to stay invisible, and I wouldn't be any good at any brilliant and cunning maneuvers because . . . because I can't. I can't afford to get involved, Willie, believe me. I won't even consider it. I'm sorry. I'm not engaging in any battles here —I don't have an inch of footing."

"I thought I'd ask. No harm in asking."

"Not at all."

"Forget it then."

"It's forgotten."

But I didn't forget that easily. I thought about that conversation a lot while I was down the shore today, and I concluded that I really can't afford to get involved. It would be a mistake. I've been maintaining here in Newark. I can't afford to draw attention to myself and I can't afford to engage. Now listen to yourself as you write this. Mr. Excitement has given up his practice. In fact, maybe I should back off from Willie. I should just stay in here and write this journal.

When I got home today I poured some homemade cherry liquor, knocked it down, poured another. I put the albacore in a washtub of salt water, dropped crabs in boiling water, poured some more cherry liquor and sat on the fire escape.

I ate the crabs with just a little lemon, lemons I got from the trash behind The Embers. I made pasta with garlic and oil.

Now, sitting at the typer with liquor I made from cherries I gathered down the shore last year and tea made from mint I gathered from people's yards, I don't feel like such an evil person, but that could be the alcohol.

5

IT WAS A REAL PROFESSIONAL WHO WORKED ON JAMES ROBinson—a real artist.

Where Robinson's cheeks had become sunken, they were filled out somehow. The bags under his eyes were gone—stretched or tightened. With his mouth closed, the gaps where his teeth had fallen out could not be seen. Because he was lying down, the arch in his backbone that developed over the last year could not be noticed. His eyes were closed, of course, so people were graciously saved from looking into the abyss that took over there when all desire, meaning, purpose or whatever else clutters the eyes of humans vacated James Robinson. Even the fear that was for so long stuck there like a parasitic worm had dropped off the dying body in the final months. James looked healthier as a corpse than he did before his suicide, when heroin moved in and life moved out.

The death was odd, the way they had it laid out there, like a holiday of death, like a springtime of death, with death on the pedestal as the centerpiece for the feast of death. And death was all dressed up for the occasion, all scrubbed and on its best behavior. The flowers were lovely and the music was groovy and the funeral director was the most. What a time we had—the guests in their black and blue basics. Everybody touched each other's hands. There was the thickest of carpets—everybody milling around three inches off the floor, like angels mill around, like understanding grieving angels mill around at a funeral parlor. I never thought black people could be so white, milling around three inches off the ground in dark conservative suits and dresses: no saxophones, no trumpets of Gabriel, no white patent leather shoes, no beautiful old man just a-moanin' on the fractured edge of some gospel tune so effortlessly it makes you cry—and no tears, not a tear—and this white music having the gall to filter down from the tinny ceiling speakers.

Then the littlest girl started wailing, and she heaved a big spasmodic sigh and wailed again louder, her hands wringing, trying to wring out all the whiteness, I think, and get down to the black of her genes, but a woman came up to tell her to stop crying, in a comforting sort of way, and a man came up to help. They knelt beside the littlest girl. The girl hushed her wailing, stifled it, tightened it into sobbing, and the man and the woman managed to hush the sobs, leaving them in there for her to digest, so that she might be nourished in the ways of funerals, in the modern sense. They walked the littlest girl to a bench along the wall and left her there.

"You can cry if you want," I said to her.

"I can?" she asked.

"If it's sad, you're supposed to cry."

She looked across the room, rubbed her eyes with the back of her hand, kicked her leg back and forth, "It's very sad."

"Then cry if you want. I'll stay here with you." I kicked my leg back and forth with hers. "What's so sad?"

"James."

"You're sad because James is gone?"

"Yeah. I'm scared because he'd dead."

"No need to be scared. Death may be sad, even boring, but it's not scary."

"It's not?"

"I've peeked in. I've been there and put my foot in the door, looked around, talked to a few friends, then came back."

"Did your friends think it was scary?"

"Nah. They said it's okay. They said it's a little boring but it's okay."

"You haven't been there."

"I've been right up to the door, on this side of the door, I'm tellin' ya, and I talked to some people there, and they said it's kind of like being born only there's nothing to do and no place to go but it doesn't hurt and it makes more sense."

"Uncle Albert said it's 'cause of God, 'cause God wanted James."

"How would Uncle Albert know that?"

She shrugged, looked up at my face, " 'Cause he's a grownup man."

"He's just guessing. Grownup men don't know anything."

"They don't?"

"Does Uncle Albert know God? Of course he doesn't. Then how would he know God wanted James? Grownups don't know anything."

"Then how do you know it's not scary?"

"I told you, because I've been there. Besides, was it scary before you were born?"

"Before I was born?"

"Yeah."

Uncle Albert had moved within earshot. He stepped up and said, "What are you telling this child?"

"That death isn't scary."

He put his hand on the child's shoulder and moved her away from me. "Of course it isn't scary," he said. "You go home to Jesus when you die. I'm not sure the child's mother would approve of your views, and you're probably confusing the little one, so I'll thank you to leave her alone."

The girl began to cry again.

"I don't think she wants to be alone," I said.

"You let us take care of it."

She gasped for air and still crying said, "That man said people aren't scared when they die, Uncle Albert."

"Jesus meets you and takes you to God, child. Never you mind about what this man tells you."

"Who wants to be met by some bloody dude with holes all over him?" I asked.

The man took the child by the hand and led her away.

Before Uncle Albert could say boogie man I stepped up to the coffin and opened the half of the lid that covered the legs so the entire box was open. I rolled the body onto its side to make room, climbed in beside Robinson and closed the lid after me.

Uncle Albert tried to lift the lid, but I held it down by the lip around the edge. He sent someone for the funeral director.

The little girl started crying louder. I heard Uncle Albert tell her to leave the room, but she wouldn't. In a few minutes he told her again. I listened to her wailing, thinking nothing, holding tight to the coffin lid.

The funeral director sounded gay. He asked me to come out. James was quiet. I got out.

I walked in the hot southern California sun to some fern bar. The place was full of skylights and blonde waitresses with deep tans. Brie and chablis for the bored and beautiful. I ordered a George Dickel and sat there blankly.

It seems like a lifetime ago when I lived in California, when the biopsy determined that the white spot on my throat was malignant. It was not hip to have cancer in California. And adjusting to death by cancer was not an attractive idea.

Sitting in Newark now, under the overcast Jersey sky, remembering it all on the typer, it seems like a fictitious character I'm writing about, and my memory of what happened in California is foggy and disjointed. When Robinson died it had already been a year since debriefing, and I still wasn't sure I'd survived the war—it was a daily matter—and that was before I knew about the cancer. There were frequent suicides among combat vets, and some among the guys I knew from the therapy group.

And James Robinson, in his silken repose, in his newly manicured opulence, in his sweatless luxury, had captured behind those indifferent eyelids a poise and self-composure that couldn't be denied.

In Nam, fear—some kind of primordial fear—was so indistinguishably tangled with survival that death somehow became a companion— a calm word amid the perpetual howling. What returned in me from Nam is irrevocable and irreconcilable. I'm a carrier of a mutant perception. I doubt we are a civilized society at all, beyond the rules that we agree to play by, that say we must believe we are civilized.

While trying to find a life in southern California at the time, I was still hearing the twig snap in the trees and assault rifles blast into the branches like a pack of mad dogs. Often it wasn't determined whether the shredded meat that fell was a VC sniper or a monkey, but at least you could pull the trigger and fear would burst out of you a clip at a time.

As we got closer to the target hamlet we couldn't react to snapped twigs, but had to stand and wait to see if one of us got zapped before we gave ourselves away with gunfire, even if it was the distinctive popping of AK-47s.

But the serious problems were not the bad dreams or the imaginative reenactment of horror. More serious, more problematic was the everyday living—that was the real mind-fuck—the ordinary comings and goings and errands and jobs and people. I knew that people were icebergs. What I saw on the beach, under umbrellas at poolsides, on tennis courts, on campuses, at parties or on the job were the tips of icebergs, unaware of their own submerged bulk. Under the murky forbidden water, roots of unfathomable instincts were gnarled in the deeper strata of the brain.

These instincts had tasted human blood. Superstitions, rituals, ceremonies, spells, ghosts, curses lived in the protein of that blood. I saw the blood splattered in the strangest places—in my salad bowl at a vegetarian restaurant, on my shoe, on the dining room window of a tennis club, in the white foam of the ocean waves.

Death is not sterile, removed, institutionalized or abstract down in that blood. It's attendant, over the shoulder. It's functional. It informs the living about how to live. It has a vital need to cherish every little bug of life as a part of its body.

I believed that, yet I'd discarded human life like trash in Nam, and even then, in Hollywood, I cherished nothing. The world transformed daily, distorted before my eyes, as though the white malignant spot on my throat, like the thumbprint of death, was a hole through which altered perceptions of the commonplace would enter and exit. Every trendy fad imaginable was flourishing simultaneously in southern California, and every one of them made it that much more difficult to go on. The triviality of business as usual depressed me. I wanted everyone to tear their hair in anguish and spit their teeth in despair.

I was drunk every night for months at a time, and every morning I woke up about six and went to the bathroom to vomit. I'd been mixing beer and whiskey every day since Robinson died—shots and beers—and I thought that was causing it, so I cut out the beer and drank whiskey with a water back, but the next four mornings I woke and had to vomit immediately. Then my legs started aching, which I couldn't understand because my legs were strong—I was still in good shape.

I didn't drink a drop one night. In the morning I got up and vomited. I quit drinking completely for three weeks, and seventeen of those twenty-one days I woke up at dawn and made the trip to the toilet to vomit, so I went to a doctor at the VA hospital in L.A. In fact, I went back three times. He did a series of tests, but he couldn't find a thing wrong with me. I figured the illness was related to the wound, but the doc said he was sure that it wasn't. He assured me that the surgery had been successful and the wound was healed and there was no reason for it to ever give me any trouble. He gave me some medication for nausea and sent me on my way.

Then one morning I woke up with something hard in my mouth. I'd broken a tooth in half while sleeping. The dentist said, judging from the looks of my other teeth, that I probably ground my teeth every night —"Either that or you've been eating nails," he said.

It was the dentist who discovered the cancer. He noticed the white spot and urged me to have it checked out.

"It's malignant," the doc told me over the phone, "but it may be operable, and if it's not, we've had some success arresting this type of cancer with..." And then he said it. "Chemotherapy." I'd been waiting in dread for that word. The cure was worse than the ailment. And I knew it was no cure, not for a spell, a curse.

I'd had enough of the hospital already with just the tests. I was abjectly afraid of being killed by the chemotherapy—captured, sedated and weakened. As I recall, there was no decision involved. During the week following the diagnosis I developed the morning ritual. The ritual was born of desperation—a byproduct of helplessness and confusion. I had cancer; it was that simple, and I couldn't consider putting myself in the hands of experimental science. Yet, after daily summoning the energy to force the decision to survive, I couldn't simply do nothing and let the cancer have my body.

Frequently, after completing the ritual, I'd go lie on the beach and read, all the time conscious of the onus I wore on my throat, trying to find the mental footing to confront it.

The hip chic beaches severely depressed me, and the family middle-class beaches weren't much better. They both triggered cynicism and bitterness in my already ailing mind. I began going to a beach in front of a private swim and tennis club that belonged to the wealthy.

The staid, slow-moving deliberate rhythms of the place were soothing.

It seemed barren to me, incapable of producing any changes in the routine. Though I knew it was nothing that could help my condition, at least it was not aggravating. Two aspirin and some rest.

The club was populated by people who were removed from as much of the world as they wanted to be—that was the way I understood wealth —so far into the extreme of what contributed to my depression that they seemed to emerge absolved from the other end in the soft indirect lighting of confidence and control. They dealt in the luxury of choice. They seemed to be—or thought they were, or acted like they were— in control of the game. It was amusing. It didn't bother me.

I'd watch the silver-haired elders from my spot on the beach as they glided sure and unhurried across the dining room behind the tinted glass coolness. I'd watch them eating their low-calorie lunches of shrimp or abalone or veal or fresh salmon. They maintained excellent diets—I was sure. Saw the best doctors, played tennis, swam, walked the golf links. They got lots of sunshine, never overexerted themselves and lived a grand life of control and moderation. They were well-informed, stimulated, active, charitable, articulate, well-traveled. They knew their geography firsthand, their history through economic trends and their literature through the casual and disciplined use of an abundance of time to themselves.

This is the way I saw them, anyway, from my sweaty seat in the sand. I deduced all this from the way they moved, greeted each other, sat in the sun, laughed, chatted over lunch. Surely these are the gods, I mused rhetorically, who have acquired a place in the world—a cool place in the sun. Never a bead of sweat, a discouraging word, a soiled hand or a desperate twinge unless by the controlled adventure of choice. The landed gentry of mental balance and wholesomeness. It didn't bother me. I was twisted. Flirting with the fringe. Beginning, I think, to destroy the pathogens of reason.

I met a good-looking young woman there one day. She came up to me on the beach with this confident and educated jive—too cool to be cool, or beyond cool, or fashionably uncool—I never did figure it out. But she was nice, really nice, and smart, pretty smart. We sat in the sun and got blasted on Heineken. I remember talking about Swinburne, never having read him. I'd swallowed just enough Heineken to know everything about Swinburne. I'd run across his name reading the socialistic novels of Jack London. I just conjured up an image that I thought London would like. The way I had it figured, Swinburne was okay—too romantic, of course, but we gave him that much. He was likeable, really, for all his naiveté.

She had actually read Swinburne in a literature class at Smith or someplace—in the same college where she'd never read Neruda and never heard César Vallejo mentioned. Even Galway Kinnell she thought was one of the Aran Islands off the northwest coast of Ireland. But she took me into the club, into the room of tinted glass where I'd never been, and we drank more imported beer and swam in the excellent pool, making fools of ourselves with loud drunken laughter, turning the cool eyes of the sedentary up from their tall drinks clinking in the shade of poolside umbrellas.

I fell to my belly beside the diving board, slithered across the tile to the water and, with arms held to my sides, slipped noiselessly over the side. I remained underwater for almost a minute, swimming with undulations of the torso, then surfaced just my head from nose up. I was a few inches from Karen's thighs. Underwater, I reached for her thigh with my tongue, but she dove to the side, her slim body arching away in the bubbles.

It was after we swam and dried in the sun that I entered the room of tinted glass, following her lead, venturing only as far as the lounge area around the near end of the bar while Karen ordered two Heinekens on her father's number. The blood was splattered from ceiling to floor on the window. The sea sloshed, mute and sullen beyond, a miscolored TV blue from the tinted glass. On the inside of the glass people shifted languidly in the cool blue of a tinted sun. It was late for lunch, and the room was hushed. Just a few groups lingered at the tables along the windows. They looked just as fine, just as calm in person, I thought, as though they were luminaries I recognized from the cinema. Because I had thirty hours of beard on my face I felt uncouth. I felt they sensed the squalor in my mind. A tall trim man in white pants, deck shoes and terrycloth shirt turned to look at me. I saw the blood soaking the legs of his pants. The room got quieter. I stood awkwardly a few feet from the bar, neither at the bar nor situated in the lounge area. I took a few steps toward the door. I was chilled by the air conditioning, damp under the arms, and the distant unintelligible murmuring began again in the room as I turned my back.

"Can you handle two?" Karen asked too loudly.

I walked to the foyer without answering, and out into the sun that made my head pound. The blood, like a heat mirage, pooled on the tennis courts. The sun lay on the horizon—a bloated corpse burning and stinking. I sat on the curb, drunk in the afternoon heat, in the brightness. Yes, I could handle two.

Drinking became the foundation of our relationship. Also, I'd been confined to bus routes because I'd totaled my '53 Chevy in a drunken accident south of Mendocino. I couldn't afford to buy a car. So, because Karen had a car I gained a new mobility. We visited her friends in Manhattan Beach, cruised up to S.F. to eat at a Japanese restaurant, over to Sausalito for rum cookies. The confidence with which Karen carried herself, which I both doubted and envied, I came to understand as a trained thing, a condition of her station, a gesture from the tip of the iceberg. Still, the mobility alone seemed to help me, and the companionship did not hurt.

I remember it was the seventy-fifth day of the ritual. By then I'd lost my job. After a week of showing up an hour late the bar manager told me I was gone. I'd begin the ritual at five in the morning and couldn't finish any earlier than ten, even though I never really did anything during the final hour and a half—I'd watch the neighbor in the bungalow below my fifth story window yell at her kids in Spanish or I'd sit on the front stoop of the apartment house and read or I'd walk to the café for coffee. I could just as easily have been at work setting up the well and cleaning ashtrays. So I figure losing that job must have been a part of the ritual that was out of my hands—a kind of divine intervention.

Actually everything was just out of control, and I didn't know what I was doing about any of it, including the ritual.

I only worked three days a week at the bar, so it wasn't any great loss. I did try to explain the situation to the manager, but it was difficult to explain a ritual in a world of miracle drugs and chemotherapy. And he didn't know how to deal with cancer. Cancer is easiest to remove from the mind, which, in this case, could be accomplished simply by firing me one minute and forgetting me the next, which made sense to me too.

I managed to hold on to a part-time job as a late night jock at a public radio station. The place was empty at night, so I didn't have to deal with anyone. All I had to do was play music and read the play list over the air between sets. I didn't get into any patter about the music. I just tried to play good music and put it together well. It was therapeutic, really, and eventually I incorporated the ritual into the radio job.

At the end of my Sunday shift, actually Monday morning at one, when I signed off, I would leave the power raised after sign-off while I filed records away. Then I'd boost the power, pot up the studio microphone, put the headphones on so I could hear myself, close my eyes and sit quietly, listening to my breathing in the headphones. When I felt like a lot of my scattered energies had been gathered, I'd begin a variation, an end-of-the-week extension of the daily morning ritual.

Seventy-five days before, I'd dug two holes in a fenced-in vacant lot behind a taco stand a block away from my apartment building on North Normandie in the low rent district of Hollywood. The holes were oval, about six inches deep and spaced six inches apart. Each morning I'd stand in the holes while the sky was still dark but beginning to lighten in the east. I'd squat, with my feet in the holes, in a position that the Vietnamese use to rest or eat, and raise my eyes to the moon, trying, usually unsuccessfully, to be serious.

With my eyes fixed on the moon I'd draw all the electricity in my body to the white spot until the eastern sky was washed with light. Then, slowly, with careful control and trying not to laugh or forget what I was doing, I'd send the electricity down my backbone and gather it again in my groin. Then I'd release these laserlike beams from my heels, sending them down, at the speed of light, to the earth's core. There they would stop. The electricity in my body would travel down these beams to the center of the earth. How 'bout that.

I'd deal with this fantastic and abstract notion matter-of-factly, as though it was both beyond and unworthy of any questioning or scrutiny. It was often a source of amusement—a private black humor that made me laugh out loud at times.

I was, after all, living in the heartland of quasi-psychic hocus-pocus, and my cynicism was sufficiently developed, so it's only because of what followed, which is undeniable fact, that I allow myself to detail this ridiculous process that I still find hard to believe.

I'd keep this electricity flowing, down the spine to the heels to the center of the earth, until I sensed energy from the earth's core rising into my groin simultaneously with the emptying of the body electricity. I don't know how I sensed this rising energy; I guess I made up the sensation and just went with it, riding the indulgences of the imagination into power and efficacy. I didn't have any belief or faith in anything I was doing. The motivation to continue so routinely was simple: since I wasn't pursuing any medical treatment, I had to do something. To do nothing was to give up my body, which had to be out of the question, considering the energy I'd already invested in staying alive.

The mumbo jumbo I engaged myself in at the studio microphone on Sundays was similar to the daily version, and, similarly, I had no notion of faith in it. With the static and the breathing in my ears I concentrated the body electricity in the white spot and brought it to the larynx. When the larynx could no longer contain it I potted up the microphone to the maximum position and screamed a gutteral and bestial sound into it. The modulation meter would leap to the red zone and remain pressed there by the scream converted to electricity. When an FM signal overmodulates it can escape the atmosphere and, sometimes, skip off the ionosphere and land somewhere on the earth's surface thousands of miles away. I entertained the notion that I was dispelling the cancer from my body and jettisoning it into space or dispatching it to some faraway part of the globe.

This seventy-fifth day began no differently than the rest, but a significant detail developed.

I got up and showered as usual. I always had the feeling that the cancer had difficulty with its work while the mind wandered aimlessly in dream; it seemed to thrive on the waking, rational state. I went to the counter by the hot plate, switched on the small lamp there, and began the seventy-fifth ritualistic breakfast.

I opened a new supply of cosmic herb tea that I bought from some whacko who ran a head shop cum apothecary. I'd asked her if it would cure cancer, and she said it would if I had faith, so I always added two shots of George Dickel for faith.

In a blender I mixed bananas, apple juice, fresh carrot juice, debittered brewer's yeast, a bit of soy flour, figs and molasses. I then downed the first of the ten glasses of water I would consume before drinking the pureed mixture. With the tea I ate a handful of almonds, some pine nuts and a bagel with butter and peanut butter. This is what I'd eaten each morning for seventy-five days before I walked to the holes in the vacant lot behind the taco stand.

That morning, the seventy-fifth, before I left I went to the bathroom mirror to inspect the cancer with a flashlight. I saw that the white spot was considerably smaller. I closed my mouth, looked into my eyes, rolled them a little, shook my head and went to put on a shirt.

The moon had waned to a thin crescent. I stepped into the holes and tilted my head back. I laughed, thinking about skipping this part of the ritual for the day, but began the ridiculous routine once again.

6

THINGS HAD BEEN UNCOMPLICATED HERE IN NEWARK. Then, suddenly, I make my social debut at Willie's for chicken wings. Maybe I shouldn't have gone. A few months ago I wouldn't have considered it. I may be risking too much.

Tuesday morning, the day after my trip to the shore, two days after Willie invited me to dinner, I got up early and took some soup stock out of the fridge, skimmed the fat off the top and walked down to Jeanie's to buy soup makings. I was thinking about cream of asparagus or mushroom as a special treat for dinner at Willie's that night. Either one would go well with chicken wings and potato salad. But the fresh asparagus were so expensive that I got annoyed and left without anything.

So I went out back to my small garden and pulled some onions, parsley, chives and six or seven carrots. I was still wondering about what kind of soup to make when I spied the rutabagas. I hadn't pulled a single rutabaga yet. The greens were healthy, and, judging from the tops that stuck out of the soil, it looked like there were some fat rutabagas underneath.

I grabbed the base of the greens, started to pull, then let them go. Up from the lost years in my mind came a Navajo harvest song I'd once read in a book called *Technicians of the Sacred*. The song lingered on the singer/harvester's hesitation to pick the vegetable, a hesitation that seemed to provide for a brief meditation on the precise moment of the picking. The song seemed to ask the harvester to consider, not only if it was the correct moment to pick, but whether the vegetable should be picked at all, demonstrating a reverence for the mystery of growth and a deep gratitude for the plant. The song went: *"Shall I? Shall you? Shall I pick it? Shall you pick it? Shall I pick the fruit of the great corn plant?"* Something like that. It's been a long time.

"Shall I? Shall you?" I said, looking down at the rutabaga. "Shall I pick it? Shall you pick it? Shall I? Shall you?" Could I in these seconds of superficial meditation understand gratitude for a plant? Why not? I thought, though I felt like I'd picked an Authentic Indian Prayer from a Cracker Jack box. But maybe it was a joke to the Indian, too. How can we trust these white man translations, anyway? Maybe it was a big, ironic irreverent Indian joke.

Then I pulled at the rutabaga and suddenly remembered Willie sitting on the stoop of the Blue Eagle News Stand. There was nothing left of the rutabaga, just a chewed stub end. The entire root had been consumed. I dug into the soil and saw a few potato bugs scrambling into the dark.

I grabbed the greens of the next plant in the row. I tried to feel something for the plant—anything. How pathetic. I was bent over there, in the middle of a concrete city, zooming out from myself, seeing an aerial view of myself bent over a tiny plot of earth amid the geometry of concrete, the symmetry of madness, trying to use a few words from an exhausted alien culture to feel something—anything—for a rutabaga before I unplugged it from its socket in the mother. "Shall I? Shall you?" I said and snorted a little spasmatic snigger. I pulled a nice fat rutabaga from the dirt.

I pulled nine rutabagas that way, violating the Navajo song as I worked down the row. Four had been eaten and one was half gone. I took the four whole and the one half and washed them with the carrots, onions, chives and parsley.

I peeled and cut up the rutabagas, carrots and onions and cooked them in butter in my iron soup pot for about five minutes. I sprinkled in a teaspoon of ground coriander seeds from my herb garden. I grated some ginger root and peeled a few cardamom seeds and ground them and added them to the pot. After the spices cooked a few minutes I poured in the stock with some salt and brought it to a boil. I then poured in a cup of uncooked brown rice, put the lid on until the soup was simmering, adjusted the flame to low and went for a walk.

I walked downriver to the city bridge, then back up along the canal, staying between the backyard fences and the wire mesh fence along the bulkhead of the canal. This narrow strip of city land is littered with cans, plastic bags, cardboard—all kinds of trash. I searched among the debris as I walked, looking for anything useable, picking up a few bolts and washers. I was conscious of the sound of the river—a muddled, infused amalgamation that, like a yard full of crickets, emitted a pulsing rhythm of repetitive precise amplitudes.

I passed Jeanie's Market on the other side of the canal, thinking I should have walked the west side so I could check the trash. Just past Jeanie's I saw a black man in a wheelchair reading in the shade of a maple. Miles.

I stopped almost involuntarily, looking at the river, glancing up to eye the black man in his yard.

He looked up from his book. I looked down at the river. I threw a few stones at the bulkhead.

He looked up again and continued to watch me. Rather than look away again, I gave a little lazy salute. "Hey, grunt," I called.

He hesitated a moment, then wheeled down the incline toward me and stopped across from me, the two eight-foot wire fences between us.

"Say what?" he said.

"I said, 'hey, grunt.' I was at a loss for words."

"That's what I thought you said. And who are you, General William C. Westmoreland?"

"Navy SEAL."

"Yeah? Do you bark for fish?"

I didn't reply.

"I know," he said, "SEALs are prime meat. I've heard the stories.

Elite honky crazies. Tougher than fucking nails. Don't know if I believe it. What did you do, sit on a boat and float?"

"I sat on a barge in the Mekong."

"Thought you was 'sposed to be frogmen or some shit. Underwater demolition."

"All the latest Bang and Boom, as the CIA calls it—remote detonation devices, silent weapons, assassination techniques." I threw a stone into the canal. "We did our frogman bit in the irrigation canals."

"I wouldn't trust no Navy—wouldn't trust nobody over there. The guy behind you could trip and shoot you in the back. Got caught in a crossfire once between Navy jerks floating up the river and friendlies, all bustin' caps like madmen at each other."

"Is that where you caught it?"

"No, I caught it in Khe Sanh. I was lucky."

"What did you do to the bus driver?"

"What?"

We were both talking loudly over the noise of the river.

"I said, what did you do to the bus driver?"

"You a friend of Willie?"

"Willie told me about it."

"I didn't do nothing to the bus driver."

"You didn't fuck his woman or something?"

"I gave him some shit 'cause he gave me some shit."

"What kind of shit?"

"Chocolate. Chocolate shit, man."

I threw another stone over the fence and into the water, then looked back at him.

"Second time I rode the bus," he said, "he tells me this joke. You know why so many niggers died in Nam? 'Cause when somebody yelled 'get down' all the niggers stood up and danced."

I threw another rock.

"Funny, right?" he said.

"Funny," I said.

"Well I didn't mind the joke, but then he gives me shit about lifting fucking cripples. Not in his job description. In front of the whole bus, man. I didn't even feel good about riding the bus to begin with. This one-legged bullshit is fairly new to me, man. I lost it in Nam, but it didn't come off till a year ago."

"So you what—threatened his life?"

"I grabbed him by the balls and hung on, trying to reason with him, you know."

"I know."

"*What* do you know? You don't look like no SEAL. You're a shrimpy fucker. Thought SEALs were so big and tough. Maybe you weren't even in Nam, pretty boy."

"Okay, I wasn't then."

"Then don't call me grunt."

I spread my fingers on the mesh of the fence. "I hear you got a job," I said. "That's good."

He nodded, then shrugged.

"What are you reading?" I asked.

"Book," he said.

I tried to read the cover, my head pressed against the fence. The book was propped open across his knee. He looked down at it, then back at me. Then he picked it up and held it out so I could read it.

"*Invisible Man,*" I said. "Never read it. Who's it by?"

"Ralph Ellison," he said.

"Ellison," I said.

"It's a classic," he said. "You should read it."

"Take care," I said, nodded and walked on.

From down the bank a-ways I watched him wheel the chair back up the incline.

When I got back home the vegetables and the rice were cooked. I ladled it all into my yard-sale blender and pureed the mixture. I chopped the parsley and the chives, hung my head over the soup and inhaled deeply. "Shall I? Shall you?" I said, amusing myself, stirring the soup like a witch's brew. I filled my hand with chives and passed it over the soup a few times. "Shall I? Shall you?" I said, and spread the chives across the surface. "Shall I? Shall you?" And dropped some parsley in. "Shall I?" And grated in some black pepper. "Shall you?" And stirred.

I filled the ladle, lifted the soup to my mouth and blew on it. "Shall I? Shall you?" I said, then sipped the soup. "Shall I add more salt?" I said mysteriously, laughing silently. "More salt," I said with affected seriousness, and passed the shaker over the soup. "Bad for the blood pressure."

It was ridiculous but amusing. I had nothing better to do, so I spent the day brewing a special soup for Willie and Bernie.

At five I started for Willie's, the soup swinging at my side by the handle of the iron pot. I stopped at the liquor store to pick up some beer.

"Whatta ya got there?" Kurt asked as he hit the register.

"Rutabaga soup," I said.

"Rutabaga soup?" he repeated, handing me change.

"Rutabaga soup," I said.

"Somebody dying?"

"Whatta ya mean?"

"That's the only time people eat stuff like rutabaga soup. They save it till you're dying, then they spoon it down."

I stopped at the Blue Eagle to buy a cigar.

"What's in the pot?" Chuck asked.

"Rutabaga soup," I said.

"What the hell is rutabaga soup? Soup made out of rutabagas?"

"Yes," I said, "soup made out of rutabagas."

"What are you going to do with that?"

"Feed it to Willie and Bernie."

"Do they know that?"

"No."

"You better catch 'em soon—they just walked by a while ago with a bottle. Lemme see what rutabaga soup looks like."

I lifted the lid, exposing the tepid, velvety golden soup. A strong odor emitted that was almost embarrassing. Two men who were standing at the rack thumbing through skin magazines looked over.

Chuck wrinkled his nose. "Phew," he said, waving his hand in front of his face, "that's strong medicine. You sure that stuff is legal?"

I passed Kelly's on the way to Willie's. Johnny from Nutley was out on the corner smoking and jingling change.

"Whatta ya got in the pot there?" he asked.

"I got some rutabaga soup."

"You gotta lotta nerve walking around with rutabaga soup."

"Want a whiff?"

"I'll pass. I just ate."

Dave from the wire factory was getting out of his truck across the street. He started toward the bar.

"Hey, Dave," Johnny yelled, "want some rutabaga soup?"

"Some what?"

"Rutabaga soup."

"Rutabaga soup?"

"Whole pot of it going down the street there."

Dave looked. "What would I do with rutabaga soup?" he said.

"Fuck if I know," Johnny said.

I went up the stairs to Willie's second floor apartment. There was a woman standing there.

"He's not home," she said.

"He's not?"

"But there's a ballgame on in there. He's probably hiding like a child. Hiding won't do him any good. You can't hide from God."

"Why not?"

"You can only turn your eyes from Him. What's in the pot?"

"Rutabaga soup."

"Never had it."

"You should try it. Adventure is not ungodly."

"I'm not crazy for rutabagas."

I knocked on the door. "Are you with the Jehovah's Witnesses campaign?" I asked.

"I'm with God's campaign."

"Please don't tell me anything about it."

"You prefer to hide too, like Mr. Sykes in there?" She raised her voice. "Ignorance will not save you."

"I don't think Mr. Sykes is home," I said.

I walked down the stairs with the woman. She went on her way. I went through the alley to the backyard and up the outdoor stairway to the porch. I looked in the door and saw Willie hiding behind the kitchen door. I opened the back door.

"Are you trying to hide from Jehovah, Father Sykes?"

"Jesus Christ! You scared me. I thought she went around back. I've been waiting for her to do that."

"Where's Father Bernie?" I asked.

"Is she gone?"

"She'll be back, Willie. You can't hide from Jehovah."

"She's gone, Bern," Willie called.

Bernie came out from the bathroom. "I think she knew you were here this time," he said.

"Damn Jehovahs," Willie said. "Why can't they leave a man in peace?"

"She wants you, Willie," Bernie said. "I think she likes you. I think she craves you. I think she wants to convert with you."

"I like her too, Bern."

"She's real cute," Bernie said. "You should let her convert you. Maybe she has a bankroll."

"I'll burn in Catholic Hell first."

"That you will do, regardless. You haven't been to church since Maggie died. And lookit here"—Bernie aimed his thumb at me—"he actually came."

"Can't turn down chicken wings," I said. "Anybody need a beer?"

"I need a whiskey," Willie said. "That woman drives me to the bottle."

"And that's her only good point," Bernie said. "What's in the pot?"

"Soup," I said.

"Campbell's I hope," Willie said, then laughed.

"Campbell's hasn't evolved to this flavor yet," I said.

"What flavor is it?" Bernie asked. "I love soup."

"Rutabaga."

"Rooty-begger?" Bernie said.

"See, I told you," Willie said to Bernie. "He's got this weird thing about soup."

"I'll eat anything once," Bernie said. "I haven't eaten rutabaga since my mother shoved it in my mouth from a Gerber's jar."

"You ate it over here two weeks ago," Willie said, "only I pressure-cooked it."

"So that's what that stuff was—I was afraid to ask."

"Give it a chance, Bernie," I said. "It's powerful stuff. Make the dead get up and dance."

"Chicken wings is powerful stuff," Bernie said.

"Beans," Willie said. "*Beans* is powerful stuff. Especially canned beans."

"Beans is," Bernie said. He pointed at me. "Got some Kessler's whiskey in there—cheap and cheerful. Help yourself."

I put a low flame under the soup. Bernie stuck his nose under the lid. "Whoa!" he said. "Rooty-begger."

We went to the front room. I poured some whiskey in a water glass and walked around the room looking at things.

"Who's winning?" I asked.

"Who cares?" Willie said.

"Yanks," Bernie said. "Five to zip. That's why Willie doesn't care."

"Thought you liked the Yanks?" I said, picking up a wooden bear from a shelf.

"If you came to see the Yankees," Willie said, "you missed it—by about twenty years."

"He's a turncoat," Bernie said.

A milkglass vase of plastic flowers was centered on top of the TV, probably untouched since Willie's wife was alive. A bookshelf stood next to the TV. Sherlock Holmes, a few Zane Grey, a boxing encyclopedia, a book on James Cagney, *For Whom The Bell Tolls* and *East of Eden* in hardcover, *The Naked and the Dead,* two Jimmy Breslin novels, other assorted paperback novels. On the shelf in front of me where I stood with my drink was a small boxing trophy beside an old framed photo of a man in a fireman's uniform. There was a snapshot of Willie when he was about thirty-five. Square shoulders. Almost bald. Hair still black. Sitting at the breakfast table in a tee shirt. Sleep still clinging to him. A glass quart of milk and a newspaper on the table. The highlights showed the harshness of artificial light. Ceiling lamps. It was probably before dawn. He looked tired, worn down. His face was not anticipating a leisurely day.

"They were all so hysterical," Willie said. He was looking over my shoulder. "Everybody. My in-laws lived next door. Even my kids were hysterical then. Everything was a calamity. Somebody was always yelling or crying about something. I just trudged through it like a machine. I left the house at five and got home at seven. Sometimes going home I passed myself going to work on the other track. On weekends I taught the kids how to play ball and ride bikes. I was older then than I am now."

"Who's the fireman?"

"My father. Captain."

"Where?"

"Right here in Newark. We used to meet him at the bus-stop when we were kids because we loved to walk down the street with him when he was in uniform. It was a big deal. I couldn't keep my eyes off those brass buttons. Once in a while he'd stop on the way home for a few shots. We used to go in the bar with him, my brothers and I. I remember one time a fight broke out over something. Pretty soon everybody was into it, breaking it up or whatever. My father had this chicken in paper that he was bringing home for dinner, and he was belting people over the head with it, holding it by the feet. I'll never forget it. Laughing and belting people with this chicken. By the time it was over he had nothing but the two legs and feet in his hand. Chicken all over the bar. He was a good guy."

"He the boxer?"

"No. Me. Golden Gloves. Got some clippings from the newspaper in the drawer over there. I did okay for a while."

"Where's this?" I pointed to a photo of five men in army combat dress posing arm-in-arm.

"Marseilles."

"That's you, isn't it?"

"It was then."

"How come it says Mike on your helmet?"

"That's what I called my wife, Maggie, sometimes—Mike."

"Maggie was a good gal," Bernie said, getting up from the sofa. "I'm gonna check them coals."

Bernie returned, and we all sat down to watch the game. We'd each had four or five shots of Kessler's and as many beers when Willie brought up the Miles affair.

"Yes, I've been thinking about it, Willie," I said, "and I decided I really don't want to get involved. Miles isn't exactly crazy about me anyway."

Bernie went to the kitchen and came back with a bowl of soup for each of us, placed them on the coffee table near us and sat down with his in his lap. "I've eaten some weird things before," he said. "I married a Greek, you know. But this is strange stuff. I like it."

"That's not much of a testimonial," Willie said. "You'll eat anything that doesn't jump off the plate and bite back."

"That's true," Bernie said.

Willie turned to me. "We wish you'd reconsider. We need some help organizing this shit." He paused, folded his hands. "So you talked to Miles, huh?"

"Willie married a mick," Bernie said. "He's lucky he ate anything but potatoes and canned peas and roasts."

"I can't do it, Willie, believe me. I just can't." I picked up his can of tobacco from the coffee table. "Besides, Miles doesn't trust me. He's smart."

"That's the end of it then," Willie said. He tossed me the rolling papers.

"Eat your soup, boys," Bernie said.

A full inning went by.

"I believe I'll have a little more of that soup," Bernie said, groaning as he rose from the sofa. "Rooty-beggers. Them rootybeggers is okay. Wanna eat the wings out on the back porch?" He looked back and forth from Willie to me.

"Sure," I said.

Willie nodded.

"So be it," Bernie said. "I think them coals are getting close to perfect. Can I get you boys another bowl of rootybegger?"

"Half," Willie said.

"Not me," I said. My stomach felt odd all of a sudden—not full, but not hungry.

We moved out on the porch. Willie opened a beer for each of us. Bernie put the Kessler's on the small table against the railing. He had thirty or forty wings piled on a platter, all salted and peppered and waiting for the coals to be perfect.

"Tell him about that poker game that Christmas with Raymond and Ace Pooley," Bernie said to Willie.

"You know Raymond?" Willie asked me. "He lives over the paint store."

"Never met him," I said.

"Good fella," Bernie said. "Used to work out at Bendix till they shut down."

"We were seven hands into progressive Jacks-or-Better," Willie said, "and still no openers, and the pot was bigger than when Shorty Nelson's brother-in-law was visiting that time, wasn't it, Bern?"

"It was. But we had money then. Most of us were working when Shorty's brother-in-law was here."

"That's right. But this particular game everybody was short. It was the night before Christmas Eve—the money was spent. Raymond was out of work. I'd just retired. Shorty's fridge was on the blink, and he'd just bought a new one. And Bernie never had any money. His old lady took it all."

"Greeks are like that," Bernie said. "Ace was flush, though."

"Yeah," Willie said, "Ace was flush. He was working as a security guard in a mall somewhere."

"Way up in Paramus," Bernie said. "Imagine that—Ace Pooley a security guard! That's like hiring the fox to watch the chickens."

"It's like hiring Bernie to see that the chicken wings don't get eaten," Willie said.

"Similar," Bernie said.

"We'd been playing all night," Willie continued. "Well, it was about two in the morning. And we're seven hands into this Jacks-or-Better five card draw, and still no openers. I don't remember why the bet limit was busted open, but there we were, up to our balls, the ten-buck, three-raise limit a thing of history. We'd progressed up through ace openers, back down to jacks, and up to aces again, the ante up to five bucks. It was serious shit all of a sudden."

"And Ace opens with twenty-five bucks," Bernie said.

"Twenty-five bucks," Willie said, pouring each of us some whiskey.

"Mexican Sweat," Bernie said. "That's where the bet ceiling busted open—in that game of Mexican Sweat."

"Raymond was going on karma," Willie said.

"Fucking Raymond and his fucking karma," Bernie said.

"Raymond's daughter had told him about karma. She was a Buddhist or some shit. Raymond started believing in karma when his landlord cheated him out of thirty bucks, and a month later Raymond had occasion to sell his landlord's ladder and power drill."

"He was always talking about karma down at Kelly's," Bernie said. "It was kind of a joke. Raymond gets stuck on things—he's got ruts in his brain. If you didn't buy him a drink he'd say, 'bad karma,' and you'd think about it, you know what I mean. You might even buy him a drink a little later."

"Raymond liked the idea of karma," Willie said, "and he was sure it would work for him in that poker game 'cause Ace Pooley is such a smelly bastard—a real shyster—cheap as the day is long."

"Hasn't sprung for a round of beers since his mother-in-law died," Bernie said.

"Raymond figured Ace Pooley had to have some of the worst karma around."

"Raymond told us later he drew a jack to his two pair," Bernie said. "Full boat—aces and jacks."

"He thought he was in like Flynn. He was sure of it."

"Hell," Bernie said, "there must have been three hundred and fifty on the table, not to mention a wedding band."

"Let's not mention the wedding band, Bern."

"That's another story," Bernie said. "Don't ever lose your wedding band if you're married to a Greek."

"I'll try to remember that," I said.

Willie sipped his whiskey. "When Raymond bumped twenty-five bucks everybody folded. Everybody but Ace Pooley. We were all cursing and snorting. Ace just tossed in the twenty-five and bumped him fifty."

"Raymond was in a sweat," Bernie said.

"Raymond was having cardiac arrest," Willie said. "He only had a fiver in his pocket, and Raymond has this . . . moral problem"—he drew quotes around the phrase—"with IOUs. Besides, he felt an IOU would be bad karma."

"Plus," Bernie said, "you don't want Ace Pooley holding paper on you. So what does he do—he bets his mother's Christmas gift. Talk about bad karma!"

"Raymond says to Ace, 'I just paid fifty-seven fifty for this gift for my mother. I'll call you with that.' So Ace asks him what it is. 'A shawl,' Raymond says, 'an imported lace shawl from Italy.' 'What would I do with a guinea shawl?' Ace says."

Bernie laughed. "Willie tells him he can give it to Alice, and Willie's sitting there batting his eyes and scrambling up his face with both hands like this." Bernie scrambled his face. "It was really funny. I almost peed."

"Awful Alice," Willie said. "Had to be the ugliest woman in the world."

"Stop a clock," Bernie said. "She worked nights at the White Castle for a while. God, make you lose your appetite."

"But Ace Pooley was no Tab Hunter," Willie said.

"Ace Pooley smelled like canned farts," Bernie added. "The trees would bend the other way and the leaves would curl up and die when he walked down the street."

"Now you're exaggerating, Bernie. Have a little more whiskey." Willie reached over and poured some in Bernie's glass. "So Ace turns over his ace openers, teasing Raymond. Raymond needs a resuscitator by this time. Everybody's thinking Ace has the full boat. Raymond told us later he saw two queens and a king in Shorty's hand when Shorty reached for one of Bernie's smokes. So Raymond thinks his odds are good. Chances are slim Ace has a full house with aces and kings.

"But that's what he had," Bernie said. "Raymond nearly shit."

"He nearly died is what he did. Poor Raymond couldn't figure how his karma could be that bad. Not only did Stinkbomb win, but *he* lost, and lost his mom's Christmas gift to boot, imported from Italy. There is no God. That's what I was thinking—there is no God. Either that or Raymond's got some serious karma problems that we don't know about."

"Raymond just stuffed his mouth with pretzels and sat on the sofa in a trance until Shorty's wife told him to go home. It's already three o'clock, right, but me and Willie and Shorty go to the diner, and we're there till dawn trying to figure ways to help Raymond out. You know, it was fucking Christmas!"

"And we know that Raymond has this moral problem"—he drew quotes again—"with accepting charity, so we can't just buy the shawl back. It wasn't gonna be that simple."

"After the hundred and seventeenth round of coffees," Bernie said, "Willie gets this idea. It wasn't a very good idea, but it was all we had."

Willie sipped at his whiskey. "We knew Ace Pooley stopped at Kelly's every day after work. That was a given."

"Meanwhile," Bernie said, "Raymond comes up with this plan of his own. Luckily me and Shorty ran into him in the morning and he told us what he was going to do. It was a great plan: walk into Bam's and steal something nice. Real Polack strategy."

"Goddamn Bamberger's on Christmas Eve," Willie said. "The place is crawling with floor detectives, and Raymond, burdened with all these moral problems, is about to go make some bad karma for himself."

"But we weren't sure Willie's plan would work, so we decided to improve on Raymond's—Shorty and I."

"Bernie and Shorty—six foot three and five foot four, right—are in there faking this fist-fight while Raymond is sliding a few items under his coat."

"Right in the middle of lingerie," Bernie said.

"Great plan, right?"

"I got the idea from an Elvis Presley movie—*King Creole*, I think."

"You never told me that."

"But some asshole . . ." Bernie held his hand over the coals. "Perfect."

"Some upstart bucking for manager saw Raymond," Willie said, "and Bernie had to put the kid up against the wall—"

"The coat racks—up against the coat racks." Bernie started laying the wings on the grill.

"He had to threaten the kid's life before he shut up."

"But the whole thing scared Raymond," Bernie said, "and he dropped the booty and made for the street. Time for plan B." He walked to the kitchen door. "Give him plan B, Willie. I'll get the beans and potato salad."

"I met up with them at Kelly's. Ace Pooley was there, sure enough, a bottle of Bud and a pack of Pall Malls in front of him as usual. 'I was gonna wear my new guinea shawl,' he says to Raymond, 'but I got transmission fluid all over it this morning.' I mean, this son-of-a-bitch is nasty."

"So Willie tells Ace," Bernie said through the window screen, "since it's good and greasy, why doesn't he shove it up his ass and run the hundred-yard dash to some other bar. You're a regular comedian, Willie."

"We had a few rounds," Willie continued, "giving Ace a rash of shit the whole time. So Ace leaves to go eat dinner at the Essex. Now, Jim Kelly has no love for Ace Pooley, so it was easy to enlist his help. He reaches under the bar and plants the pack of Pall Malls on the bar where Ace had been sitting."

"See," Bernie said, coming through the door with a covered pot and a bowl, "Willie bought the Pall Malls and gave 'em to Kelly."

Willie took his Prince Albert from his pocket. " 'Look,' Shorty says, 'Stinkbomb forgot his smokes.' So Shorty gets the smokes and tossed them in front of Raymond. 'Here, Raymond,' Shorty says, 'I think these must belong to you.' Then Raymond offers us all a smoke. So—who was it, you, Bern?"

"I says, 'Holy Jesus and Mary, look at this,' and I handed the pack back to Raymond. Raymond looks and pulls out this silver tube, and he's looking and looking, and he doesn't know what it is."

"It was this silver sheath for a Bic lighter," Willie said, "all studded with turquoise and red coral and decorated with silver leaves. I got a good price on it off Johnny from Nutley. He owed me a favor. It was made by Indians." Willie reached over and poured more Kessler's in our glasses. "'That's heavy-gauge silver,' Shorty says. 'Must be worth fifty bucks. Your mother's still huffing on those L&M's, isn't she? You could give her that lighter holder for Christmas.' And Raymond thought his mother would actually like the thing too. We were all kicking each other under the bar. It felt like Christmas should feel. We ordered another round and slapped each other's backs. We even bought Johnny from Nutley a round when he came in." Willie licked the Zig-Zag and rolled up his smoke. "Raymond left before the rest of us," he said. "He runs into Ace Pooley outside the Essex. He shows Ace the lighter holder and says, 'I think you left this at the bar.' Imagine that shit! Raymond has a moral problem all right. So Ace says, "Yeah, I guess I did.' Of course he never saw the damn thing before, but he drops it in his pocket. I could have brained Raymond when he told me that. I could have beat the moral snout out of 'em."

"When you're hot, you're hot," Bernie said. "When you're not, you're not. The wings are just about done. Grab your plates, boys."

We filled our plates and sat back down. Bernie put the second load of wings on the grill.

"You give us one," Bernie said. "Tell us a story."

"Don't have any stories," I said.

"Go on. Every man's got stories," Bernie said. "Give us some braggin' and lyin'."

"Maybe later," I said.

"Don't talk much, do ya?" Bernie said.

"Not feeling so good right now." I suddenly felt sick in the guts. The whiskey was sitting right—it wasn't that.

"What's the matter?" Willie said.

"Don't know. Just feel sick in my guts. I don't think it's the whiskey. I don't feel loaded."

They were both digging into their food. I put my plate on the table.

"Try some wings," Bernie said. "Maybe it'll settle your stomach."

"Nah, I'll be okay in a minute," I said, but I was feeling more nauseous by the minute.

Bernie cracked another beer. "Couldn't be the soup, could it?" he said. "I thought it was great. Made me feel great. Feel like I can drink all night."

I was fighting the urge to vomit. "I don't understand it," I said. "I'm sorry."

"Hey," Bernie said, chewing on a wing, "nothing to be sorry about. A man's sick, he's sick. We been there, ain't we, Willie?"

But you don't fight the urge to vomit for very long. I stood and leaned over the porch railing and vomited.

"Hold on, matey," Bernie said. "Man overboard."

"I think I'm gonna puke again," I said. "Don't let me spoil your dinner."

"Go right ahead," Willie said. "The bathroom's right off the kitchen there." He put his plate down and got up to help me. When he saw I could make it okay he stood and pointed to the bathroom, holding the kitchen door open. "Mrs. Sheehan might get upset if you keep puking in her irises."

I no sooner got to the toilet when the soup came up again. I hadn't vomited since L.A. Even with enough whiskey in me to go blind, I never vomit. But I vomited that night, over and over for over an hour. I was almost delirious with vomiting. Every four or five minutes my stomach convulsed and I howled into the toilet. There was nothing to do but get into it, so that's what I did. I wanted everything in my stomach out, and out it came.

Willie checked in on me a few times. "I'm not drunk," I told him, "I don't understand it." "You don't seem drunk," he told me. "Are you sure you're okay?" He wanted to call a doctor, but I told him to let me crawl off and puke like a sick dog. "When it's over I'll have a drink with you," I said.

But I stayed in the bathroom for over an hour. I could hear them outside talking and getting drunk. They even sang a sea chanty, but softly, so they wouldn't disturb me. They didn't want to sound too joyous while I was so sick, but they couldn't contain themselves as they drank more whiskey. I was smiling in there listening to them.

When Willie came in again I was still sitting on the upside down trash can, hunched over the toilet.

"Hey, son," he said, "sure you're okay?"

"Yeah, Willie, I'm okay. I just don't feel like I want to hang up the big white telephone here for a while."

"Well, if you're okay, Bernie and I are itching to go over to Kelly's and raise some hell. And Johnny from Nutley owes Bern twenty bucks, and he's 'sposed to be there tonight."

"You think I'm wild about you guys looking after me while I puke?"

"The number at Kelly's is written on the wall above the phone. Don't be a hero if you need some help."

An hour or so after Willie and Bernie left I felt well enough to go home. I went right to sleep.

In the morning I ate a good breakfast, packed some bread, fruit, nuts and water in a small canvas shoulder bag and set out on a walk. I walked downriver to the city bridge, then back upriver along the canal on the east side.

Five or six miles up the canal a vast cemetery stretched for a mile along the river. Much of the bank was shaded with nut trees and maples, and there were lots of old oaks and pines throughout the grounds. The eight-foot steel mesh fence that bordered the canal stopped at the cemetery, and a high hedgerow continued in its place, dividing the bulkhead from the cemetery grounds. I found several breaks in the hedge that kids for generations had used for access to the bank for fishing, rock throwing or whatever else.

I was almost at the end of the cemetery when I found the grave of a Vietnam vet. The metal VFW insignia was planted by the headstone. He was a Marine named Alvin Johnson—killed in action in 1970. Directly across the canal from the grave was a black neighborhood. A Baptist church stood on the shady lot along the opposite bank.

I sat watching the river. There was a rural feel to the place that was strange to the inner city. The river seemed almost clean there. I ate and drank my water then napped on and off until about six. Squirrels woke me up a few times, chattering in the oaks over me. They had a route through the branches from one side of the river to the other. Squinting, I followed their silhouettes traversing the network of fine black lines that the branches made against the sun, then dozed off to sleep again.

By the time I got back it was dark. I went to Willie's place, but he wasn't home. I left a note telling him to meet me at five in the morning. I thought Willie probably hadn't been up before ten since he retired, so I printed a large IMPORTANT on the note. It was just about five when Willie turned the corner. I walked to meet him. He had no quips ready—no curses. Five in the morning was serious business. He was barely awake, unshaven, frowning.

"What's up?" he asked, applying his fingers to his temples.

"I thought we could take a walk this morning," I said, "watch the sun come up."

"Take a walk?" His voice was low in his throat. "You feeling better today?"

"I was fine when I woke up yesterday. I don't understand it."

"Musta been a bug or something."

"You know," I said, "stealing has never been beneath me, Willie. Whether I need it or not. I can steal a good meal from Jeanie's or any of several markets around here. But I usually get up at this time to look for easier game."

"I'm too tired to steal." He was padding along behind.

"Feeling a little rough this morning?"

"I'm trying to find some good humor. What in the name of God am I doing up in the middle of the night? This is not going to be another lecture on how to make soup, is it?"

"There're bakery shipments at the doors of markets now. Shopkeepers won't be there till six. And there're perfectly good lemons and oranges in the trash behind bars. They're just a little too soft for the lip of a gin and tonic, but they're just right for me."

"Don't even talk about gin. Joe Duffy broke out his birthday Beefeaters last night. Goddamn mick drinks like there's no tomorrow, and here it is, tomorrow, same as always, hung over and swearing I'll never drink again. I feel like hammered shit. Two nights in a row now. I'm too old for this shit."

"I've seen you worse."

"That's the God's truth, but it ain't no consultation."

"You mean consolation."

"I mean hammered shit, boy. What the hell are we doing? I don't want no damn lemons!"

We stopped at the Essex and got Willie some coffee to go, then set out again for downtown. Halfway through his cup he began to find humor. At least I thought it was humor.

"Now what in the holy fuck are we doing in the goddamn dark hunting for lemons?"

I ducked into an alley and turned off behind a cocktail lounge. Sure enough, there were two oranges and three lemons worth picking. The other bars nearby were dry, but on the return trip I opened a bakery shipment box and took a loaf of iced raisin bread. Willie looked once over his shoulder, lifted the lid of the waxed box and took a loaf for himself.

"That's the spirit," I said.

"Must be the passion of the hunt. Not to push the issue or anything, but why, for the fifth time now I ask, did you get me out of bed at five o'clock?"

"To invite you to breakfast on the terrace while the sun rises."

"But first we have to harvest breakfast. I don't find this funny—even interesting. What terrace?"

"I was thinking we could harvest materials to build a bridge just the way we're harvesting breakfast, but I have to contemplate this with you over breakfast on the terrace while the sun rises."

"A bridge? What bridge?" What goddamn terrace?"

"A bridge over the canal right behind Miles' place. Then he really will be only two blocks from The Embers."

"Holy fuck." He put his hand to his forehead. "No," he said, as if to say, this can't be true.

"It won't be hard."

"There's a goddamn eight-foot fence on both sides of the canal!"

"Exactly eight feet. We'll cut it."

"The city will tear it down. Why am I being so rational about this?"

"Well, we have to build it before they can tear it down."

"It won't work. I was wrong about you."

"Let's have breakfast."

We walked back to my place. The whole way Willie was going on about what a bad idea the bridge was. He compared it to Raymond's plan to steal a Christmas gift for his mother.

When we got back I toasted some raisin bread and made some tea.

"Want some cheese?" I asked.

"This bridge is not a good idea," he said.

"The terrace," I said, opening the window to the fire escape.

I brought the food out on a platter. We sat with our legs hanging over. The sun was rising.

"We don't know how to build a bridge," Willie said, "we don't have anything to build it with. It would extend to private property. The cops would go crazy. We'd get thrown in jail and fined. All our work would be for nothing."

"No, it wouldn't."

"It won't work."

"We have to start gathering materials right away. Between you and me and Bernie and Joe and whoever it shouldn't take long, but we need to be ready in one week—by Monday at the full moon."

"Oh, so you want to build this bridge at night."

"Yes."

"You're fucking nuts!"

"Can you call a meeting of the people concerned?"

"I could."

"Do it."

"No."

"Look at this sunrise, Willie. It's kind of dull."

"Cloudy again."

Just before dark we walked over to Miles's place. Before Willie could finish introducing us Miles said, "Forget it." Miles thought the plan was crazy. He wanted nothing to do with it. Miles was suspicious of me and he as much as said so. Anybody in their right mind would have thought the plan was crazy, so I never pushed it, but we went out to look at the bulkhead. A foot below the top of the bulkhead was a four-by-eight beam bolted to the bulkhead and running parallel to the top beam that was flush with the ground. We agreed that the four-by-eight would make a perfect ledge to support a superstructure, but that's about all we agreed on. I waited until we left Miles to discuss the details with Willie. For lack of a better idea, he decided to go along with the plan.

A few more four-by-eights spanning the canal, bolted to the existing beam, would come up to within two inches of the top of the bulkhead, so two-by-fours would do the trick for the surface of the bridge, making the surface flush with the ground.

The next evening the group met. We looked over what had already been gathered, scratched items off the list and made another list of what we still needed. I kept the focus of the meeting on the details and avoided any general questions about effectiveness of the plan itself. Dave had a lot of what we needed at the wire factory. Joe Duffy showed up with two-by-fours and plywood. He never said where he got the stuff, but we all knew his brother-in-law was a building contractor. They were going along with the plan on Willie's say-so.

Willie and Bernie located some railroad ties along the tracks. We planned to pick them up in Dave's truck. I borrowed some tools from Dave and took apart a section of highway guardrail in the dead of night and got pockets full of nuts, bolts and washers. I also bought some heavy-duty nuts and bolts.

On the third night, under the factory yard lights, using the edge of the loading dock and the back of a flatbed truck, we cut boards to size, drilled holes and constructed a prototype between the truck and the loading dock. It went together smoothly, and it looked like it would work, so everybody was getting excited about the adventure.

On the fourth night we perfected the components and had construction drills. We built the bridge four times, until each man had his specific job under control, then we turned the yard lights off and built it twice in the dark.

On the fifth night we cross-trained each other in our jobs. When everybody knew everybody else's job, we walked over to Miles's place, sat in the back yard drinking beer while casually studying the shadows and light we'd be working in during the actual construction.

"You people are crazy," Miles said. "Those people over there living where this bridge is going to land don't even like to see me out their windows. They're gonna love this crippled nigger wheeling across their back yard!"

"It'll be great," Dave said. "I can't wait to see their faces."

It was the first comment Dave made about the plan. It caught me by surprise. The whole group was getting keyed up. The effectiveness of the plan no longer mattered. It was an adventure, a group undertaking and a joke on the city. Everything was go.

On the sixth night we hauled Joe Duffy's flat-bottomed duck-hunting boat to Miles's place. The pieces were in place. We went to Kelly's and had a few. Joe and Dave both told me, confidentially, at different times, that they always thought I was strange and were happy to find out that I was a regular guy. We drank to that. Regular guy builds absurd bridge. Willie kept eyeing me strangely all night. Finally, just before we went home, he followed me into the john.

"You know the city will tear the thing down," he said. "What the hell are we doing here?"

"Let's just build the bridge like there's nothing wrong with building the damn bridge," I said, "like it makes perfect sense. Miles needs a bridge to get to work, so we build the bridge. The bus doesn't have to stop. Miles doesn't have to depend on anyone. The city has a new footbridge that didn't cost them a cent. It makes sense. How 'bout a little breakfast on the terrace at five, Willie?"

"Not a chance."

"Don't worry. Let them tear the thing down. Right now we're nowhere. We need something for them to tear down."

"Sometimes I don't know—I really don't know if you're crazy or not."

Come Monday, the seventh night, we met at Miles's place and played poker until three in the morning. Miles kept staring at me. Every time I raised a bet he said I was bluffing. He was nervous about the whole deal. Then he made coffee, and we all stood in the kitchen and drank a cup. Dave put his cup in the sink and said, "Here we go."

He drove to the other side of the canal while we snipped the fence with heavy-duty wire cutters from the factory. We lowered the rowboat into the canal and tied it taut at both ends, then cut a section out of the fence on the other side. Joe stood in the bow, Bernie in the stern. We handed down the first beams to them and set them in place on the four-by-eight ledge. Dave set the bolted components from the east side, Willie and I on the west, and Joe and Bernie worked from the boat on the middle section.

The only drilling that needed to be done was four holes in the bulkhead, and we did that last, after the components were bolted in place. We wrapped rags around the drill to muffle the sound.

When the bridge was secure we gathered up the extension cord and the tools and went back to Miles's place where we had more coffee and sat around talking with just a nightlight on. At dawn Miles cooked up a mess of eggs, potatoes and toast.

Dave and Joe went off to work. Willie, Bernie and I sat around with Miles until eleven, when the bar at The Embers opened.

Miles looked once over his shoulder and said, "Why do I feel like somebody's fool?" He then wheeled down the back yard, over the bridge, through the neighbor's yard and down the street to The Embers.

We had bloody Marys and listened to him practice at the piano.

Willie requested "Moonlight in Vermont"—Maggie's favorite, he said. "Moonlight in where, man?" Miles said, breaking into a boogie. He was hot stuff. The boogie deteriorated into a kind of outside jazz improv. The notes then somehow fell into melodic order again with "Moonlight in Vermont." A single tear fell from Willie's right eye and splashed into two beads on the polished piano. He sniffed, took a drink, smiled, laughed, then clapped, nodding his head to the rhythm.

The first complaint was called in by the people who owned the lot that received the east end of the bridge. They didn't want Miles wearing ruts into their lawn.

When Willie explained the situation to them after the cops left, they said they couldn't do anything about it. Willie explained that what they could do about it was nothing—very simple—do nothing. When they didn't like that idea, he offered some alternate suggestions, which got him thrown off the property. He crossed the bridge back to Miles's place.

The next day a crew from the city dismantled the bridge and hauled it away. We followed them in Dave's truck so we knew where they unloaded our bridge kit.

"So, what do we do now?" Willie said.

"Now," I said, "we turn the system loose to feed on itself."

"Speaking of feed," Bernie said, "let's grill some wings."

7

"WHAT THE HELL KIND OF LIFE IS THIS? EVERY TIME YOU turn around somebody's sticking it to you," Bob said to the TV news camera as the police pushed him toward their car. I saw it on the TV in a bar on Hollywood Boulevard. Bob lived in the same tenement that I lived in—on North Normandie between Sunset and Hollywood. Bob lived on the third floor. I never spoke to him.

After the arrest the super told me Bob had been broke for months and couldn't pay his rent. The super told me Bob had lost his job as a bus driver when somebody remembered him from an alcohol rehab center and reported it to the city. According to the super, Bob hadn't had a drink in thirteen months, but when the city confirmed the tip-off he was fired. Evidently, five years earlier he'd had a minor accident while legally intoxicated and didn't report that fact on his job application.

When he lost his job he had to stop payments on a few things, including his hospitalization and health insurance, and the policy was canceled. Of course, soon after that an ambulance took him to the hospital because of a kidney stone attack.

It had all the elements of a classic breakdown. Bob must have seen it all happen a hundred times on TV. He was sinking fast, and that made it all the more difficult to find a job.

He was stopped by a cop on the way back from a failed job interview. He was legally intoxicated—a pint half empty under the seat. He lost his license. Driving was the only way he'd ever made a living—taxi, delivery, airport limo.

Then an L.A. County motorcycle cop confronted him in Griffith Park because he was sipping from a quart that was inside a paper bag. He hit the cop above the ear with the bottle, took his pistol and pointed it at him. They sat there like that for almost an hour, according to the news. My guess is Bob was trying to explain a few things and the cop was listening closely.

Bob was lucky they didn't blow him away on the spot.

The super was upset because he was responsible to the landlord for three months rent that Bob never paid. The super was supposed to evict after rent was two weeks overdue. He told me forty percent of the tenants were one to three weeks late every month. Everybody in the building was edgy.

I was edgy myself, feeling like a fresh corpse waiting to stiffen, the white spot living in my throat. I was getting sick of the beach and tennis club and hanging out more and more on the stoop of the tenement.

Even after I had enough money to move, I remained there in the fifth floor one-room. Despite their desperation, the people in the low-rent district were less of a strain on me than the student communities or the hip apartment complexes or the Venice hippie scene or the amorphous swarm that inhabited the middle-class residences. So when I wasn't stewing in the sun or out with Karen, I was on the stoop of the tenement with the curs of welfare.

I was one of the few tenants with a job. In fact, I had two jobs—day barkeep at El Peso Bar and Grill and night jock at the public radio station. When I'd get off the bus from El Peso there'd be seven or eight tenants nodding on the stoop, most of them drunk on wine or shot full of junk. Some of them would be holding on to the railing while they dozed, like they were afraid they'd be hauled away in their sleep.

I kept to myself mostly, but I'd talk to a few of the men, and they'd come to my room once in a while to ask for food. I didn't do much cooking then, since I only had a hot plate. I kept only the stuff I needed for my ritualistic breakfast, plus bread, lunch meat and cheese for the winos. I ate dinner at a café on Sunset.

The men never stayed long after they ate a sandwich. They didn't want to make a nuisance of themselves. They just wanted something to eat, and they figured I could afford it. And I could—for a while. I even kept a bottle of whiskey so I could send them off fixed, comfortable for a while.

Then I lost the bartending job because I kept showing up late, so I was around the tenement a lot more, usually out on the stoop.

The stoop was a meeting place—and more. Some mystifying seminars went down out there. Everything began and ended on the stoop. Everyone came and left there. Problems were created and solved. There were times when leaving the stoop was a matter of serious concern for some men, and when they came back up the stoop they'd either succeeded or they'd failed—they were okay for a while or they were in trouble. The stoop had a hard judgment on those who failed. The stoop was the mother, and the mother turned her children away—put them out on the street. The people loved and hated the stoop. It was everything and nothing. It was their safe home and their exile. It was what kept them from death and what made it hard to live—a limbo between pain and comfort that charged a monthly rent. If they drank their daily quart of wine on the stoop, they were still social drinkers. The cops didn't bother them as long as they had the stoop—that's what they believed until Bob made the news. They got very drunk and very sober on the stoop.

I was actually relieved when I lost the bartending job. I promised myself I'd buy some sheets with the money I'd saved.

Then, because I only worked a few nights a week at the radio station,

I started drinking more. As I drank more, I spent more time on the stoop.

I couldn't afford any longer to keep buying whiskey, so I drank beer for a while, but I got sick of it—it made me feel bloated. I started buying sweet wine. I drank ruby port a lot.

When I was in my room, I started locking the door. When someone knocked I pretended I wasn't there.

Three or four nights a week I'd pass out on Carol's floor after Karen dropped me off. Carol lived next door. She was a chronic insomniac, so I could go there any time of the night without disturbing her.

I never bought sheets for my bed. I started cooking canned chili on the hot plate instead of spending money at the cafe. From my window I watched the red light blink on the tower in the hills. I was going down the tubes, managing to stay away from the junk hustle only because it was so poor compared to the stuff we got in Nam.

Then one Saturday night I ripped off a guy getting into his Cadoo in the parking lot of a joint on the Strip. Easy money. I bought some whiskey, a few bottles of decent wine, a turkey, some potatoes and vegetables and brought it all over to Carol's. I bought her a quart of Grand Marnier. She made an apple pie. Gary, her roommate at the time, went out for vanilla ice cream.

Below my fifth-floor window was a cluster of bungalows—flat-roofed, low-rent cubes on a gravel lot. Beyond the bungalows was an expanse of buildings rising gradually up to the hills. In the hills, the blinking red light on the tower.

Almost every Saturday night a violent argument would break out in the cube just below my window. The guy was a biker. They had a baby. The woman took a lot before she broke. It got loud and ugly, and usually culminated about three in the morning with physical violence, prolonged screaming, weeping and finally the roar of the bike fading into the woman's sobs.

Many of the tenants in my building didn't like being disturbed at three in the morning so frequently. They'd yell down at the couple, offering advice. "Kick him in the balls!" someone would yell. This only fueled the biker, and he'd scream, "Fuck you!" Then someone would yell, "Why don't you leave the no-good bastard?" Then a drunk would chime in with a slurred unintelligible litany. Then a chorus of drunks with their separate litanies. In a matter of minutes most of the east side of the building would be yelling down at the couple or commenting on the other tenants' remarks. Then the tenants in the west side of the building would start yelling at the racket on the east side.

I usually sat on my sheetless bed, rolled a joint, leaned on the sill and listened to the show. Eventually Carol would say something to me from her bed. Her apartment, because it had a bedroom, protruded out from the outside wall of the row of one-rooms. All the corner apartments did that. So the brick cranny of the corner was between our windows. We could look or talk directly at each other over this fifteen-foot span.

"I wish the fucker would get into some good smack," she said one night. I couldn't see her in the dark, but her words were as clear as if she was next to me in bed. "If he'd get into smack instead of booze it'd be a lot quieter on Saturday nights. It's offensive the way he treats her."

Carol was on welfare. She was less than a year out of a state mental hospital in Minnesota, mostly for drugs and depression, nothing too serious, so she said, though she did have self-inflicted razor scars wandering up and down her legs.

She took in a variety of male roommates to share the rent and food with somebody. She didn't get along with other women. Most of her roommates didn't last a month.

Carol and I got along. She thought I was gay because I never tried to get her into bed. I told her I wasn't gay, but she didn't believe me. We often sat on the floor of her apartment and smoked herb and talked all night. She gave me an old radio, and the music made my one-room more livable. Carol was warm and nurturing, and that's what I needed from her—not sex.

Sometimes when I'd knock she'd come to the door naked from the waist up just to irritate her present roommate. We'd laugh about it. She'd tell the guy I was gay, and we'd chat as if nothing was out of the ordinary.

"I did it for them," she told me one night, talking about the razor scars. "They expected me to do something self-destructive, so I mutilated myself for them. It was sick shit, but I was sick in there. You had to be sick to get along. If you weren't sick, they made you sick. The drugs were nice at first, but they got to be a bummer. I just sat around drooling and nodding, and when I started feeling like I wanted to do something different, they hit me with more drugs. It was really bizarre because the reason I was in there was because I took too many drugs."

It was Carol who told me that the woman who lived next to me on the other side lived alone there. For months I'd been hearing two distinct voices through the wall, and I assumed, though I'd never seen anyone but her go in and out, that another woman lived there, perhaps someone she took care of. "Nope," Carol said, "she's a flip-out. She walks those cats all over the city in that shopping cart, then goes home and spends the night having stimulating conversations with herself."

The day after I was canned from the bartending job, I had a notion to just follow my nose for a day, like a cat might wander its way through a neighborhood—a smell turns the head and the body follows, a sound alters the course again, and the possibilities unfold.

I was up early, despite the hangover. A knock on the door woke me. I still had my clothes on. A couple hundred barbiturate caps were spilled on the floor by the table. By the time I'd scooped them up and staggered to the door, whoever had knocked was not there. Since I was up I began to go through the steps of the ritual, which was becoming more absurd by the day. I was about two months into it at the time.

The only sink I had was a small one in the bathroom, so every time I cooked on the hot plate I had to wash the pots in the shower because they wouldn't fit under the faucet in the sink. There was always a film of grease in the bathtub, even with the little cooking I did at the time. That morning I decided to clean the tub before I took a shower. Unemployment had given me new hope.

I switched the hot plate on. Roaches scurried out of it. I made some peppermint tea, which I could barely stomach anymore, and scrubbed the tub. When it was clean I pulled back the window curtain and stood in a hot shower for a long time, looking down at the bungalows below and the red light blinking in the distance. I then ate the ritualistic breakfast and walked to the lot behind the taco stand. I was beginning to despise the holes behind the taco stand.

On the way back I ran into Carol at the bus-stop. Her eyes were bloodshot. She had a cup of coffee in her hand.

"I just saw you a few hours ago," she said.

"Get any sleep?" I asked.

"About an hour, I think." She held the coffee out to me. "Want some?"

I took a sip. "Why don't you dump that guy, and I'll move in with you. You can support me."

"Yeah, right," she said. "You had your chance."

I laughed. "Besides, you'll never support another man again, right?"

"I don't need to be rejected again," she said, then looked for the bus.

"I didn't reject you, Carol," I said.

"No, you just turned me down. I still say you're queer. How could you turn down this body?"

"Let's go back to your place," I said. "We'll throw that lazy Gary out of bed and make love all day."

"You're full of shit."

"I couldn't make it till three, I bet."

She laughed and put her arm around my waist.

"Where're you going?" I asked.

"To the farmer's market—had to get out of the apartment. I need some produce and stuff. Need anything?"

"Nah."

"Wanna come for dinner tonight?"

"Sure."

"I'm making curry. Gary's never had curry. He's okay—Gary."

"I know he is."

"A bit naive. Lima, Ohio."

"He's a good guy."

"I'll give him a month at the most," she said.

"A month wouldn't be bad."

"It's about right. I'll be sick of him by then anyway. I can take only so much sincerity."

"I agree."

The bus pulled up and the people there shuffled into line.

"Where're you going?" she asked.

"I think I'm gonna stick out my thumb—see where I wind up."

"Wait—I'll go buy a car. We can wind up in Lake Tahoe or someplace."

"I'll be on Hollywood Boulevard."

"See ya tonight."

"I'll pick up some wine."

"Beer," she said, "get some beer."

"I'll get some beer."

I walked a few miles down Hollywood Boulevard, then cut through a residential neighborhood, working my way toward the hills. I stuck out my thumb, and the sixth or seventh car that passed pulled over. A young woman about twenty—on her way to the dentist. She took a joint from her cigarette pack. It was good herb.

"I'm hoping I can talk him into a dose of nitrous," she said. "I thought it would be extra weird on the smoke. It's good smoke, isn't it? It's supposed to be Cambodian, but who knows? Where're you heading?"

I admitted I wasn't going anywhere. An Oriental family crossed at the stoplight. The sun was glaring off the hood. "I'm out on an adventure," I said. "Yes, it's good smoke."

"I've got an adventure right here," she said, reaching into her purse. Things like this don't happen anymore. She held out her hand to me. "Sunshine," she said. "It's clean."

I put one under my tongue.

"Want to go to the dentist with me? It won't take long."

I sat in the waiting room reading an article in *National Geographic* titled "The Mekong: River of Terror and Hope". There were photos of the power lines that run from the dam on the Nam Phong in Thailand to light the city of Vientiane in Laos. I'd seen them while flying with an Air Force FAC. There was a photo of men from the ARVN 5th Battalion standing around a VC stash in the U Minh, the Forest of Darkness. There were aerial shots of paddies and new irrigation systems, colorful Kodachromes of Lao farmers with hybrid rice grown with dry-season irrigation, American engineers studying plans for a new dam, a C-47 dropping rice and cornmeal, a Navy Seawolf gunner firing an M-60 from a chopper.

I read closely. I studied the photos. I think it said we were helping the people of Southeast Asia with agriculture, electrical power, food and medical supplies. I was happy to read that that was what we were doing. Maybe we were. I wanted to believe it. I wanted that to be my war, those colorful photos to replace the images in my head. It wasn't so bad to keep the VC at bay while we helped the people. The acid was coming on.

I left the office and walked for a long time before I got hot and thirsty and went to a bar for a beer.

I couldn't see when I stepped in the door. I heard a man laughing. I didn't want to go another step until I could see, so I stood by the door. The laughing stopped. I still couldn't see. I felt the acid pulsing in my temples, then a rush in my chest. "Can I help you?" a man said in a tone that indicated he wasn't offering help. I turned my head toward the voice.

"I can't see," I said.

There was no reply.

I reached behind me for the wall, backed up a step and listened. I felt people near, fixed my attention on them and waited for a moment, then took a few steps toward a dim light and made out the outline of bottles on the back bar. I found a stool and sat.

"What'll ya have?"

"Bud," I said.

"Bright out there, ain't it?" a man at the bar near me said. He was drunk.

I drank half the beer and put the bottle on the bar.

"Hot out there, ain't it?" the drunk said.

When my eyes were adjusted I looked around the room. There were four men and a woman at the bar, all down the other end. A man and a woman sat at a table near the bar. Two women sat at a table in the back.

"They oughta just pull everybody outta there and blow the hell outta the whole north end of the country," a man at the bar said.

The war, I thought, the war again.

"Just send me one of them missiles in there," he said, guiding his hand into the bar like it was a missile. "Fuck 'em." He was turned around from the waist, talking to a woman at the near table. "You can't talk that way about our boys. They're dying over there!"

"If they're stupid enough to go fight in the damned war," she said, "they deserve what they get."

I saw images of some of what they got.

"We don't belong over there messing with some other government," she continued. "Who the hell do we think we are, God?"

I finished the beer.

"Want another?" the barkeep said.

I was eyeing the whiskey. Drinking again, I thought. "Yes," I said.

"You don't understand the complexity of the situation," the man said to the woman.

"It's so complex that you think we should just blow the shit out of the whole country," she said. "That's the extent of your complexity."

"The war?" I said to the barkeep, raising my eyebrows.

"What else?" he said.
"Must be interesting to hear all the arguments." I didn't even know what I was saying. My voice sounded odd. I was too aware of my tongue.
"It's not so interesting," he said.
I knew it wasn't. "Barkeeps hear everything," I said. I repeated "everything" under my breath to understand how my tongue moved.
"It's boring," the barkeep said.
The man arguing had raised his voice. I didn't want to hear it.
"The hell with the vets," the woman said, raising her voice too. "They're just hired killers."
"Cheers," I said quietly to the barkeep, picking up the fresh bottle.
The drunk a few seats away offered me a Camel. I took it and accepted his light, then drank half the beer. The tobacco rush slid into the acid rush and the alcohol twinged below my ears. I was getting too high to be in a bar. The drunk said something that I didn't understand. His mouth moved grotesquely when he spoke. I thought of a grasshopper eating. His face was contorted, rubbery, drooping, bright red. I looked away from him, put the smoke out, drained the beer and walked toward the door.
"Never mind why we need to be there," the woman said, "I'm talking about right and wrong. What we're doing is wrong and evil. How do we live with that as decent people?"
I couldn't see when I opened the door. The sun blasted me and the air conditioning withdrew from my body. I squinted, dizzy from the heat and the drug. A truck roared by, throwing up a wind. "Holy hell," I said aloud. "Lemme out of here."
I got off the main road, zigzagged back toward the city, feeling better all the time, fingering this and that, molesting trees, violating flowers, being gentle with horrible insects, watching the few people who ventured out of their natural habitat cages—doing all the ponderous things one does on acid. But I was feeling okay.
It was about four when I approached the inner city again. I saw some boys throwing stones and aluminum cans down a stairway to a basement beneath a huge office building on a corner. As I passed I looked to see what they were doing. There was a square hole in the sidewalk with a stairway going down to a door. A man was sprawled on his belly at the bottom.
"What the fuck are you guys doing!" I yelled, grabbing one by the shirt.

He pulled away, and they all ran.

I went down to check the guy out and was surprised to find out it was Charles, a wino from my tenement. He was lying in a pile of garbage, so drunk he couldn't stay conscious.

"Charles," I said, lifting his head and shoulders, "how did you get so far from home?"

His face and forehead were scraped and bleeding.

"How's that?" he mumbled.

"It's your salami sandwich connection," I said. "How did you wander so far from home?"

"Can't remember. Where am I?" He tried to focus his eyes on me.

"You're passed out in a hole," I said, "way down in a goddamned hole."

"No shit," he said. "That's bad, partner. I could get hurt."

"You are hurt. Your face is all scraped up. Can you walk?"

"Sure I can walk. But I don't want to."

I lifted him to his feet and held him up.

"Fucking stairs," he said. "Just help me up the stairs, and I'll be okay. Let's go home."

"Looks like you didn't have any trouble getting down."

His shirt was torn and his arm scraped.

"I remember these stairs," he said. "Getting down's easy—easy stuff. Last few steps I lost my balance, I think. Or somebody pushed me from the top, I think."

"Get up now. I'll help you home."

His knees were buckled. I lifted him from under the arms, but he couldn't stand, so I put him over my shoulder and carried him up the stairs. He managed to walk about ten steps before he sat down, coughing and spitting. I got him to his feet again, but it was useless. I put him over my shoulder and started home.

Everyone we passed stared at us. People were stopping in their tracks to gape. Charles was hanging lifelessly, unconscious from the booze, drooling. We would have been less conspicuous if it had been dark. It was too early to be that drunk. The city was full of rush hour traffic. The smog was thick and the sky low, hanging just above the bare palm trees growing out of the sidewalk. A weight pushed down on me as I carried Charles—the sky, the traffic, the daylight, in which he had become a spectacle. People slowed me with their stares. I climbed one hill to begin another.

I'd carried him a mile when I had to rest. I propped him against a lightpost, sat down, took one of the two joints from my shirt pocket and lit it. I breathed heavily, hearing my heart pump, my lungs suck and blow. I heard people walking behind me, the cars driving by, the cars driving faster on the main street at the end of the block. Then I heard the cars on the freeway a mile away, all the people walking all over the city, all the cars, all the noises of the city surging and gaining on me. The red light pulsed on the tower in the hills.

A cop drove by. I cupped the joint in my hand as he passed. He turned at the end of the block and drove toward us. I snuffed the joint on the curb and slipped it into my shoe.

"What are you doing here?" the cop asked from the car.

I had to think for a few seconds. "This here is a drunk," I said. "Say hello, Charles. I'm trying to get him home. Maybe you could give us a ride. He can't walk. It's just another mile or so."

"Move on," the cop said.

"I've been carrying him," I said. "I need a breather."

"I said move on. You're loitering. Or do you want some trouble?"

I did—I really did. I stood up, adrenalin rising, heart pumping, acid crackling and the herb collecting it all into one unit of trouble.

Charles raised his head with much effort. "This boy feeds me sandwiches," he said. "He's a good boy. You can leave him alone. I'll take care of him."

"He's loitering," the cop said, "and you're publicly intoxicated. I'm only gonna tell you once more. Now move on."

"No," Charles said, "no, no—he's a good boy."

"You men have sixty seconds to get your asses up and out of here."

I had a joint in my pocket and a roach in my shoe. Jail seemed like a bad idea. "It's not worth it," I told myself.

"What's that?" the cop said.

I lifted Charles to his feet and held him in a standing position. "I said, it's not worth it."

"Hold it," Charles said. "I gotta piss." Urine was running out of his pant leg.

"What's not worth it?" the cop said.

As the urine ran down the crack in the sidewalk and into the gutter I saw it turn red. I stood between Charles and the cop so the cop wouldn't see it. It ran around my shoe and into the crack, a stream of blood running in the gutter.

"I'm talking to you, mister. I said, what's not worth it?"

"This is a good boy," Charles said over his shoulder.

"You," I said. "And I'm not answering any more questions without a lawyer."

"You should show some respect," Charles said, raising his voice, starting to get enraged in his drunkenness.

"Respect!" the cop said. He got out of the car. "You people are just trash on the street."

I put Charles over my shoulder. I wanted to tear the cop's throat open.

"You're a goddamn public servant," Charles yelled, then vomited, then moaned, then babbled something as I shifted his weight.

"Tell him, Charles," I said under my breath.

"What was that?" the cop said to me.

"Back in Jersey during Christmas time," I said, "the ticket collector at a university movie theatre stopped me because I had a bag of popcorn with me. It was against the law to bring in popcorn because there was a concession stand inside that sold popcorn. The guy said, 'Go back and put that where I can't see it.' He thought he was being lenient—liberal —a nice guy."

"Save your breath," the cop said. "Just get moving."

"I'm trying to explain something to you before I go. When I came back through the line again I said, 'You could have simply pretended that you didn't see it in the first place, but you chose to make me go to the end of the line, jump through a hoop, come back tame and humiliated, kiss your ass and shuffle into the theatre. You've been seduced by petty authority. You are the most dangerous animal on earth. I should terminate you before you multiply.' "

"Get in the car," the cop said.

"I'm leaving right now," I said. "I'm on my way."

I started up the hill. I was sick—shaking. Sick of feeling like a freak. I stopped walking. Sick of the images in my head, the ghosts, the blood seeping out of nowhere, the violence in my body scrambling to get behind one blow. I put Charles on the sidewalk. Sick of the dogshit on the sidewalks. In my head I put him down between piles of dogshit, the acid tightening in my groin. I walked toward the cop. Sick of the biker beating his girlfriend. I stepped out from the jungle. Sick of the guy behind me in that ticket line saying, "Come on, let's go to the movies." I stepped out from the jungle and took the cop by the throat from behind. Sick of the tiny white spot threatening me. He raised his club or drew his gun—it didn't matter which. Sick of people talking about the war as though they understood. I tore open his throat and washed my face in the blood. Sick of all the cockroaches scrambling for cover. I stepped back into the dark. I walked up the hill. Charles vomited down my pants again. The cop, with his last dying breath, unholstered his weapon and shot me in the back of the head. Charles fell next to me. An ambulance arrived. Blood flowed under me. I stood up out of myself and walked around myself three times. Charles watched me dizzily, smiling, amazed. The medic told the RTO to call for Medevac. I heard RPGs coming in. I looked down at my body—it was burning. The medic threw a poncho liner over me, then stuck an IV in my arm. I said, "What the hell is going on? Are you crazy? I just slipped and fell on this blood, and you go sticking me with IVs." "You were dying," the medic said. I picked up some blood in my cupped hand. "What's going on?" I asked the blood. "A man in the sky killed you," the blood said. "Fucking Navy jerks," the medic said, climbing into the chopper. I threw the poncho liner off me, pulled the IV, picked up Charles and started up the hill. Though the sun was getting low, it was still hot. The cop was parked on the corner where he could watch us. I was soaked through with sweat. My pants were streaked with vomit. I saw a Chinese cabby explode. I walked through the blood and the shards of windshield and the shredded flesh, up the hill to the tenement.

I was straining my legs to climb the stoop, but I kept going. "Charles okay?" a man asked. "He's okay," I said. I climbed the six flights of stairs, stopping at each landing to readjust the weight. It was 6:30 when I laid him on his bed.

I drank ten glasses of water, bought some smokes in the liquor store and walked toward the Vine Street area. My body felt weightless after the burden. I was full of false energy. The city lights were coming on. The hills were glowing with a dusky red, the tower blinking its red light.

All the street freaks were coming out at Vine. The bikers were beginning the first of their nightly laps. The sweat was drying on me as the night cooled. I stepped into an alley and urinated behind a fire escape. I smelled like tobacco and exhaust and sweat and vomit. I could taste the acid in my mouth. The alley smelled worse than I did —torn-open trash bags, broken wine bottles. I needed to sit down. My legs felt strong, but I needed to sit. My kidneys ached from the acid. My heart was pumping furiously. I needed to get off the street, disappear for a while.

Spirits of the Dead, it said on the marquee. Perfect, I thought. Just what I need. Actual footage of the actual ghosts. Fellini, Vadim, Polanski it said. I think it was Polanski—I can't remember now. I remember a decapitation in a car. I remember Jane Fonda riding through fire on horseback. A woman dressed all in black sat a few seats away from me —black dress, shawl, boots, hair—black cloth bag over her shoulder. She kept looking over at me. A woman behind me kept saying, "What's going on?" And her boyfriend kept answering, "It's Fellini."

Every time the woman in black looked at me I felt like I was being monitored. I didn't like it, but after the films I found myself following her up Hollywood Boulevard toward the Chinese Theatre. She stopped at a corner, and I stopped. She looked back at me, then continued on, slowly.

After a while she went into a café and sat at the counter. I took a seat in a booth. We drank coffee. The place was bright, the colors loud. The waitress had an olive complexion, wore a blonde wig and pink lipstick. I smoked and watched the woman in black—the back of her head, her profile when she turned to the window.

When she went to the register to pay the tab she glanced at me. She wore no makeup. I followed her back to Vine. She sat down on the sidewalk, leaned against the building and stared at the traffic. I stood on the corner.

My own odor came up around me again, and I wondered how I could have gone into the theater like that. The woman took something from a pouch around her neck. Whatever it was, she struck a match and lit it, and it burned like dried grass. She took the ashes in her hand, crushed them smooth with her finger, and put a mark on her throat with the ashes. She swung her head toward me. It was spooky shit. I thought she said something. I just stood there, watching her watching me. It was ridiculous.

There was a lot of foot traffic, but she ignored even the street freaks who stopped to talk to her. Even when people were between us I had the feeling she was still monitoring me. I didn't like it, but I lit a smoke and stayed on the corner. This is bullshit, I thought. Maybe she just wants to get in my pants. Maybe she's lonely and . . . Get in my pants! I must be crazy! Too spooky. Let me out of here before I go following my cock into something I can't get out of.

I was about to leave, retreat, break the spell, get out of the movies while the gettin' was good. A short man dressed as a woman with a purse in the bend of his elbow walked in front of me calling, "Mother, mother, I've been looking all over . . ." He embraced another man who had come out of the drugstore. The second man seemed indifferent, hard-to-get. I watched the short man's foot leave his high heeled shoe as they embraced, then return to the shoe as the second man placed his fingers on the short man's chest and moved him aside with the cock of his hip and an indignant expression. When I turned back to the woman in black, she was gone. The familiar chanting of the Hare Krishna people began a few blocks away.

For a while, out of curiosity, I looked for her, but she wasn't around, so I started toward home.

I was walking back down Hollywood looking at the sidewalk. I looked up and saw her face in front of me. We locked eyes, passed each other. I almost stopped. A sexual adventure. She'd be strange in bed. I was horny. Best way to crash off acid. Something a little kinky. But I kept walking.

There was an ambulance parked in front of my tenement, the red light flashing and refracting in the alleys and angles of the buildings. Four men were sitting on the stoop. "What's up?" I said. One pointed over his shoulder with his thumb. The red light crossed his face. He looked back to the street.

I walked up to the fifth floor, feeling the weariness in my legs. The super was at the top of the stairs on the sixth floor. He looked down at me. The red light had leaked through shaded windows, reflected off bathroom mirrors; it had found its way through doors left open in curiosity. It appeared here and there on the old wood and plaster, then vanished, then appeared again.

"What's up?" I said, looking up the stairs.

"Charles," the super said. "He fell down the stairs. Dead when I found him."

I felt something at my elbow. It was Karen. I didn't recognize her at first in that environment. She'd never been in the building before.

"I've been waiting in your room," she said. "Somebody died upstairs. This is a creepy place."

We went downstairs, out to the front stoop and sat down.

"How do you live here?" she said. "Isn't it depressing?"

"Yes," I said, "it's depressing. What are you doing here, Karen?"

"I've been trying to find you off and on all day. I wish you'd get a phone. You know, there're cockroaches in there."

"I know. What's up?"

"Why don't you have a phone?"

The door opened. Two paramedics and the super came out and stood talking. A cop pulled up—more flashing light.

"I'm having lunch with my parents at the club tomorrow, and they asked if I'd invite you—if you want."

"Sure," I said, "that sounds fine. What time?"

The cop came up the stairs past us.

"Dad plays tennis till twelve-thirty, so about one would be fine."

"I'll be there."

The paramedics carried Charles on a stretcher. He was covered with a blanket. I followed them down the stairs to the sidewalk. Karen stayed on the stoop. They put Charles in the ambulance. The five men sitting near Karen passed a pint of wine. The red light flashed across them, one holding on to the railing, one spitting between his feet.

Carol came out of the building in bare feet, walked past Karen and the men, came up to me, and we embraced.

"You should get out of this place," she said in my ear. "You can do better than this. They're dropping like flies around here."

"It has been a bad week, hasn't it?" I said.

"You missed the curry."

I nodded.

"You don't belong here." She leaned back and held both my hands. "Maybe you should just keep it on the road for now."

At seven in the morning it was already hot. After forcing myself to the holes behind the taco stand for the ritualistic abracadabra, I got on a bus to meet Karen at the tennis club. The smog was already thick, the sidewalks already full of fresh dog shit, the air stagnant, torpid. The palm trees arched up in the smog, stripped, dried and motionless—not a leaf to sway if there were a breeze to move it.

The shopkeepers were just opening up. People were on their way to work. They moved as though they were already exhausted, reluctant to begin the mounting pace that by ten would have them locked into optimum efficiency. I watched from the bus window without discriminating between single images, staring unfocused, hearing an off-sync sound track. Though moving, it all seemed to be motionless, moving like a bee flies to the back of a bus that's moving forward—all of it cast in a motion that seemed eternal.

Karen's father, after his tennis and after his sauna, joined us at our table by the window. I was sitting with my hands folded in my lap, gazing at the ocean through the tinted glass, the third Manhattan coursing in my blood and lapping at my brain. I had sat so often watching from the other side of the glass, watching people like they were fish in an aquarium, watching their mouths move in silent speech, that I was a little disoriented to be inside the room of tinted glass. The ambiance of voices and clinking glasses and silverware did not sound like the distorted sound track I had superimposed over this too.

"Well," Karen's father said, truly invigorated, "what's for lunch?"

"Something light," Karen replied.

"The avocado salad is very nice," her mother suggested.

"I had the avocado salad last time," Karen said.

"How was your avocado salad?" her father asked.

"It was very nice," Karen replied.

"Well, good. I think that's what I'll have." He glanced up from the menu and caught my eye. "Would you like another drink?"

I did.

"That's a Manhattan?"

It was.

"I've never cared much for Manhattans," he said. "I think it's the vermouth."

I was dripping alcohol into my blood the way an IV drips morphine into the vein. I was enjoying the way words were floating out of our mouths like a simple melody played with one finger by a child on a toy piano. The people on the beach moved silently, in slow motion. The flowers on the table colored Karen's face with washes of yellow and pink. A scale of words fluttered up around me.

"Are you still tending bar?" her father asked.

I told him I'd been laid off.

"Those jobs are a dime a dozen," he said, and asked me if I had any idea what I would do next.

I didn't. I wanted to say "eat"—my stomach was empty. I told him about the government checks and the radio job. He was fascinated with the idea of a radio jock, then asked me to play some tennis with him, since I had some time on my hands. I look like an athlete. I'd pick it up quickly. It's good for the appetite. He was a nice man. The lunch was good. I felt relieved to be out of Hollywood.

"I certainly don't mean to encourage you to go out and find a job right away," he said, "especially if you don't have to. We work too much in this life. In fact, I'd much prefer to have a tennis partner. But if I can be of any help to you, as far as trying to scare up a job among the people I know, give me a call, and I'll see what I can do."

I thanked him. I'd keep it in mind.

"Did you get any training in the Navy that will help you?" he asked.

"Yes," I said, "I did."

"Good," he said.

We drove to their house after lunch. It was a spacious place, decorated tastefully with contemporary paintings and etchings. After a brief chat and lemonade near the lemon trees on the patio, Karen's father retired for his afternoon nap. Karen and her mother decided to take a walk. I declined their invitation to join them and asked if it would be okay if I spent some time looking at the artwork and relaxing on the patio.

The old man fell asleep. I could hear his heavy breathing coming from the lounge chair on the deck. In Vietnam, standing in a dark hootch in a VC stronghold hamlet while the entire family of the target lay sleeping, I had to learn to read any changes in the breathing patterns to determine if my entry had wakened anyone. I'd know what bed the target was sleeping in. The guy behind me had a duckbill shotgun loaded with four-buck. If anyone woke, he would talk to them softly in Vietnamese, telling them to remain calm and quiet or get blown away. But most of the time no one woke. I'd pinch the target's nose, and when his mouth opened I'd stuff a knotted bandana back into his throat and put a razor sharp K-bar knife to his throat. If he struggled he was done, and he knew it. I'd have him out of the hootch and passed to a prisoner-handler without disturbing anyone's dreams. We'd booby-trap the hootch door and disappear into the dark jungle. I was recalling the distant explosions of those grenades as I opened a few cabinets in the kitchen looking for liquor, listening to the old man's breathing for pattern changes, feeling the ghosts hovering around me.

I poured some Jack Daniels in a water glass and walked to the far end of the hallway. Noiselessly, I entered the bedroom on the thick carpet. There were bath and dressing rooms off a short hall to the right, and to the left was an adjoining office with a view over the sun deck to the sea. I could see the old man asleep in the shade of the awning.

I began going through the drawers of his desk. I read his ledger, his checkbook entries and his credit card statements. I copied down his telephone credit card number. I read a few of his business correspondences and inspected his list of things to be done. He didn't have a single appointment or chore for the remaining two weeks of his vacation.

The next day I went to the radio station to work on a news brief I was producing. There was an envelope addressed to me in the mailbox there. I started a cassette tape dubbing onto a reel, sat in the production room and read the note.

> *I've heard about FM signals traveling great distances. I volunteered for a while at a campus radio station. It's called skipping, I'm told. Something about this or that condition in the ionosphere.*
>
> *Well, I was driving across Pa. on my way to Jersey at about 3:00 A.M. (about midnight there), and I picked up your signal for a few minutes. I heard a bit of music (I think it was Miles Davis from the Kind of Blue album), then your name, the station ID, an announcement about a local theater group, then you saying, "We began with the music of . . ." Then the signal faded right on cue. I really wanted to know what else you'd been playing. We don't hear much good jazz on the air out here. In fact, we don't hear much good anything —just commercial junk.*
>
> *It was so mysterious—a familiar and favorite tune coming all the*

way from the west coast. The ionosphere is a strange place, I think. Just wanted to make contact. Have fun. I'll be listening.

> Cheers,
> Diana Farley
> West Orange, N.J.

I remember being fascinated by this letter, totally distracted from my work on the news tapes. I began editing and splicing, but after ten minutes I set the blade down, punched up the air signal on the board to hear the music being broadcast, then browsed through the record stacks in the production room.

Among the stacks was a collection of old 45s that belonged to the program director. I'd looked them over a few times, but never had the urge to play them—as soon as I read the titles I could still hear them playing in a worn groove of memory.

I unsheathed Frankie Ford's "Sea Cruise" and punched up turntable 1. "I got the boogie-woogie like a knife in the back," sang Frankie, and I cued up "Lover Please" by Clyde McPhatter on turntable 2, then closed the production room door and potted the speakers up high. Then Little Eva, tough as nails on "Keep Your Hands Off My Baby"—you *know* Little Eva could kick ass.

I went through the stack, searching for titles that would signify a specific feeling I faintly remembered. Suddenly I wanted the marrow of that feeling exposed, the bone cracked open.

The vinyl was cherry. This guy must have bought two of each disc and kept one in a drawer unplayed. He probably already knew he'd someday be a radio jock.

I played Troy Shondell singing "This Time," then Gary U.S. Bonds with "Quarter To Three." Clyde McPhatter made me want to hear The Platters, so I cued up "Smoke Gets In Your Eyes." I was cueing one after another, on a search to find the one single that would deposit me back —the one tune that was the perfect encapsulation, the mystical embodiment of a sensation that lingered just beyond my ability to actually feel and know it. I wanted to glimpse a whole aggregation of sensory junk and connect with that person—before he was kidnapped.

Young killers are the best killers. Initiate them in blood, and they desire blood. They don't think much and they don't feel much, and if they happen to do either, it can be drilled out of them. Put one in a war plane with bombs and napalm and cannons that fire one hundred rounds a second, and put one on the ground to mop up. I killed a man in cold blood with a knife for my initiation. It was called "getting wet." The back of his body was touching all up and down the front of mine. I stuck a knife in his throat and opened the vein. I got wet.

I rewound the news tapes, my hands trembling as I boxed them. I was talking to myself, laughing to myself, snickering while a tumor swelled up from my groin and pressed against my rib cage.

On my way out of the building I stopped in the men's room to inspect the white spot on my throat under the fluorescent light. When the light fell on the back of my throat and my eyes focused there, I snapped my mouth shut. I'd better open my mouth for another look, I said to myself; on first inspection I hadn't seen it—this prominent white eye that had stared back at me menacingly every time I'd looked at it. Where had it gone? Down my throat? I opened up again, tilted my head into the light, looked closely. It was there, but it was definitely smaller and less opaque, almost flesh-colored at the center, more like a dull ivory circle, like the glow around an eclipsed moon. "What the hell does *this* mean?" I said aloud, staring myself in the eyeballs.

When I got back to the tenement a man and woman were packing Charles's belongings in boxes. I went to my room, fell on the bed, jumped up, swallowed some Dexedrine and ran down the stairs. Men were out on the stoop with a new jug. It was unbearably hot. The men were bunched at the top of the stairs in the shadow of the building. A group of people stood at the bus-stop down the block on Sunset.

"What are we waiting for?" I said to the men.

Only one of them looked at me. No one answered. The palm trees, bald and ridiculous, were waiting too. The blinking red light on the hill was barely visible through the smog. It seemed to be blinking more slowly. I sat and waited too, for the Dex to come on.

After a while Carol came up the street with a bag of groceries. I was thinking about getting a bottle of wine and going up to her apartment. She stopped in front of me.

"Did you join the club?" she said, cocking her head toward the men seated next to me.

I smiled, but she didn't. Her lips were pressed tightly together. I didn't say anything. She stood there looking down at me.

"We're waiting," I said finally.

"That's great. Don't hold your breath." She continued up the stairs and into the building.

I caught her on the second flight. "What's the matter?" I asked. She kept climbing.

"Carol," I said.

She stopped, turned.

"I'd love for you to stay here," she said. "You're one of the few lights in my life right now. Forget the sentimentality. I feel better just knowing you're next door, even if you won't fuck me, you queer. But I can't stand to watch you go down the tubes. Next you'll pull a gun on a cop, like Bob, and they'll lock you up. You'll burn someone else for their wallet and you'll be too fucked-up to pull it off. I don't want turkey and Grand Marnier that badly." She turned and started climbing. "Go find a life somewhere—this ain't no life."

I began my board shift that night with Miles Davis and John Coltrane—the tune titled "So What" from the *Kind of Blue* album—the signal power and the volume attenuator raised slightly higher than normal, the meter reading at a continual overmodulation, the Dexedrine running in my chest like a rat on a wheel.

I let the album play through "Freddie Freeloader" while I pulled more records from the stacks. I pulled some odd records—all music I knew would be inappropriate for the strict classical and jazz format of the station.

It was an abrupt segue from Miles's blue jazz to Danny and the Juniors doing "Sometimes (When I'm All Alone)," and for some strange reason I cued up the sound track from the old *Victory At Sea*. When the part came around where the big guns are firing and the radio communications are crackling underneath and war planes are buzzing over, I faded in the title cut from Dylan's *Highway 61 Revisited*. The hysterical slide whistle that begins the song worked perfectly with the whistle of bombs falling on the American fleet. I let the two albums play simultaneously, then slowly faded out *Victory At Sea* and cued up "Zippity Doo Dah" from the Disney movie about Uncle Remus and that trickster, Br'er Rabbit. I had to laugh as the bluebird on Uncle Remus's shoulder sang crisply over the L.A. airwaves. The Dex had me strung tightly, spinning me in the swivel chair. The segue into Tiny Tim's "Tiptoe Through the Tulips" was fairly smooth, I thought. I'd never before appreciated the abandon with which Tiny leapt for his falsetto.

I spun in the chair, rifled the stacks, dove for more musical oddities, cued up an album of ancient Chinese wooden flute, and when Tiny was finished I did an ID break and a public service announcement. The log called for a pledge break—a request for sponsorship subscriptions—which I usually kept as brief as possible, but the Dex had me by the tongue. I knew something was coming but I didn't know what—it was pure discovery.

I reminded the mostly college-educated demographic group that the station was listener-sponsored and noncommercial. I asked them where else they could hear music as diverse. "I know it's odd not to hear ads every few minutes," I said, "but if you give it a chance you can get used to it." I put the responsibility on them to protect this valuable source of music and information. "After all," I added, "this is radio that's almost free of the meddling of real estate maggots, almost free of the bland noncommittal fluff of radio under the thumb of the business community, almost free of the bloody claws of war industry . . ." That was the one that did it—I cringed, laughed and continued. "Almost free of the gangsters of politics. You can help protect this freedom by pledging your support. Tune in daily and judge for yourselves. I don't want to convince you of anything. I mean, who am I to tell you how to spend your money? In fact, I *am* this slime that I speak accusingly of, friends and listeners—no, I'm their dog—attack dog for the slime. There is no denying the magnitude of my corruption, music lovers. A killer sent by killers to kill killers—a kidnapped kid sent to kidnap. And I'll tell you the truth—why not?—this is public radio. I am deathly afraid of this kidnapped man squatting inside me, who by his sheer spiritual superiority over me might emerge magically from his bindings or his wounds or his death and strike me dead. And I'll tell you the truth—this imprisoned man has a plan of escape. I can be your nightmares, music lovers. But until then, here's more jazz for you, beginning with some ancient Chinese jazz played on the wooden flute. And remember, oh demographic computer model—it has been determined that if we play only classical and jazz you will give more money, so give now, if only to stop the blues set I have planned."

I faded the music back up and spent the rest of the shift bouncing in and out of the blues—Otis Spann to Seamus Ennis with a slow air on the Irish pipes, Josh White to Japanese koto music, Professor Longhair to klezmer music, Phil Ochs to zydeco—any combination that struck me, no logic applied.

After sign-off I prepared for the ritualistic screaming into the mike by boosting the power. I was interested in making contact with Diana Farley again. How was I to know the station manager was hurrying across town in his VW bug?

I was falling headlong into a deep gutteral howl, sending the cancerous electricity into the ionosphere, when I felt eyes upon me and looked up to see the station manager staring at me through the glass partition. I remember he looked embarrassed. I felt the beams of electricity snap back into my body. He opened the control room door. He's a soft-spoken guy.

"It's part of a harmless ritual I use to heal my throat cancer," I said.

He put his hands in his pockets, jerked a little, took his hands out, spread them in front of him, looked them over, then put them back in his pockets.

"It doesn't hurt the equipment," I said. "I checked with Roger."

"What about this little speech on the air tonight?" he said.

"It was a whim."

"We don't have whims on the air at this station," he said calmly. He was standing stiffly, looking down at me, his shoulders hunched, bouncing nervously.

"I thought this was public radio," I said.

"And we don't segue Jimi Hendrix with Kabuki Theater."

"You caught that, huh?"

"I heard it in the car. I got eleven phone calls in twenty minutes, mostly from employees and listener-sponsors."

"Why doesn't Hendrix segue with Kabuki Theater?"

"We don't even play Hendrix on this station anymore. You are, I assume, aware of the format changes that went into effect over six months ago? I think we should discuss this tomorrow. Now shut down the transmitter and lock up."

"What time tomorrow?"

"Anytime after three. I'll be in my office."

"*Hendrix* is not a *classic?*" I asked.

He wanted to smile but he said, "What's the matter, man?" There was a new injection of compassion in his voice. "We've never had any problems before."

"I knew better but I did it anyway," I told him. I walked past him and out the door. The Dex had me grinding my teeth and chewing my tongue. Sleep was out of the question. This small man imprisoned in me had done a heck of a board shift. I was feeling cocky. From the station, which was just west of U.C.L.A., I headed west.

I started running and jogged all the way out Sunset to Santa Monica beach. The moon illuminated the sea near the cliffs to the north. The white water was glowing. After a rest, I stripped, ran into the ocean and swam out past the breakers. As I bobbed around in the swells I thought about the note from Diana Farley. Maybe I need to go back to the home soil, I thought. I should have known the cancer would land in New Jersey, gravitating instinctively toward home. Maybe California is just a stop on the way from Asia to home. Maybe I'll have to resurrect all the dead Indians and unlay the Great American Railroad on the way. Maybe I need to ground my energy in Jersey—that was a good one. Mr. Excitement was flailing. Maybe Diana Farley will lick my wounds—I sure hope so—make me a pallet on the floor. "Ah, if it were that simple," I said rhetorically to the full moon.

I stayed in the water over an hour, playing hard, body surfing the glassy waves and tumbling in the luminescent foam. Despite the abuse I'd put my body through, I still felt strong in the water. I swam as well as when I was in underwater demolition training in the Navy.

I washed up in the surf, exhausted but renewed, and crawled onto the beach. I filled my lungs with air, spread my arms and legs and watched the moonlight on the sea until the breeze dried me.

I walked all the way back to Hollywood, and by four o'clock, though my heart was still tossing and rolling, I fell into some kind of sleep on my sheetless bed.

The following day about noon I met Karen at the club. After a few beers on the beach I suggested we visit her parents for the afternoon. She jumped at it. I told her I wanted to talk to her father to see if he could help me find a job.

At Karen's house I accepted her mother's invitation to dinner. The old man went out and came back with lobster and abalone. In the bathroom I confirmed that the white spot had definitely shrunk, and a healthy pink color was coming through the white. Mr. Excitement felt nearly wholesome. He ate hearty, told jokes, lied.

After dinner, while we were watching the TV news, I excused myself and went to the bathroom. I waited a moment and opened the bathroom door quietly, went to the old man's office and, from his desk, where he kept his wallet, took his driver's license, two major credit cards and three hundred and sixty dollars in twenties that were stacked in the top drawer, listening all the time for the first utterance or movement from the TV room.

I found a .22 magnum and a box of shells in the bottom drawer, opened a window screen and dropped the pistol to the ground.

It was about eight when I told Karen I had to leave. I thanked her folks for everything. When Karen started the car I jumped out, ran to the office window, stuffed the pistol down my pants and ran back toward the car, stopping to pick a flower from the garden on the way.

"What are you doing?" Karen asked.

"Went to pick you a flower. Your mom will never miss it."

"How nice. Thank you." She smelled it.

"Thanks for the nice day," I said, sliding over next to her, imagining a lizard's tongue coming from my mouth as I licked her beneath the ear.

I asked Karen to drop me at a bar. I ordered a George Dickel and called a guy I knew from a VA therapy group. From him I got the number of another vet who dealt in various controlled substances. His name was Sam. He was a decorated Marine who spent some time on search and destroy.

I called Sam and told him who I was and where I got his name. He didn't want to talk on the phone. We agreed to meet at a bar in Hollywood. He said he'd probably be the only black man in the place, and if I was still not sure, he'd probably be the only person with a VC tooth hanging from his earring.

I took a taxi to the joint. He was with two guys.

"I have a fair quantity of heroin," I told him, "and it ain't Mexican. I need to dump it right away, so I'll let it go very cheap. I have to get out of town."

"How hot is it?" he asked. "And what exactly is a fair quantity?" He looked down his nose with his head cocked back.

"It's not hot," I said. "I have to leave town."

The bar phone started ringing. Sam looked toward it, then back to me.

"How hot are *you*, man?" he said.

"I have the feeling some people are going to be on my ass tonight."

"I can appreciate that, bro, but I don't know why you should be worried, from what I've heard about you from McNeeley. Do you need an M-16? Some frags? Maybe we could work a deal."

The light over the booth was reflecting off his forehead. Someone finally picked up the phone. Sam lit one Kool after another. His friends were silent, watching the door, watching me. The whole place seemed a little uneasy with our presence. I think he chose the place for that reason.

"This stuff is uncut," I said. "Ass-kickin', war surplus. I have three ounces. It's not hot. I can sell it to four other people if you don't want it."

"Three oh zees! Unstepped on? Mutha-fucka, man. Sweet Saigon White?"

"Can you get the cash? It's dirt cheap."

"Why me? For what do I deserve this privilege, bro?"

"Let's just say it's a gift from Uncle Ho," I said.

"Uncle Ho! Shee-it, man. I can get the cash no sweat, brother. We'll have to inspect it, of course. Where do we go?"

"I'm carrying it. Where do you have to go?"

"He's carrying it, he says! Uncle Ho is fucking carrying the shit. Man, where did you get your balls?" He wagged his head back and forth. "If you allow me to make a phone call, we can go right over to my place and square this deal."

"Phone call to who?"

"Bucks, baby—my man will meet us there."

In an hour we were sitting in an apartment in El Segundo. A white woman sat at the kitchen table, visible from where we sat in the front room. She had a black baby on her knee, a joint in her hand, and she was reading *Soul On Ice*.

Another woman kept entering the kitchen from somewhere out of sight to stir a pot of something on the stove. Blind Faith's "Can't Find My Way Home" was playing on KRLA.

In another room a child was crying, and two women who sounded black were talking and laughing.

Sam and his two friends and I all did a few lines of coke, and one of the guys was crumbling Thai stick into a pipe. We were waiting for the money to arrive.

"Now, brother," Sam said, "you understand we have to taste this stuff."

"You can knock yourself out, but first I have to see the cash," I said.

Sam smiled wide and took the pipe from his friend. "Now, we brothers, ain't we? Ain't we been through some shit? I've heard about you from Bobby Mercer—McNeeley too. Even some of the brothers I deal with in Watts say you're okay. You must get around, bro."

"Not much anymore. Who's in Watts?"

Sam laughed. "No, man—'Watt's on first.' " He grinned, toking the pipe like a satisfied man. Sam liked to sit back and wait for people to make mistakes—I felt like I knew that about him, and I kept thinking back to Nam to place him.

The door opened. A young white guy walked in. He greeted everyone and handed Sam a zippered cash bag. He looked to be about seventeen. The pipe was passed to him, and he took a seat on the vacant sofa. He jived a bit—"What's happening?" "Everything's cool." "Good group at the Whiskey tomorrow." He was obviously a courier, and obviously on speed.

"How does that honky joke go, Glen?" Sam said to the kid. "Who's on first?"

"Yeah, right," the kid said, " 'what's on second.' Abbott and Costello or some shit. You guys telling jokes?"

The kid looked at me. I looked at Sam.

"Is that the cash, or am I leaving?" I said.

"Clarence Wilson lives in Watts," he said. "He was a Navy SEAL. You remember Clarence. They call him Rube. He don't like Whitey, but he like you."

"Clarence is a good man," I said.

"I wouldn't turn my back on him," Sam said.

"Of course you wouldn't. What's he doing in Watts with a degree from Irvine?"

He passed the pipe to me. "What's he doing in Watts? What's he doing in Watts, Jay?" He turned to look at one of his friends.

"What?" Jay said. "What's who doing in Watts, man?"

In minutes we were all ripped on the Thai stick. Sam's friends started their jive on cue. They got very testy, feeling me out—stoned jive, half serious, half joke—all geared to test my reactions.

One of them left his seat on the arm of a chair and was standing behind the high-backed chair that Sam was slumped in. The other guy I knew had a pistol in his pocket. I could tell by the way he guarded it. The child came in from the back room. The courier kid, Glen, was playing with him on the floor. Everybody was stoned. Jay was chewing his lip from the coke.

"No, listen," Sam said to me, "I wouldn't fuck with your head, bro. The cash is right here." He sat up, opened the zippered bag and laid a stack of hundreds on the table between us. I reached over, picked it up and counted it.

"This is only half of what I told you I need to get," I said.

"Well, the other half is my business. It's in the drawer of that desk."

He stood, took a few steps toward the desk and stopped. "I can't believe you're walking around with three oh zees on you. This is a dangerous city."

"It's a serious risk," Jay said from behind the chair, "with so many bad dudes in town."

Sam stood next to the open drawer with a stack of bills in his hand. He grinned.

"It's not much of a risk," I said to Jay, "because I don't really have any junk." I smiled.

They all laughed.

"Did you hear that funny joke?" the courier kid said to the child, grabbing him in the ribs until he started to laugh.

Not Jay—the other guy—started moving toward the door behind me. I reached out to block his way.

"I can't handle people standing behind me, bro," I said, "unless you want me to tear your nuts off right now."

The phone rang.

"That'd ruin your whole day, wouldn't it?" Sam said to the guy, grinning wide. "You're so unsociable, man," he said to me. They let the phone ring. "We give you all these good drugs and you want to leave right away. Here's the cash, man. Now lemme see the junk."

The white woman came out of the kitchen to get the phone. Sam was still grinning, poised like a cat when I took Karen's father's .22 magnum from my pocket. The guy behind the chair went for his pocket, and I popped one off into the flesh of his thigh. Sam had a handgun out of the desk drawer, but I already had the .22 on him. He raised his arms slowly.

The child on the floor was screaming, the phone ringing. The two black women burst into the room. One ran to the guy who was hit. He was leaning up against the wall. I kept the .22 pointed at Sam's head. He was frozen, hands in the air, the money in one hand and the handgun in the other.

"Now everyone calm themselves," I said. I was including myself. "He's not hurt bad—no arteries, no bones. I want everyone face down on the floor with their hands behind their heads, or Sam's gonna be a dead man, and that would be a shame, after Nam and all that." I pointed to the white woman. "Except you. You answer the damn phone."

"Hello," she said. "Yes. Can you hold a minute?"

"You couldn't stop Super Nigger with that peashooter," Sam said. "That's a gentleman's gun, for shooting gentlemen, but I'll get on the floor just the same—just for you, bro."

"Open your hand and let the pistol fall," I said. "Now kick it over here. Now drop that money on the table and get on the floor."

I stuffed both stacks of bills in my pants pockets and picked up the pistol. The child was still crying and screaming. One of the black women was trying to hold him and stay prone at the same time.

"You wouldn't mind if I borrowed your wheels, would you, bro?" I took the keys off the table.

"No, man, go right ahead," Sam said, "just be careful now."

"I'm in a hurry or I wouldn't ask," I said.

"Don't mention it," Sam said, "what's mine is yours."

I ran outside and pulled the coil wire on the courier kid's car and tossed it in the back seat of Sam's Mustang. The front door of the house opened and Sam's head stuck out. I swung both pistols at him—the door closed.

I drove to Hollywood and dumped the Mustang in a garage driveway between two buildings, then ran the four blocks to my tenement. I said hello to the four men sitting on the stoop, handing them each a fifty dollar bill, ran up to my room, grabbed a vial of uppers, a change of clothes, the five hundred dollars I kept beneath newspaper under the rug, packed it all in a small shoulder bag and split.

The men on the stoop were still holding the fifties when I dashed down the stairs. "You heard me say I was going down the Baja," I said. "Adios," one of them called as I ran away.

8

I WAS TALKING ALOUD TO MYSELF BY THE TIME I HIT HOLLYwood Boulevard and turned toward Vine. I liked the drug combo—it was doing just fine. "It's like a goddamn B movie," I said, amusing myself. "Quite a profit on that drug deal. I'll mix in with the street creeps at Vine, make my way to the Chinese Theater, linger in the crowd till the downtown bus comes, ride to the bus depot, get the first bus to the airport and be gone." It seemed reasonable enough—I'd seen it done in the movies.

The homosexuals were cruising, honking their car horns or whistling their code calls at men walking the sidewalk. A car drove by me slowly. I waved to the driver. He pulled over to the curb.

"Need a lift, Marlon?" the driver said.

"Yes, I do," I said, huffing a bit from the excitement.

"Why such a hurry? Get in. We'll talk it over." He looked me up and down and pulled into the traffic. "That's a stunning outfit. Where'd you ever find it? Very smart."

"Navy-issue baggy pants," I said. "Cool cotton, dark blue for night work, lots of room for movement—practical and carefree."

He laughed. "Yes, indeed."

"Plain old black tee shirt," I continued, "never needs ironing."

"Yes," he repeated, "the perfect outfit for the fashion-conscious active man."

"Thanks for noticing," I said. "I spend a lot of time, you know."

"It must be the pants—you look like the young Brando. Pants are so tight now. Not everybody can wear them, but everybody is. I like the baggy pants. It shows the mind of an individualist, which is a polite term for a deviant. Are you a deviant? And why are you huffing and puffing? Shouldn't hurry through life. You'll get ulcers, like me."

"Can you spare a smoke?" I asked.

He handed me one. "Where you from? New Orleans, I bet—behind the Quarter, on the fringe, a steamy night, baggy pants, the young Brando leaning out the window with bourbon in a water glass, no ice. Where's your tattoos? I thought sailors had tattoos."

I looked at him and said nothing.

"Did your boat stop in Southeast Asia?"

I remained silent.

"The brother of a friend just got back from there. It must be terrible. I hate guns and I hate dead people, not to mention snakes and bugs."

"You mean you don't get off on a little rough trade?" I asked.

"No, I do not, sailor! I definitely do not! And you can get out right here. Or I'll scream rape." He looked in the rearview and swerved toward the curb.

"I was kidding," I said.

"Violence makes me extremely ill!" He opened the door as we rolled to a stop. "Please get out—or I'll scream bloody murder."

"I'm just incredibly stoned," I said. "I was just giving you shit—that's how you can tell I like you."

He stood outside the car, lit a smoke and looked at me with his eyebrows raised, waiting.

"Relax," I said. "I rediscovered my sense of humor last night and I'm not sure about how to use it yet."

"Where did you find it, under a rock?"

"I think it was Tiny Tim."

"We're not going to get anywhere, are we?"

"I just need a ride," I said.

He got back into the car cautiously.

"I have a feeling someone is following me," I said. "I'll pay you to drive me up to the Chinese Theater. I don't want to beat on you."

He pulled away slowly, keeping an eye on me. "I can't be wasting my time on good-looking men who don't put out. And I can smell violence on you."

"A little violence in the right place in not a bad thing."

"Like in the villages of Vietnamese peasants? I'm sorry, but . . . I don't believe that."

"Beginning with the head and moving down, I can kill you seventeen different ways before I reach your heart. I can kill you with that pack of smokes, that pen, the gearshift lever. I can paralyze you with a glance. I can make your head explode by chewing that piece of gum there. I can . . ."

The car was at the curb again. "Shall I scream?" he said.

I opened the door and put my foot on the curb. "I'm not only violent—I'm straight."

"I can smell that too." He had his brow raised again. "That's the way it is then. Maybe you can find a way around it."

"Just getting out of bed is a violent act, just walking to work. Suppose we admitted we live by violence?"

"Suppose we did?"

"It would be a place to begin." I peeled off a hundred from the stack of bills in my pocket. "Here, I'm giving these away tonight."

"My God! Who did you roll?"

"Jesus said, 'The kingdom of Heaven is taken by violence.' Buy yourself a good woman."

"I could buy a little boy with this—if I were into such things."

"No rough trade, no little boys—you might be straighter than I am."

"A sailor who quotes Jesus and gives away hundred-dollar bills—this could only happen in Hollywood."

"Hell, I'll quote anybody. I picked up one of those southern evangelists on the radio the other night. That's where I got the quote."

"What did Jesus mean by that?"

"Fuck if I know."

"Sure you want me to keep this?" He held up the bill, still sensing the undercurrent of violence.

"Of course. This is a B movie," I said. "The money is just a prop. Thousand, ten thousand, couple hundred thousand—it just depends on the plot. A hundred is enough for this plot. I didn't mean to upset you. I'm very stoned. I'm talking just to find out what I'm going to say. It was nice to have met you. Be careful." I closed the door and waved. He arranged the bill in his sport coat pocket like a hanky, then drove off.

There was no reason to expect Sam and his friends to find me, but I kept looking over my shoulder at every car that passed. Soon I heard the Buddhists chanting hare krishna in the distance. The herb, the coke, the adrenalin and the paranoia all rushed up behind me. Behind the chanting I heard an M-16 busting caps. A ghost—the one in the Hawaiian shirt—ducked into a doorway. I ran up to a dingy little bar and went in to get off the street.

I sat at the end of the bar near the door. Men were lined up on the stools, turning their heads back and forth between the TV over the bar and a movie screen on the wall behind them. I ordered a George Dickel. Nixon was on the TV, on half of a split screen. He spoke over a telephone to Buzz and Neil, who were on the moon, of all places, and on the other half of the TV screen. I poured a little Tennessee sour mash into the chemistry of that historic moment. Opposite, on the movie screen, in Super-8 color, a woman climbed onto a table. She was naked. She spread her legs and arms like a specimen, and a man, naked too except for black socks, mounted her. "For all Americans this must be the proudest day of our lives," Nixon said.

The astronaut jumped; the man in the black socks pumped; the heads at the bar swung back and forth; Nixon rejoiced in the Oval Room with his cosmic telephone, talking to the moon, his shingles beginning to itch beneath his socks, and the woman and the moon were silent, submissive. I knocked down the whiskey and pointed for another.

The world is undoubtedly some kind of hell—that's what I was thinking during that giant step for mankind. I saw movement like fish through the frosted glass bricks and I knew the ghosts were gathering at the door. I am a P.I. for the devil in this hell—Evil is My Business. My hands curled from this guilt, turned upward in my lap and opened, my fingers reaching up gently then like petals of two tulips, and I felt the weight of the AK-47 there.

Mr. Excitement couldn't contain himself—his heart was a poison pill dissolving in his chest. "Which is the kingdom of Heaven?" he asked the man at the bar, swinging his arms from TV to movie screen. He wanted to walk up the wall and across the ceiling for them, but he finished his drink, went to the door and opened it cautiously. The ghosts had vanished, those inscrutable Orientals. He continued up Hollywood toward Vine.

On the next block a huge searchlight was mounted on the back of a truck. It panned the sky, advertising the opening of a strip joint called The Batcave. I was watching the swath of light cut through the darkness above the city when a car turned the corner too tightly in front of me and stopped short at the curb. I jumped behind a wire trash can, gripping the .22 magnum in my jacket pocket. A man's head craned around from the driver's window.

"Hey, sailor," he said, "where'd you go?"

I stood up.

"What are you doing crawling around in the street? Did I scare you? I'm glad I did."

I was eyeing every car that passed.

"I can be a frightening fellow, too," he said.

"I thought I smelled like violence."

"An obvious misconception," he said, "now that I see you clutching a weapon of some sort in your pocket I'm sure I was mistaken."

"What do you want?"

"I'm bored, actually. This cruising is for shit. I have a strong intuition that you're being pursued. I thought I'd pluck you from peril, sweep you away to safety. You have me worried. Who is here to rescue you but me, and that has me worried the most. You probably just strangled seven nurses for that money, and I'm driving around looking for you. Why? My name is Anthony." He cocked his head toward the car. "Get in."

"It was queers, Anthony. Seven queers with a snake—with a four-foot cobra."

We were both eyeing the cars that passed.

"You'd better hurry up and get in," he said. "I'll take us somewhere for a strong drink—no strings attached, sweetheart, so you don't have to worry about your cherry. Unless I decide to take you by force. But hurry, please, before I have an accident in my pants."

I got in the car and he pulled away.

"A four-foot cobra," he said. "Is that what you hide in those baggy pants?"

"I wish you could get your mind off my pants." I fished in his shirt pocket for a smoke, lit it and looked behind us.

"I'm doing rather well, actually," he said, "for a queer in a B movie."

After a few blocks I felt almost relaxed, as much as the drugs would let me relax. The Dickel was getting an edge on the coke and the Thai stick was cruising smoothly. We passed Vine. The street creatures were out for their promenade. "The circus," I said, looking at all the weirdos. "Don't you love it?" he said. I spotted the woman in black—she was sitting on the sidewalk between two famous footprints, conjuring some magic with two sticks. She had added a black cloak to her outfit. She looked up as we passed—I couldn't believe it. As I turned my head to watch her a wire trash can, the contents on fire, passed between us. "Weird movie," I said.

"Well," he said, "personally I think it's better than some heady, existential German New Wave cinema where we're all trapped on the San Berdoo Freeway, driving back and forth between life and death until something metaphorical happens, something based on Heidegger's wet dreams or something—political underpinnings, rain."

"I agree. We should be coming up to the high-speed chase scene any minute now—that's where we leap flaming trash cans in your . . . what is this boat?"

"It's a Buick." He searched the rearview.

"No headlights closing on us yet?"

"No."

"I think I got clean out of this shit."

"Watch them as they escape the clutches of boredom, men caught in a contemporary drama where right and wrong are not so easily delineated—Mr. Excitement and his sidekick, Anthony. Did you make a bundle?" He looked over at me.

"Just some traveling money."

"Where're you going?"

"New Jersey, I think."

"New Jersey! My God! Why? A man of your resources?"

"For the climate, the scenery, the drinking water, the fresh air . . ."

"How thoughtless of me."

"Did you know we're conquering the moon right now?"

"I heard the rumor."

"Well, that's why I'm going to Jersey."

"Is that supposed to make sense?" He turned into a parking lot.

"I trust that it doesn't. What is this place?"

"It's a bar."

"It's a fag bar."

"It's not a fag bar—it's a mixed bar."

"Let's go further."

He pulled onto the street again.

"You're chasing some woman to New Jersey, aren't you? Of course. This *is* a B movie. Where could it lead? Rehash romance. It's sad," Anthony said.

"I might not be able to find her anyway."

"Of course you won't. Well, maybe you will—some people do. But if you ask me you'd be better off here for a while—you need to find the female inside you first."

"What, so you can poke me in the peaches?"

"Forget it. It's beyond you. You're a roughneck. You need to learn to cook or something. You can't go on dealing with—"

"She's dying of cancer, Anthony."

"Oh, Jesus!" He looked at me, his mouth open, his whole face open. "I'm sorry. I should keep my mouth shut. I'm really sorry. I thought—"

"It's okay." I played it deadpan.

"Jesus, that's awful. How are you going to get there?"

"You could drive me."

"There's no way. I mean, I'm really sorry to hear about your friend, but . . ."

"I was just kidding you about her. Actually I need the toxic waste dumps in Jersey. I need to find the source of the poisons, the heart of the enemy, so I can eat it. Come with me, Anthony, as my sidekick—the chemicals will make us immortal like Wu Ch'eng-en's Monkey in the Chinese folk tale."

"Like who?" My sidekick was exasperated.

"Like Monkey in—"

"I do not like to be manipulated! You are fucking with my mind—another form of violence! Why did you tell me she is—"

"Anthony! Immortality! Like Monkey we can con our way up to the heavens! Fuck some angels! Imagine that!"

"No thanks."

"Fucking angels on a fucking cloud, Anthony! Ripped on the best herb in Heaven! Then we could cruise down to Hell—we could use the Buick—drink at The Batcave, fuck some she-devils under the eerie glow of the big searchlight. He-devils for you. Then we could erase a few names off the Books of Hell, raise the dead, incarnate some ghosts, dispatch some *agents provocateurs* up to Heaven. We could leap off the brink of doom into another world, Anthony!"

"Actually, I wouldn't mind a little travel.

"That's the spirit. This is the perfect machine for it—the Buick from Hell. We'll have to get some tinted windows."

"About this person dying from cancer—what's the point of telling me—"

"I need a drink, Anthony."

"I'm looking," he said, trying to be patient with me. "The place we passed is a biker bar."

"Let's go there."

"You must be kidding."

"No—it'll be great."

"You're not dragging me into this violence of yours."

"I murdered children, Anthony—bikers would be nothing. I've never dragged anyone into the murderer rap before. What is this place, the patio set from the Valley?"

Anthony parked and turned the car off.

"When was the last time you had a drink with a murderer?" I asked. "What is this place?"

"This is the naugahyde lounge," he said, "and I'm not going an inch further—alcohol is alcohol. Murderers gather here—you'll like it. Murderers, queers and the patio set from the Valley. Actually I've never been here in my life. I just need a drink."

The place was like a Holiday Inn in Somewhere, Nebraska. I settled into a George Dickel. It was perfect. A hack piano player sat in the corner belaboring the ivories with a Beatles medley. The ambiance of colorful polyesters highlighted by the indirect lighting exuded a sterile secure calm. The bottles twinkled on the glass shelves in the mirror of the back bar. The deep red naugahyde and the exaggerated heaviness of the ceiling fixtures seemed to anchor the place—nothing unexpected was due to happen beneath those hewn-look imitation wood beams.

After the second Dickel I was enjoying the pop schmaltz that followed the Beatles medley. Anthony was rambling on in a soothing tone about the female movie stars of the forties, reciting lines from their films.

"Tell me something about yourself," I said. "To hell with the movies."

He shrugged his shoulders. "I'm still wondering if it was your official duty to murder children—or if you were just jerking my chain like you did with the poor girl dying of cancer."

"I made movies for the Navy—besides murdering children." I motioned to the waitress for another round and drained my glass.

"I'm sorry," Anthony said, "I didn't mean to drag you into this."

"Before I was dragging you—now you're dragging me. I was a scout—that was my official duty. I made movies even in bad light. I played around with infrared stuff. I started doing all this in-camera editing—dissolves, wipes, fades, cut to medium shot, cut to close-up—getting artsy with recon shit. It was never appreciated much, but I did it anyway. It was good for a laugh. I bought a nice sixteen-millimeter over there—for personal use. Haven't used it much since I've been back. I don't see anything I want to look through the lens at."

"You should use it. Make a film of the Vine Street scene. You could shoot some weird stuff down there."

"That I could. It's a nice camera—a Doiflex—made in Japan, telephoto and everything, pistol grip."

"You should really use it, you know. Start a project."

"You think it would be good therapy, right?"

"I think it would be a good thing to do, a productive thing." He snuffed his smoke and drew his shoulders back. "I'm going to tell you this if it takes me all night, so you might as well not interrupt me this time. I don't like to be manipulated like you did with that cancer bullshit."

"But I'm so good at it."

"Don't do it to me."

"But there's no one else here."

"I don't like it."

"You're so sensitive. How do you get through life. Doesn't everyone manipulate everyone else?"

"Just because you're that cynical doesn't mean everyone else is."

"I'll tell you a story—a parable about manipulating people. There's this guy named Gene. I wanted to whale on him since the first day I met him, so I screwed his wife's ass off instead."

"See," Anthony said, getting excited, "that's what I'm talking about! I can't understand that! I've never—"

"Who said anything about understanding it?"

"I've never wanted to beat on anyone. And I don't understand sex that way."

"It's not really a true story. I'm making it up. It's an illustration. I didn't beat on him or her, all right. And I'm not saying I understand sex that way, just because I did it."

"You did it or you didn't do it—which is it?"

"They don't even exist, so relax. I'm making it up. Where the hell's the waitress?"

Anthony looked around behind him. She was nowhere in sight.

"This guy pissed me off," I said. "He dumps all his violence on his wife—and I like his wife. She's a sweetheart—and a victim. I wanted his ass. His whole way of life depended on exploiting her gentleness."

"What you did is no better—I mean, who are you to pass judgment on this—"

"I was Monkey, and Monkey wanted his ass."

"Who is this Monkey?"

"So Monkey whaled on the jerk. 'The culture is rooted in violence,' Monkey declared, 'but it's wrong to express that violence.'"

"As it should be. As it must be."

"But Monkey doesn't care."

Anthony hit the table lightly with a loose fist. "You're bullshitting me with this Monkey jive, and I'm trying to be serious. If it's all a joke to you, say so, and we won't have to listen to your parable."

"I'll be serious. This guy, Gene, I'm talking about—he thinks he knows the way things *really* are. He's the logical type. *He fucking understands*—whatever it is, he understands it. He knows how everybody is supposed to feel about everything. He knows how everything should be, from his wife's vegetable soup to foreign policy to the Ram's goal line defense."

"Well—you're describing an awful lot of people."

"I wanted to crack the logic and pour in chaos."

"So you, too, victimized his wife."

"Right."

"And you're just making up all of this, of course."

"An illustrative example, yes. I had this conversation with his wife. She called me and asked me to meet her for coffee . . . to tell me, as it turned out, that she had to end this affair we were having. For her own sanity, she said. I liked her a lot, which is partly why I didn't like her husband. He treated her like shit. And I liked having her around, and she liked being around. But we were pushing our luck at that point anyway. It'd been going on too long. Gene was about to flip out. So I meet her for coffee, and she says all this stuff like, 'What's been going on with you?' and 'Have you been happy?' and 'You seem so distant lately.' 'If you want to talk to somebody about it,' she says, 'I want you to know that I'm here to listen.' Then she tells me that she can't see my eyes. I had these mirror sunglasses on. I was hung over, and the lenses reflected the light and eased the pain a bit—we were in this outdoor sidewalk café coffee joint, and the sun was killing me. It was too early for serious discussion.

"I tell her I'm hung over and the sun's too much, and we sit there sipping coffee. I take the glasses off. I don't need to say anything. It's her move. She called the meeting, and I'm silent because I know something is about to come down, and there's no sense in making it easy. I'm Monkey, right, posing as God—Monkey in his God costume, sitting in judgment."

Anthony hit the table like a powder puff again, sighed and looked at me. "You *can't* really think this way. You must have some responsibility to . . ."

"Don't get overexcited, Anthony—I'm just making it up. But listen. She's sitting there quietly. She doesn't know what to do. Maybe she's having second thoughts about breaking it off. Who wants to be dutiful and loyal to an oppressive husband in the face of Monkey? So I start telling her about this Fellini film—I think it's Fellini—where his gigolo is taking this sweet naive woman for a ride. He's nice to her at first, charming her, setting her up, of course, and he's coming off as a likable guy—kind and gentle—the audience likes him. Then, when he's about to turn the tide, when the shit is about to hit the fan, they're dining out on this veranda café overlooking the Med somewhere, and he takes these mirror sunglasses out of his pocket and puts them on. So at that point in my story I put the glasses back on, right. I'm illustrating."

"You're fucking with her mind is what you're doing. You like to do that." He lit a smoke. "But go on."

"So there I am fucking with her mind, and I explain to her that from that point on the Fellini character—it might have been Mastroianni—but from that moment on he's an entirely different person, and he really pulls it off beautifully. I'm telling her all this, right—how he's completely detached, cold, indifferent, not even there, and I have the glasses on. I feel like I'm dealing with her the way I'd seen her husband deal with her. I'm understanding his ugliness through my own, and I'm beginning to feel this violence toward him—and me. As I fade further from her I'm feeling more violent, and at the same time I don't want to lose her—as a lover or a friend. I'm realizing this emptiness—this need. I feel like Gene is taking her away from me."

"But Jesus Christ," Anthony said, "she's his wife!"

"Gene knows about this affair, you see, and he's freaked-out because he can't *understand* what to do about it—there's no logical solution. Monkey likes to have Gene in this position. Sure she's his wife, Monkey says, but so fucking what. Monkey, he don't understand shit. He just Monkey. But where was I?"

"You were sipping coffee and being ugly, stewing in your own emptiness."

"Right, and she's still not talking. I think she's guilty over the affair and wants to be blamed. It'll be easier for her to break it off if it's a penance for her sins. But I want to keep fucking her if I can, you see, if it's not too much trouble. That's what's going on in the back of my head. Actually, I was just going quietly crazy, I think. This was right after I got back from Nam. I was spending my time on the beach by myself. I'd recently found out I had cancer in my throat. And I'd met this woman named Karen at the beach, so . . ."

"Wait a minute. You have cancer in your throat?"

"Yes, but that's all over now—I think."

"You had cancer, but now it's gone."

"It seems to be."

"Is this the same kind of cancer the girl in New Jersey has?"

"Anthony, you're so fastidious about the details. I'm trying to tell you something."

He motioned for me to continue and looked around for the waitress again.

"I need your undivided attention, Anthony."

"And *I* need a drink. And what makes you think you deserve my undivided attention?"

"Because I give you mine. Now listen. Finally she opens her mouth and tells me how she's working things out with her counselor, and . . ."

"That's more than you're doing."

"And she realizes, she says, that she has to be able to be angry with me. She needs to get in touch with herself as a woman, think about herself for a change, make sense out of her life, get to the bottom of woman's roles in society, stop living to please men—all this therapy horseshit. So I tell her she can whip me next time if she wants to get mad—walk on me with spiked heels."

"How sensitive of you."

"She didn't think it was funny either. Then I knew it was over. I tell her it's okay, we'll always be friends—it's not necessary to fuck—but, you know, the glasses are on, and I'm fading before her eyes. I'm way back there behind the mirrors, and my mouth opens, and the words come out, and I tell her how the sex I had with her was important stuff —all in the past tense now—how it was this deep libidinous balm, right, freedom to express the innermost, healthiest . . . this lie and that lie. It's the taboo that makes it, I tell her. Take that away, and you're fucked-up like normal people. Through that kind of sex, I tell her, you come to your true sexual self, see God, make peace with the natural world, come to grips with death—all this shit you wouldn't *believe*, but somehow I'm believing it all, and this relationship has suddenly become important research for nothing less than the survival of the species. I'm feeling the emptiness again, and the cancer. So she starts telling me about how she's too much into pleasing people, as though it's a flaw or a weakness to be guilty about, and how she should please people only when she wants to—when it's her choice. This is no doubt coming from her frustrated counselor, who is no doubt a woman, and is no doubt talking specifically about pleasing men, and probably jealous of her affair. The counselor is trying to make her into a fucked-up normal fucker. I was fucking with her head as much as the counselor or her husband. I needed to keep the affair open if I could, but I don't think I knew that. I figured I didn't need anybody, and if I did, I had Karen, and one is as good as another. If it was just a whim of hers to end the affair, that was okay, as long as it opened up again. I needed to keep that possibility open. I started telling her that it was all my fault . . . I fucked everything up—our relationship, their marriage, my relationship with Gene, the peace and general well-being of the entire cosmos . . . me. I'm the one who fucked up the world—the guy behind the mirror sunglasses. A decent person wouldn't have done what I did. A good person lives according to social standards. You don't fuck around with another man's wife."

"I wouldn't argue with that," Anthony said.

"So, of course, she then tries to convince me I'm not such a bad person. She's not quite at the pitying stage, but I can't let it go any further. I'm seeing through myself and her, and it's scary, so I go numb. Who gives a shit, I tell myself.

"Then I say, look, when we're sixty I'll probably come over when Gene's at work—we'll talk dirty and do something kinky and play hide the hot dog—so don't worry about it, we'll get over it. I remember thinking that that was the first thing I said that made any sense.

"But she says, 'You're just filling me with longing.' I'll never forget that one. It came right out of a movie—probably a movie her counselor saw. But I agreed that I was trying to fill her with longing. Then she tells me that it just doesn't feel right anymore, and we have to cut it off. And I think right then I decided I would kick the fucker's ass—Gene, that is. That's the way it works. I think I realized for the first time that I was in love with her, and that love was an actual possibility for me, an important thing, especially then. We're fucked-up, complicated people, but I think our motives are simple, almost primitive. They just seem complicated because of all the possibilities we've invented.

"It was the very next day, I think—the day after that conversation—so it was still on my mind. We were at this barbecue at the house of a mutual acquaintance. I didn't know most of the people there. There were a lot of older folks too. It was a birthday party for the father of this girl we knew. We were all invited because a bunch of us helped him move all this heavy shit after he had a minor heart attack. So all these people are there in the back yard, and we're all drinking.

"So, Gene, he's basically this militaristic mad dog suppressed inside a quasi-literary type—putting up this fashionable facade of passivism and mellowness. I get into an argument with him over a film.

"The hero of this film is a pro-war, red-blooded American hero disguised in all the trappings of the hip, and, of course, he's a stud with the ladies, and this asshole Gene is identifying like crazy with this movie hero. It was making me sick.

"So I go on to prove, to the apparent satisfaction of all listening, by use of examples from the film, that Gene is basically a dumb fuck and was taken by all the hip culture images and manipulated into identifying with a hawk in dove's clothing. I'm proving it's a jingoistic propaganda film—he's insisting it's an anti-war statement.

"Eventually I all but call him a dumb fucking shit-brain asshole in front of a lot of people. An hour later—we're both drunk—he starts this shit with me over nothing. It had to come down to this, and he's expediting matters. After some prodding I got him to call me some nasty name, so I overreacted and started yelling at him like a lunatic, calling him a jerk-off and telling him to get out of my sight like he was a leper or something. So he takes a swing at me, a drunken swing. I damn near killed the fucker—knocked his ass all over the patio."

"And this you think is funny," Anthony said.

"The funny part comes next. I remember telling the host—this girl's father—that I was going to rip Gene's balls off, and that I was sorry if that would ruin the party though I didn't think it should. I was calmly telling the old man this while Gene was trying to pick himself up and people were trying to stop the bleeding with napkins. I went over and knelt in front of Gene. People thought I was going to apologize, I think. We're civilized people, right? I took a hamburger bun and wiped his bloody nose with it and put a burger on it and took a bite. Some people thought I should leave after that."

"I would have been one of them," Anthony said. "This is no parable—this is a confession. Do I look like a priest? What is the meaning of all this? And do you have any more of this coke? It must be very good, judging from your line of chatter and your warped sense of humor."

"What it means is, I haven't talked to anyone in a long time. It can't be a confession because I made it up. I don't have any coke but I have some black beauties."

"I gave up speed when I couldn't remember how to tie my shoe. I'm happy to talk to you."

"You think I'm pretty fucked-up, Anthony?"

"I don't understand violence."

"I'm growing out of it. Even an innocent little bean seed has to break up out of the ground."

He nodded, looked me in the eyeballs, nodded again.

"How 'bout you?" I said. "Tell me something about yourself. I've bared my soul here, and it's sickening."

"It's too boring. I don't mean you've been boring. I don't know where to begin. It's all rather uneventful."

"Sounds like a personal problem—maybe you better keep it to yourself."

"I have nothing to say."

"Make up lies. That's what I've been doing. I've never been to Vietnam."

He studied my face while I smiled back.

"Lies about what?" he said.

"How did you get to be queer?" I asked.

"Just lucky, I guess. We prefer the word gay."

"I know." I saw the waitress and flagged her. "Did you ever have a woman?"

"Some of my best friends are women."

"I bet you've never had a woman."

The waitress arrived.

"This is Anthony," I said to her, "and he's never had a woman."

"Nor do I want to," he said, a bit flustered. "No offense, dear." He put his hand on the back of hers. "It's a matter of taste. Some people love oysters, for example, and some people can't eat them."

"Oysters?" I said, laughing. "Two more of the same," I told the waitress. "Anthony, I bet you've never even seen a woman."

"I've seen them in strip joints," Anthony said.

"You know what they say," the waitress said, "turn them upside down, and they all look the same."

Anthony gasped a bit overdramatically. "How can you talk like that?"

"Ten years of cocktailing," she said. "It's a joke. No harm."

"Well," Anthony said, "they don't excite me either way."

"What were you doing in strip joints then?" I asked.

"Getting young men hot," he said.

"Are you hot yet?" the waitress said to me, changing the ashtray.

Anthony put a few dollars on her tray. "You have a wonderful sense of humor to tolerate the crudeness at this table," he said. "Thank you."

"You're pretty funny yourself," she said. "Thank you, gentlemen." She moved to the next table.

"Well," I said, "how did you get to be gay? Correspondence course?"

"My, we're all funny tonight, aren't we?"

"Tell me the truth, Anthony."

"The truth? Well. It was like this. I once was madly in love with this older woman, but I couldn't bring myself to tell her."

"You're bullshitting me."

"Yes. Actually I did tell her, but she rejected me. She was indifferent."

"Was she a stripper?"

"No, she was not."

"A cocktail waitress?"

"Then I ran into her having breakfast one morning and sat in a nearby booth so I could watch her. I loved the way she put her makeup on so thick to cover the wrinkles. She was beautiful. I ordered poached eggs and tried to think of something to say to her that would . . ."

"I usually have poached, too."

"No grease."

"But they're overdone a lot."

"That's true. That's why you have to find a place that's consistent with poached and go there exclusively. They take care of you if you're a regular. It's the cook, of course. I followed one cook from a Denny's Restaurant to a pancake house and wound up in a Walgreen's at a little dead mall every morning. It was a ghost mall—people'd come in once in a while for discount tissues or something. That's where I ran into this woman. It was so sad. I was staring at her face when she looked up at me. She eyed me for a few seconds while she lit her cigarette—not even a nod. She'd tried to quit smoking at least a dozen times. She blamed the tobacco for the wrinkles around her eyes. She'd gotten up early that morning to escape from the man who was sleeping next to her."

"How do you know that?"

"I can know if I want to. She hoped he would be gone by the time she returned. She was a miserable person, and I loved her."

"You're sick. I thought you were going to tell me something about yourself."

"That's what I'm doing."

"This woman is your mother and the man she woke up next to is your father."

"Lord, no. They are not. I'm telling you about this woman—I was in love with her."

"But she's your mother, right?"

"She is not my mother, so you can forget that, really."

"She's America. This is a parable, isn't it?"

"Oh, Jesus!"

"The Holy Mother."

"No, not the Holy Mother."

"Aretha Franklin."

"I'll ignore you."

"Well, who was she?"

"Is this what you call undivided attention?" He lit a smoke. "She opened a fresh pack of cigarettes. Chesterfield Kings."

"Strong poison."

"Thinking about her wrinkles, she began to daydream back to when she was twelve, pure, pink-lunged. She remembered a boy she knew who showed her the boys' hide-outs and where they hid the dirty magazines."

"I get it—you are the boy."

"I am not the boy. *I* am sitting in Walgreen's watching her smoke. She sat under the railroad bridge reading a story in one of the dirty magazines. It was about a man who entered a woman's apartment when she was out. He was going through her drawers when he heard her coming. He—"

"Going through her drawers when he heard her coming, Anthony?"

"Coming up the walk. He climbed—"

"Was he sniffing her drawers, Anthony?"

"He was rolling them and smoking them. He climbed—"

"You are undoubtedly this man, you sneaky pervert."

"He climbed into the attic crawl space and spied on her from the trap door. The woman was 'voluptuous' the magazine said, and she removed her clothes in full view of the man in his secret perch."

"Of course. I think I've read this story."

"It became obvious by the woman's behavior, if you know what I mean, that she wanted a man."

"Do *you* know what you mean, Anthony?"

"Just listen."

"Well, which woman? It became obvious by which woman's behavior that she wanted a man?"

"The one who took her clothes off, of course. The man watched—"

"Are you sure, or did the woman in Walgreen's bat her eyes at you until the heat from inside your pants overcooked your poached eggs? But when she took you home you couldn't perform, mainly because your father caught you and beat the snot out of you for diddling around with his wife."

"You are a sick man. Do you have some problem about incest that you'd like to talk about? Or are you just—"

"I'm just obsessed with decoding this cryptogram."

"I do not respond well to Freudian analysis, especially such clumsy dullwitted application."

"Yeah, yeah—on with the story."

Anthony sipped at his drink. "Shall I laugh or be indignant?"

"I love you when you're indignant, dear."

"The man watched her on the bed." He sipped from the drink again.

"This is where she is . . . ah . . . making it obvious that she wants a man. Is that right, Anthony?"

"Yes, but the story ends with her asleep in the dark and him hiding in the cold attic."

"This is an allegory, is it then?"

"This is not an allegory. This is just what the girl is reading in the magazine."

"That's right. What did she do then?"

"She started home through the orchard, still thinking about the story. The woman, as she sat in Walgreen's, thought she could still smell the apples fermenting in the grass and the musky wet paper of the magazine. She remembered how soft her skin was before the wrinkles. The girl ran through the orchard to a ditch where a large drainage pipe surfaced in the undergrowth."

"Good detail."

"The woman wanted the girl to feel everything around her so she could feel."

"Who could feel?"

"The woman in Walgreen's."

"She couldn't feel?"

"No. She tried to have the little girl waken her senses—every little sense node—to the sounds and smells and the light of the autumn orchard, but, when the woman could recall those smells and sounds the way they were, she wanted something more immediate, more provocative, something she could actually feel instead of imagine she was feeling, instant gratification, not this imaginative bunk. So she remembered how the girl began to stroke herself through her panties."

"Of course."

"But the woman was almost embarrassed by her own thoughts."

"Nonsense. You can think anything. Go on."

"That's right. So she did."

"That's the spirit."

"The girl didn't want to stop stroking herself when she heard the DDT truck approaching."

"The DDT truck?"

"Yes. It sprayed the orchard to kill insects and worms and things. She ran between the rows of trees, and as she ran the feeling between her legs climbed into her. When she reached the road she turned and ran back into the orchard. The sprayer turned up the row and into view. She crossed over into the next row and ran toward the cloud of DDT. The orgasm began as she reached the cloud. When she emerged on the other side of the cloud she turned and ran into it again."

"Can a girl have an orgasm while she's running?"

"You would think so, wouldn't you?"

"Why the orgasm in the cloud of DDT?"

"Because that's where it happened. When you start having an orgasm you can't really do much about where you are."

"So what did she do, follow the truck around all day sniffing DDT and having orgasms?"

"She went home, and when she got there no one was there."

"Now we're back to the woman in Walgreen's. The man was gone."

"No, the girl. The afternoon sun was drenching the back yard and the old shed and the woods beyond were rich with yellow light. She went in the front door of the shed and closed it behind her. She opened a small door on the back wall and looked out into the woods. Light poured across the dirt floor, vibrating with the movement of the leaves' shadows. The aroma of the crates of apples mingled with the must of old wood that remains in darkness most of the time."

"I get the picture—it's very sensual."

"Very. Without understanding why, and without the desire to understand—"

"Good for her."

"—and despite an impulse to go back in the house and eat a piece of strawberry-rhubarb pie, she removed her clothes and hung them on a nail inside the back door of the shed."

"It's a kiddie porn story. She's back in the dirty magazine. Aren't you embarrassed by your own thoughts, Anthony?"

"We are not in the dank, musty and base magazine—we're behind the shed in the daylight, cleansed by the natural world. She stepped outside the shed into a swath of light that was teeming with the movement of leaves above like a creek laden with fish."

"Didn't you already use that image?"

"Well, I didn't use the fish. I like the fish in it."

"So what does she do there, naked and nubile, and having rejected the material world of strawberry-rhubarb pie?"

"She ran into the shelter of the first trees in the woods and stopped and looked past the corner of the shed to the house."

"This is where you enter, you dirty old man."

"She crouched for a moment at the edge of the woods, then ran toward a—"

"This is where I enter. Make me enter here. I'm in the woods tending my herd of pigeons."

"And she ran toward a clearing that she knew well, and through the clearing to a dense sheltered part of the woods—kind of a thicket where the laurel snarls engulfed a small niche. The ground was covered with moss there. She sat and peered through the thick laurels, her arms wrapped around her knees, tucked up in a ball in the small hidden place. She didn't know what to do there."

"And you don't either." I laughed a kind of drunken laugh and bounced my drink on the table. "*You* don't know what the hell to do there."

"I do too—she dug a hole with her hands and—"

"And she made pee-pee." I couldn't help but laugh again.

Anthony was holding back laughter, persisting in a mock seriousness.

"She made pee-pee in the hole, right, Anthony? And that's the end of the story."

"She dug a hole with her hands and crawled in."

"And what? What did she do?"

"And that's all. That's the end of the story."

"How could she dig a hole with her hands?"

"She just did—just like that. Then she gave birth to a litter of furry animals and encircled them with her legs where they all clutched together on the moss."

"Then she gave birth to you, and that's how you got to be gay."

"No. Then the waitress refilled the woman's coffee cup, and she looked up at me again."

"And you were abusing yourself through your panties under the table." I thought that was funny and laughed.

"Don't be crude and sophomoric," Anthony said. "It doesn't become you."

"Sometimes I get crude and sophomoric when I drink sour mash on top of Thai stick and uncut Peruvian toot. You'll have to excuse me. I apologize, but what about the girl in the hole?"

"She just stayed in the hole, all curled up like a snail, waiting."

"Pseudo-mystical bullshit! Waiting for what? Was she waiting for the poison cloud of her autoeroticism to make her blind?"

"Heavens no. Nothing like that."

"Then what has this unrestrained indulgence led her to?"

"It's a story about how I got to be queer. Isn't that what you wanted to hear?"

"Yes. And what about the woman in Walgreen's?"

"She went home, and the man was still there, and she never did quit smoking."

"I love it, Anthony. I really do."

Anthony finally laughed.

We had more whiskey, clouds of cigarette smoke billowing above our heads. We requested bad music, split the cost of a round for the house, bragged, complained, lied and, at closing time, left without an argument.

9

AFTER THE BAR CLOSED WE MANEUVERED THE BUICK BACK to Hollywood for coffee and poached eggs. Then, back on North Normandie, the sun glaring about eyeball high, Anthony waited in the car, squinting behind his sunglasses as I ran up to my room and grabbed the Doiflex and some film. I slipped a note under Carol's door, telling her to take what she wanted from my room before the landlord got it. I ran down the five flights, threw my junk in the back seat of the Buick, then ran back up to my room and flushed down the toilet a couple hundred barbiturates that were in the fridge.

"There it is," I said to Anthony, "one-hundred-foot daylight loading spools, pistol grip, telephoto . . . Nice, huh?"

He took it and looked through the viewfinder, aiming down the street and panning the stretch of Sunset. "I don't know why you don't get some sleep first," he said. "I can take you tomorrow."

But there was no stopping the momentum. We were still jabbering and lying when we swung off the freeway at the airport exit.

"Listen," Anthony said, "I have a dear friend in New Jersey. He's a truly wonderful person—a quiet person. If you get hung up, go there. Tell him I sent you. He'll put you up for a while. His name is Jimmy Rosenthal. We call him Jimmy Rose. He's a beauty. I'll call to let him know you might be stopping in. He keeps a low profile in the gay community because he works for the city as a social worker, so don't make things too exciting for him. And be careful with him—I mean, I'm trusting you with a precious friend."

When we parked at the terminal he wrote Jimmy Rose's address on a pad while I got my junk together. I took the .22 magnum from my jacket pocket and put it in the glove box.

"I was wondering what you were going to do with that," he said.

"It wouldn't fit down the toilet."

"I'll dispose of it."

I extended my hand. "Anthony," I said as a complete sentence.

"Mr. Excitement," he said, extending his hand.

"I love you," I said.

He tried to hurt my fingers with the grip of his small hand. "I love you too, sweetheart."

I booked a 10:45 one-way to Washington, D.C., on Karen's father's credit card. I had an hour before the flight and I couldn't sit still for a minute. I loaded the Doiflex and moved to the big windows where there was a flood of morning light. The place was full of people, but there was nothing going on. Everyone was simply waiting—every person involved in that same functionless process—except Mr. Excitement, who couldn't wait. Mr. Excitement was filming, stalking people in the viewfinder and capturing them in the act of waiting.

Despite the fact that some people were offended and others tried to avoid or ignore him, he knew he was helping them, providing a service. In the viewfinder these people were no longer merely waiting, no longer drifting drowsily at the depths of this functionless sea—they were metamorphosed onto film, alchemized by silver nitrate and light, and their barren act of waiting was fecundated with the camera.

A woman was sitting in the plastic chair, one hand on her suitcase, staring vacantly across the throng of waiting bodies. Mr. Excitement fecundated her for a good sixty seconds. She smiled, showed her profile, brushed her hair back with her hand, shook her head gently and tilted it to study her hands, then smiled again, fecund and stimulated. Mr. Excitement was pleased.

A man in a safari-style jacket was given, by the camera, reason to be offended. The benevolence of this instrument fascinated Mr. Excitement. The man went about escaping with much overtly articulated purpose. Conspicuously he disappeared to another waiting area.

Even the light coming in the windows, as it cleaned up the hard edges of the room and exposed the lack of textures, dramatically illuminated the possibilities of that moment in that room filled with unoccupied people.

Then Mr. Excitement fell in lust at first sight. She was heading down the hall toward the main terminal. She was so beautiful he heard himself groan—a sound that rose up from his groin and resonated in his chest. It hurt him. He ached. She was bounding into the forest as quickly as she had appeared. He pursued, keeping a fix on her off-white linen jacket as she darted among the people. She was heading for the people conveyor.

One of those electric shuttle carts was coming toward him. He pulled a twenty from his pocket and waved it at the driver. In seconds they spun around and were speeding toward the people conveyor.

"Parallel the conveyor," Mr. Excitement said excitedly. "I need a smooth tracking shot here. See the woman in the white jacket? Stay abreast of her."

The woman looked annoyed as he filmed her—it was perfect. His heart fluttered. He heard music. She walked casually with her long legs as the background flew by behind her, as she flew by people walking in the foreground, as the shuttle cart continually gained slightly on her.

"Full speed ahead," he called, and they sped to the end of the conveyor, where Mr. Excitement jumped off, steadied himself and aimed the camera down the conveyor, ready to fecundate her further as she came at him.

She stepped behind a man so he couldn't get a clear shot, but it only added to the drama. The man moved to the side, not wanting to be in the way. She became fully exposed and didn't try to shield herself again. She was brilliant, gliding like an angel toward him.

Mr. Excitement opened his mouth as she approached, trusting that some kind of captivating words would come out, and they were about to, just as she said, "No, thank you," and stepped around him into the arrested pace of unassisted walking.

Whatta snot, thought Mr. Excitement—I'll just have to fecundate her from behind.

And I did, all the way to the ladies' room, where she escaped.

Mr. Excitement couldn't wait a minute, and he let her slip away—his true love, perhaps—the most beautiful woman he'd seen all day.

In D.C. I paid cash for the first Amtrak express to New York, stowed my junk in a locker in Penn Station and went to a bar on Eighth Avenue, where I stayed until closing, talking to four Puerto Ricans, listening to stories about the Umbrella Man.

At last call I swallowed two black beauties with a swig of beer, walked over to Fifth and up Fifth to Central Park, sat on the fountain in front of the Plaza Hotel and lit a smoke. I watched the occasional passersby, waiting for the speed to pick me up. The darkness was soothing and the confusion of drugs was disorienting enough.

Only the nocturnal creatures were out. I felt a kinship with them. There was no brightness to contend with—nothing that had to be done at night. In the trash behind the Plaza, thought Mr. Excitement, surely there is a champagne cork—with that cork and the matches in his pocket he could easily reflect less light. In the layers of receding trees in the park and the darkening shades of gray in their leaves there were traces of a map, traces he could begin to decipher only by crawling around in the dark where he couldn't see them but maybe smell them, only by working their scent into his skin then letting the dew set on him.

Mr. Excitement was articulating a bad attitude for himself as he headed for the darkest trees. I should find some niche, he thought, some hole in which to be sick or molt, some crate in an attic in which to remain suspended in the undead during daylight until the quality of that darkness reveals the map to where good and evil are indistinguishable, where it makes sense that what is Godless and inhumane of one man is valiant and necessary of another. In this *place*, revealed by this *map*, Mr. Excitement told himself, skeptic that he was, every particular of the world would be renewed and become frighteningly and beautifully luminescent in the dark connecting tunnels of the brain. He could see how it would be staged in a musical comedy. He told himself that the molten core of the individual, where innocence and goodness can readily be smelted into the hardware of torture, would be exposed to air and burn out and then wither in the sun. There would be no need for one pulse to lie to the next so that the heart might continue its work. He sang himself this song, considering possible choreographic interpretation.

"More psychobabble," sang Mr. Excitement quietly, pausing to reflect briefly on the space junk orbiting in his brain. "Let's be more practical and to the point," he said. "Now, how can a murderer use his skills productively?" He raised his left hand, palm up, to answer the question. "By taking money from some creep in deep cover to murder a Libyan college student living in Colorado?"

Isn't it true I've seen beyond the veil of civilized behavior? he thought. So, in a practical sense, can this be turned to my advantage? Is it self-pitying and therefore self-defeating to think I was kidnapped, duped, exploited, used up and tossed away? Poor Mr. Excitement. It's true that I've witnessed, to a greater or a least more dramatic degree than most, the ugly side of humanity. And I have been terminally disconnected from a part of myself, or so I've been told. So, was this disconnection necessary to the mastering of my trade? Must Mr. Excitement now find a way to sort of trick himself into showing himself a glimpse of this estranged, abducted, mythic, stunted Jungian figment? And why bother with this reunion, even if theoretical, when it might make it all that much harder to survive? I mean, wouldn't this wan homunculus most likely be another burden, with his wimpy sincerity and compassionate understanding? It would be a neat trick I'd have to pull on myself, considering my deft defenses against this pest. Mr. Excitement sang himself this song for a while.

As he reached the first shadows of Central Park and his brain began to clear and he no longer felt insoluble in the digestive acids of the dark, he said aloud, with a nod of completion, "I am a murderer who was sent by murderers to murder murderers—but this can't be the end of it."

The nocturnals passed, some of them slow-footed, bovine, others hurried, preoccupied, parting the emptiness. Most were solitary and silent.

When I spoke to one, and a word came back to me, it was a marvelous and magical act, as though a bird had spoken.

This person had ducked under a stone footbridge in the park and didn't see me standing nearby in shadows, sheltered from the rain. The person was half man and half woman, wearing a long coat over heavy breasts and a kerchief tied under a sparsely bearded chin. The face, except for the beard, was feminine. The hands and shoulders were masculine. The voice was brittle, magical.

"Hello," I said, stepping out of the shadow, "I'm standing out of the rain. How you doin'?"

The person nodded from across the walkway. "Hi," the person said sullenly, not quite cowering, shuffling a few inches.

I stepped into the dim light of the lamppost, not close enough to threaten but close enough to let the person see me clearly. I did a little dance step as I stood there, as though it were cold, but it wasn't—hands in my pockets, shoulders hunched a bit. I took a pack of smokes from my pocket and extended my arm with the smokes in my palm. I waited, expecting the person to inch toward me cautiously like an animal. The trees glistened where the lamp light reached into the lower branches, the black-green hillside disappearing in the mist, buildings invisible except for smudges of light floating and diffused high in the yellowish fog. I felt the light rain falling on my face. "Want one?" I asked.

The person walked over and bowed close to my hand to remove a smoke from the pack in the dim light. There was no caution. The bowed head was vulnerable. The person produced a match from a coat pocket and turned to shield the flame from the breeze.

We smoked and said nothing. I watched the reflections of the lamp lights on the wet walkway curving into the fog. When the rain let up the person mumbled something I couldn't understand and left, rocking slightly from side to side into the puddles of diminished light.

I stepped into the shadows, fell to my belly, slowed the cardiovascular noise, turned off the broadcast, moved with my chin brushing the wet grass, chest a few inches off the ground, elbows pointing up, fingers spread on the ground like a lizard, the lizard sensory discs activated in my temples.

I prowled through the park, staying in the darkest shadows, shrinking the world down to my immediate surroundings—a sphere of territory that I scanned for intrusion.

I heard voices and crawled toward them to locate the source. The men in the dark by a footbridge radiated purposeful energy. They were lying in wait for prey. I moved closer, growling deep in my throat, rattling the roots of my voice in a slow dull vibration.

"¡Ay, por Dios!" one of them said, then "What was that?" in a Puerto Rican accent.

I could almost hear their hearts kick into high gear. I raised the pitch of the growl, adding a human tone to it. They hurried off, almost running. I paralleled them in the dark, scrambling noiselessly on all fours, grumbling restrained snorts and snarls. When they started running they kept running. I listened until they were out of earshot then leaned back and roared as loud as I could.

I realized then, kneeling in Central Park, that I could survive in New York City as in the wilderness, by hunting prey at night, by finding shelter where I could, by utilizing my skills and finding resources in the spoils. I remember feeling a primitive security. In my new life I had quickly discovered one possible way to survive. The foundation had been established—I could build up from there—I could always return if I had to.

Just after dawn, cranked on the speed, I took a subway downtown. I found a café with strong espresso coffee to put a cutting edge on the amphetamine.

From the café window I saw a Chinese man with a parasol held over his head. He pulled a wagon behind him that was loaded with parasols. I confronted the man, geared up on the beauties, walking circles around him as I spoke. That impulse began the first in a series of moneymaking scams that I continued for a long time.

At first it was just nickle-dime operations, and more for the sport than anything else. I think I was trying to lose everything, trying to bottom out to cause some crisis and wind up with nothing.

It seemed that because I didn't care about the money, because it was all a rolling of knuckle bones on a game board, because there was no compulsion to gain any profit, because it was an unrealized scheme that I made up as I went along, I couldn't lose. It wasn't any big money—not at first. My profits varied from a quick twenty dollars to buy food or a bottle to five-hundred-dollar deals. The parasols, for example, I considered a remarkable investment at first.

They were well-made, handcrafted parasols of wood and thick painted paper. The man was on his way to sell them to an import shop in Soho, hoping to make a few retail sales along the way. I bargained with him, driven by the speed, and didn't give up until I got all fifty parasols for three dollars a piece.

I boxed the parasols and put them in the locker at Penn Station where I'd stowed the camera. I removed the Doiflex from the case and walked aimlessly for miles, stopping from time to time to shoot film. There were people who balked at the sight of the camera. They were the people I held the camera on, flipping the turret to the telephoto lens to capture the discomfort in their faces.

I filmed a black man from the opposite side of the street. He was walking quickly, and I paralleled him for a block. I liked the way the cars passed in front of the lens, the man shooting glances at me between them. At the corner he crossed the street and approached me.

"Who the fuck are you?" he said.

"CIA," I said. "Can't you tell by the concealed camera and my surreptitious behavior?"

"A smart-ass dude." He changed his weight to the other hip. "Am I right?"

"Yes. And who are you, a Black Panther on your way to an underground bomb factory?"

"Maybe. And maybe I just don't like being filmed."

"There's no film in the camera. I'm just practicing smooth tracking shots."

"Suppose I smash that thing open to see if there's film in it?" He put his hands on his hips and leaned toward me. He was as big as a door.

"I bought it in Nam," I said. "They're new on the market. I liked the pistol grip."

He stared hard at me, brows shrouding his eyes. I looked down, turned the turret and looked back up. He was silent, still staring.

"Where were you—Hue, Khe Sanh, Ia Drang?" I asked, looking him in the eyes.

"Who says I was in Nam?"

"I can tell by the way you walk," I said. "Your asshole is still puckered from the sound of 51s and B-40s."

He pointed at the camera. "That's an invasion of privacy. Point it at somebody else."

"I'm making a documentary of business as usual in real life," I said.

"Leave me out," he said and walked away.

I filmed him as he walked away. I got a room in a hotel that was cool and quiet and slept deeply. When I woke I ate in the hotel restaurant and drank coffee and brandy while planning the parasol scam.

From the Port Authority building I took a bus to Jersey City and found Jimmy Rosenthal's apartment—Jimmy Rose, as Anthony had called him. He wasn't there. I returned later and found him home.

Jimmy Rose was not in a good way. He explained right away that he was trying stubbornly to recover from a six-month cocaine habit that had left him strung out, unhealthy and nearly broke. He was obviously depressed. Still, he was a gracious host, had lots of questions about Anthony and tried to make me feel as comfortable as he could under the circumstances.

I stayed there a little over a week. He put me up in a spare bedroom that he used for a study, cooked dinner every night, gave me a key to the place and even had me drop him off at work so I could use the car during the day.

The apartment was full of artwork that he'd purchased over the years. He loved to browse through galleries in Manhattan, then look up artists whose work he liked. These artists would introduce him to other artists. He even corresponded with artists in Europe. He owned several pieces done by a printmaker in Amsterdam who was beginning to make a name for himself. Jimmy Rose had an impressive collection—all contemporary, tasteful and subtle. It was his pride and joy.

On the second day I was there I dropped Jimmy off at work and drove to New Hope, Pennsylvania, a town north of Philly where I knew there were lots of novelty shops, galleries and boutiques. Between New Hope and Philly, by two o'clock I'd sold all fifty parasols to retail shops for ten dollars apiece, and through the owner of a boutique I found some local greenhouse herb that had the kick of good Oaxacan. They were selling pounds for one hundred and ten dollars. I left with three and a half pounds for the three-hundred-fifty-dollar profit I'd made on the parasols.

During the following few days I used Jimmy's friends and contacts to sell the herb by the pound as Oaxacan for four hundred a pound, which was a decent price for good Oaxacan. I made fourteen hundred dollars, a twelve-hundred-and-fifty-dollar profit on my initial investment in parasols. I bought Jimmy Rose an antique Chinese woodcut print of a house in the mountains, a bottle of V.S.O.P. cognac and a dinner at a good restaurant. After dinner we talked for hours over Grand Marnier and coffee. We both enjoyed the time together and the dinner, but Jimmy couldn't surface through this emotional funk he was in.

Then one night—I'd been there a week—I came home about ten and found his mood suddenly transformed. He was with two friends. Judy Garland was on the stereo. The three of them were in the kitchen whipping up a chocolate mousse. It was the first time I'd seen Jimmy Rose happy. He was gadding about animatedly and separating eggs, a goblet of wine beside him on the counter.

"This is a friend of my great friend, Anthony," he said to his friends, extending the goblet toward me.

Everybody shook my hand enthusiastically, including Jimmy Rose.

"What's the occasion?" I said. "It's so festive."

"It snowed," one of Jimmy's friends said. "Show him, Jimmy."

Jimmy Rose disappeared into his bedroom and returned with an antique enameled box. He brought it into the light in the kitchen. In the box was an ounce of coke in a plastic bag.

"Want your nose fixed?" he asked me.

He spread some lines on a slab of polished agate and handed me a silver tube. It was exceptional coke. They all refixed their noses too.

"There's enough there to make a lot of chocolate mousses," I said.

"There's plenty," Jimmy said, "but actually I have to sell three quarters of it to pay a debt."

"Borrowing from Peter to pay Paul," one of his friends scolded, "and he's already got his nose in it."

"Maybe we should have waited," Jimmy said, smiling.

They all laughed.

"Right," one of the friends said, "let's wait."

They laughed again.

"At least it's just going through the nose this time," Jimmy said.

"The Rose smashed his needle," the one who'd scolded him said.

"Only to buy a new one tomorrow," the other one said.

"Why not put it in the mousse?" I said.

More laughter. There was a lot of laughing for the next few hours. The Rose was talking on and on, rambling and digressing and returning. We ate the mousse at midnight and settled in the living room for a bowl of hashish. Jimmy ceremoniously unveiled the Chinese print to much overdramatic acclaim.

After his friends left I asked Jimmy questions about certain pieces of art in his collection, and he went through almost every piece, explaining where he'd found it and what he knew about the artist.

"How can you afford this stuff?" I asked.

"I spend every spare cent on it," he said, "which isn't much, but I don't have many expenses. At least I didn't before I got into coke. But that's over—I mean, as a habit. Some of it is already worth four or five times what I paid for it, though I doubt I'll ever sell a single piece. This gift from you is the first addition in quite a while. It's an incentive. I'm very grateful."

"It's my pleasure," I said. "I'm happy you like it."

"Let's take a walk," I suggested. I was tired of all the talk. The city was sleeping by then. It was a warm night, a cool breeze in the air.

"Let's do some more coke," he said. He began chopping some cocaine on the agate. "More coffee," he called when the lines were up our noses. He poured two cups and fired up the hash pipe. The night was young again.

"I don't know what I'd do without this stuff," he said, still talking about the artwork. "I depend on it, really. It's the only thing I do that means anything to me. I'm comforted by all the beautiful clutter, and the hunt for the stuff gives me something to do. It's good for me all around. It's a lot more than a hobby or a love of art. It—"

"I like this," I said, pointing to a carved ivory fish in a glass case. The fish was detailed down to the texturing of each scale and the ribs of the fins. Looking at the detail made me nervous. I wanted to get outside and move around.

"That's the only piece I didn't buy," he said. "It was given to me by my grandfather."

"It's great," I said. "Let's take a walk, want to?"

"He made it. It's my favorite piece. It's funny you picked it out of all this because it's Anthony's favorite. He made me promise to will it to him in case I die before he can steal it. My grandfather was a wonderful carver. This is the only fish he ever made. As detailed as it is, it's one of his simplest pieces. I especially like it because the fish is an ancient Chinese symbol for no-mindedness. Not mind*less* or careless or something like that—not unconscious but consciously no-minded. I think it's like without the mind's recognition of the workings of the mind—pure unthought or some such thing. I have a feeling for what it must mean. I've always been interested in ancient Chinese culture—their poetry, art, philosophy. Anyway, I particularly like this fish."

"It's beautiful," I said. "No-mindedness, huh? I'm gonna take a walk." I took a step toward the door.

"The idea reminds me," he continued, opening the glass case, "of the brass spheres on the Buddhist temples in Kyoto in Japan." His coffee cup was already empty. "They're said to represent the eye that sees everything but itself."

I walked toward the door. He followed and handed me the fish.

"It's made of aged elephant ivory," he rattled on. "My grandfather had a whole tusk. I had the stand made for it. It's fourteen karat gold —worth a lot of money."

I couldn't bear another sentence. Mr. Excitement was pounding on the inside of my rib cage. "Why do the Buddhists in Kyoto construct objects to represent *what is not?*" I asked. "It's stupid. They have material representing nonmaterial. Why?" I opened the door. The trees rustled. I didn't care one way or the other about the ancient Chinese or the Japanese Buddhists or the ivory fish. "Why don't they *not* construct the brass spheres? It would be a more interesting ritual, and wouldn't that better represent that which is not—no-mindedness? They could not build the temples, too—leave the hillsides to whatever nature has in mind for them—let that be the representation of no-mindedness. Or would the absence of the brass spheres then necessarily represent *mindedness?* If the fish is beautiful, what do we have if we take the fish away? Does the space left in the glass case represent ugliness? Do we need all these words and symbols to know what can't be known—to tell us where we go after we die or something. Does it matter whether the brass sphere is there or not? To *whom* does it matter, Jimmy Rose? I don't really understand any of this, especially when I'm stoned and there's a breeze blowing. I'm going for a walk. Why don't you come?"

"It's too late," he said. "The city is dangerous at night."

"I'll protect you. Come on." I stepped onto the small porch.

"You know," he said, "just what you were trying to express, I think that's what was behind ancient Chinese philosophy. They thought—"

"Yeah? Did they just talk on and on about it, or did they live it?"

"I don't know. Judging from the translations of the . . ."

I jumped off the porch to the sidewalk, tilted my head to the sky and yelled: "Maybe our *minded* mind could lead us to an understanding of the *no-*minded mind that would render *minded* descriptions of the *no-*minded unnecessary."

"Quiet!" he said, laughing and closing the door.

I made a tour of alleys, backyards, docks. . . . It was a taste of what would take over when I got to Paterson.

It was the next day that I found a small apartment in Montclair. At dinner that night I told Jimmy Rose I'd be leaving on the following day. I told him I was going to Florida to find work on the boats. He told me he enjoyed my visit and welcomed me to come back.

The doorbell rang four times, quickly.

"Who the hell is this?" Jimmy said, getting up from the table. "Always at dinner." He went to the door and opened it.

A guy about twenty-five walked in, brushed past Jimmy and swaggered into the living room. I heard a car running outside.

"How ya doin'?" I said.

"I'm not doing well," he said. He was a cocky one. He paced in a circle.

Jimmy Rose was obviously worried. "I asked you not to come here again," he said to the guy.

I went to the kitchen window to look at the car. A guy was in the driver's seat.

"You don't ask me nothing, fag," the guy said to Jimmy. "You're done asking."

I returned to the living room.

"I told you I'd have it in two weeks, and I will," Jimmy said.

"That's what you said two weeks ago. Do I look like a fucking fool, man?"

I almost answered him.

"I explained the situation on the phone this morning," Jimmy said.

"I don't want no fucking explanation. I want the cash."

"I've always paid you before," Jimmy said.

"I need the cash now, fag. I can't operate without cash. You think I'm running a credit company?"

"I don't have the money," Jimmy said. "I won't have it for two weeks. I told you that."

"Suppose I start taking pieces of this art shit until I think I have twelve hundred dollars worth." He looked around the room.

"I'll get it to you in two days," Jimmy said.

"I need it now, fucker!"

"You should be more polite, pal," I said.

He pointed at me with his thumb. "Who the fuck is this?" he said to Jimmy.

"I'm just crashing here," I said. "I'm a friend of a friend. I have nothing to do with him or his deals, but I think you should be more polite."

"Polite!" he scoffed. "I'm done being polite."

"Two days—or two weeks—is not a long time to wait," I said.

"Keep out of this," he said. "This is between me and Jimmy the fag."

"They why didn't you keep it private?" I said. "You saw me standing here. You're a sloppy operator, pal."

"I don't need to explain myself to you, fucker." He picked up a bronze sculpture of a gypsy playing a violin. "How 'bout if I start with this? Who is it, some fag?"

"Put that down," Jimmy said and took hold of the guy's upper arm.

The guy dropped the bronze, grabbed Jimmy by the throat and shoved him against the wall. "Keep your hands off me, fucker!"

When I moved toward him he pulled a pistol from a shoulder holster beneath his jacket, keeping it pointed at the floor.

"You're cranked up too high, pal," I said. "Too much profit up the nose. You're going to make a mistake." I took a wad of money from my pocket, counted out twelve hundred and handed it to him. "Twelve hundred," I said. "Now leave us alone. We're in the middle of dinner."

When he started to count the money I jumped his ass hard, dropped the pistol, hit him with a combination of blows, bounced him off the wall and hit him again. He went down.

"Enough enough!" he yelled.

I picked up the pistol, and when he tried to yell to his buddy in the car, I stuck the barrel in his mouth and shoved it down his throat. He gagged, eyes bugged out, panicky.

"Bang," I said.

Jimmy was still against the wall holding his throat. I wristlocked the guy, yanked him to his feet and told him to pick the money up. He picked it up and stacked it, cowering against the wall.

"You come back here and I'll kill you," I said.

I took the bills from his hand, folded them lengthwise, grabbed his head, yanked it back and pinched his nose closed. When his mouth opened I stuffed the bills in and grabbed him by the hair. "Say thank you to Jimmy Rose," I said.

He grunted a thank you.

"Now get out of here." I moved him toward the door. "You ever come back and I'll hack you to death with a machete."

I dragged him downstairs, threw him over the hood of the car and pointed the pistol at the driver. The car squealed away with the tough guy rolling up over the windshield, twelve hundred dollars sticking out of his mouth, his fingernails trying to hold on to glass.

"You're gonna get me killed," Jimmy Rose said.

I handed him the pistol.

The next morning I thanked Jimmy Rose and told him I'd send an address when I got one. After he left for work I opened the glass case, removed the fish from the gold stand and put the fish in a paper bag with two bronze pieces, including the gypsy violin player that the coke dealer had tried to take. I made a sandwich, kicked over some furniture, dumped a few drawers, busted the lock on the glass slider in the living room with a screwdriver and a hammer, scrawled the word *fag* on the wall with a felt-tip pen and walked to the bus-stop. I ate the sandwich on the bus to Montclair.

When I got off the bus I tossed the paper bag with the fish and the two bronzes into a dumpster on the way to my new apartment.

The apartment was a block off Bloomfield Ave, the second floor of an old house. I spent a week scrounging in the trash for furniture and usable items. What I couldn't find of the necessities I bought dirt cheap in a church thrift store.

Brookdale Park is large and full of trees and fields. I started running and stretching there a few times a week. I cut down on the booze too, and there was a college in the city, so I was looking into courses in botany, but I never got around to enrolling. As it turned out, this notion of being settled turned out to be an illusion.

I guess I'd been in Montclair a few months when I ran into a Sears salesman in a joint called Tierney's. He invited me to a poker game, a game that had been going on steadily every Friday night for over four years. The game was frequented by local regulars, plus it was one stop on a circuit traveled by serious poker players from as far away as Philly.

It was one of these games that caused me to move out of Montclair in a hurry.

The games were generally held in the back room of a sporting goods store. Boxes and other assorted items were stacked against the walls. There was a permanent place cleared in the center. A felt-topped table stood there. An overhead lamp hung from an electrical cord. Old stuffed chairs and end tables were scattered around to accommodate onlookers, backers and women who accompanied the players. Along the back wall a makeshift bar was set up with all manner of mix and match accessories.

The crowd varied from week to week, depending on who was in town and who was on a junket to Vegas. At times, none of the heavies would show up, and the local small-timers who otherwise made up the onlookers and partyers would have the table to themselves. That was when I usually sat in. Those games were the best—all the local losers gathered excitedly under the lamp.

For many, the games were just an excuse to party—always lots of booze, women, stolen merchandise and general rowdiness. I made a habit of going with this guy Rich, the Sears salesman, who was a poker fanatic. He loved to play with the big boys, when I usually sat around drinking and lying.

Occasionally I backed Rich. If his luck was down, and he needed to buy some room in order to come out a winner at dawn, I'd front him enough on the sly to help turn the tables.

Then one night, stoned on good hash, I started studying the game. I studied the behavior of the players, trying to second-guess their hands, read their bluffs, determine their patterns of folding and raising.

I went through extensive training in experimental psychology and psychic awareness with the CIA and the Navy when I was being prepared for my job in Nam. Evidently I demonstrated an exceptional facility for various kinds of ESP, especially telepathy in the auditory sense—that is, I could receive or "hear" with consistant accuracy. It was discovered that I could increase the rate of accuracy through certain concentration techniques and through simply trusting in my abilities. They worked with me in developing these abilities, experimenting for months with me, their remote jungle unit that they would soon dispatch into the Jungle of Darkness on its proto-mission. For example, my ability to become "invisible" is a product of their training. I'm sure they had big plans for my future after the war.

So I began experimenting with these techniques while playing poker. It became a game within a game, and I was able to achieve some success by combining the application of these techniques with the kind of observation and concentration that any serious poker player practices.

The experiments began to pay off. There were times when I simply knew the betting man's hand. I just saw it in my mind—three jacks, a ten-high straight—there was no explanation. The real betting was with myself.

When I did lose, which was rare, it was usually because I was more involved in drinking and partying than betting, and the loss meant nothing to me.

Just after Christmas a lot of heavies were in town. A big game was inevitable. The rendezvous was moved to a spacious split level in Wayne to accommodate the holiday spirit in the air. Most of the players came with an entourage, and a party was in full swing while the game was being played in the dining room.

I was more intent on drinking than on betting. I did have a thousand dollars backing Rich, however.

Sometimes about one in the morning, I guess—I was pretty loaded by then—a guy told me Rich was losing badly. He said Rich had lost the thousand plus several hundred of his own and was getting deep in IOUs. I went to the dining room to watch for a while. Rich looked uneasy. He was playing against himself, psyched-out. I walked to the far end of the room to pour a drink, and a woman met me at the bottles.

"Having a good time?" she asked.

"Having a drunk time," I said.

"Wonderful," she said melodramatically with an upward swish of the hand, "and boring."

"Sounds like you haven't had enough to drink," I said. "What can I get you?"

"It would be fun to lose a lot of money here," she said. "Then I could drink and enjoy it."

"Are you making money here?"

"Fatso is." She pointed to the game table. "He's the only one winning. Except Skinny there—I think he's a pittance up."

"Is Fatso your boyfriend?"

"He's my old man." Her lip curled like she was disgusted by the thought of him. "My loving spouse."

"Sounds exciting," I said.

"Wonderful." Her hand swept upward again. She didn't need another drink.

"My man's losing his ass tonight," I said. "What are you drinking?"

"Gin and grapefruit. Who's your man?"

"The young guy."

"He's your friend?"

"Yes."

"He's cute. I wish he'd break old Fatso down to his smelly socks."

While we were talking I noticed Fatso kept looking over at us. Nervously, he'd look from his cards to the cards showing to the players and back to his hand. Then he'd shoot a look at his wife. I moved closer to the woman and turned my back to the table, placing myself between Fatso and his wife. I freshened her drink and handed it to her with a napkin.

I remained in that position talking small talk for ten minutes or so, then I asked the woman to sit on the sofa across the room. I was drunk enough to talk some good trash, so I started laying it on, making sexual innuendos out of everything that was said.

I clinked her glass in a toast, making sure that her husband was looking, and said, "I like nice underthings myself."

"Who said anything about nice underthings?" she said, leaving her mouth open at the end of the question.

"I thought you did," I said.

"You're full of shit, aren't you?"

"Yes. Actually I was just stimulated by your lavender panties."

"I don't have lavender panties on." Her mouth was left open again.

"Yes, you do."

"How the hell would you know that?"

"I especially like fine slips," I said. "I like to put on a sheer slip and dance in front of the mirror taking dirty to myself—oh, you slut, you jezebel, stop that prancing and strutting and come over here to me."

"You're fucked-up," she said, laughing loudly.

Her husband shot a look at us.

"It's the truth," I said.

"I'm fucked-up, too," she said. "At least we can admit it."

"Admit it!" I said. "I advertise."

"Oh? And where do I find your classified?" That petty little mouth was open again.

"Why, in my pants, dear, of course. You'll have to excuse me for a minute."

I found the guy who told me that Rich was losing. I handed him five hundred and fifty dollars and asked him to pass it to Rich and tell him that everything was cool.

I poured Fatso's wife a fresh drink and brought it to her, then coaxed her outside for some air, slipping my hand around her waist as we left the room. I could feel Fatso's eyes burning into my back.

Outside in the back yard behind the arbor we fumbled with our clothes, joking and laughing drunkenly. We played "hide the hot dog" up against the garage. I could sense the sweat beading up on Fatso's forehead and feel the increase in his blood pressure. I heard his mute anger in the pulsing of my temples.

We went back in and sat on the sofa again. Fatso had already begun to lose. I poured us two more drinks, and we gadded about the room together while I kept one eye on the progress of the game. Fatso couldn't keep his eyes off us. He lost several hands in a row and excused himself to use the bathroom. He stopped in front of us.

"Are you winning lots of money?" she asked him with a cock of the head.

"Not as much as you can squander in a day," he replied. "What are you doing?"

"I'm getting happily drunky," she said. "Oh, this is my new friend. I didn't catch his name."

"Hi," I said. "It's great to be alive, isn't it? Have you ever thought about the fact that Jesus died for your sins? How's the game going? Very nice to meet you. Are you superstitious about gambling? Jesus said to the Pharisees that—"

"Watch the booze," he said, pointing his fat finger at her menacingly.

"I sure will," I said. "Thank you."

He left for the bathroom. I walked the woman into a conversation with two men in the living room and went to the game table. Fatso was back. He'd just lost a large pot on a full house in a hand of seven card stud. I stood behind Rich exaggerating my drunkenness, being loud and obnoxious, bragging and lying and talking dirty.

A player stood up, saying he wanted to sit out for a while, so I bought in.

When the deal came around to me I dealt a riotous hand of holy cross, laughing and nearly misdealing over and over.

When it was my deal again Fatso complained about my antics. I dealt a hand of seven stud, low spade in the hole wild, feigning a sanctimonious attention to the possibilities of every card as it fell. "A three to the gentlemen's seven. Both hearts. Possible straight flush. Or maybe just a straight—or a flush. We'll have a better indication with the next card. Ah, the four of spades is now burned. Who's got the low spade, gentlemen?"

"Deal the fucking cards!" Fatso said.

I bet carelessly, raising at every round. When Rich won the hand of stud, Fatso slammed his fist on the table.

"Enough of this nigger poker!" he said. "Next we'll be playing fucking no-peek."

Fatso couldn't win a hand no matter what we played. I kept betting against him and raising the betting when I felt that Rich had a good hand. When the deal came around to me again I said, "Chinaman sweat."

"What the fuck is Chinaman sweat?" Fatso said.

"It's no-peek with deuces, one-eyed jacks and the card after the queen wild," I said.

"Jesus fucking Christ!" Fatso said. "Do we have to play this nigger poker?" He looked around the table for support.

"It's his deal," Rich said. "He can't help it if he's fucked-up."

Nobody complained. Some of Fatso's chips had been finding their way around the table.

"Are you in?" I asked Fatso.

"I'm in," Fatso said, trying sloppily to contain his anger.

"Then ante up," I said. "The game is Chinaman sweat."

By dawn the fat man had lost over three thousand dollars that was dispersed fairly evenly among the four other players and myself. Rich was about five hundred ahead of the fifteen hundred I fronted him. I was already anticipating a week of fine restaurants and expensive booze.

The fat man came over to me before he woke his wife, who was passed out on the sofa with a contented smile on her face.

"I know you fucked with that game," he said. "What I don't know is how. If I find out—and I probably will—you'll be a sorry fucker."

"I think that, one, you're accusing me of cheating," I said, "and, two, you're threatening me with physical harm. I don't take either one lightly. Am I hearing you right?"

"I don't intend to repeat myself. You're a wise-ass punk playing with fish a lot bigger than you. You may have gotten yourself in big trouble here tonight."

"I am a wise-ass—I'll grant you that, fatfish, but you were losing before I even sat in. You're a bad loser. The cards fell, and I didn't have anything to do with it."

"I know you did. I just don't know how, or you'd be a broken fucker right now. There was no reason for me to start losing steadily like that. The game was fucked with, and that's serious business."

"There are many things that happen without reason, and don't threaten me or I'll . . ." I brought my hand to within a quarter inch of his balls before he could react fast enough to look down, and when he did he was looking wide-eyed at my thumb and forefinger poised ready to blind him. ". . . or I'll tear your balls off and throw you across the room blinded."

"I'll see you around," he said, and pulled his wife up by the arm.

"Drive safely," I said.

"Fuck you," he said, and pulled her out the door.

"Thanks very much," I said, waving goodbye.

A few months later I found out through the grapevine that Fatso's wife told him I'd doctored her behind the garage with the painless meat injection, and I'm sure Fatso still suspected that I'd cheated somehow that night. Also, by strange coincidence, on the way home from the game the brakes in Fatso's car had malfunctioned, and he'd narrowly avoided an accident. He remembered me telling him to drive safely, and he thought I'd done something to the brakes. I guess you just you don't treat the big shots that way, and word was out that Fatso had some goons out to break my ass as soon as it was convenient.

For months I never left the house without expecting sniper fire. I'd been threatened before, and I knew that most threats are empty—just verbal catharsis for the impotent. But I also understood that among small-time gangsters there is an edict of revenge necessary to maintain respect and credibility.

Yet I was hesitant to leave Montclair. I was feeling settled for the first time. After a month went by and no shadowy figures had followed me, I grew more lax, though I hadn't really let down my guard in several years.

Then one night while walking home from Tierney's I turned around to see a man carrying a small baseball bat coming up behind me. I stood and widened my stance. "You're going to get hurt," I said. He raised the bat and approached cautiously as a car pulled to the curb and four men got out. Two carried bats. The others had their hands in their pockets like they held pistols.

I ran.

Three of them ran after me. Two ran to the car.

I outran the three in a few blocks. As the car closed on me I ran up the stairs of a tenement, down the hall and out the back door. I climbed a few fences and dashed down an alley and emerged on a narrow residential street. I hid behind some trash cans behind an iron grill gate.

The car came around the corner and pulled over halfway down the block. The two men got out. One stood by the car while the other walked away from me, toward the corner that they'd turned. When he disappeared around the corner I took my jacket off, dropped it and began walking toward the man stationed at the car. I put my hands in my pockets and whistled loudly.

The man watched me, tense and still, trying to see my face in the dark. When I got within twenty feet of him he reached into the car, came out with a bat and called for the man who was searching around the corner.

I ran at him. He swung the bat clumsily. I hit him hard in the throat and face. He staggered back, and I followed and kicked him in the guts. A .22 fired and hit the brick porch behind me, shattering sheets of glass in my brain—I saw blood pumping from the body at my feet, though I knew he wasn't bleeding. Before the chips of brick hit the sidewalk I was into the mouth of an alley, hoping there was a way out the back.

The alley took a left turn and stopped at a high cement wall that separated a small backyard from what looked like a warehouse or a small factory. I heard footsteps coming down the alley. There was no time to figure a way over the wall. The man running down the alley was obviously not shy about using the pistol.

Two trash cans stood next to the small cement porch, and next to the trash cans, a large plastic trash bag, stuffed and fastened at the top.

Behind the bag, with my legs hidden behind the bag and the cans, I lay on the concrete, my upper body extending out beyond the bag. I turned my face to the foundation of the building, pulled my arms in front of my chest and stomach and worked my body into the corner where the building met the ground. I slowed my breathing, cleared my head and opened myself, shut down the brain waves, receiving but transmitting nothing. In dark clothes, and with no skin showing to reflect light, I concentrated on becoming a roll of tar paper in the shadow. By the time the footsteps arrived, I wasn't there.

The man stopped, leaped at the high wall. I heard two more men running on the sidewalk out in front of the building. The man with the pistol was standing two feet from me. He pivoted once, then ran the few steps to the mouth of the alley and yelled for the others. I heard their footsteps start down the alley toward us as I sprang out of the darkness, disarmed and disposed of the man with the pistol and ran up the back porch steps. The door was locked. I put my elbow through the door window, reached in and opened the door. Inside a young girl and a woman were peering out the kitchen window. Another girl was seated at the table. The woman screamed and clutched at the girl near her. I ran through the kitchen and into the living room. A man had just stood up from a chair, a newspaper still in his hand. "Hey!" he yelled. "Sorry," I said, running out the front door.

The man I'd attacked at the car was still on the ground out front. A group of men stood outside the tavern on the corner. They were looking down the street toward me. I ran four blocks, cutting over from one street to another, sprinting west a block, then north a block. A city bus turned the corner a block away. I ran across the street and flagged it, rode to Caldwell, went into the lounge of a restaurant and ordered a George Dickel.

"Do you have an aspirin . . ."
I turned to the voice.
". . . by any chance?"

She was beautiful. I couldn't even speak.

"Did you ever hear of a bar that didn't keep aspirin?" she said loud enough for the barkeep to hear, rubbing her temples.

"I'm sorry, I don't," I said. "How about a lime soaked in bitters? No, I guess that's for hiccups. How about a month in the Poconos?"

"I hate the Poconos."

"I'll buy you a Singapore Sling, and we'll pretend we're in Aruba," I said.

"I'm with some people and I'm married and I hate Aruba."

"I was just being polite, not pushy," I said.

"Men are so defensive about being polite these days." A tiny smile sneaked into her lips.

"It's very trying for them these days," I said. "The patriarchal power is leaking out of them. It's complicated."

"You think so?" She rubbed her temples again, her eyes closed.

"No, not really. In my experience I've found that they just think it's complicated. It comforts them as they decline. They've blown it, and they know it, and women are restless."

"And what *is* your experience?" She propped her elbow on her hip and raised her glass to her lips.

"I'm a psychiatrist," I said. Mr. Excitement felt a surge of elation over his new profession. Without hesitation he dropped the Mr. and inserted the Dr., turning a penetrating leer into her stunning eyes.

"God, not another one."

"Is this a convention?"

"It's just that I've spent half my life with analysts. My husband has a lot of money, and it's fashionable to be in therapy these days, don't you think?" She kept her ironic tone restrained and subtle. "Am I revealing too much about myself too quickly?"

"Not if you want to unload your headache," I said, "and therapy as fashion is going out now." I paused to sip the whiskey. "It's going to be a physical one-upmanship next. You know, jogging and tennis for pain and profit. That's my prediction. Building endurance to devour the competitor in the final stretch."

"The final stretch? Sounds apocalyptic."

"I always manipulate conversations around to a sense of impending doom when I'm out of the office."

"And you're so objective—that luxurious, aloof, removed perspective.

They think it's complicated. It's trying for *them*. *They've* blown it, and it comforts *them* as they decline."

" *'Let it be known that I was not one of them.'* Swinburne said that, I think. Or was it Lord Byron? Yes, George Gordon Lord Byron."

"A cripple, wasn't he?" That tiny smile again.

"That's fraught, really," I said.

"Fraught?" She sipped her drink.

"Really," I said.

"So after analysis comes jogging toward the apocalypse?" she asked.

"Exercise for killers," I said. "It's big in California already. And after that, more analysis, more conundrums, more confusions, more diversion. Jogging, in fact, will be elevated to a form of therapy. It will be thought of as unwinding, and it will be another form of competition. People will take pride in how unwound they are."

"And Michael the Archangel's sword shall fall, dividing the joggers from the non-joggers?"

"It will not be that easy. He will have to go in with a scalpel. It will not be clear to him. He will be confused. Gabriel will be blowing a new bebop that nobody understands."

"Michael the Archangel will need an analyst," she said.

"He will be incapable of making the necessary final judgments," I said.

"That explains why a man with your foresight and cynicism would go into psychotherapy. It has a lucrative future."

"They will be paid handsomely to keep people confused and deluded, which will come natural to them. It will be a disappointing and disorganized Judgment Day, for sure."

"So when the scalpel falls," she asked, "who will be saved and who will remain to burn? What should I do to save myself?"

"Well, really, I mean, who am I to judge . . . mere physical material and electronic information systems floating aimlessly in the void? I'm not capable of such understanding. Isn't that how it goes? I don't have enough information to make intelligent guesses. But don't worry. There will be many people ahead of both of us on the burn line, and watching them burn will make it worth our suffering. So is your husband a bank president, a corporate lawyer or a politician?"

"A politician."

"And quite wealthy, huh?"

"Politicians have ways of getting wealthy."

"It must be very unsatisfying for you."

"Such a poignant observation, Doctor. And I bet you know how to satisfy your patients, don't you?"

"For a fee," I said, laughing and signaling the barkeep for another drink.

"Whore," she said.

"We must not give away the secret knowledge! Even the engineer who designs a parking lot must keep his secret knowledge locked and coded in the blueprint. Otherwise any damn fool could design a parking lot. And where would we be then?"

"This is an enlightening conversation, Doctor, but I regret that I must tear myself away and get back to my friends."

"Going away unsatisfied, are you?"

"Always."

"Can I buy you an aspirin?"

"I'm married, as I've said, and my headache's gone."

"No charge."

"Are you married?" she asked.

"Yes, I am. How about another drink?"

"I'll buy you one," she said.

"I'll drink it," I said.

She ordered us both a drink.

"So," I said, "are you getting anywhere in therapy?"

"No. In fact, I've gone through four shrinks this year. I enjoy it, actually, and as long as John can afford it . . . It gives me something to think about and it gets me out of the house twice a week—away from the TV and the country club and the malls and the hairdresser and all that awfulness. I should get back to my friends before the rumors start. You're welcome to join us if you like."

"And meet John?" I don't think so. I'm not really dressed for it—the country club set and all."

"Why, that's a stunning black tee shirt, and John's not here."

"Out making lots of money, is he?"

"Probably. He's in Newark, actually, of all places."

"Colonizing the heathens? Teaching them English, giving them jobs in factories, exporting their food and giving them Christianity in return?"

"Not quite. He's at a waste dump, if you can believe that—in Newark at a waste dump. Some people will do anything for money."

"Let's go then." I shrugged and followed the woman toward the table.

"I'm Judy Oswald," she said.

"I'm not really sure," I said as we approached the table, "because things have been happening too fast tonight, and I'm a bit disoriented, but I think I might be in lust with you."

She just looked at me oddly with that nearly invisible smile. We were standing before her friends. She extended her hand toward me to introduce me. "This is . . ." She paused. The smile flowed into her lips. "Who are you?"

"George," I said. "George Dickel." It was as good as any.

"This is George," she said to her friends. "He's a headshrinker. I thought we could use him over here."

The only man at the table extended his hand. "Where do you shrink heads, George?" he asked. He was dressed in an expensive sport coat and Oxford cloth shirt.

"Over in Angleton, near Paterson," I said. It was as good as any.

"You have a head for business, sir," he said. "I'm Tom Scarlatelli."

"So you know the place, Tom?" I asked.

"We're all from Angleton," the young woman next to him said. "We just ate dinner here."

"I just moved there this month," I said. I'm not completely set up yet."

"You'll do well," Tom said. "All the ambitious overachievers from Paterson and Passaic live in Angleton. All the cutthroats success stories who can't move too far from their mommies and daddies."

"That's not completely true, Tom," the middle-aged woman across the table said. There's a lot of good people there—just hard-working folks who climbed out of poverty—into debt."

"With blood on their claws," Tom said.

"And there's nothing bad about staying near family," the woman added.

"Except they'd rather be in Marin County or Aspen or someplace," Tom said.

"Where do your mommy and daddy live?" I asked Tom, smiling genially at him.

"Two doors away!" the middle-aged woman blurted out, then laughed.

"I'm aware of the idiosyncrasies of the social stratum to which I belong," Tom said. "Mama is a real guinea. She wouldn't let me leave home without hauling a dump truck of guilt and egg pasta along with me. Great for the cholesterol of the brain, right, Doc? And as for the overachieving—a middle-class ginzo from Paterson does not make it through Yale law without such an ailment. So, you see, Doc, we have it all figured out at this table."

"That's too bad," I said. "I was out trolling for some patients."

"You people will never get me to own up to anything," he said to me.

We drank for a few hours. Fortunately they never asked me where in Angleton my office was located. Judy Oswald had to leave before the others because her husband was expecting her. Before she left she asked me, amid a barrage of razzing from Tom, if I was taking on patients yet. I took her number and told her I'd call her after the office was set up.

In the morning I gathered some things from my apartment in Montclair, took my money from where it was stashed and rode a bus to Angleton. I was in the market for a psychiatric couch.

I found a small house for rent in the paper that was in the vicinity of professional buildings and doctors' offices. It was perfect, actually, and this twist of fate convinced me to see the plot through. I could move in on the first of October, which was the next day.

I immediately commissioned a sign painter to make a shingle that read "George Dickel, M.D." and underneath in smaller letters, "Psychiatry."

10

I SNATCHED THE CAN OF PRINCE ALBERT FROM WILLIE'S pocket and said, "But the thing about the media is, it has to make money like any business, and in order to make money it has to have a marketable product."

Willie Sykes stopped chewing his egg sandwich and scratched above his ear. "What, a bridge?" he said. "A torn-down bridge?"

It was a balmy day in Newark. Wind had blown the smog away. All the Newark wildlife was out in the sun. The sky was blue, thick clouds gathered in the west. It was like some other place, some other climate —a Colorado morning.

Lately it has been overcast every day—showers every afternoon—definitely Jersey. One two-hour break in the clouds would mean a lot to me right now.

"That's right," I said to Willie, "a bridge. But we need to do some legwork. Do you and Bernie have any room in your schedules?"

"I think my next appointment is with Jesus," Willie said through a bite of sandwich. He sipped some coffee in with the egg and hardroll and spoke through all of it. "And he can wait for this crusty bastard. But legwork, I don't know. No, I don't think so—no room for any legwork. I'm retired."

"Not legwork as in legs," I said. "Telephone work."

"Let me see. No—no room for any telephone work."

"I have a list of all the TV and radio stations, newspapers, social services and civil liberties groups in the area, including ABC and NBC news bureaus. We have to call them all."

"I'm not much of a telephone man."

"We have to make believe we're reporters and call the U.S. Marine Corps, the Veteran's Administration and senators and congressmen galore."

"I'm better with the actual legs, come to think of it," he said, fishing a speck of something out of his coffee.

"Then we have to make copies of Miles's medical records—lots of copies—and copies of the letters from the surgeons who testified that the military surgeon caused the problem that resulted in the amputation years later."

"I don't know."

"Then we have to steal our bridge kit back from the city."

"I'd be better at that kind of stuff, I think," he said.

"We'll do that together. Then we have to call the family of Alvin Johnson."

"Who's Alvin Johnson?"

"He's buried in that cemetery up the canal. Then we have to take Miles to church."

"It won't work," Willie said, taking another bite.

"Here's a list, step by step, of everything you have to tell everyone you talk to on the phone."

"No matter where we build the bridge"—he put the coffee on the sidewalk and took the rolling papers from me—"they'll tear it down the next day. This shit has gone to your head."

"We'll build it up in that cemetery," I said, "extending from Alvin Johnson's grave, which is private land, across to that black Baptist church up there on the bank."

"What the hell are you talking about, son? That must be four or five miles up the canal."

"Six point four klicks."

"The damn city bridge isn't anywhere near that far! If Miles can't go down to the city bridge and back up to The Embers, how the hell can he go six point four goddamn klicks?"

"None of that matters now, Willie."

"I think you're a brick light of a load here, pal. I just wanted to raise a stink with the city council, not build bridges for NBC news in some shine neighborhood. This is too much. You can get killed in that neighborhood! I went along with this harebrained bridge the first time, but this is too much."

"But we're still building the bridge, Willie. We can't stop in midair."

"No we ain't building no damn bridge—not me, anyway."

We set up an office at Joe Duffy's kitchen table until his wife threw us out.

We moved to the wire factory for two days, but when the owner stopped in on his monthly checkup he threw us out. The office was too small there, anyway, and it was noisy outside the office. We couldn't get any work done.

There was no alternative but to use the phone and tables at Kelly's Tavern. Jim Kelly wasn't crazy about the idea, but Joe Duffy convinced him that it wasn't any different than collecting money for the IRA, which Kelly had done on occasion, including half of his St. Paddy's Day take for the last fifteen years. So Kelly felt an obligation to put up with us, though he never did understand the connection. When we all chipped in to have more phones installed, Kelly came around. He liked having three phones in the place.

After they broke the ice with hesitant stammering and stuttering, Willie and Bernie actually enjoyed the persistent business of hounding secretaries until they got through to various political and administrative big-shots. They couldn't figure out why they hadn't done it before, if only to speak their minds.

During the third day of work at Kelly's, Willie and Bernie came in wheeling Miles at a dead run. They were all whooping and hollering, calling for a round for the house.

"It's Martin Luther King!" Bernie yelled, his thumb pointing over his shoulder.

"What are you talking about?" Joe Duffy asked. "What's going on?"

"That Reverend at the shine church," Bernie said, "he was involved in all that civil rights stuff in the sixties. He sounds like Martin Luther King himself—quotes and statistics and hundred-dollar goddamn vocabulary words—plus he knows all the wheels in town. He's an official of some sort in that national colored's thing—the N - W - A . . ."

"The N - double A - C - P," Miles said, a bit indignant.

"That's the one," Bernie said excitedly.

"It's not a *shine* church," Miles said to Bernie.

"Well, you know what I mean," Bernie said, "Baptist or something."

"I'm gonna shine the floor with your head one of these days, man," Miles said.

Bernie danced a few steps out of reach, behind the wheelchair. "Just because his hair is curly," he sang, "shoo-be-do-bop." He rubbed Miles's head. "That's why they call him shine."

Miles pivoted the chair and went for Bernie, but Bernie danced behind a table and held up his palms. When he saw that Miles wasn't playing he went to the far end of the room and sat down.

"He says he'll join forces with us," Willie said to me, "and use what influence he has to make a big stink. The guy knows his stuff—I mean it."

"He's a good dude," Miles said, "for a shine." He scowled at Bernie. "He was talking about getting some reporter from the *Washington Post* he knows personally. He knows a lot of people. This could turn out to be a real circus."

Everybody set to work with new vigor. Some of the Kelly's regulars pitched in. Others clung to the bar and scoffed. Some exhibited a determination they probably hadn't felt in a long time, trying to get through the barriers to pull on the coat sleeves of important people. It was something they could do with a few drinks in them.

I watched Willie chewing on some politician's ear for fifteen minutes, one hand on a glass of whiskey, the other on a pencil, the phone tucked in his neck like a violin. He had stumbled onto the magical power that lives hidden in tone of voice, sounding more important, more in control, more vital than the voice at the other end. He seemed unaware of everything going on around him, his palm rolling a pencil against his bald head as he spoke about the diminishing services for veterans.

I didn't know what to make of it all. I didn't like being in a position of leadership, which is where they wanted to keep me. I kept slipping into depression. When Alvin Johnson's mother called to confirm her family's support and said she'd do some organizing of her own, the energy in the bar climbed a bit higher, but I worried about being that much closer to an episode I would subsequently regret. I was risking my obscurity, blowing my cover, threatening my survival. I knew better, but I did it anyway.

After Alvin Johnson's mother called I walked along the polluted Passaic to get out of Kelly's for a while. The river offered no consolation. It was just brown, sluggish, defiled—a dumb god that in its indifference made me feel stupid for going there harboring some hope of solace, reinforcement, direction, recognition or any other abstract, conceptual and impossible interaction between a river and a man. The barren inanity of the experience should have been significant perhaps—the river should have given me something in its indifference, some enigmatic Zen inkling or some such claptrap, but it didn't. It was only irritating. I felt like climbing into the slothful gunk of poison and floating away, but instead I got down on all fours and vomited onto the oily gravel by the tarred bulkhead, pop-top rings blurring in my watery eyes.

I knelt there, remembering the morning we built the first bridge. I'd stood on the bridge just before dawn. If I looked upriver I saw what was yet to come down—the unknown—and if I looked downriver I saw what I'd managed to survive, and either direction did not inform the other —either did not prepare me in any way for anything.

If I looked over the bridge to the other side, then back to the side from which I'd come, I also saw nothing, either way, that shed light on my position at the center.

Standing there at the crux in the center of the bridge I was bathed in that moment of void. I thought: this is where I begin—with nothing. It was an old thought that I already knew. It didn't comfort me.

I wanted to vomit again, and I did. I'll not create another victim, I thought. It's not my life I'm laying down to span the river of poisons.

Fatso and his goons never found me, if they even continued to search. It couldn't have been too long before Fatso had to throw his weight in another direction. But John Oswald, Judy's husband, is another kind of man, plus I did give him more reason to be more persistent, and he is a less forgiving animal by nature than Fatso at his worst. If Oswald finds me, he will find what he thought he'd gotten rid of.

As it turned out, the bridge building was a conspicuous event. The big networks even sent a crew.

Willie and Bernie were so excited they couldn't shut up. As the media were gathering, Willie and Bernie moved from one reporter to the next, speaking to all at length, championing Miles's cause and telling all about the first bridge building and the city's reaction.

There were reporters and camera crews from college newspapers, public radio, the TV giants, magazines and the local daily newspapers. It was amazing. Newark hadn't made such news since the riots and the chemical fire. And the reporter from the *Washington Post* did show up.

Alvin Johnson's entire family was there. His mother was not shy about the media. They filmed her standing next to her son's headstone. She'd done some preparation and was articulate about her anti-war sentiments.

The Reverend from the Baptist church spoke eloquently to a group of reporters about how the war machine discriminates against the poor and black, supporting himself with statistics and quotes. He said the poor were twice as likely to see combat. "If the sons of the rich were dying," he said, "the war would have ended years sooner."

But the real impact came with the procession.

I stayed in the background in the cemetery and spoke to no one except cameramen. I told them what was coming so they could position themselves.

Then it was time to begin. Willie signaled, Dave backed his truck up to the canal, and the men went to work building the bridge. They lowered the rowboat into the canal and secured it to the bulkhead with bow and stern lines. There was no fence to cut this time. On the cemetery side there was a gap in the hedge wide enough for Miles's wheelchair to pass through—nothing in the way on the church grounds. Three picnic tables stood along the grassy bank in the churchyard—a stone barbecue under a stand of maples.

"Lower it down," Dave called from the boat, and the first beam was set on the ledge below the top of the bulkhead. As the men fit the components together the cameramen moved closer. Their instincts for good video got them involved in the precision and speed with which the men worked. Willie and the men were well-rehearsed, and the cameramen were able to film much of the construction without using a lot of tape. Likewise, the reporters knew they had some prime grassroots liberal copy, and the soundmen seemed to love the ambiance of the men working. "Keep those two-bys flush," Bernie called amid the whacking of three hammers.

When the procession emerged from the back hall of the church the cameras never stopped. It looked like something out of *Amos and Andy.*

The Reverend led, dressed in a black suit, followed by a white Catholic priest holding an American flag. The Reverend moved forward with grace and poise. He was a refined and elegant looking man.

Miles followed. He sat in his wheelchair, which was chocked securely atop a large dolly borrowed from the wire factory and painted with white enamel for the occasion. An old upright piano sat on the dolly at his fingertips. He wore a white choir gown. The collar of his Marine dress blues showed above the gown. His black hair glistened. His face was serious, intense.

The dolly was rolled by three black men on one side and Willie and Bernie and Joe Duffy on the other. They were dressed as they always dressed.

The church choir, dressed in black and white gowns, followed the dolly.

Behind the choir marched an honor guard of vets—both black and white—in full dress uniforms.

Bringing up the rear was a group including a Democratic Congressman, a woman who was the president of a civil rights organization, two professors, a representative from the County Social Services and three clergyman from various denominations.

The Reverend halted at the bridge, turned to the procession and raised his right arm. The crowd gathered in the churchyard hushed. Miles played a little blues run, and the choir began to sing a well-rehearsed, exaggeratedly slow gospel-blues version of "Rally 'Round the Flag Boys," complete with harmony and soulful flourishes, the likes of which could only come out of a black Baptist church choir in the heart of Newark before the camera eyes of the nation. *"Hurrah, boys, hurrah,"* they keened, *"Down with the traitor and up with the Stars,"* dragging the phrases out into a dirge.

The soundmen jockeyed for position. Everybody was getting great tape. This was national news.

When the song was finished the Reverend, in his practiced pulpit oratory, delivered a brief address before crossing the bridge.

"Alvin Johnson," he said at full voice, as if summoning the soul of the man, "your soul is at rest in the Lord. We ask you now, Brother Johnson—we, your brothers and sisters in the world of the living, ask of you one more deed, one more holy deed for Brother Miles Stanley and for all veterans, living and deceased, lame and tormented, heroic and frightened, exploited and abused. We ask you, Alvin Johnson, if we can, for this one moment, to disturb your eternal peace one time in the name of the Lord, almighty God—to reach up from your sublime repose, Brother, and receive, to the world of the unseen, the broken limbs of Brother Miles, the torment of all our souls who have been at war and the prayers of this congregation before the Lord, in the spirit and hope of freedom for all of God's children. Amen."

"Amen," the congregation chimed.

Miles struck a chord, and the choir repeated the final verse of "Rally 'Round the Flag Boys." *"We welcome to our numbers,"* they sang, *"all the loyal, true and brave, shouting the battle cry of free-dom, and although he may be poor, not a man shall be a slave, shouting the battle cry of free-dom."*

"Amen," the Reverend intoned.

"Amen," the congregation replied.

The Reverend walked to the center of the bridge.

"Standing here at the crux of truth and glory, brothers and sisters," he said, "I beckon you to follow me to the far side of this bridge built of man's desire for peace among all men—and rejoice, bereft of complexity, rapt in clarity, unburdened by illusion, free at last, as humble visitors to the world of the unseen, as a guest of our brother Alvin

Johnson. Now baptize yourselves in this moment!" He bowed his head. It was an odd prayer, I thought.

"Now commence," he said, and continued over the bridge, and with that the piano led the choir into a spirited gospel song as the procession crossed the bridge to Alvin Johnson's grave, each person stepping squarely in the middle of the mound of earth.

The Reverend greeted Mr. and Mrs. Johnson, Miles broke into a boogie-woogie, and food appeared from nowhere. Blankets were spread among the graves and covered with fried chicken, potato salad, barbecued ribs, baked beans, blackeyed peas, bread, cheese, cold cuts, salads and baskets of garden fresh tomatoes, cucumbers, lettuce and watermelons. There were jars of pickles, pickled pigs' feet, bags of peanuts, gallons of wine, fresh fruit and tubs of soda and beer on ice.

Bernie's eyes were bugging out of his head. A black woman handed him a chicken wing to tide him over, and he sat down on the grass to chew and wait until the entire spread was assembled.

The choir, with Miles at the lead, sang blues, gospel, Otis Redding, Leadbelly, Josh White, Smokey Robinson, The Temps, Muddy Waters, The Drifters—whatever anybody requested they took a crack at. Then Miles did a few of his arrangements of Bob Marley songs. They sang until about two in the afternoon, then broke up to eat and drink, but a man named Old Hodas sat at the piano and the music continued.

By evening there was a party of over two hundred people in full swing in the cemetery. It spilled over into the church grounds and into the streets of the black neighborhood beyond.

I bet Willie and Bernie never danced with a black woman before in their lives, and I bet they never danced with each other, either, but they did both that night, and they couldn't figure out why they'd never done it before.

At about ten o'clock Joe Duffy and Dave from the wire factory got in the middle of a conga line that congaed through the church, down the street, in the front doors and out the back doors of every house for three blocks before it broke up on the corner by Cool's Bluebird Lounge, and Joe and Dave found themselves at the intersection of white taboo and soul street in the dark heart of Afro-Newark, jiving and hand-slapping going on all around them, pint bottles of Thunderbird and Tiger Rose and Ten High bourbon and Schenley whiskey extended toward them, a conflagration of laughter and chatter crackling up and down the block under the blinking and faltering and half-lit neon.

"Even the smells were different," Joe told me later. "I could smell the cooking lard," he said, "and cigars, lots of cigars and I don't know what else. Black smells—good smells—we had a great time down there, Dave and I. We really did. Dave was nearly shittin' his pants till he slugged some of that whiskey and started talking to this black guy about tuna fishin'. I felt like I took a trip to New Orleans or something—I don't know—right here in Newark. Strange night."

At about one o'clock when the party had calmed down some, Bernie was propped against a maple smoking a smoke with old Ezra Judd. Willie staggered over and said to Bernie, "Whatta ya doin', Bern?" Bernie yanked his head up and said, "I'm sittin' on my ass." Bernie extended his hand to Willie, and Willie grasped it to pull Bernie to his feet, but they both wound up sitting on their asses. I laughed to myself and went over to join them.

"Have you seen Miles?" Willie asked me. "Bernie and I have about had it."

"He's over there," I said, "with the Reverend."

"Miles," Willie called, "come over here a minute when you get a chance."

When Miles came over he pushed the chair up between Willie and Bernie and patted them each on the back. "What's happening," he said.

Willie grabbed Miles around the ankle and shook it a little. "I was wondering how you feel about all this," he said. "Was it an embarrassment to you, or do you think it was worth the hassle?"

"I dug it, man. I'm still digging it. The party's not over yet, is it?"

"Bernie and I are gonna head home," Willie said. "I was just wondering . . ."

"If nothing else comes of it," Miles said, "it was still worth it. How can it not be? Good food, a little music . . . just gettin' all these folks together . . ."

"I'm glad you feel that way," Willie said.

"I enjoyed myself thoroughly, man." Miles looked at me. "You know," he said to me, "all this has gone down, and I haven't spoken ten words to you, or you to me. We should have a few things to talk about, don't you think?"

"We should get together for a beer someday," I said.

Bernie snuffed his smoke on the ground and said to me, "I thought you told me and Willie that you and Miles had a long talk along the canal one day. Didn't you tell us that?"

"I was lying," I said.

Willie's head bowed. He picked at the grass.

"Well, why?" Bernie asked.

"It seemed like the right thing to do at the time, Bernie."

The Reverend walked up. "I'm gonna call it a day, gentlemen," he said. "I'll be in touch. Miles, can I give you a lift?"

"Sure," Miles said.

"We were all about to leave," Willie said. He stood and pulled Bernie to his feet successfully this time.

Everyone said their farewells and parted. Willie and Bernie walked off arm in arm, over the bridge, toward the black neighborhood where they hadn't set foot in thirty years.

I ran and caught them in front of the church and walked toward home with them.

"You know, this is a nice neighborhood," Willie said.

It was noticeably greener than most of Newark.

"Maybe you could rent a place here, Willie," Bernie said. "You could change your name to Willie Mays."

Bernie thought that was real funny. He laughed and stumbled along searching his pockets for smokes.

"Watching Alvin Johnson's old man," Willie said, "I've been thinking about my son. He was at the State College during Vietnam, and that kept him out for a while, then he managed to keep his own butt out, thank God."

"Mickey-boy," Bernie said.

"He grew up to be a decent person," Willie said, "like I knew he eventually would. There were a few years there when I really didn't like him much, I must admit. He was a punk—he really was. But it wasn't easy for him growing up in Newark, nothing like when we were kids, Bern. But he turned out to be a decent person."

"Hell, yeah, Willie," Bernie said.

"I remember when he was a youngster," Willie said, "maybe ten or twelve. I never really hit the kid, you know. Oh, maybe I whacked him a few times on the butt when he got too smart with his mother, but I never really hit him. Thank God. But this one time—I don't even remember what it was about—the kid really got to me. He really got me mad. I can't even remember why—isn't that something? But I whacked him a good one—open-handed, you know—smacked him one on the back of the head. Left hook—wham—and Maggie started screaming at me. 'Don't ever hit him on the head!' she screamed, 'I told you, never hit him on the head!' And the kid runs in and throws himself on the bed and starts wailing like he's hurt. I knew I didn't hurt him. I didn't hit him that hard. Just a whack. The skull is tough. But he's in his room carrying on and on like he's in pain, like he's got some damn injury, playing his mother against me, trying to make her think I hurt him. I really resented that for a while. It was a bad time anyway. Money was tight and there was tension between Maggie and me. And the kid was getting in trouble all the time. I think even years later I was still holding on to that incident, holding a grudge.

"It was a shitty thing to do, faking being hurt like that, causing all that grief between Maggie and me. It hurt me. I held on to it. It lingered in my brain even after I didn't want it there anymore. I guess I didn't think it was a very honorable thing to do, and it bothered me to see it in my own son, my only son.

"It still comes back on me because I never dealt with it, and he lives with it too, whether he knows it or not. I mean, it's no big thing. It could be a lot worse. It's just that, well, I keep coming back to this word dishonor. I thought we were friends, my son and I—I thought we could support each other—and I had a hard time thinking about him as dishonorable. I never could think of him that way and feel comfortable with it, and I never could talk to him about it, and it keeps coming back on me.

"Right then when it happened I should have realized that my son, even if he is one of my own, is capable of dishonorable acts. Hell, I mean, it was cunning, right?—it was clever. We get rewarded for that kind of shit in this world. But I never loosened up with him like I would like to—never told him a lot of what I wanted to. I suppose it's the same for him. Maybe it's the same for all fathers and sons, maybe it is. It was probably that way for Alvin Johnson and his old man, and that's probably why we have these fucking wars.

"And now Alvin's gone, and so is my son, really, and I can't blame him one bit for leaving Newark. I see him maybe for a week at Christmas time, and it never seems right to bring up anything too serious then. I guess that's just the way it is."

"It's not worth getting sad over," Bernie said. "It's happy, really. You always got along better than most families."

"Oh, sure—you're right, Bern. You're absolutely right, but in Alvin Johnson's case it's sad. It's very sad. I'm sure my son understands my difficulty in expressing myself in such matters, Bern. He knows I love him, and I know he loves me. Don't you think so, Bern? He's a bright fella."

"Are you kidding, Willie," Bernie said. "The kid idolizes you. He's a good kid. He had good folks."

"But Alvin Johnson's dead, Bern. Dead as a doornail. And maybe it's because we can't deal with the fact that our country is capable of dishonorable acts, that it can make wrong decisions, that it can hurt us and leave us with that hurt to live with."

There was a silence for a few minutes. Willie looked up at the stars through the tree limbs. Bernie blew his nose in his hand and wiped his hand on his pants.

"Goddamn, Bern," Willie said, "I'm drunk."

"We built that damn bridge, didn't we, Will?" Bernie said.

The following evening we gathered at Kelly's to watch the news.

The story had already come out in the morning *Ledger*, and while most of us were sleeping off the party the A.P. wire carried the story all over the country. The National Public Radio satellite network broadcast recordings through its member stations. Even the internationally distributed *Stars and Stripes* ran an edited version.

Bernie was so nervous over the possibility of seeing himself on TV that he drank nine or ten beers in an hour while acting as the official greeter for people coming into Kelly's to watch the news. His adrenalin was cooking, and he wouldn't shut up. He even called his daughter down the shore and told her to watch the news.

The festive energy of the party carried over, and Dave and Joe both took the day off to nurse their hangovers with a few hairs of the dog.

By six o'clock there were thirty or forty people in the bar to watch the seven o'clock news. Jim Kelly wore his green tie with the shamrocks on it.

A hush came over the crowd as the news came on.

Then most of the news was over, and the story hadn't been on, and the crowd was impatient, chattering and milling around the bar and tables. Bernie had consumed three more beers.

Then a hush again after the commercial.

Then noisy again with everybody hushing everybody else.

Then a female commentator on the bank of the canal, the church in the background. "Miles Stanley is a Vietnam veteran," she said.

"Miles!" Bernie yelled, rubbing Miles's woolly head.

Half the people in the bar yelled, "Shut up," and the place fell silent again.

The camera cut to Miles wheeling along the canal, and the commentator continued: "Miles, during an appeal for an increase in his disability compensation, offered the testimony of three top orthopedic surgeons as evidence that the problem which resulted in the amputation of his right leg stemmed from a surgical error during an operation performed by a military surgeon after Miles was wounded by shrapnel. A little over a week ago Miles and some of his friends built a bridge over a canal in Newark, New Jersey, so Miles could get to work. He'd been unable to . . ."

"There you are, Willie-e-e-e," Bernie yelled.

The commentator had strolled over to Willie, who was standing next to Alvin Johnson's grave.

"Bernie-e-e-e," Willie yelled. His image on the TV put an embarrassed smile on his face. He laughed across the room to Bernie.

"Shut up!" chimed the crowd.

". . . but the bus driver, day after day, wouldn't stop for Miles," the commentator continued.

"Goddamn right," yelled Willie, "The bastard."

"The camera cut to a close-up of Willie. "I called the city four times," Willie said on the TV, "and each time they told me the driver would be told to stop, but he never did.'

"I bet he's wishin' now that he fucking stopped," Bernie yelled.

"Shh-h-h-h-h," from the crowd, "shh-h-h-h-h."

"I bet he's making the *Big Stop* tomorrow," Willie called across the room to Bernie.

"The Big Stop!" Bernie howled with laughter. "The Big fucking Stop!"

Ten or more people yelled at Bernie to shut up.

"Yous shut up!" Bernie yelled back.

"Well," Willie said on TV, "the city tore the bridge down, so we decided to build another one."

"Yous didn't build no bridge," Bernie yelled at the crowd in the bar. "Don't tell me to shut up."

"Shh-h-h-h-h," from the crowd.

"Yous didn't have nothing to do with it!" Bernie yelled. "*We* built the goddamn bridge! Willie and me and Joe and . . ."

The crowd clamored again. A man climbed up to raise the volume.

"Go ahead and yell if you want, Bern," Willie yelled. "Fuck the news! Go ahead and yell!"

The crowd tried to hush the two friends again, but by then Joe Duffy had joined their defense. The procession was crossing the bridge on TV.

"We don't need the news," Joe yelled, "because we was fucking *there!*"

"Joey-y-y-y!" Bernie yelled. He was standing on a chair.

Then Dave, who'd been quietly drinking, and who is generally a quiet man, started to laugh uncontrollably, which started Bernie laughing. Willie was yelling at somebody who was yelling at him, and soon the whole place was standing up and yelling or sitting down and laughing, and the TV couldn't be heard over the laughter and anger.

11

BY OCTOBER THIRD DR. DICKEL HAD PURCHASED SOME FURniture, and the front room of the house in Angleton was almost ready for business. This was the consultation room. It contained two seating areas, one with four stuffed chairs positioned around an oval coffee table, and another more formal arrangement with a desk between two chrome and leather office chairs. Some people would respond better in the formal roles, I speculated—very considerate of Dr. Excitement. On the far wall was the psychiatric couch. Just looking at it made me horny.

Except for a coffeepot and some other necessaries in the kitchen, I left the rest of the house empty. I closed the doors and lived in the consultation room and the kitchen.

I had the shingle up the next day, and the following day I called Judy Oswald from a bar to let her know I had some room in my schedule. I gave her an appointment for a few days later to give myself some time to pick up some etchings or something for the walls of the consultation room and contemplate the artifice necessary to embark on my new career.

That same day a woman stopped by who'd seen my shingle while driving by. "Hello, Doctor Dickel?" she asked. "Yes," I said, holding the door open. "Can I help you?" Her name was Marie. I gave her an appointment for twelve days later.

I sent each of my clients a questionnaire, requesting that they return it immediately. It asked for the expected personal data like age, address, occupation, medical history, and I provided space to answer a few subjective questions. The first was worded like this: When was the last time you took a walk in the woods? Describe the circumstances surrounding your walk.

I pondered rather superficially for about one minute over the questions I asked. I figured that would be the best way to assure a puzzling lack of purpose. I got a chuckle out of the first question, since there weren't any woods to speak of for several miles in any direction.

I also asked the question: What do you think of dogs?

Despite my scheduling, my first session was with Marie.

I'd been pacing between the kitchen and the consultation room when she arrived.

I was doing a lot of pacing at the time. I didn't like living in Angleton—it was a heartless sprawl of private residences. Also, I was expecting Fatso's goons to show up any day. I didn't want to be found. I wanted to be lost. I was pacing and bouncing a rubber ball and squeezing it, first in the right hand, then in the left. The brain was wobbling in its orbit again. The ball bounced while the mind ran amuck. What was Dr. Excitement doing in Angleton?

I was staying up almost every night, unable to sleep, walking the streets or sitting in the bars until closing. I'd finally curl up on the psychiatric couch just before dawn and sleep until ten or eleven. I've never had such fantastic dreams as I did sleeping on that couch—it was as if they came with the thing. I flew in a lot of the dreams—soared over towns, around steeples, landed delicately in wide greens. I began sleeping more to dream more, eventually rolling out about two in the afternoon.

Three times I went to Judy's house and lurked in the shadows, trying to get a glimpse of her through the space between the blinds and the window frame. I found that by climbing to the roof I could see in one of the dormer windows to the hall that led to their bedroom and watch her as she went back and forth from the bedroom to the bathroom preparing for bed.

The spacious, professionally landscaped yard was surrounded by a high wooden fence. Behind the large house there was a swimming pool at the edge of a palatial patio that was furnished with rattan, adorned with flower beds and joined to a screened breezeway at the south end of the house. A burgundy Cadoo and a light blue Mercedes were kept in the garage. Judy's Datsun was parked in the bay of the driveway.

One night I sat on the roof smoking and dreaming until four o'clock, then took my clothes off and slipped into the pool for a swim. Before I left I urinated at the foot of a chaise lounge that was under a purple plum tree that grew through the flag stone.

"What have you been doing for the last thirty minutes? In detail."
I lit a smoke and sat in my desk chair.
Marie shifted in the chrome and leather chair.
The consultation room looked pretty good, I thought. I flicked my smoke in the Guinness ash tray I'd swiped from a bar.
"Actually," she said, "minutes after I decided to come over here I began to feel better, and by thirty minutes ago I could hardly remember what was wrong, though I'm sure something was wrong."
I stood and walked to the center of the room, bouncing the rubber ball, watching it return over and over from the floor to my hand.
"I hope you don't mind me coming over like this. I couldn't find your number listed. I just didn't feel like I could wait till Wednesday. I was scared and . . ."
"That's fine," I said. "I'm still waiting for my phone installation. Credit problems."
"I hope I didn't mess up your schedule."

"It's okay, really," I said, still bouncing the ball. "I can always make room for special situations. Now, go on, please."

She was silent for two or three minutes. Her right hand picked at her left hand. I continued the rhythmic bouncing of the ball for the entire duration, fixed on the motion of my hand snagging the thing from its path.

"Yes?" I questioned, turning to look at her, simultaneously snapping the ball out of the air.

She looked down at her hands. "I . . . ah . . . really didn't do much. I ate lunch and . . ."

"What have you been thinking about during the last thirty minutes?" I asked.

"Well . . . since I made the decision to come over here I kind of stopped thinking. I figured it would be best to wait and talk to you."

"And what did you want to talk about?" I asked.

She was silent again. Her head hung. She stopped picking and folded her hands.

"Move around if you want," I said, "physically and mentally," I paced the length of the room, bouncing the ball ahead of me. "Begin anywhere. Think anything. Sit anywhere you like. Would you like some coffee or tea?"

"No. No, thank you." She stood and walked to the window and pulled back the drape, but the silence continued.

The profile of her face frightened me. Despair, I thought, deep despair. Dr. Excitement was getting bored. I caught the ball, turned to the woman and said, "That's all for today, Marie. I think we'll keep it short the first time. You won't have to pay for this visit. When can you come back?"

"I have some time on Friday," she said, "in the afternoon."

"How about three?"

"That'd be okay."

"See you then, Marie." I needed to get out of the house. My heart was clamoring against my chest.

"Doctor," Marie said, "it's not easy for me. I have to be guided. I haven't had much therapy before. I don't know what to do. Do you think you could ask me some questions or something?"

"What questions, Marie?" I bounced the ball off the wall and caught it on one bounce.

"Any questions," she said.

"I asked you what you'd been doing for the last thirty minutes, but all you told me was that you were calm and you had some lunch. I want to know the details. What do you do when you're calm?"

"Well, after I decided to come talk to you I made some lunch. I was hungry. I couldn't eat last night and I didn't have any breakfast because I had to take my husband to work because the Ford is on the fritz. I made a sandwich of leftover roast beef and ate it in the dining room by the glass slider. Then I checked the oil in the car and . . ."

I bounced the ball off the wall a few feet to the left of where she was sitting. Her head jerked up watching it. I missed it on the return and followed it to the far wall, reaching under the psychiatric couch on my hands and knees to retrieve it. I walked back toward her squeezing the ball hard, working the ebbing anxiety into the rubber. I had three hours before Judy Oswald would arrive for her first appointment, and I had to get out for a drink.

"It's time for us to stop today, Marie. We can continue fresh on Friday." I figured I'd worry about Friday on Friday. I wasn't sure I'd be around that long. "I think it's important to end here. Do you understand?"

"Yes, okay," she said, "you're the doctor. I want to cooperate, I really do. I had some problems with my last analyst. It's just that last night I . . ."

"I'm sure we'll do fine, Marie. I feel strongly that we should end here today."

"Um, how do I call you if you don't have a phone—if I need to . . ."

"It's supposed to come tomorrow."

"We didn't get very far."

"Yes, we have. You think about it. That's why I want you to go home and rest now, and think about what has happened here today."

I walked to the bar and had a sandwich. After three beers I switched to Dickel and had three. My heart began to ease back down in its cage.

On the way back I stopped in a pawnshop and found there an old Bell & Howell 16mm movie camera. I checked it over and it seemed to work, so I bought it with a thirty-day guarantee. I also bought a portable cassette recorder that was almost new, then hurried back to meet Judy Oswald.

I knew from my questionnaire that Judy had a long history of therapy. Before we even sat down she told me she'd been seeing female analysts for a few years but felt that certain developments in her relationship with them seemed to impose limitations on the progress of the therapy. The second thing she told me, offering it up as stock background, was that she'd been raped as a ten-year-old.

She described her former analyst as a freewheeling, sexually liberated bohemian type.

Her marriage, she said, was not bad as marriages go, but basically boring. They performed well in bed and with average frequency, but she feared that over the past few years some destructive associations and behavior patterns were establishing themselves in her psychosexual relationship with her husband. The specifics she would go into later, if she decided to continue therapy with me.

She thought she'd try a male analyst again in hopes of finding some new perspectives on herself, in general, and on the situation with her husband.

Having gone through two miscarriages, she added, she was, as yet, childless.

Her husband, John, a Princeton graduate, was a local politician, and well known in the area for his fundraising abilities. He'd served as city purchaser, two terms as county clerk, two years on the mayor's advisory council, and was, at the time, preparing to campaign in the mayoral race. Big shit.

Dr. Excitement was not impressed.

Judy also mentioned in passing that he'd been an Air Force pilot during the Vietnam War, stationed in Vientiane, Laos.

"Partly I decided to see you because you're new in the city," Judy said after we sat in the stuffed chairs around the coffee table. "Through one function or another I know nearly all of the professional people here. It gets a little sticky. I wanted to talk to someone from another place.

"Also," she said, "probably from seeing female analysts, I'd been thinking that my blocks are primarily 'female' problems, but I don't think so anymore, and I'm sick to death with all this quasi-psychological trash out in paperback about all this women's bunk."

I bounced the ball between my legs where I sat. Then I stood and bounced the ball in the center of the room. I couldn't sit for more than a few minutes, and I was further unsettled by her sincerity, her intention for a professional relationship. I was sinking into the reality of this elaborate scheme—the ridiculous extent to which I had gone to actualize an erotic fantasy. I shuddered inside, floundering in the design of my own stratagem, the back of my head and neck burning with momentary gravity. I was still unsettled from leaving Montclair so abruptly, with Fatso's goons on my tail. I was afraid I was slumping into the condition I'd suffered in L.A. I'd only been a psychiatrist for a short time, and I wasn't sure if I liked it.

But I liked Judy Oswald—I knew that. I could smell her feral odorless glandular secretions from across the room. I had to do something about all that sincerity. I had to guide the therapy toward my new psychiatric couch. My heart was beginning to fidget and thrash about again.

"I can't deal with these female problems," I said, "I don't understand them. I don't deal with male problems for the same reason. Unless you don't mind that I don't understand, then we'll have a go at it. I like to operate beyond the male and female bullshit, and into the carnal flesh-on-the-bone, animal reality."

"But I thought psychiatrists understood everything," she said with a cock of the head and a playful tone in her voice that threw me back to the cocktail lounge in Caldwell.

"That sounds quite serious," I said, "especially after having been to so many shrinks. This could take a long time to untangle, though I prefer the expedience of the sword through the knot—figure out what happened later."

"You mean you're admitting a certain . . . lack . . . in your professional competency, Doctor?" That invisible smile awakening in her lips again.

This was more like it. Dr. Excitement's excitable heart twitched.

"Not only that," I said, "but to tell you the truth I don't understand much, but at times I think there isn't all that much to understand. I don't know whether I'm stupid or brilliant. Most things are simple, I think. Actually, I'm fairly confused. I sometimes get depressed."

"You're kidding, Doctor. That's so . . . human of you."

"Basically, I think I'm a bad person because of things I've done, but I resist assuming the guilt for those things, and I'm unwilling to accept punishment for them. I still have a lot to learn about therapy, I must admit, though I have helped some people—made others worse. With some people, well, I've ruined their whole day. Besides all that, I'm a liar. But I haven't lost a patient yet this year. That's why I stayed out of surgery."

"You're also one of the younger shrinks I've seen. I have some question about trusting your experience."

"Don't trust me, really. No, actually I burned through university and med school in a neurotic, work-obsessed drive, sublimating for dark and instinctual suppressed needs."

"Sounds too oversimplified to me, Doctor."

"You've been in therapy too long. Things *are* simple."

"Classic overachiever." The smile shaped her lips this time.

"Not really," I said. "I'm making all this up. I graduated with honors. I then had two years of clinic experience and one year in a hospital psych ward in Baltimore under the renowned Dr. Millard who, besides being the papa of modern psychiatry and famous for his research with rhesus monkeys and his red clam sauce, blew a mean bebop tenor sax in a club downtown on weekends. Then I worked in two other hospitals, and I've had a private practice for three years now. I was a child genius, and now I'm an adult genius. A Syrian palmist told me I have a mind like Einstein and I'll never have to worry about money. It hasn't been easy. I'm unable, like many of my patients, to adjust to society. I'm basically sociopathic, and I like it that way. I have a criminal mind and a massive clot of subconscious guilt. If I lived in Russia I'd be in prison. Here I'm a psychiatrist. I have no moral standards to guide me—as a matter of professional stance—and I see civilization and civilized behavior as a hoax, and I see peace of mind and honesty as luxuries of the deluded. Most of the time I feel like a mythic character trapped in a funny and tragic fable or a B movie script about an unwilling evolutionary agent who is a slave to his genes."

"It sounds too classic," she said, "but it's more than I know about my last two analysts after two years—that is if you're not making it all up. Maybe if I see you twice a week we can get to the bottom of this. I do think there are very positive signs in your behavior. We may as well begin now."

"I thought we had."

"Yes, of course we have," she said. "I lost my head."

"Try to be a little more attentive, Judy."

"I'll try, Doctor."

I bounced the ball. "And no smiling, please," I said, "even the invisible smile. This is supposed to be painful. All manner of childhood trauma must be summoned up—intricate dissection of the sub-, un-, collective un- and superconscious—all complemented with profuse eidetic imagery. I introduce mnemonic devices, dream analysis, great drugs, some brie cheese, a nice chablis, primal lie therapy—the plot thickens—people are cured, the dead walk, your husband becomes mayor. Everyone escapes unscathed, almost, for a while."

I found a custom lab that sold high-speed 16mm film.
The consultation room had two large windows on the north wall—more than ample light.
With a thin-gauge copper wire I built a circuit from a battery to the contacts of the Doiflex drive motor. I simply taped the shutter trigger in the on position so the camera would run constantly until the circuit was broken. I ran the circuit wire through a silent switch and mounted the switch on the underside of the psychiatric couch. The next task was to mount the camera where it wouldn't be seen or heard.
I hacked a hole in the wallboard and mounted it between the studs, but the two-by-fours didn't allow enough room, and the lens of the Doiflex protruded past the wall. I searched the shops for something with a concave back to hang over the hole and conceal the camera, but there was no easy solution, so I hacked another hole in the bedroom wall behind the one I'd already made and adjusted the camera so the back of it extended into the unused bedroom and the lens was within the wall. I then ordered a one-way mirror from the back pages of *True Detective* magazine.
I drilled a small hole just above the baseboard in the consultation room, directly below the hole I'd hacked in the wallboard. I managed to feed the tiny copper wire from the camera contacts down behind the wallboard and through the small hole above the baseboard by wrapping it around a stiff wire that I bent at a right angle at the bottom.
I pulled the circuit wire through the hole, ran it along the baseboard and up the leg of the psychiatric couch and connected it to the switch.
When the mirror arrived I hung it over the hole.
I tested the system by shooting some film of myself. I loaded the Bell & Howell and the Doiflex, sat on the couch and started the Doiflex with

the silent switch. I removed my clothes, stood on the couch, aimed the Bell & Howell at the mirror and shot I jumped from the couch and began stalking the mirror, cautiously and stealthily moving closer while the Doiflex filmed from behind the mirror. When I reached the near limit of the depth of field of the lens on the Doiflex, I continued to aim the Bell & Howell into the mirror while I moved in what I imagined to be a primitive tribal dance, contorting my face and jerking my body violently.

When I got the film back from the custom lab I paid a fee to use their editing machine and cut the two films together in sequences, mostly just to practice splicing, which I hadn't done in a long time.

The film I shot in the mirror was, of course, in reverse of the film shot by the Doiflex. When my positions, movements and especially my exaggerated facial expressions were interfaced on the editor screen, it created a strange effect, alternating back and forth between one perspective and the other.

The system was crude, but it worked.

"I was twelve when my father died," Judy said. We were almost two hours into our fifth session. The cassette recorder was running beneath the coffee table. The microphone was taped in a hole in the tabletop and covered with the tablecloth. I'd gone shopping for a fantasy and bought a job. I couldn't tell anymore who was stringing who along. Every effort on my part to trivialize the conversation and get it back on the right track—the track to my new psychiatric couch—was deftly redirected, redesigned into a new game plan and bounced back at me, oddly resembling the actual process of therapy. This was some elaborate psychological foreplay. I kept bouncing the ball and bantering and countering, and it was all accepted with gratitude and credence, as though it was actual insight, then hurled back at me with an invisible smile. Was this still sincerity? Was this an actual professional relationship between a doctor and a patient? I had no idea. Whatever was going on, I didn't need to know. I just played along looking for chance openings and opportunities for parody and burlesque of the talk therapy process. Monkey in the doctor's office.

Judy pushed on: "I'd been to the movies to see a Dracula film. When I got home—my girlfriend's father drove me home—I remember it was raining and blowing like crazy, just like in the film. I walked in the back door and sensed something—I smelled something odd. A huge man— he must have been six-five—was walking toward me. I'd never seen him before. He had on these gray and black striped pants and a black coat. I thought—I mean, I really believed for a few seconds that he was a vampire. Evidently I became hysterical. I don't remember much. He was the undertaker. My father had died of a heart attack. He was pretty young, but he had diabetes. I was sure the vampire had killed him.

"I remember I never went back to school that year. I saw a psychologist once a week. It seems like I've had a therapist of some kind ever since. Except for the two years I was on my own between my third and fourth years of college—that's the best I've ever felt. My own place, my own time, my own money, no schoolwork, my own responsibility for my own state of mind.

"It was the situation—the coincidence, the combination of events, the Dracula movie, which I think would have affected me even if my father hadn't died that night. It was my age maybe—puberty and all that —hormonal confusion. The vampire in the film bit right into my awakening libido and fucked things around in there, and somehow it all got connected with the death of my father and my sexuality. And, of course, that was only two years after I was raped. And the man who raped me was all in black with a black wool watch cap."

"Have you tried garlic?" I asked.

She looked up out of her recollections and cleared her eyes of the memory mist. "Why, no, Doctor, I haven't." It was one of her instant transitions from seriousness to playacting the naive innocent, the sultry, erotic innocent.

I loved the playfulness.

"A little dab between the breasts and behind the ears?" she asked.

"That would do it," I said.

She crossed her legs and exhaled audibly through her nose.

"You should have tried garlic before spending a fortune on all these shrinks," I said. "They're all phonies. Garlic works very well in these cases."

"You've had cases like this before, have you?"

"There was one now-famous case I recall about twenty years ago. I was called in on the case when the previous psychiatrist was found drained of his blood with two punctures in his throat."

"How fortunate it is, then, that I've found you. Will the Shoprite variety do?"

"No. Never. It must be wild garlic gathered at the full of the moon by a procedure that is kept secret and only survives today because of one eccentric old man in Lithuania who went to great lengths to secure the ancient books. He had them entombed with him."

"Of course."

"It wasn't until the man's corpse was exhumed, by order of the high courts of that country, following lengthy litigations pursued by my client, that the ancient knowledge became available for discriminate professional use. As good fortune would have it, I have access still to these well-guarded texts. What was my surprise, my dear Mrs. Oswald, when I learned the nature of your suffering?"

"When can we begin your treatment, Doctor?"

"At once, my dear. I can't wait another minute."

The invisible smile. "Your journey will be so perilous, Doctor. How can I ever thank you?"

"What journey is that?"

"To Lithuania for the well-guarded, ancient texts."

"Oh, the ancient texts. I happen to keep them in a hidden compartment in the psychiatric couch." I extended my hand toward the couch. "Let's take a look."

"You'll have to make that journey alone," she said. "I'm on a schedule today, and we've run over." She checked her watch.

"Alone! In that case, I shall make the necessary preparations and go off to Lithuania. You leave me no choice."

"How can I ever thank you?" She pulled her shoes on and stood. "I go strengthened, Doctor, and wondering—am I paying for this extra thirty minutes of bullshit?"

"No time for petty details. What your husband doesn't know won't hurt him. Besides, he gets more satisfaction out of paying for your therapy than taking you to Club Med. He likes to keep you ill, wan, frail, hindered, etcetera. Now, if you'd accompany me to the hidden compartment we could get the ancient books and figure out what to do about him, too."

She picked up her coffee cup and took it to the kitchen sink. I followed.

"You've made this diagnosis of my husband by remote, have you?"

she said. "There's been some remarkable advancements in psychotherapy."

"Actually, I observe him through the window from the roof of your house."

"You do, do you?" She put her jacket on.

"Yes."

"And you've determined this from just watching him through the window." She walked to the door and stood there with her hands in the jacket pockets.

"From the corny pajamas he wears." I took her hand and kissed it, lingering there, inhaling deeply along her arm. I turned her hand over and gently bit her wrist, then stepped back holding my brow. "I don't know what came over me," I said, melodramatically short of breath. "I was overcome by an urge to fill a snifter with your blood."

"Does raw T-bone do the same thing to you, Doctor?"

"Only when it's hanging around a woman's neck."

"You're sick, Doctor." She opened the door.

"Wednesday at three, Mrs. Oswald, and better bring your crucifix."

"But I don't think I could, Doctor." She stepped onto the porch.

"You must continue to protect yourself, Mrs. Oswald. I cannot say that what just came over me will not recur then."

"But, Doctor, I can't make love with Jesus in the same room. It's another hang-up I have. You see, this priest, when I was a girl—it was after mass in the sacristry, and. . . ." She took a step backward.

"This can become a much more serious affliction if left to root in the fallows of the mind. Come back in here, Mrs. Oswald. You must be administered to immediately."

"But I shan't, Doctor—I have a tennis date." Another step backward, the invisible smile.

"But you can't say things like that and leave. It's not healthy, and that's my professional opinion. Look at me shake."

"You'll get over it."

"How?"

"You'll think of a way." She turned and took a few steps. Then, over her shoulder: "Use your imagination."

"That will make it worse."

"Then use your hand." She walked toward her car.

"That's dirty, Mrs. Oswald."

"Never gave me pimples," she called from the end of the walk. She opened the car door. "You should know about that, being a psychiatrist."

"I'm not a psychiatrist, Mrs. Oswald. I'm a vampire."

She put the key in the ignition and rolled the window down. "You're just fucked-up," she called.

"How can you sleep with a man who wears such corny pajamas?" I called as she drove away.

She waved her pinky.

Sure I was in lust. I was infatuated and enchanted. I loved the way she moved, her grace, her lines, her loins, her aura, her sun sign. She exuded a careful ration of come-jump-on-me. I was intellectually stimulated. I wanted her to devour me. And I wanted to get to her husband.

But besides all that—besides everything—I wanted to marry her.

I wanted to live with her, change her oil, be generally handy around the house, do the grocery shopping together in the easy listening of the afternoon, embark on a classic kill-the-husband plot together, a flawless one.

I lay in bed fantasizing about how it would be—I cooked fantastic meals for us, all the while keeping up a clever, entertaining line of chatter. We rarely went out at night, content to simply be together, doing whatever we did, watching TV, working on our separate projects while enjoying a sense of harmony and general well being.

It was something about the way she smelled. Maybe it was possible for me to be married to her—maybe she was that fucked-up. Maybe she'd spelled my mind into thinking it was possible, or had I done that to my mind? It was crazy, and I wanted it. Happily married. A seemingly, outwardly, apparently normal life together. Could we raise two children and be happy in our odd way? He was deluded, father Excitement, sweetly and painfully, consciously and not.

She must have known I wasn't a shrink. Maybe I allowed myself that deception—that I had her fooled—as she deceived herself as well. I'm sure she was in it for the adventure. She seemed to nurture, through the lack of any substantial guilt or moral tenet, a rather kinky sexual sublife that was always there awaiting the opportunity for sexual variety. I liked that.

* * *

After the bars closed on the following Sunday morning I went to a diner for poached eggs and ran into Judy Oswald and her husband there. I sat with them for an hour or so. We were all pretty loaded. They'd been to a party at the home of an orthopedic surgeon. I'd been shooting eight ball for dollars in a dive in downtown Paterson.

John Oswald seemed quite friendly after Judy introduced me as her therapist. She'd obviously talked to him about me. "I don't trust doctors who don't drink," he told me. That was supposed to ease the guilt I was supposed to have about being a drunk psychiatrist. This guy was a jerk-off, and Monkey was drunk.

"You know," Judy said, "you probably won't like this, but I was talking to Doctor Moore about you tonight."

Her tone of voice made me nervous. Had I been exposed for the quack I was? I instantly prepared to give up the quest for Judy, give up psychiatry and leave town at the first opportunity to excuse myself from the table. "About me?" I said. "Why?"

"Well, I don't think I ever thought too much about it before, but suddenly tonight, as I was talking with Doctor Moore, I couldn't stop thinking about you bouncing that rubber ball all the time. At the moment it seemed significant. I think it was the champagne punch."

"I just do that to exercise my grip." I was back on the quest again. "In case I'm ever hanging from the cornice of a building some day, or I need to swing from the upper canopy of the jungle on a vine to tear open the throat of an antelope."

"I was suddenly wondering tonight," she said, "if it's some kind of method—some hypnotic or calming technique you work with—and I asked Doctor Moore if he'd ever heard of such a thing."

"I assure you, Judy, it's no technique. I'll stop it if you're too conscious of it."

"It really doesn't bother me. It seems to help loosen up my thoughts. Maybe because I think you're more interested in the ball than in what I'm saying. It helps having only half your attention. And Doctor Moore said he'd heard of methods *like* that, but never the bouncing ball."

"Actually, I'm preparing a paper to introduce the bouncing ball therapy to the psychiatric community. I came across the method in some ancient Lithuanian texts on sortilege and different kinds of magic and mystery."

"They had rubber balls way back in ancient times, did they?" she asked.

"Evidently left here by visitors from space," I said.

John Oswald laughed. "Maybe you've stumbled onto something, Doctor."

"Perhaps I have. Please call me George."

"You two seem to get along well," John said. "Judy tells me you've gotten further with her than any other therapist."

"Well, frankly," I said, "that surprises me. I haven't gotten very far yet. I hope to get a lot further."

"We're very grateful that we've found someone she can work with," he said.

"I'm glad to hear that. I feel confident that in time we can work some things out once and for all. Judy's an intelligent woman."

"Yes, she is. That's wonderful. I've never heard a psychiatrist expect such concrete results. Judy must be making some headway."

"God," Judy said, "I feel like I'm not even here the way you guys are talking about me. Headway? What, am I being housebroken or something?"

"Nonsense, dear," John said. "We're just concerned. We're happy you're having some success."

"Nonsense, dear," Judy replied.

"Let me ask you," John said to me, "how do you feel about socializing with your patients?"

"Oh, I generally let things run their course and feel about them as they happen. I don't think there's any inherent harm in it. In fact, given the right situation, it can be . . . well, productive . . . rewarding. It can alleviate certain pressures."

"Good," John said. "The reason I ask is, Judy and I are throwing our annual Halloween party next Saturday, and I want you to know that you're welcome to come if you're so inclined. Judy and I have discussed it, and it's fine with her. You may find it interesting. I know you're new in town, and besides being one of the wildest parties you can find in this sleepy town, I have several friends in the medical profession who come every year, as well as professional people from many other fields. You might take the opportunity to meet some of your colleagues. But it's usually great fun besides all that, if you're into such silliness."

"I have nothing against silliness, believe me," I said, "and I thank you for the invitation. I'll keep it in mind. Halloween is my favorite holiday—good for the psyche, you know, to take on a different persona. Off the record, that is."

"You mean I can't quote you on the invitations?" He laughed heartily. " 'Good for the psyche—Doctor George Dickel, psychiatrist.' " He laughed again.

"Please don't," I said. "I have enough trouble with credibility as it is, being less than gray-haired and erudite."

"I don't know—you have a little gray around the temples, sir, and I don't find you an unlearned man."

"I can move in most circles, I guess, though I do find you slightly patronizing, considering you don't know me, so I take your kind of flattery with saltshaker in hand."

"As you wish. Personally, I've learned to take anything I can get. No harm in a little flattery."

"We're being so fucking polite," I said. "Do you hear us?" I looked back and forth from Judy to John. "There's a crust on this conversation. Who the hell talks like this?"

"Politicians," Judy said.

"Judy has a problem with politicians," John said.

"Whereas I have a problem with basic social politeness," I said.

"Maybe we should talk about it when we're a bit more sober," John said.

"But you haven't always been a politician," I said. "Judy tells me you were a fighter pilot."

"Judy should maybe tell you more about herself and less about me, but, yes, that's true."

"She also told me you wear corny pajamas."

"I did not say that!" Judy snapped. "I don't know why I feel like this conversation must periodically trivialize me."

"I was just being impolite," I said, "just lying. Actually, I walked past your house the other morning on my way to the park. I peeked up over the fence and caught John tracking down the morning paper in his pajamas. They *are* corny pajamas."

John put his fork on the table and studied me.

"It's a beautiful house, though, and enormous," I said. "It must be nice to be out in the clear. I'm still paying off med school debts."

"I've had several successful investments," John said.

"That's why people get into politics, isn't it?" I asked. "There are opportunities for investment. Do you mind if I smoke?" I took a smoke from my pocket.

"Not at all," John said. He was eating his pie.

Judy was smiling behind her coffee cup.

"So you were in the Vietnam conflict?" I asked.

"Yes," John said. "Were you?"

"No. I'm afraid I was a draft dodger."

"Yes, well, some of my best friends were," he said.

"So you don't have any moral problems with that?" I asked.

"I don't have moral problems with much of anything," he said.

"That's interesting." I sipped my coffee. "I assume you weren't drafted. You went in as an officer after graduating Princeton?"

"I enlisted—that's right. Do you have a moral problem with that?"

"I have a moral problem with almost everything," I said, "but, to tell you the truth, some of my best friends enlisted. You read a lot of Hemingway in American Lit. 303?"

"Yes, okay, that's right—I wanted some adventure. I didn't want to sit behind a desk while the war was going on. I was fascinated by jets. I qualified for flight school. And it was easy to upgrade your rank in Nam."

"Especially for an Ivy Leaguer, I guess."

"Sure, that's true."

"Get to know some important people, upgrade your commission, drop some bombs, make some noise, raise some hell, give it the old college try, pick up some medals, come back a man."

"It's not hard to figure out," he said. "There was a certain bravado to it. I have military men in my family. I was young, ripe for a bit of derring-do."

"Something to write the first novel about," I said, "use those Princeton connections, be a man of letters with a warrior background to keep that knowing ironic edge."

"I never wrote a novel," he said, trying to flag the waitress.

"Why not?"

"Because I didn't want to."

"Because you would have expected yourself to tell the truth, in one fictitious way or another, in the tradition of other men of letters."

"What are you driving at, sir?" He gave me only half his attention, still trying to call the waitress and eat his pie.

"What does it feel like to kill people?" I asked.

"It feels better than being killed."

"You're pretty safe in an F-4, aren't you?"

"They are very fast fantastic airplanes, of course. People were killed in them just the same."

"Where were you stationed?" I asked.

"I was moved around quite a bit."

"Secret war in Cambodia?" I asked.

"No."

"Laos?"

"No. Nothing like that—just blowing the hell out of the jungle."

"Napalming the jungle?"

"That's right."

"No people down there?"

"Yes, there were people down there—it was war. I didn't see them very often. I'm not ashamed of what I did."

"And I guess you shouldn't be, John. Did you ever kill any friendlies by accident?"

"No." He sipped his coffee, trying to maintain his diplomatic cool. "No. I sure didn't. I wish you'd get to the point of whatever's bothering you."

"I've heard that sort of thing happened," I said, "a lot of incompetence and confusion, and a lot of covert CIA bullshit that cost American lives."

"I never saw any of that," he said.

"A superior officer in Laos, and you never saw any of that? I thought the CIA ran the war in Laos."

"I said I wasn't in Laos," he said, "and I never saw anything like that. I'm sorry to disappoint you. And what do you know about the CIA? What do you know about the war? What, did you read a book?"

"Ever kill any friendlies on purpose," I asked, "or, rather, because you were ordered?"

"Come on!" He put his cup down with emphasis. "What is this shit?"

"Maybe you've been misinformed," I said. "Or disinformed."

"It never happened. I can assure you."

"Or am I being disinformed now?" I asked.

"This conversation is taking an . . . unsociable turn," he said. "Why the hell would pilots target their own men?"

"Well, did you ever *not* hit Charlie when you knew grunts were being overrun by them?"

"What the hell is this—interrogation? I'm not even supposed to discuss these matters. And why the hell would we choose to not hit Charlie?"

"To avoid revealing intelligence infiltration," I said. "If you hit Charlie they'd know there was a leak, and if you don't want them to know there's a leak because there's a grander plan coming up in the near future for Charlie, then you don't hit Charlie so you don't blow the cover and spoil the grand plan, even though grunts are getting overrun."

"And where the fuck did you get this information?"

"It's just stuff I've heard, and I wondered if it was true. I thought you'd be a good person to ask. It's important to know the truth when I'm working with vets as patients."

"Well, you may never know the truth, sir." He moved his cup so the waitress could refill it. His neck was red and his hand shook slightly. "Believe me, George, there's a lot of disinformation about the war. Spread around by both sides."

"What two sides are you talking about?" I asked.

"Spread around by groups with vested interests in disinforming the public."

"I hope you'll excuse my forwardness and my directness," I said. "I work with a lot of very disturbed vets. I can use all the data I can get."

"And I hope you'll excuse my quick temper—and my reluctance to give you any specifics. I'm sensitive about the subject, obviously, and I do have certain restraints on me. I mean, for all I know, you could be with the CIA. But I know one thing—you can't trust the words of every grunt in a psych ward."

"I guess officers had more accurate information," I said.

"Of course. Rumors were rampant among the grunts, and there was little respect among them for their superiors."

"That's what I understand."

"You can't run a war that way," he said, "and you, having never been there, cannot understand. You really don't know what you're talking about, sir."

"I'm sure."

"I'm sorry for my tone of voice," he said, "but it annoys me—civilians thinking they know what went on over there. We didn't even know what was going on over there!"

"Then why do you consistently pretend you do? That's what I'm curious about."

"God have mercy, man—eat your eggs."

"What I need to know is if we should be punished—if there's a curse on America now. That's important to know when dealing with demons and ghosts like I am, because if there is a curse, we should find out how to remove it. If we'd admit that we feel we should be punished, then we'd know where to begin—with witches and magicians—certainly not with politicians and psychiatrists. We should begin with people who know about curses, not with people who don't believe there is such a thing."

"I don't feel like I should be punished," he said.

"I don't either," I said.

"Well, there you have it."

"But many of my patients do."

"Then the curse is on them."

"Yes," I said, "and if they're that stupid—to hell with them."

"I didn't say that."

"But if they were smart they'd have the same opportunities you have. They deserve what they get because they're stupid. You are among the chosen people, and your so-called success is the proof, and they are among the damned, proven by their failure. It's simple for you, isn't it? You have it figured out. You understand, don't you?"

He put his fork down again, chewed hurriedly, swallowed and said, "I understand that I'll never get anywhere by feeling guilty and cursed."

"That's right," I said.

There was a silence—not an uncomfortable silence: too much alcohol in us for discomfort. Judy still held the coffee cup to her mouth with both hands.

"But I am happy to hear," I said, "that pilots were never responsible, by design, for the death of American soldiers. I'm glad I asked—I needed to hear that from you."

"Rest assured, Doctor," John said, looking down the aisle, out the windows, down the highway.

"Good. That's great to hear. I mean it. I believe you. I trust what you're saying is true."

His eyes came back to the table. "You can trust me."

Judy's eyes narrowed and she began to peer at me over the coffee cup.

"The first day I was back east I learned a lesson in trust," I said. "From a person in Central Park who was half male and half female. Some people have to say a lot to teach a lesson—this person didn't say anything. A little mumbling maybe— nothing I could understand. This person trusted me—the person knew right away that I could be trusted, at least at that moment, and as a result, I trusted this person. And hardly a word passed between us."

"Half man and half woman?" Judy asked.

"That's right. I'm sure of it."

"This was a street person?" John asked. "A freak, a bum, a bag person of some sort?"

"Yes."

"It's simple then. The person had nothing to lose."

"That's right. And no place to get to."

"You can lose your *life* in Central Park," Judy said. She swung her head to John. "Is that *nothing?*"

"Well, yes," he said. "No, a life is certainly not nothing, but George here does not exactly look like a killer. What I mean is . . . Well, you both know what I mean." He directed his index finger to the table top. "You can trust me this far—to my knowledge, pilots were never responsible, by design, as you say, for the deaths of GIs."

"Thanks for repeating that," I said.

"How could we live with ourselves?" he said, curling his index finger back into his fist.

12

ACTUALLY HALLOWEEN IS NOT MY FAVORITE HOLIDAY. THE doctor does, however, recommend dressing up whenever the urge may strike.

Halloween reminds me of some grunts I new in Nam. They were usually LURPS or special teams of some sort—search and destroy units—the kind of soldiers who wore VC ear collections around their necks. I'd seen guys, when the mood would strike them, dress up in bizarre, always primitive-looking costumes, as though their long treks into the jungle had released some weird medicine from a juju bag deep in the brain.

I was always expecting to hear that they were eating the hearts or livers of the dead VC like some primitive cultures did as a spiritual psych-out or to ingest the strength and bravery of a warrior—witchery inflicted magically on the enemy.

Then I saw it happen with my own eyes—a liver removed, a bite taken out of it—strong magic that horrified the Vietnamese, made to look like it was done by the VC. Word of that one bite of that one liver traveled in-country quickly and completely, as though the image had risen into the brains from every individual brain stem.

We laughed when we saw it happen—this guy with his mouth full of human liver. We didn't know what else to do. Bad magic.

After that I saw the VC ear necklaces as talismans. There were numens in the forest that could be summoned with these ears or with sacramental drugs or with any number of personal rituals of divination.

Halloween hasn't been the same to me since. I can feel its historical origins, the connection with the spirits of the dead, with ghosts that walk the earth, with living witches who know the business of dealing with ghosts.

I saw these ghosts hovering and quaking around men who would be dead hours later. I heard the ghosts at times. I had firsthand dealings with them, crouched at the edge of a hamlet at night, in the viscera of VC turf, waiting motionless for the sounds of sleep to overcome the place, the disembodied faces and limbs of the enemy or dead buddies or death itself laughing or stomping or wailing in pain all around me—the whole mephitic swamp of characters and organs making a racket while I was trying to silence even my hearbeat.

I placated them, reconciled with them, fought with them, made deals with them, pleaded with them to keep quiet. I made offerings to them. I worked for them and stood motionless, listening for hours at a time with them. I blasted Jimi Hendrix tapes into the jungle for them. I buried myself in dung to hide and wait with them. At one time All Hallow's Eve must have been a day designated for this kind of business—a necessary business, an unavoidable business—witness me now. And witches must have been the necessary go-betweens.

There was this SEAL from Pittsburgh named Doug. He'd been in and out of the brig for various thefts and drunken brawls with officers and MPs and Marines. He was a good man. He'd watch your back. He was hunkered down at the bank of this creek, hugging an M-60 machine gun. We were all under cover—as much cover as we could find in daylight. We weren't used to working in daylight. The five of us, thirty minutes before, had hit a regimental point unit, which wasn't our line of work. The M-60 was cradled in Doug's arms as he whispered to this guy, Juan, from Jersey. "Is this fresh or salt water?" he asked Juan.

Juan pointed inland and whispered, "Fresh that way," then pointed the other way, toward the mouth of the Mekong, and whispered, "Salt that way. Catch trout that way," he said, raising his inland arm again, then switched his arms again and whispered, "catch tuna over there—if it was in the States. I don't know what the fuck they catch here, man, except them big ugly *pla buk* monsters."

We all listened to the jungle for a minute. Nothing. Clean job. The regiment on its way.

Then Juan raised his inland arm again. "Comes all the way down from swamp to woods to reeds to grass to cattails to boardwalk to the honeys on their beach blankets to the sea. Crabs, man—herons, bait fish, osprey nests all along the way. Apples, peaches, watermelon, pizza, hot dogs, cotton candy, Italian sausage sandwiches, man. Fucking peppers, corn, tomatoes—*Jersey* muthafuckin corn and tomatoes! Charcoaled cheeseburgers with a slab of onion, Philly steak sandwiches—Jesus! And lots of traffic, beautiful sweet Jersey traffic. Lotta people don't know that about New Jersey, that there's lots of wild traffic. Did you know that, Doug, man? That's the natural habitat for traf—"

There was something in Doug's face that made Juan stop. Doug was listening hard. Then we all heard it. Doug raised the M-60, pivoted toward the creek on his heels and stood halfway up to peer through the foliage, and just then his head flew up in the air and blood sprayed from his back.

We'd thought the NVA had taken the loss of the point unit and moved on, but a handful of scouts were right on our ass. Juan never spoke above a whisper after that, even back on the barge, except when he'd scream and yell and curse the worst curses he could think of at anything—himself, a wet pair of socks, friends, officers, whores, the jungle rot on his ankles . . .

It was Juan who whispered it to me. "Remember that day Doug got it," he said, "and you told me that morning you saw his ghost following him?"

I did remember. Only it was more like the ghost was half out of him in the back, jerking around clumsily like it didn't know whether it was in or out.

I didn't see Judy Oswald again until the Halloween party. She left a note on my door, canceling her appointment for the week after I'd seen her in the diner with John because her sister-in-law was in town. She reminded me about the party on the note. That afternoon I searched the thrift stores for a costume. I wanted something I could disappear behind.

I found a pair of knee-high riding boots at the Salvation Army store, removed the torn sneakers I was wearing, pulled the boots on behind the shoe rack, took a tux jacket off the rack, paid for the jacket and walked out with the boots.

At a church thrift store I found a red silk scarf, a black, knee-length wool coat and, among the junk jewelry, a small heart-shaped pin made of red glass.

I also bought plastic fangs, white greasepaint, spirit gum, black hair dye, eyebrow pencil, lipstick and fake fingernails.

On Saturday morning, the day of the party, I removed the sleeves of the coat at the seams and sewed the arm holes closed, then cut the collar points square and turned up the collar.

A few hours before the party I opened a quart of George Dickel, took a few belts, dyed my hair black and darkened my eyebrows with the pencil. I snipped some hair, fashioned it into a widow's peak, applied it with spirit gum and combed my hair straight back. I applied the greasepaint heavily for an opaque whiteface effect and put on a thin layer of lipstick to accent the fangs. I glued on fake fingernails and whitened the backs of my hands with the greasepaint.

I drank some more whiskey and pulled the riding boots over a pair of white pants, then arranged the red silk scarf around my neck and tucked it like an ascot into a white silk shirt. I pinned the minute red glass heart to the black satin lapel of the tux jacket.

When it was time to go I put on the black tux jacket and threw the altered coat over my shoulders. When I looked in the mirror I knew the vampire was in me. He had risen from the same mountainous country of the brain where the vampire mythology itself was born and became undead. And it was from those crags that the beast crept down into the rumblings in my throat as I made my way through the dark neighborhoods to the Oswalds', sipping from the quart of Dickel all the way.

When Judy saw the vampire her mouth dropped open—she froze as though she'd been turned to stone. The vampire was half hidden between a mummy and a scarecrow. The vampire's eyes widened and his lips rose a little like a dog beginning a growl, exposing the tips of his fangs. He growled low in his throat. The mummy and the scarecrow both turned to him, the mummy pausing at mid-sentence.

Obviously shaken, Judy turned back to her guest, who reached to touch Judy's arm with concern over her sudden paralysis. Judy nodded slowly to the woman, as though a momentary spell had been lifted, but the vampire knew she had not fully recovered.

When Judy glanced back at the vampire he covered his face with the cape and spun around into the crowd, disappearing into another room that was also crowded.

In there, in the corner near the finger sandwiches, he hunched his shoulders, drew the cape around himself, parted his lips and growled. People looked at him and smiled, but he was not smiling. He was trying to contain a force, an energy that seemed to swirl around him—he was trying to keep the swirling in check before it displayed itself openly there by the avocado dip.

People moved away from him. The eyes of a woman were drawn into his glare. Two men stood their ground. The vampire saw their eyebrows drop. He smelled the release of the scent of fear on them. One forced a smile then spoke.

"I never saw a vampire in whiteface before," he said.

"I thought it would be more theatrical," I said. My voice sounded odd to me, deeper, with stronger resonance in the cartilaginous walls of the larynx.

"It works," the man said. "The theater is magic."

"Yes," I said, and left to pour a drink.

When the vampire confronted Judy again she was looking for him. He seemed to glide over the floor, pulling a silk hanky from his sleeve. The swirls were engulfing him again.

"Hold still, my dear," he said to her, "you have a speck of dried blood on your lip."

She lurched away from him.

"Your lips are so full and red," he said, stepping close to her, drawing the silk across her lower lip. "And your neck . . . " He touched her beneath the ear.

"Who are you?" she said, restrained anger in her voice. She was visibly trembling.

"Your dead father returned from the grave and lusting for you," the vampire said.

She gave a shallow sigh, fractured with nervous apprehension. "You're freaking me out, George," she said. Her jaws were clamped. "Your voice is so weird." Her voice was quaking. She lit a smoke with trembling hands.

A whirlpool drained my head. "Sorry, Judy," I said. "I was getting into it."

"I noticed," she said, inhaling deeply. "You son-of-a-bitch!" Her voice raised in volume until by the end of the sentence she was inappropiately loud. The anger was finding its voice. "How could you do this! Is this supposed to be some joke?"

People nearby turned to look at us.

"You may think this is funny," she said, "but I don't." She took two quick steps away from me, then stomped back and stuck her face in mine. "I feel like punching you in the face!" She raised both fists, dropping her drink and her smoke, and beat me once on the chest with both fists, then bit the flesh of her hand and sobbed to hold back tears.

A man approached us. He was looking around for John as he took Judy by the arm. "Is there a problem here, Judy?" he said.

"No, it's okay," she said, picking up the glass and snuffing the smoke against an ice cube.

"Are you sure?" He looked at me warily.

"It's okay," she said. "He's my doctor."

I bared my fangs at the man. He tried to walk her away, but she resisted.

"Bug off, baldy," I said to him.

He was about to blurt something silly and impotent when Judy put her palm on his chest.

"Please leave us alone, Alan," she said. "Thank you."

He hesitated. I showed the fangs again. He left. I lifted the cape to shield my eyes from a group of people who were watching the scene.

"Let's get out of the spotlight," she said. She was still upset.

We went into the foyer and stood by the staircase.

"You're a strange person," she said. "I'm not sure I appreciate this."

"Only as strange as your imagination," I said. "I'll be a good vampire and go mingle with the guests. Where's the blood?" I eyed my empty glass.

"Looks like you already found it," she said. "This was a fucked up thing to do, George. I can't tell you how much I . . . "

"Oh, yes, I forgot. In the other room. There's some weird people in that room. Can I get you a fresh one?" I took her glass, raised the cape and backed away.

There was no Dickel at the bar, so I went downstairs to look, but none there either, so I poured some Jack Daniels and took a seat on the sofa, looking to the women on each side of me slowly, mouth slightly parted to expose the fangs.

"I'm Grace," the woman to my left said, extending her hand.

I growled in my throat, taking her hand and turning it over to inspect the veins. She was dressed like Jackie Onassis was dressed on the day John Kennedy was shot, complete with blood stains. My head sank slowly toward the blood stain on her lap.

"What's your name?" she asked. "What are you doing?"

My head stopped inches above her lap. She shifted her legs away from me. I snapped my head up. Her smile drooped. I turned to look at the other woman. She smiled shyly. I saw blood on her too, where there was no blood—it was dark, almost brown, and making the material stick to her right side. I got up to stalk Judy, stealing toward the point of no return.

At the top of the stairs two men leaned close to each other. The taller man captured my attention. He was in heavy blackface makeup that was completely opaque, covering all exposed skin. Black moustache, black inside the ears, black Ray Charles shades camouflaged against his face, which rose up out of a white-on-white collar like a nebulous field of black energy, no eyes, a little dark lipstick—all obscured beneath a rakish brimmed hat. Dyed black hair showing at the sides and back. Hands also black, with pink nail polish. Black-and-gray pinstriped pants held up with suspenders—a paunch added to fill out the waistband. Black vest over the white-on-white shirt. Black, red and white diamond-checked tie. Large black hands dancing around him as he spoke, taking from his mouth, then leaving there a big cigar. Silver rings with black jade stones on each hand. He stepped to and fro to a rhythm in his head, his mouth playing the melody with words. He was talking to a slim Christ in robe and sandals—natural black-and-gray beard.

Looking into the other room and away from this black man, I moved closer to him to listen to the rough throaty melody of his speech, phrased to accompany the to and fro of his body, the head bobbing and weaving the grace notes. This was the only music in the place, except distant periodic TV jingles from some portable auxiliary unit yakking away in a back room somewhere. I could tell from his voice that he'd turned his head toward me. I kept my back to him, standing at the fringe of the crowd in the living room. When I heard him call, "Hey, bloodsucker," a suspicion that had been tingling in my gut rushed up my spine. I turned. "Hey, blood," I said to him.

"You got a match? Jesus here doesn't smoke."

His cigar had been lit a few minutes before.

"No," I said. "Why'd you snuff it if you wanted it lit?"

He just looked me up and down. "What color are you underneath? I'm beginning to notice a lack of brothers here. I wonder if I happened into the wrong party. This is East Orange, isn't it?"

"I thought this was Jerusalem," Christ said, regarding his drink. "Doesn't this tour go to the Wailing Wall today?"

"I was just telling brother Jesus here," the black man said to me, "that he best keep his jive to hisself." He turned back to Christ. "I mean, if I were you I wouldn't send out no announcements. They string your ass up again before you get to heal one single blind dude."

"I might say the same to you, Leroy," Christ said. "The same warning."

"I hear ya, brother. Hey,"—Leroy hit Christ on the shoulder with the backs of his long fingers—"you ever see Ray Charles's piano?"

"No, I haven't," Christ said.

"Neither has he," I said, stealing the punch line.

Leroy turned the cigar in his mouth. "That's my point." He pointed the cigar at Christ but he spoke to me. "You go giving my man, Ray, his sight, he may never play again or—worse—he might start playing some kind of elevator music. You can't go messing with blindness and get away with it."

"It'll do no good to warn me," Christ said. "It's destiny."

Leroy scoffed. "He don't know what we know, do he, brother Drac?"

"What's that?" I said.

"They just dispatch some CIA muthafuck"—he took matches from his vest pocket and lit the cigar—"and it's all over but the resurrection. All you gotta do, brother Jesus—all you gotta do is start that shit again. You be dead in a week, seated at the right hand o' God, the Father. They eat your ass alive and worship it later. Check out your act, brother—you don't even have the threads for it. You look like a beggar. That won't get you nowhere these days. And you're slim too—you can wear nice rags. And look at you—sackcloth and Jesus boots. Who gonna listen to you dressed like that shit?" Leroy jerked his chin at me. "Now this dude—nice threads, right? Silk shirt, satin lapels, leather boots . . . He lookin' awright. That's what it's all about—ain't that right, brother Drac?"

"That's what what's all about?"

"Survival, man—nothing less."

"Nice threads?" I said.

"Yeah, baby. You sort of a survival expert—ain't that right?"

"How do you know that?" My head was filling, then draining, the swirling erratic, uneven, off center.

"From what I hear, you boys don't even have to come up for air," he said, rotating the cigar between his teeth.

"What do you mean?" Dr. Excitement and the vampire were noticing a certain confusion of perception. "Am I about to have a breakdown?" Dr. Excitement asked the vampire, but the vampire was preoccupied with this guy, Leroy. Leroy has an odd scent, thought the vampire. The costume is too good, the character too well conceived. He was too slick—a professional. His eyes followed me too closely as I came up the stairs, like he knew what he was looking for. And why did he go out of his way to corner me? Dr. Excitement was no help at the moment —he was losing brain cell after brain cell of control, thinking that if he got Leroy down and rubbed the makeup off, he'd uncover his own face. And this scent—was it fear? Was it my own brain smoking? I'd been drunker before—this was something else.

"What I mean is," Leroy replied, "I hear you boys can cruise in the undead, stay in the coffin till you need blood, sneak out at night, waste some innocent villagers, make it look like a routine murder and steal back into the darkness. Ain't that right?"

"Who are you?" I asked, but the vampire didn't even care.

"I am Leroy," Leroy said. He studied his glass. "Some class whiskey around here. White women. Some intriguing pâté." He drained his glass. "I'm gonna pour me another glass of this Tennessee sippin' whiskey and see if I can entice some white women with this lump in my sock." He started to bop away.

"Did Oswald sic you on me?"

"I beg your pardon, brother. Should I be insulted?"

"You're a spook."

"Hey, now, bro—watch your slurs. I didn't go calling you no white trash honky, did I?"

"You know what I mean."

"I have a feeling *you* don't know what you mean." He started to walk again.

"I'm talking to you," I said.

"Now let me get some more juice, will ya? I'm not going anywhere." He left a cloud of cigar smoke and descended the stairs toward the bar.

"Who is that guy?" I asked Christ.

"I don't know," Christ said.

"Then what good are you?" I said, annoyed, deranged, drunk.

"Look," Christ said, blowing his nose, "I don't even know what you guys were talking about."

I wandered off to stalk Judy.

She caught me by the arm in the kitchen.

"I'm sorry," she said. "I think I needed another drink to see the humor in this. You gave me such a fright—such a strange feeling. It seems so calculated—this costume. I was not kidding that day about the intensity of that experience when my father died. Sometimes I think you think I dramatize everything."

"Sometimes I think you think I think you think," I said, "when it's perfectly obvious. Let's avoid the obvious."

"Yes," she said. "You're drunk." We watched the side of her foot drag across the linoleum. "What's this costume all about?"

"It's Halloween, my favorite holiday. I could ask you why you're dressed like a fairy princess."

"You're playing with my head, George."

"I'm treating you, remember? I'm your doctor, back from a perilous journey where I walked every step of the way with death at my back, just to get the materials necessary to cure you, and you tell me I'm . . ."

"For Christsake, George!" She took a step away, then back. "I wish it was as simple as your jokes—some witch doctor mind-fuck conjured over bourbon by a goddamn lunatic shrink who—"

"It *is* that simple. Either it's that simple or it's so un-fucking-fathomable—so-o-o-o-o inscrutable, so *gnarled* and *deep-seated—much* too complex for any shrink. Your own private malaise can't be understood by *any*body, let alone treated. Twenty years of shrinks can't cure your comforting hearth of problems—can't untie your crying towel of knots, can't—"

"Is this another of your dubious professional opinions, or is this the bourbon speaking so severely? Just what I need—a drunk shrink." She exhaled forcefully, watched her foot scuff the floor, then looked right in my face. "You seem to insist that I have some evil spirit inside me that needs to be exorcised or something. Why are you being such an asshole? The last thing I need is some quack to fuck with my head. I may as well call a priest! I need help, not more games to play!"

"Actually you've had too much help. And a good priest *could* trace these knots to their source, but removing the knots and their source is the task of the magicians. My professional opinion, dubious as it may be to you, is garlic, as I've told you—until I come up with the cure. A bit in each corner of the house, a little down between your breasts, a tad behind the ear, a pinch between lip and gum . . . But you're convinced of some Freudian conumdrum because it reinforces the complexity of the problem, giving it the power that you believe it must have in order to keep you hindered the way you think you are. And to keep you occupied, as you've said—away from the TV and the coffee klatches. If you'll excuse me, I think I need some more blood. Can I get you a fresh one? Here comes Freud."

John Oswald stepped up, taking Judy by the elbow.

"Fun party, John," I said.

"Well, thanks," John said. "I'm glad you're having fun. I just wish I knew who you were. Is there a problem here, Judy? Alan said there was some kind of problem."

"*This,*" Judy said, "is my analyst."

"My God!" John said. "Well." He extended his hand. "I'm so glad you could make it. I would never have guessed. Great costume. I was hoping you had no hard feelings from our last encounter. To tell you the truth, George, I don't talk about those things enough—never, really. Leave it to a shrink, right?"

"I'm not your analyst," I said to Judy. "I'm the vampire."

She scoffed me with a short hiss, then cocked her head to fling the hair away from her face.

"Are you two having a disagreement?" John asked.

"I was going to freshen our drinks," I said. "Can I get you one, John?"

"No, thank you," he said. "Are you getting around all right? Meeting some people? I'll introduce you around when you come back."

I nodded. The swirling was beginning between us. His eyes darted away.

"I'll introduce you to some single women," he said, glancing at Judy, "or some married women for that matter." He laughed.

Judy frowned.

I spotted Leroy in the doorway to the dining room.

"Who's that guy in blackface?" I asked.

"He says his name's Leroy," Judy said. "We don't know who he is."

John looked at Leroy uneasily.

"Hey, Leroy," I called, waving him over.

He relit his cigar and bopped over.

"Brother Drac," he said, nodding to me.

"You make a good brother," I said.

"How would you know? And don't patronize me, man." He looked Oswald up and down then turned back to me. "What are you, another doctor? I ain't never seen so many doctors in one place. Makes me nervous. 'Spose I get sick! Could be the end of me." He laughed his Negroid laugh. "I keep checking for my wallet. They all walking around with a scalpel in their pocket and new lawn furniture in their eyes. Gives me the creeps."

"I'm a hemotologist," I said.

He laughed again. "From way back, right?"

"From before the fall to external medicine."

"I remember that," Leroy said. "My racial memory contains images of that black face pierced with bones, painted with fat and ochre, chanting that hoo-doo. We've come a long way since then. Today they offerin' free x-rays at the hospital to scan the kid's trick-or-treat bags for razor blades. Damn liberal of them. Next thing you know they be shovin' socialized medicine down our throats." He puffed his cigar. "If you can't afford your own x-ray machine, then fuck ya!" He looked at Oswald. "Ain't that right, my man?"

Oswald cocked his head like when a dog hears a cat on the TV. "I don't know how to take you, Leroy."

"I'd give you a clue," Leroy said, "but you wouldn't know how to take that either."

"Leroy," I said, "have you met John and Judy Oswald?"

"Pleased to make your acquaintance." Leroy extended his hand to John.

John looked at Leroy's hand as he shook it.

"Don't worry," Leroy said, "it doesn't rub off." He held John's hand and turned to Judy. "Say, baby," he said to her, taking her hand in his free hand, "hows about a little dark meat tonight? See that lump in my sock?" He dropped John's hand and pulled his pant leg up to expose his black banlon, then held both his hands about a foot apart. "Leroy's about like that, little sister, and about that big around." He put his thumbs and index fingers together to form a circle. "That ain't no myth livin' in there."

Judy dismissed him with a look of disgust.

"You will not speak to my wife that way," Oswald said, puffing up. Judy dismissed her husband with a look of disgust, too.

"Who are you?" Oswald demanded. "Have we met before?"

"Sure, sure—that's right," Leroy said. How could you forget? At the country club, right?"

"I can't place you," John said.

"Sure, you remember me. I was kitchen help there. I was the jellyroll baker. I bake some sweet jellyroll. Then I got sent up fo' murder in the first degree. But the judge's wife call—she say, 'Let Leroy go free—because he's a jellyroll baker—he bake the best jellyroll in town.' Den I invent de banjo. Den I go blind. Den I take up de piano. Den I gets de TB. Den I rape de white womens with de meathook. Den I ask de hairball how comes I dance so good. Now you remember, Missah Oswald?"

I'd been thinking Leroy was one of Oswald's dupes, but he was cutting too close to the bone—unless Leroy was very slick. Two-bit security men don't come that slick.

"Leroy," I said, "you're fucked-up, brother."

"I am." He grabbed me by the arm and squeezed.

Either I was too drunk or this guy, Leroy, was a master of mixed signals. I liked him and I didn't trust him. I felt he was a kindred spirit and an enemy. I felt I should leave the party at once to get out from under the scrutiny of his shrewd professional eyeballs and I wanted to stay to observe him.

"So what are you," I asked Leroy, "a gynecologist?"

He smiled, looked at the floor. "I'm a Negro."

"What do you do for a living?" John asked, trying to inject a practical and cordial seriousness.

"My job is to serve as a bad example," Leroy said. "Somebody has to do it."

John set his jaw and stuck it out a bit. "I think your job, from what I've been hearing around here, is to ridicule everyone you meet. Excuse me, but this is my home, and I'd like you to identify yourself."

"Well, ain't this some kind of Halloween party—a man has to identify himself when his costume is too good. I should have known better. There is no conviction here—nothing is real, not the ghosts, not the trollops, not the clowns. . . . What's sadder than a fake clown? What about the vampires?" He cocked his head at me. "Real?"

"I'm getting there," I said.

"Thatta boy—you stay in the undead, bro. The undead are bound to be more alive than the living around here. These people are extinct and don't know it. But I love it. It's so typical that the undead are more alive than the living. Isn't the whole world in reverse like this, Oswald?"

"Maybe you'd prefer another world," John said.

"One that ran forward instead of backward would be a pleasant change," Leroy said. "We would grow healthier and stronger as we grow older, instead of deteriorating. We would grow more childish. Going forward, as we grew we would believe less, not more, until we just plain *didn't* believe. No faith. No answers. No Heaven. Nothing. Eventually we would say 'goo-goo' and gurgle and chortle and somebody would take us into their arms, feed us, rock us to sleep, and we'd slip into an infant dream and be born in reverse."

"You have some very basic problems with the world, don't you?" John said condescendingly.

"I am really fucked-up. But I do my part to reverse the world."

"By making generalized judgments on the way people live their lives?" John said.

"Yes," Leroy said, "and by not working—except as a bad example, of course."

John was looking around the room for a way out of the conversation. "But you are self-righteous enough to think that your bad examples are actually good examples—and you'd rather complain about the way things are than work to change them."

"Now you're catching on," Leroy said. "Next maybe you can give up your crooked job."

"You'll understand," John said sternly, "if I ask you to leave. There's only so much a man has to take in his own home, especially from a sociopathic party-crashing malcontent with nothing to offer but negativity."

"Oswald, you just routinely assume that I am negative—that's about as far as you can get."

"May I have the pleasure of knowing who you are before I have the police remove you from my house?"

"You have no sense of humor, Oswald."

Judy put a hand on John's shoulder. "Surely we can work this out between us. There's no need to call the police."

Judy looked so beautiful at that moment that I ached and let out a groan. The three of them looked at me. It was at that moment that Dr. Excitement figured out the first step to Judy's cure, and it was obvious that John would have to take some medicine too.

"You'll have to excuse me," Oswald said. "I need to make the rounds among my guests." He turned to Leroy before he walked away. "I hope you'll remember you're a guest in this house. The host is perhaps too gracious."

"In that case," Leroy said, "brother Drac and I will try to coax your lively wife into a kinky *ménage à trois.*"

"Good luck," Oswald said as he walked away.

"Do you need to be excused too, Mrs. Oswald?" Leroy asked.

"I'm thinking about it," Judy said.

"You don't like this discussion?" Leroy asked.

"It's a vapid discussion," she said.

I gathered their glasses and took John's empty from the table top. "I'll get some more verve and sparkle to save the conversation," I said. "Until then, do the best you can. Don't let her get away, Leroy. I'll be right back."

On the way to the bar I locked myself in the upstairs bathroom. The vampire watched me from the medicine cabinet mirror. The party was ripening with potential. It was beginning to flow like quicksilver in the alchemist's crucible. Dr. Excitement needed to take advantage of this transitional liquid-metal state. He opened the medicine cabinet to consider a prescription. Lots of good medicine: Darvon, Valium, Percs, codeine in two forms, Ritalin and an economy-sized vial of heavy barbiturate sleeping pills. The doctor swallowed five or six tabs of Ritalin to get in touch with the proper spirits, then looked at the vampire, who was rising to the occasion.

The doctor pushed the highball glasses aside and opened four caps of the barbs, emptying the powder into John Oswald's glass. He opened three more and poured them into Judy's glass. He ran a little water into each and swirled the glasses until the powder dissolved. He looked into the vampire's eyes until they weren't there—just the swirling escaping from him again.

Judy and John were both drinking rye and ginger with a wedge of lemon squeezed in. Both glasses were tall highball glasses. At the bar the doctor squeezed half of a lemon into each glass to hide the taste of the narcotic, dropped in just a few ice cubes, added a shot and a half of Old Overholt to each and filled the glasses with ginger ale. He tasted both drinks, poured some Jack Daniels for himself and Leroy and went back downstairs.

He found the Oswalds talking quietly together. The doctor intruded. "Some very friendly and quite attractive woman helped me with your drinks—we got carried away with the lemon." The voice sounded remote to him.

"There's a fifty percent chance they're single or divorced," John said, taking the glasses and handing one to Judy. "If there's one thing I've learned it's how to plan a party." He laughed his forced laugh. "Thanks very much, Doctor. I was just looking for my glass."

The doctor lifted his cape over his face and stepped back into the hubbub. The vampire went to find Leroy, but Leroy was nowhere to be found.

The vampire was coming up the stairs after checking the bar a second time when he felt a breeze, pushed through some people and saw Oswald standing at the front door. "Have you seen Leroy?" he asked Oswald. Oswald said nothing, closed the door and returned to the party. The vampire stepped outside, into a shadow in the yard that was full of darker shadows of trees and shrubs. He thought he heard Leroy's voice from the direction of the street, beyond the hedge and the fence. He heard car doors close as he maneuvered through the shrubbery. "Leroy," he called. Another car door closed. He glimpsed lights through the hedgerow. "Leroy, it's me, brother Drac." Still no answer. The lights moved, and as the car passed the driveway he saw it was a new model, long, dark, no chrome.

It wasn't the type of crowd that goes on until four in the morning arguing for fun in the kitchen. By midnight some people had already left. The vampire watched the Oswalds become exceedingly drunk on the booze and barb cocktail. Leroy was nowhere in sight.

John loosened up and actually had some fun. He knocked over a lamp, fell on his ass trying to pick it up and laughed for five minutes until his face was wet with tears. The vampire almost liked him then for a moment as Oswald sat bawling like a child on the shag carpet. Then Oswald started chasing a woman dressed like a sheep around the coffee table yelling something about virgin wool. He took the jewel from his sultan's hat and tried to put it in the sheep's navel by reaching down the neck of her wooly costume. When a large man dressed like a shepherd intervened, Oswald reproached the man for keeping the pleasures of sheep to himself for so many centuries by making it taboo. "I bet God invented women," Oswald said, "because sheep can't cook," then laughed uncontrollably at his joke. A few women admonished him for his comment and the shepherd grew more insistant. Oswald responded by shifting his interest to an Indian princess in a slit miniskirt who was surrounded by four men. There he spouted political rhetoric with his respect-commanding tone of voice until he'd made a sufficient fool of himself. A most gracious friend walked him into the kitchen for a conference.

Judy was staggering, trying desperately to stay in control. After a few verbal duels that left prominent men of the community flailing defensively, she passed out on the sofa in her fairy costume, looking like Sleeping Beauty, showing a little leg, a look of peace on her face.

When John couldn't manage to carry her to bed, the crowd decided it was time to leave. An elf and a ghost carried Judy and John to their bedroom.

The vampire retrieved his quart of Dickel from the shrubbery and started through the shadows and alleys. He stopped often, tucked in a particularly dark niche, decompressed his brain and regulated his body, adjusting to the depths of his abandonment.

When he got home he lit the small lamp on the desk and the candle on the coffee table and gathered some necessary items. The rhythm of insect song pulsed in his inner ears as he worked. Over the candle he heated a straight pin by holding it with a pliers. When the pin was red hot he snipped the head off and pushed the pin into the plastic fangs until just the point stuck out from the tip of the fang about an eighth of an inch. He did the same to the other fang, then secured the pins in place with glue.

He put his black pigskin gloves in his pocket and stood on the back stoop drinking in the darkness. There was enough wind blowing to make the cape flap like a bat's wings. He jumped from the stoop and started back to the Oswalds' place, leaning forward into the shadows, almost running to keep up with himself.

On the way he encountered a group of people leaving a party. He spread his cape for them, looking to the sky for possible fringes of daylight. They laughed, but he was not laughing, even to himself.

A cop slowed his car and directed the spotlight at him. The vampire pulled the cape over his eyes and cowered from the light, and the cop gave a little salutelike wave and drove on.

As the cop passed the vampire heard a moaning growl from the root of his own throat, and the hair on the nape of his neck stood erect. He ducked into a back yard and disappeared. He put his hand to his mouth and found he was slavering. His nostrils flared; his eyes dilated, and his heart, which had been throbbing, held itself still in the dark until it found repose, then urged forward, barely beating, cautious, sure.

He squatted at the edge of Oswald's yard, keeping still, listening and smelling for a long time before he crawled to the back door. He entered noiselessly, though he knew there was no chance of waking them with the barbiturate coursing sluggishly in their brains.

He made his way to the bedroom, twisted the gooseneck lamp on the night table toward the ceiling, switched it on and crossed the room to open the doors to a second-story balcony. There were no trees nearby —no escape from the second story.

He went to the side of the bed where Judy slept. He realized his breathing was loud and silenced it. He smelled his own odor rising about him. Something glinted before him from the lamp light, and a wet spot formed on the sheet near Judy's shoulder. He put his hand to his mouth and felt that he was drooling again. His breathing was loud again, almost a wheezing. He wiped the slobber from his mouth and the snot from his nose.

He went down to the back yard, found a garden hose rolled in a wheel rack and unrolled it. He looked up at the balcony, went back in the house and began going through kitchen drawers until he found a drawer full of tools and tape and other odds and ends. There he found a ball of twine, which he tied to the nozzle of the hose. He tossed the ball of twine to the balcony.

Kneeling on the balcony, he pulled the hose up with the twine, untied the twine and removed it. He wove the nozzle end of the hose around one of the wrought iron railings and pulled in the hose until the nozzle had descended to the ground. After returning the twine to the drawer, he went back to the bedroom.

He wiped his mouth and nose again, climbed onto the bed and stood between John and Judy. His breathing percussed the quiet, moths flapping at the window screen. "My bride," he said, then began jumping up and down, flapping his cape like wings.

When they began groping through the drugged stupor toward wakefulness, he summoned the germ of the growling up from his groin, gathered it in a rumbling in his guts, then drew it up to resonate in the roots of his throat. He tasted the sourness on the back of his tongue. He grabbed each by the hair and shook and jostled them roughly until both were awake as much as they could be awake with their systems so full of booze and downers. A thin membrane seemed to hang there between them, trembling with their breathing. He reared back and ruptured the membrane with a bellowing roar that pierced their semi-consciousness.

John's face contorted. Instantly he began to pass out again.

Judy was trying desperately to focus her eyes. Her body jerked once spastically.

The vampire smacked John's face and shook him hard. He kept them both conscious until they were looking up at him in the dim and eerie light, but they could barely raise their arms to protect themselves.

Judy screamed, a look of terror on her face.

John struggled to his knees, grunting and panting and spitting at the edge of hysteria.

The vampire handled him as easily as he would a sleepy child. As John reached for the vampire's throat, he was forced to his back—a portion of the sheet was stuffed in his mouth. Another portion went into Judy's mouth. The vampire held her by the hair while straddling John's chest, pushing him down each time he tried to get up. Then, throwing his head back, the vampire howled again, baring his fangs and drooling and grunting like a beast above them.

He pulled Judy to her knees, put his foot in John's gut to hold him down, ripped open the front of Judy's fairy dress and sank the points of his fangs into her breast. He pulled her on top of her husband and held her head over his chest. Both struggled helplessly against the drug and the vampire's adrenalized strength. Before John's bugged-out eyes, the vampire sunk the fang-needles into Judy's neck.

He hung there like a heavy worm, sucking and gulping, drawing small drops of blood and lapping at them, then returning the suction to bleed her more, stuck like a leech, tasting the salt sweating out of her and the metallic smack of blood. The more he tasted, the more he wanted. The longer he hung there, the longer he wanted to remain, and he curled up in the profane heat like a child in dreams.

John was already going back under. The vampire heard their hearts beating above the whimpers and cries and utterances strangled with fear. He smelled Judy's odor, then John's—then the smell of the three of them. The taste of her neck, the blood, the sweat and heat of them spellbound and transfixed him. He heard moths batting against the screens. The pulsation of the crickets in the yard below flooded the room and throbbed inside and outside the room like a heart both inside and outside the body. The trees along the hedge below the window flurried, then hushed again. Judy and John slid beneath the narcotic. The vampire pulled his knees to his chest, embraced them both and lay curled there, sucking and lapping at Judy's neck.

Faintly, as though from beyond the yard, beyond the neighborhood, the vampire heard a cardinal whistle, then sing with the high-pitched chirping. Though still dark, the fringe of dawn stirred in his backbone. He shook Judy and John, waking them, and sprang to his feet on the bed. Both began to pant. They watched him, confused and helpless, struggling to their knees on the bed as unconsciousness tugged at their eyes, drawing them back under as their legs struggled to stay beneath them.

The vampire embraced their heads, pressing them to either side of his, then slapped their faces and sprang from the bed. He stood in the doorway to the balcony, let the wind blow his cape as he held it out, then screeched a terrible cry that widened the eyes of his victims. He climbed over the railing, took hold of the doubled hose in one hand and raised the cape with the other. As John Oswald stumbled toward the vampire and Judy knelt at the edge of the bed, trying to focus her eyes on the demon, the vampire leapt from the balcony into the night.

Grasping the hose with both hands, he swung under the balcony, slid to the ground and stood noiselessly in the shadows. He heard John's slurred and frightened utterances.

In less than a minute there were no sounds coming from above. The barbiturate had taken them back under. It was silent then except for the crickets. Clouds passed over the moon. Wind waved through the maples near the garage. A car passed a few blocks away.

When the wind stopped, the vampire heard John's heavy breathing.

He pulled the hose through the railing, wound it back on the spool and moved through the darkest shadows of the yard toward the alleyway behind the house, pausing along the way to urinate at the foot of the chaise lounge under the purple plum near the pool.

Sometime after noon the next day I was making coffee when the back door opened and Judy walked in.

"You are fucking strange!" she said. She was angry. She paced to the center of the kitchen, then returned to the place of her pronouncement. "What did you dose us with? And what in the fucking hell . . ." Her hands grasped at the air between us, then were flung violently downward. "John is still sleeping!" She paced again. "I couldn't even get a cup of coffee down him! What did you put in our drinks?"

"Some of your own medicine," I said, pouring the coffee.

"None of your cryptic bullshit, George! I want to know what you . . ."

"I was being literal," I said, "as I usually am."

"That'll be the fucking day! You're about as literal as you are subtle. It's outright melodrama! Like last night! Gothic fucking schmaltz!"

"Just playing with the recipe—a little magic, a little terror, a little sex, a dash of blood. By the way, you have . . ."

"What did you dose us with, damn it? I want to know!"

"By the way, you have the most full-bodied delicious blood I've ever . . ."

"George." She took a deep breath. "What did you dose us with?"

"Just some barbs you had in your medicine cabinet. I used to take barbs for kicks a long time ago. I knew how much I was giving you."

"Do you realize that John will be over here with the entire goddamn police force as soon as he figures out he wasn't dreaming, and you're having yourself a leisurely cup of coffee!"

"Would you like a cup?"

"What the hell is wrong with you? Are you serious? Are you insane? Are you sick?"

"Undead."

"I even bent the goddamn lamp back down, as though I was covering for you, as though John might actually think it was a dream!"

"I don't think he'll be coming over here today," I said. "I've been thinking about it, and I don't think so."

"You bit my fucking neck with something!"

"Just a flesh wound."

"You also bit my breast, you asshole! Who the fuck do you think you are, ripping my clothes off?"

"I only opened your dress. It was purely medical."

"You're crazier than hell, George. What are you going to do about this? Stand here and drink coffee? What's going to happen when the sultan opens his eyes and it's two o'clock in the afternoon, and the last thing he remembers is a vampire flying off the deck?"

I laughed.

"And how the hell did you fly off the deck, George?"

I laughed again. "Sorry, it's a funny image."

"I don't even know how much of it I dreamed."

"And John won't either. Besides, he's about to begin his campaign for mayor. Imagine what great press this would make if it got into the hands of the opposition. One party that wild can ruin a man's career. Not to mention what a good lawyer can dig up on a man to persuade him to stay out of court. None of it would look good, Judy—making a public scene and not going through with it—some weird story about drugs and vampires. No evidence, no motive, no nothing. The press would have a ball. So I don't think John will touch this right now. Later, yes. I'm sure he'll find a way to settle out of court, so to speak, but that's later. Now is now, and I see you've come without a crucifix."

I handed her a cup of coffee. She held it, glaring at me with her lips tightly pursed. I watched her lips, hoping for the beginning traces of that invisible smile.

"There's one thing I want to know," she said, "and I want to know now—no bullshit, no cryptograms, no mythology, no ancient texts. Did you fly from the deck?" Her lips wanted to smile.

"The vampire did," I said. "Vampires can do that. How 'bout some milk?" I offered her the milk carton.

"How did you fly off the deck, George? And no vampire bullshit "

"Milk?" I asked.

She held out her cup. *"How?"*

"I just did it. I flew. I surprised *myself*, really."

"You couldn't have possibly jumped from there. Did you have a rope?"

"I had a cape. I just pushed off and flew. I can if I want. You've seen it before. The cape spreads and turns into bat's wings, and that's it. It's simple."

"I'd also like to know which of all those pills you dosed us with. I haven't had so much fun in a long time." The smile finally broke into visibility. "I've never seen John so loose. Maybe those pills could improve our marriage."

"A potion of illusion evidently," I said.

The smile widened, and all was well.

"What does that mean?" she said.

"Eye of newt, twist of lemon. All that good shit. More cryptic bullshit. It was a recipe I got from those ancient texts I told you about. Basically the extract from a common berry native to Southeast Asia. I went to great pains to get it. While you were busy with your sister-in-law I was hard at work with the oracles."

"You're full of shit. I told you I don't want to hear about the ancient fucking oracles."

"The oracles said you'd come to me after the potion was administered, and here you are."

"And what did the oracles say I would do about your rude behavior and your disrespect for people's privacy?"

"They don't concern themselves with such things. They just said you'd do as I request."

"They did, did they?"

"And I request that you take charge here. Be decisive. And I request that you show the oracles some respect. They contain a knowledge that was brought back from the fringe of death, a place where you haven't been. Now do as I say and take charge."

"Isn't that a contradiction, Doctor?"

"Contradictions are legitimate, even kind of immaculate, according to the oracles. Come with me." I extended my hand.

"I thought I was in charge," she said.

"You are. I'm at your mercy." Taking her by the hand, I walked to the psychiatric couch and sat.

She stopped, still standing. "What did the oracle say I'd do with you?"

I sat back against the wall. "I don't want to hear about the oracle," I said. "Now we can simply consult *you* when we need to know what you want. So, do you want to do as I say and take charge here?"

"Does this all *mean* something, Doctor? Are we getting deep now? Are we role-playing our way into this contradiction?"

"Don't be alarmed," I said. "We'll come out the other side, and it won't have meant a thing."

"And you think I should do as I'm told?"

"Do as you tell yourself. Don't you see me twitching?" I twitched. "That twitch doesn't mean *I* need help—it means *we* need help. You do want to cut through all this superficiality. We're at least free to *think* whatever we please in the privacy of our own minds, aren't we? Let's take it from there. We can go anywhere from here. It's one place to begin. Talk dirty to me and take your clothes off, but take charge here, because I know what I'm doing, whether we believe it or not. Or would you rather I question my professional integrity, doubt my methodologies and regain some moral standards at a crucial time like this, when our health is at stake? How am I doing? Tell me about your dreams. How many times have you used the Lord's name in vain since your last confession?"

I kicked off my shoes. "When you get down to your panties," I said, "pick up that camera over there." I pointed to the Bell & Howell. "And shoot some film—and do it with feeling. I can determine many profound things from the nature of this film. As the film runs backwards in the projector I turn tarot cards and talk dirty to myself, drawing the seminal viscous secretion of the eternal spirit into my groin area. In general, the film will be very useful in your treatment."

I removed my shirt. "My obscene acts with the projector work to purify you. You are freed from the propaganda that separates all things, including life and death, and you submit to the pure, guileless, naive, unsophisticated, artless, simple, impeccable, brilliant admission of the perplexing, incalculable, imponderable, indeterminable, inconclusive, floundering, shilly-shallying, flexible, open-minded, open-ended, always questioning, ever changing, unfamiliar, unexplained, unexplored, incognizant quandary of the innocent terra incognita of the beautiful and truthful human soul. And you become responsible for your own acts. Because, when you come down to it, you either take off your clothes or you don't. Or . . . *you* can boss *me* around and see if I play along. Go ahead. You give me orders, and I can refuse to be told what to do and remain horny but with principles. What do you think?"

I took my pants off. "Would you like me to fall on my knees and plead? I mean, there are alternatives. I could get dressed, for example, instead of sitting here like a naked idiot, spouting the essential confusion of the universe. But first, take off your clothes and shoot some film. Then we can talk about it and begin some remedial process. How am I doing?"

She pulled off her shoes and socks. "Don't make me seduce you, Doctor." She stepped out of her slacks. "I won't report a word of this to the AMA." She unbuttoned her shirt and walked to the camera. "I won't do anything with this film that might incriminate you or threaten your practice."

As she took one arm out of her shirt sleeve she shot me from the hip with the other hand. She then switched the camera, removed the other arm, dropped the shirt and shot me from head to toe.

Before we were finished she used up fifty feet of film.

Meanwhile, the Doiflex behind the mirror shot selected scenes, my finger on the switch beneath the couch doing some creative in-camera editing. I used up most of the one-hundred-foot magazine.

Most of the footage Judy shot was of me. She tried to intimidate me with the camera at first, pausing to pass it across my body, but she couldn't resist involving herself in the event, and panned the camera across her body, being careful not to film her face. She eventually used the camera as a device that accentuated the pleasures of making love—a kind of mechanical voyeur. If I'd thought further I would have had the cassette recorder talk dirty to us.

I found a studio that would develop the film. I could also rent time there on the editing machine.

Weeks went by, and I never heard from Judy or her husband. I spent the time editing the film into seven action-packed minutes. When it was finished I spliced onto the beginning the best thirty seconds of the two perspectives of me doing my primitive dance as I stalked the mirror with the Bell & Howell.

I then took two cassette tapes of therapy sessions with Judy to a local campus radio station, told them I was a doctor of psychiatry, showed them my FCC operator's license and paid them a token fee to let me dub the cassettes onto a reel and edit the tape down to seven minutes. The result was a concentration of Judy's comments about her husband.

Under these comments, on a master tape, I mixed a recording of me typing the words "think anything" over and over for seven minutes. The typing provided a repetitious rhythm while the session tape droned on in a depressed monotone. In the background of the session tape, serving as a little extra texture, was the sometimes rhythmic, sometimes sporadic bouncing of the rubber ball.

The session began:

> *He really doesn't even like me that much. I'm not aggressive enough. I don't care to meet all the important people and impress them and pick their brains for how they might be of some use to me. I'm just a showpiece. I'm good-looking, stylish, a hostess for his parties, part of his public image—you know, handsome man with graying temples and beautiful younger woman. It cuts a good image for his career.*
>
> *When the last guest leaves the party I always want to leave with them, rather then stay to watch his shit-eating grin drop as the door closes and deal with his belligerent drunkenness.*
>
> *He's such a typical smalltime politician—thrilled with little crumbs of petty authority, always thinking about how his influence and clout and political decisions will benefit him, all the while putting forth this public servant bullshit. It's really disgusting to watch from the inside, making coffee for him and his cohorts while they plan the demise of Western Civilization.*
>
> *And I guess, as a result, I think so little of him, and less of myself for playing the game and pandering to this cold, calculating lizardlike creep. But it's a difficult situation after so long. I know his lawyers would leave me with nothing. That's a shitty way to think about it, but I do have to consider that. I've become somewhat dependent on this way of life. It's very comfortable and secure. But can you imagine living with someone who you feel this way about?*
>
> *But the real hook is, he's convinced me that I'd ruin his public image and destroy his career if I left him. He's big in the Catholic Church and all that hypocrisy—just for political purposes. A stable and forthright man has to be affiliated with a church—and all the other hypocrisies too—the country club, this shit, that shit. I can't stand any of it. A man is supposed to have a woman at his feet to*

bless his corrupt manipulations. You know, the family as moral facade.

It was quite funny when a check from one of his secret accounts bounced at the massage parlor and fell, by accident, into my hands. I wonder how they all avoid running into each other at those joints. Or maybe they go together, the priest too, and it's all a club, a joke, a big fucking joke. It makes me sick. That's exactly what it does— I'm a sick person from it all. I can't even go into the specifics of what he's involved in with this toxic waste dump. Now, on top of everything else, he walks around paranoid that the FBI is investigating him.

I need to take the cure. You have any potions for this?

I went back to the film studio and dubbed this soundtrack onto the magnetic strip on the film.

I taped a note to the reel that said, "Please playback on a sound projector."

I sent the film to John Oswald.

I had no copy.

On Monday, a few days after I mailed the tape, I received a letter from Judy. It was the first I'd heard from her since the morning after the party. It read:

I'm sure now that you're not a doctor but some bizarre imposter. I think I knew it all along but for some reason refused to admit it to myself. John used all his connections but could find no record of you in the AMA or anywhere else. He is positively insane with anger and strangely suspicious. No one has ever dared to outrage him so completely. I love it. The visitation of the vampire and the mickey you slipped us had him climbing the walls, but the film! The film was nearly the end of him. In fact, in a way, it was the end of him for me.

I left John the day after the film arrived—it got too weird. He got rough with me, and that was the end of that. He doesn't know where I am, and he won't for a long time. At the time I thought I would die, but now I've never felt better in my life. I feel relieved and freed and almost "cured," if you can believe that.

But listen—this is a warning, do not take it lightly: John is

> making the necessary arrangements to have you "dealt with," and I'm not kidding. He's an ugly man. In fact, several years ago he had a man "dealt with," so I don't doubt his intentions. My mention of the toxic waste deal on the soundtrack is apparently heavy shit, not to mention what the film alone could do to his career. The only reason he hasn't acted already is because, as you suspected, he's afraid to get involved with you, legally or otherwise, before his campaign—besides, he doesn't know who he's dealing with. He's so suspicious of you after being unable to find any records on you that he's actually hoping for a ransom note to arrive soon. It would relieve him to find out that this is only blackmail for money. He's been suspicious of you since that conversation in the diner about Laos and all that.
>
> I'm sure he'll go to every extreme to "tidy up," as he says. My advice is to move far away, give up psychiatry and go into porn films. You have a natural talent.
>
> Thanks for the good times and the exciting, if not authentic, Halloween.

The letter was typed and unsigned.

I took Judy's advice—I gave up psychiatry and moved, but I didn't move far away. I moved to Paterson where I rented the house from Mrs. Horney, who grew the yellow poppies. I stayed there until the hearing, until I was caught at Ellen's place. Then I moved here, to Newark, and started this purge of words, this bragging and lying, this spell against ghosts and pathogens, this sacred bullshit.

I've never heard from Judy or her husband or the police or any of Oswald's thugs. In Paterson I stayed invisible and nocturnal most of the time, and when I moved to Newark I took precautions to assure that it would be difficult to track me.

It wasn't long after leaving Angleton and psychiatry that I discovered the poppies, and that year went by in the nod of the head.

For a while I kept tabs on Oswald by visiting his house while he was at the office. I found out there that when Judy began divorce proceedings she let him know where she was living.

As much as I knew I had to stay away from her, I did visit her house a few times, once while she was sleeping. It was that night, while she slept, that I discovered the torn-up letter from John. It was funny. When his lawyers tried to cut Judy out of everything, she blackmailed John to get what she felt belonged to her, claiming that I'd given her a copy of the film. I loved it. I loved it so much it tortured me—I wanted to carry her away. Her face was so pale in the moonlight as she slept—but I dragged myself away.

I never did look for the woman who'd received my errant radio signal off the ionosphere—Diana Farley. I'm not sure I ever had any intentions of finding Diana Farley. I knew it couldn't be as simple as that.

13

I WENT BACK TO THE CEMETERY AT THREE IN THE MORNING and torched the bridge the day after it was built. I sat on the hill in the cemetary and watched it burn.

Since then the neighborhood has returned to its usual uneventful comings and goings. I've been avoiding Kelly's and anyone connected to the bridge building. I still see Willie once in a while.

The first hint of the end to this peaceful stay in Newark came through a woman who's preparing to open a shoe-repair shop across the street from my apartment. Last week Willie and I helped her unload a pickup full of benches, shelves and tools. I've talked to her on the street a few times since then, and a few days ago we took a ride to the shore together. We had a good time.

I've been expecting some shadow tailing me out of the past to find me here since the bridge building. Even though my face never appeared on TV, I didn't think I would get away with it. It was too indiscreet of me, too public, too lax, too casual, too easy, too benign, too charitable, too socially conscious of me—I knew better but I did it anyway. So I'm not surprised that the first woman I've felt comfortable with in a long time is the harbinger of what I fear will be a malignant tide.

I've been trying to work on the journal a lot lately, trying to trace the currents that left me washed up here in Newark, trying to fill in the gaps, sensing a time of lesser stability ahead, but it has been hard to avoid

Willie since the bridge building, so the writing has been interrupted by his frequent visits.

It was the day after we unloaded Susan's pickup that Willie came over in the morning. I was busy writing so I chased him away. "Get out of here!" I yelled through the door. "I'm busy!" He probably thought I was masturbating because he left without an argument, which is unusual, but he returned in the afternoon with two greasy tea bags and some stale bread.

We made some tea and toast, and I told him about how I'd lost my shirt in a poker game because some son-of-a-bitch took my drunk wife out in the yard and bumped uglies with her while I was playing.

"Bumped uglies!" he said. "Hee hee hee, that's a good one. That's when you were playing ball, huh?"

"Right," I said.

"Think you'll get married again some day?" he asked, walking to the typewriter.

When I didn't respond to his question he started reading from the paper that was rolled in the carriage. " *'You're so unsociable, man,' Sam said. 'We give you all these good drugs, and you want to leave right away. Here's the cash—now let me see the junk.'* " Willie rolled the carriage a little and continued. *"Sam was still grinning,"* he read, *"poised like a cat when I took Karen's father's .22 magnum from my pocket. The guy behind the chair went for his jacket pocket, and I aimed the .22 for the flesh of his thigh, but I couldn't fire. Sam had the handgun out of the desk drawer and aimed at my head. The courier kid was holding the child tightly. We stood and faced off like that, three pistols aimed and ready to fire."*

"You writing a drugstore novel or something?" Willie asked.

"Or something," I said. "I'm going to change that scene around though. I might try the skin-magazine market. Maybe I can make a little money."

"Drugs and guns—you got the right ingredients," he said. "This isn't from real life, is it? From when you were in the chips in Frisco?"

"Just making it up, Willie."

He sat in the stuffed chair. "Saw you talking to Susan a couple of times. She's a good-looking filly."

"So her name is Susan—I didn't even know."

"You don't work too fast, do you?" he said. "Name's Susan. I used to know her daddy, but not so well. Joe Bovenzi. He lived down neck. Had a shoemaker shop there. Italian guy. Married an Irish girl from Nutley. Susan looks like her mother. Her mother and my Maggie, rest her ornery soul, were both in the Rosary Society. I met her daddy at these church breakfasts that the women used to drag us to. They were good people. He was a good ball player, as I remember—built like Yogi Berra. I used to run into him in Branchbrook Park once in a while. But I don't know about this shoemaker shop across the street. People just throw their shoes away when they wear out these days."

"Not around here they don't," I said. "I'd bet they don't, or if they do it's because there's no shoemaker in the neighborhood. If she doesn't charge too much she might be okay."

"Maybe she will, maybe she will. Used to be one right around the corner. Two doors from the Blue Eagle. Joe Bovenzi had it. Used to run the sports tickets out of there. Everybody called him Jobenzi. Then he got arthritis and just ran the numbers for a while because he couldn't fix shoes no more. Then he picked up and moved out like a lot of people did. That place has been boarded up like it is ever since."

"Somebody told me that place was a barber shop," I said.

"Nah nah nah nah," Willie said, "never a barbers—wasn't *ever* a barbers. Barbers was two blocks down—Angelo's place—where it's all burnt now. Right there where it's all burnt." He pointed over his shoulder with his thumb. "Never at Jobenzi's place."

There was a knock at the door.

"Who the hell is this?" I said. No one ever comes to my door except Willie and the woman who runs the dry cleaners downstairs, and it was Sunday, so the cleaners was closed.

"I bet it ain't Rocky Colavito," Willie said.

I put my tea on the table and sat there, a queer feeling in my gut. I didn't know what to expect. If it was bad news I didn't want Willie in the middle of it.

"Want me to get it?" Willie asked.

"No," I said, "I'll get it." I prepared myself and opened the door. Susan was standing there. I invited her in and offered her some tea.

"I'd love some tea," she said.

"Million things to do," Willie said, "half a million things." He finished his tea and stood up.

"Thanks for the toast," I said.

"You bet," he said, closing the door.

"The reason I came," Susan said right away, "is because yesterday afternoon after you helped me with the truck load, two men kept driving past and looking up at your window. It was right after you went out—when you waved to me. They finally stopped down a block and waited there in the car. One of them had binoculars. They waited over an hour, looking at every man who walked by with the binoculars. It's none of my business, and I don't want it to be any of my business, and I hope you aren't offended, but I wanted to catch you in case you'd like to know. That's all."

I thanked her, explaining that the men came to collect my installment on a debt from an old poker game. I told her the men come around every three months, and after I give them a payment they go away.

"So it's no big deal or anything?" she asked. "You've dealt with them before?"

"It's fine," I assured her, "but thanks for telling me. Now I can have some cash on hand and get rid of them as soon as possible."

"I didn't like the look of them," she said. "They reminded me of men who used to come see my father once a month when I was in high school. So you have the money and all? I mean, can I help in any way? I don't mean to pry."

There she was offering me money after having talked to me only a few times on the street. She stayed over an hour, and I heard myself laughing over and over. It was a strange sound. She had the ease and good temper of a person who had removed a burden from her mind, radiating a kind of excitement that I haven't been around in a long time. After accumulating useless humanities degrees for fifteen years at three universities, now she wants to be a shoemaker in Newark. I have trouble understanding why a good-looking young woman would want to live in Newark. Everything has seemed strange since the second bridge was built.

"Aren't you wary of me?" I asked on an impulse.

"Wary of you? Why?"

I was tempted to give her a few reasons. "I don't know," I said. "Sometimes I feel like some kind of geek or something. You know, before this bridge incident, which I'm sure you've heard about more than a few times already . . ."

"I saw it on the news before I even got here. Then I found out it was built by people right here in this neighborhood. And you're right—I've heard it over and over from everybody I run into. In fact, I just heard today that Miles . . . Is that his name?"

"Miles. Right."

"Well, he reopened his disability case with the help of an ACLU lawyer."

"I know," I said. "That's great."

"You were saying?"

"I was saying that—"

"That you bite the heads off chickens," she said.

"Yes," I said. "A geek. There's no future in it. I think I need another degree."

She laughed. "Don't do it, really." More laughter. "Sorry. What were you going to say?"

"I was saying that, before I got involved with the bridge the people around here thought I was some kind of weirdo—I mean, they still do, and I still am. I don't talk to anyone besides old Willie Sykes. I don't have a job. I live in this one-room dump. I think weird thoughts. I don't . . ."

"I live in a one-room dump too," she said, "and we can think anything, can't we? I haven't worked a job in over a year. I had a winter rental on the beach, and I never spoke to anyone hardly."

"What did you do all winter?"

"I worked on my act."

"What kind of act?"

"Biting the heads off chickens," she said, laughing.

"What a twist of fate," I said. "Two geeks cross paths in Newark, New Jersey."

"Actually," she said, "I read, cooked great soups, played the violin, walked the beach and learned how to make and repair shoes with my father's tools—not much other than that."

"It must have been a nice winter. Maybe we could take a trip down the shore someday—if you like. It's nice down there now, and I need a few things. After Labor Day all the vacationers are gone and the water's still warm, as I'm sure you know. We could take a swim, go crabbing . . ."

"I'd love to do that," she said. "I really would."

"You would, huh?"

"I'd go tomorrow," she said. "You find that so strange?"
"I'm finding everything strange these days. Let's go tomorrow then. How about the shop, though? Don't you have a lot to do tomorrow?"
"I have everything still to do," she said, "but so what? *Hoy jugamos. Trabajeramos. Mañana,* man. *Mañana* for that."
"No savvy Spanish," I said.
"Today we play. Tomorrow we work," she said. "The guy I traveled with used it a lot in South America. It made him friends in the *cantinas.*"

In the morning we packed a lunch and started out for the shore in Susan's pickup. It was a clear day with a scent of autumn in the breeze. I approached thoughts that I felt I should both enter and depart from immediately as I watched her face, joking and jiving down the Garden State.

As we were approaching the shore area I saw a large bird in a tree along the Parkway. It shifted and raised its wings as we passed. I saw the white underbelly flash in the leaves. The dark posterior was broken up with more white at the side of the head. We passed so quickly that I couldn't be sure, but the bird looked like an osprey, a fish hawk that was once abundant in the shore area. I hadn't seen an osprey since I was a kid—so long that I didn't believe I'd seen one. Some other kind of hawk, I thought.

"Did you see that hawk?" Susan asked. "It looked like an osprey."
"I saw it," I said.
"There used to be tons of them when I was a kid," she said. "Their nests were in the dead trees along the river and the inlets near the bungalow my family used to rent for a month every summer. In fact, the telephone company had to nail branches to the tops of all the telephone poles so the ospreys couldn't build their nests there."

I remembered watching them catch fish when I was a kid. They'd fly inland toward the woods with fish in their talons.

"Incredible fishermen," Susan said. "I used to watch them come up from the water with big bluefish in their talons. It was always an amazing sight to me. I'd be in the back yard of the bungalow, hear that sound, look up, and in the sky an osprey with a fish would be flying, sinking a little in the air after each downward thrust from the weight of the fish.

I knew where a few nests were, and I used to go there often. There were fish bones all over the ground. As I got older I saw them less often. By the time I was thirteen they were gone. I think I started believing that the ospreys were only dreams flying in my childhood imagination."

"They were nearly killed off by poisons," I said.

"DDT," she said. "They used to spray it all over the place from these trucks to kill mosquitos. It caused the ospreys to produce eggs with thin rubbery shells. They couldn't reproduce. Now there's a ban on DDT."

"And now the blues are full of Chlordane," I said. "If the ospreys are back, it probably won't be for long."

"Just a brief remission you think, huh?"

"Bandaids on the corpse," I said.

We turned off the Parkway at Asbury Park and walked the boardwalk from Convention Hall down to where Madame La Rue's palmist booth stands during the summer. We looked in the windows at the old wooden carousel, then crossed the footbridge to Ocean Grove and bought some macaroons in the bakery there.

We drove further south, driving along the ocean when we could, past Bradley Beach, Belmar, Spring Lake, and when we stopped we swam in the ocean for an hour or so. The water seemed clean—no seaweed, no jellyfish, no briny foam where the waves rolled up on shore.

The trawlers were coming in the inlet, so we sat on the jetty and watched them turn into the mouth of the inlet and ride the swells. The sea made a gulping sound in the jetty rocks. The warmth of the sun and the smells of the sea and the dried salt on my skin filled my senses, forcing a turgid smile on my face as I squinted into the flecks of sun on the water.

"Where does the inlet go here?" Susan asked. "Do you know?"

"Into the river," I said. "Or, rather, the river goes into the inlet. There are lots of marinas back there. Then it winds up through marshes and into the narrows. It's fresh water back there. You can catch trout."

I suddenly thought of Juan. One more time I saw Doug getting wasted. I should have shut them up. Goddamned Juan jiving about home. It was bad medicine, thinking about home at a time like that. Doug's ghost was falling out of him anyway. Nothing could be done. Change the subject.

I spread out on a flat rock like a starfish, closed my eyes. Warm. Safe. Waves crashing. Gulls complaining behind the boats. My fingers clung to the rock—I felt the earth turning, and the texture of the rock and the sand as my feet stroked each other and the taste of salt on my lips and the beautiful and various sounds were not to be taken for granted. There was a chill in the air that made me realize there were apples on the trees. They would be a bit shy of perfection, when the first frost had them ready to drop off the tree, but some of the MacIntosh, especially, would be tart but sweet enough for eating.

I knew exactly where to go, and we set off on foot for the railroad tracks that, a few miles inland, pass one of the few wooded areas left in the region. Nestled in those woods were three orchards.

I found the groves of pine as I remembered them from childhood, their floors covered with seasons of needles and free of undergrowth, and I found the tangles of laurel and the fields of feed corn, some harvested, some left for the deer. I found the broad clearings where as a kid I moved cautiously, crouched and ready to run from the farmer or his Puerto Rican pickers. Though the clearings were exposed and risky to travel through, I was drawn into them by the waves of golden grass.

As the sun got low in the sky the breeze stopped and the wood was still. I moved out of the cover of the wooded perimeter and into the grass of the clearing. My instincts to return to cover were even stronger than when I was a kid, but I ventured out toward the center of the clearing. Susan turned around as she walked, gazing at the sky and the trees. "It's hard to believe we're in Jersey," she said.

When we reached the first orchard I remembered where all the different kinds of trees grew—the yellow delicious, the winesaps, the tart pie apples, the big apples that remained green all season—and I headed for where the best Macs grew.

We filled my shoulder bag with apples, found a soft place in the wood under some pines and opened our lunch. I could hear a few varieties of thrushes singing. A woodpecker knocked at a tree nearby. In the distance tiny sparrows chirped among the fallen apples.

The smell of apple blossoms in the spring would almost make me drunk as a kid romping through row after row of pink and white—it will never leave my senses—it's encoded in my genes. If I had children I'm sure their grandchildren would be haunted by vague indecipherable attacks of longing for the world as it once promised to be—a promise made with the intensity of an orchard full of blossoms.

"What do you think will happen with Miles?" Susan asked.

"I think he'll get enough money out of them to forget about working."

"I heard the second bridge burned down," she said. "It's too bad because the paper said since both ends were on private property there might have been a court battle over tearing it down."

"The Reverend was planning to use the courts to make a few public statements, but it would have come down. The second bridge was way the hell up the canal. The city bridge is closer to Miles's place. It doesn't matter if it's burnt down. What mattered was building the bridge. Miles should be able to get a specially equipped car out of the deal if he's got a smart lawyer. Plus the bus stops there every day now, whether he's out there or not. And he can work The Embers any time he wants because he's a local celebrity. The Embers even got some publicity out of the deal."

"How did you get involved?"

"Through Willie. He asked for some help. They could have been hassling with the city council over that bus driver for a year. The bridge was just absurd enough to make the news, though I wasn't really thinking that way at first. It was just instinct or something—an irrational kind of head-on maneuver. It just seemed right. I couldn't think about it much. I suppose they couldn't have thought about it much, either. It was a good team. But I really think it was the music that did it. When that black choir started wailing the blues with Miles's piano behind them, the power just couldn't be denied. I was watching the camera crews and the journalists. They didn't know what the hell to record next. The music just moved the whole issue into an emotional area that couldn't be argued with rationally, and I swear the spirit of Alvin Johnson himself got up to boogie. It was amazing stuff. The Reverend doing the boogaloo at the foot of Alvin's grave took the issue right out of the hands of the law or the Marine Corps or the city council or the idiot bus driver. The Reverend knew, he knew it was working—he was inspired—like the spirit of the Lawd entered him."

"I can't believe that bus driver wouldn't stop," Susan said. "What the hell is wrong with people?"

"I can believe it. Too much trouble. Maybe Miles ripped him off one time. Maybe Miles took his girl. Maybe he sold the guy some bad dope, raped his sister, beat on his brother. Who knows? Then maybe the bus driver's just an asshole. That's certainly possible."

"What do you think of Miles?"

"I don't know Miles," I said. "He seems like a nice guy."

"You don't know him? I guess I was assuming you were friends."

"I saw a lot of him around the time we were building the bridges, but I never really talked to him much. I don't even think Willie knows him very well. I'm not sure who knows him."

"I just figured you were friends—him being your age, and both of you vets."

"Who says I'm a vet?"

"Willie told me."

"Willie? I never told him that. He was pulling your leg, sister."

"He said you were wounded, too."

"Ha! What a jerk he is."

"You're not a vet?"

"No. Only in Willie's imagination."

"I saw a scar when we were swimming."

"That ain't from no war."

"What's it from?"

"From when I wrecked my '53 Chevy near Mendocino."

"Willie's not so dumb, you know. He's not dumb at all."

"I know he's not."

"Well." She bit into an apple.

"Well, what?"

"Well, why would he tell me that?"

"I was probably telling lies to him one day, and I told him I was in the war. I've told a lot of lies around Newark. When Willie's not around I lie on the typewriter."

I threw a half-eaten apple away and leaned back on my elbows. I turned to look at her face, which I hadn't been able to stop doing all day. She was looking toward the sky.

"Look!" she said, pointing up.

"I'll be damned," I said. I shielded the sun with my hand. Through the gap in the tree branches we saw an osprey flying.

"It's beautiful," she said.

"What kind of fish is that?" I asked.

"I can't tell," she said.

"It's not a blue. I'll be damned."

"They're big," she said.

When the hawk passed behind the branches she looked at me, her face beaming with a smile. "How 'bout that," she said. "Maybe it's a good sign."

"Maybe," I said. "There must be a way we could see it as a bad sign."

She laughed. "I guess we could think of a way."

"We could," I said. "Maybe it means they're gonna start spraying DDT again."

"You're a delightful fellow." She looked me square in the eyeballs. "Maybe we could steal some more apples before we go."

"We should. We should also stop on the way back to steal some tomatoes."

"Where can we get tomatoes?"

"We passed a place along the tracks," I said. "It's in a-ways. You wouldn't have noticed it. We'll have to be careful. It's near the house."

"I'd love some fresh tomatoes," she said. "Free fresh tomatoes."

"There're three things you can't get any better anywhere in the world—Jersey tomatoes, Jersey apples and Jersey sweet corn."

"And Jersey sub sandwiches," she said. "That's the lot of it."

"That's right. God, I know where we could get a classic sub not too far from here."

"Really?" she said. "Where?"

"Sorrento's in Spring Lake. You can't get a better sub anywhere."

"Better than Scotellaro's?" she asked.

"Where's that?"

"Right in Newark! You've never been there?"

"I've never heard of it," I said.

"You're kidding! I've got to take you to Scotellaro's. Best I've ever had. The real imported prosciutto."

"The real stuff, huh?"

"All of it. Besides, the guy's a regular poet. You have to check it out."

"Scotellaro, huh?"

"Rocky," she said.

"Rocky?"

"Rocco," she said.

"Rocco Scotellaro," I said. "A real poet of the sub, huh?"

"He's a kick, really," she said. "He has the glass of guinea red next to the slicing machine. He stares hazy-eyed out the window between slices of provolone, having visions of essential reality. Then he harangues his customers about their insensitivity to this or that. 'You Americans take too much for granted!' he yells. He's only eight years off the boat. 'You people are too passive, too comfortable, like sheep in the pasture. You do not love your country enough to hate it!' He goes on and on like that. But my God, what a sub! And people keep coming in, abuse or not. They wait in line and laugh at him behind his back. There's something about that oil and vinegar dressing that's distinctive, and all the ingredients are top quality. It's just a little dive. I'll take you there."

"The essential sub, huh? Through the creation of which the artist glimpses . . ." I raised my arms in an all-encompassing gesture. "Glimpses what?" I grasped at the air. "What is it he glimpses with his eyes cast up over the slicing machine and his face like a Giotto fresco, rapt in that special Florentine spiritual awe? The essential what?"

"That's what he glimpses," she said. "The essential What, which somehow, through devotion, no doubt, enhances that dressing, and the result is no ordinary sub. I kid you not."

"I'm not sure Tony Sorrento can compete," I said.

"I really doubt it," she said.

On the way back up the tracks we sneaked into the farmer's field and picked a dozen tomatoes. We sat between the rows and ate one, comparing spaghetti sauce recipes. She never showed any fear of being caught or chased but hunkered down in the plants eating and whispering with excitement. I noticed that her ears were sensitive to the same sounds that I scanned for possible alarm. I couldn't keep my eyes off her face; she seemed as unconscious of herself as the plants around her. Lithe, athletic, weird.

"Sagittarian, no doubt," I said.

"No, Catholic," she said, smiling wide. "How about you? Pisces?"

"No, feces," I said.

She started laughing uncontrollably, covered her mouth with her hand and rolled onto her back. I played up and down her ribs with my fingers to help things along.

When she stopped laughing long enough to speak she said, "What else can we steal?" This woman was all right.

It was dusk when we got back to Newark. I heated some leftover potato soup. We ate at the table by the front window. Newark was quiet. We could hear the jukebox throbbing faintly from the open door of Kelly's Tavern.

After we ate I poured some homemade cherry liquor from a quart canning jar, and we climbed out the side window onto the fire escape. The sky was still gray and smudged with pink in the west. The streetlights came on, somehow softening the cityscape. Beyond the angular rooftops and chimneys in the hazy wash of gray, the glow of neon accented the subtle hues of the muted sunset. The occasional car horns and a distant siren were almost musical.

"Where does the Passaic begin?" Susan asked.

"In the Great Peace Meadows," I said. "I guess it seeps out of the ground—the water table surfaces. You know all those swamps and ponds out near Parsippany or somewhere?"

"Here we go again, but it must be incredibly polluted," Susan said.

I laughed. "Now you've gone and ruined the romance—just when I was going to ask you to walk with me over to the river bank and sit under those willows." I pointed to piles of junk metal along a wire fence in a warehouse yard near the river canal.

"If you can see those piles of junk as willows, I'm not going to worry about ruining the romance," she said. "What do you see the river as?"

"A wound bleeding poison back into itself . . . a heat-seeking missile coming at us from deep space inside ourselves . . . a white blip on the horizon."

Susan looked at me and said nothing, though her eyes were trying to speak. She looked back to the river. "Very romantic," she said. "Are we obsessed with poison today or what?"

"We are saturated with poison," I said. "It doesn't make for great conversation."

She fell silent, looking at the ground between her legs, which hung over the edge of the fire escape.

"It's been on my mind a lot," I said, "partly because there's a waste dump nearby, over in the Ironbound section. They store dioxin there, one of the most deadly substances man has yet created. This particular dump is the by-product of the manufacture of agent orange. They don't know what to do with it. Though the authorities deny it, some people think it's seeping into the environment, into the Passaic, into the water supply, back yards, swimming pools, vegetable gardens, canneries—you name it—into the essential submarine sandwich."

"How do you know this?"

"God told me. It's the revealed word of God. In the beginning there was the word, and the word was death. Death was nature, and nature was decay and indifference. And man hated nature and went about controlling it and destroying it with poisons and gas-powered lawn repressors. Man declared war on crabgrass. And now that nature is poisoned, it truly and obviously is a threat, so man hates it even more."

"Enough abstract oversimplification. How do you know about this seepage from the waste dump?"

"I've been looking into it. People are making money off it, I suspect. There's big money in toxic waste. It's cost effective to keep everything hushed."

"Is that what you do in your spare time—investigate toxic waste dumps?"

"I've come across some information," I said. "I have reason to believe that extremely poisonous substances wind up along miles of state highway, spilled from the open valves of trucks."

She sighed heavily and sat back against the building.

"There's big money in poisoning ourselves," I said.

"Tell me something I don't know," she said. "Tell me about the willows on the river bank." She pulled her knees to her chest and looked away. "All things die."

"Tell me something *I* don't know," I said.

"Well, we don't have to dwell on it."

"You're right. In fact, there must be a way it could be a good sign," I said, recalling the osprey we'd seen fly over.

"I guess we could think of it that way," she said.

"I often feel like an agent dispatched in a foreign land with no specific assignment," I said.

"You don't have a cigarette stashed somewhere, do you?" Susan asked.

"I have some tobacco and some rolling papers," I said.

"That'd be great."

"I'll get them." I climbed through the window and went to a drawer for the Prince Albert and the papers.

"A secret agent, huh?" she said as I climbed back through the window.

"Yeah," I said, "but I don't even know what I'm supposed to be doing here. It's like they erased my memory and dropped me here. 'Let's observe what he does,' they say in the think tank, 'see if he adjusts, if he infiltrates instinctively. Plant a bug on him and let him behave as if he were free. We can learn a lot that will help us in the future with more serious investments into peoples' lives. He will be our prototype of the Free Man Unit. From him we will learn where to point our genetic engineers.'"

"Sounds like lapses into acute paranoia to me," Susan said. "Besides, it's been done already in a number of sci-fi novels."

"Damn! I was hoping to sell the idea to the film industry, make a lot of money, move out to the real world in the burbs, put in a swimming pool, a gas barbecue and live like a—"

"This *is* the real world, damn it!" she said, jerking her head toward the street.

—"And live like a white man," I continued.

"You can have it." She looked away toward the river.

"And keep you locked on a chain long enough to reach the microwave."

"Fuck you!" she said, then smiled with her eyes flooded, then cried, then laughed, wiping her tears on her shirt sleeve.

"I was kidding," I said.

"I know you were kidding. What the hell is wrong with us?" She popped open the can of Prince Albert.

"I wouldn't worry about it."

We were silent as she filled a paper with tobacco and rolled it up. She lit the smoke and inhaled deeply, leaning back against the building.

"I'm frightened because I don't want to get away from you after an hour," I said. "I hope that's okay. I really don't want to get in the way of whatever you have planned for yourself here."

"I didn't come here to be alone," she said. "I came here because I was alone. I want to fix shoes, work with my hands, live simply among simple people. Why should we be apologetic about liking each other! There's something awfully sad about us."

A car had stopped out front. We could see the back half sticking out from the corner of the building. The brake lights were on. Susan stared intently at the car.

"That looks like the same car I was telling you about," she said, "the men with the binoculars."

I heard two of the car doors open and close. I climbed through the window and switched on the lamp on the table. Susan came up behind me and looked out.

"That's them," she said. "I'm sure of it."

The two men looked up, saw the light in the window, got back into the car and drove off.

"What was that all about?" Susan asked.

"I'm not sure," I said. "As soon as the lamp went on they headed back to the car."

"Who are they?"

"I'm not sure."

"The guys from the poker game?"

"Maybe."

"Why didn't they come up? It gives me the creeps. They thought you weren't home at first—that's what happened. Why would they come up if they thought you weren't home?"

"I'll take care of it tomorrow," I said. "Want some more cherry stuff?"

"Sure." She took a seat at the table, still looking out the window. "I was telling you that I didn't come here looking for solitude. I really don't want to try to explain—I'm getting tired of explanations. But you're not disturbing a dream for an austere life as a shoemaker in Newark, despite the way it may seem."

"I'm not?" I poured us each some cherry liquor. "I guess I'm just having a little trouble with all this," I said. "I've felt like . . . I don't know, a potato or something for so long . . . just lying in a dark drawer being dusty and vegetablelike and tuberous and slothful and bland."

"All that?"

"And more. Lots of sluggish adjectives—a warehouse of undesirable qualities."

"Well, I don't find potatoes bland. I love potatoes. They're one of my favorite foods. Perhaps you are more like an eggplant."

"The eyes of potatoes are poisonous."

"The theme of the day. Tell me how bad you are for me."

"They are poisonous, aren't they?"

"Wive's tale. Or actually it's probably a husband's tale. Women know more than that. Let's look up the derivation of that phrase. I bet it was a man who came up with it."

"A househusband, perhaps," I said.

"It's a househusband's tale," she said.

"I've always thought the eyes are poisonous. Are you sure? I think they are."

"Did you cut them all out before making your soup?" she asked.

"I always do," I said.

"You're kidding!"

"No, really."

"You know, they used to think tomatoes were poisonous, too," she said.

"Iodine is still poison, right?" I said.

"Iodine is essential for good health," she said.

"I bet you could drink a goblet of the assassin's poison and laugh in his face," I said. "Are you a mythical creature who has come to give me three tests?"

She laughed and poured another glass for each of us. "No tests," she said, "please. No damn tests."

14

ALMOST THREE MONTHS HAVE PASSED SINCE THEN, AND I haven't seen Susan once. So much for romance amid the ruins.

I probably should have left Newark when those goons showed up— I should have moved on again—but this time moving seemed out of the question. I stayed to confront the goons, as though the battle had suddenly become territorial and therefore newly significant. And, though the feeling hadn't quite jelled at the time, I realized I wanted to spend more time with Susan.

The goons were Oswald's goons, as I suspected. It took him a long time to find me. Oswald is more obsessive than I figured. Even the fat man from the poker game probably found forgiveness in his beefy heart eventually, unless he just gave up looking for me. Oswald is a more insidious animal—Dr. Excitement wanted his ass.

It's quiet here most of the time, and there are people around to entertain me. I have a lot of time on my hands to put the fragments of this tale together, and I'll remain here until I recount what happened with Oswald's goons, then I'll leave, though I'm not supposed to leave.

They're finished putting the electric back into me, and they've left me alone, mostly because I've left them alone. I'm supposed to be more passive now, and maybe I am.

Dr. Excitement may have gotten too out of hand in the delirium of paint asphyxiation. Maybe I suffered some minor brain damage—it's hard for me to tell. Before I was able to recover from the paint, I was delirious from thorazine and, later, from the electric.

Evidently I caused some problems when I sneaked off the ward in the hospital, found the intensive care ward in the middle of the night, and was found chanting some ridiculous hocus-pocus over a dying patient. It was described in the report as "irrational, repetitive raving and delirium." I have no doubts.

I feel kind of silly about that. It was unimaginative, but I guess it was the best I could come up with under the circumstances. They moved me over here to the state facility for thirty days observation, which resulted in electroshock therapy. I can't remember all the details.

Then a month ago I was released to this less restrictive area of the institution. I've made up for lost time.

I'll continue to play their game for a while. I'm now allowed to walk the grounds during the day. I can blow this place anytime I want to—no problem—but as I said, I intend to stay for a while. I get three meals a day, and there's no responsibility, and the drugs provide a state of mind that allows for some interesting psychic experimentation, and the doctors are alert and dedicated subjects for these experiments. Even the food is decent if I don't expect much.

This morning I was walking the long winding path through the green on my way to the alameda, where I like to sit and watch my fellows. At a bench under some trees I came upon some outsiders with a box of brownies. They were offering a brownie to this guy from my ward.

I walked up and looked blankly at them, swinging my gaze from face to face, moving close enough to break the bubble of accepted social distance, shoving them into a psychological disadvantage. Out of awkwardness and some noticeable fear they offered me a brownie. I took it, feigning clumsiness, and remained silent. I took a larger than acceptable bite, fulfilling their expectations, stuffed the remainder into my pocket and reached into the box for another. I took three.

"Save some for Steven," the man said, talking to me as though I were a child. "We brought these brownies for Steven."

"Fuck Steven," I said and reached for another. "Steven hates nuts in his brownies. You know that."

Steven did not seem concerned. He was rocking back and forth on his heels, his chin on his chest, his lips pursed, his eyebrows fluttering around his fat face like two moths around a light bulb.

I grabbed the box of brownies and stood fast with an intimidating look. "For how much of this mess are you two responsible?" I said, extending my hand toward Steven. I pivoted sharply and came back here.

The brownies are good brownies—not from a mix.

In a few hours I get another meal.

I have all the paper I can fill up.

They gave me this big dull pencil like kids get in the second grade. I suppose it's so I don't stab myself or somebody else. They think it's good for me to write. Good therapy or something. The assholes. Right now I'm being watched again—observed, rather—by one of the resident shrinks. The white shrink I call him. He seems to have a special interest in my case. At first I thought he was gay. Then three times he asked if he could see what I write with my big dull pencil that I can't stab him or myself with. I gave him a flat no. It's driving him crazy. I don't know what he expects to find. Yes, I do. Something he can "analyze" for a publication credit in a professional journal or for his book on fucked-up vets that the black shrink told me about. I should slip him a dissertation on The Bouncing Ball Therapy. But the less the shrinks know the better. He'll probably try to commandeer the papers eventually, or he'll steal them when I'm not around. Then I'll have to start an issue about patients' rights and throw a tantrum—or I'll kick his fucking ass all over the fucking ward. This fat pencil could easily be sharpened into a better weapon than a regular pencil. As if I need a weapon to waste the bastard. Or myself.

But I should calm myself—be more passive—sit back and stir the soup and relax. The white shrink is not worth the hassle. When I'm ready I'll just walk into those woods I can see from this barred window, out across the well-kept grounds, and be gone like some apparition.

As far as I can tell I'm paying only one price for my room and board here. The white spot has returned to my throat. It's been so long I thought it was gone forever, but that's naive I guess. They conjured it with their electric. So my stay here can't be too long. In time I'll have to leave to start the ritual again to remove the electric.

I'm confused about that right now, but in time my head will clear. I don't know whether I'll have to go back to L.A. for the ritual to work, and I can't really remember what state of mind I was in then, or whether it's even necessary to get back to that state for the ritual to work. I don't even know anything about how the ritual worked in the first place, and I'm having a hard time imagining going through that routine again. Just beginning seems difficult now—like trying to remember the way to a place I've never been. But in time my head will clear.

The white spot has gotten bigger already since the day I noticed it. Sometimes I think the ritual worked because of the time and the place —the era—all that crazy energy all over the globe at the time. The universe was receptive to such things then. The state of unrest is the state of potential. Maybe I can think of some other way to deal with it this time.

But for now, I have some time on my hands and a box of brownies —and I need some rest—so I'll scrawl on with my big dull pencil.

The morning after Susan and I saw the car stop out front I bought a gallon of bright orange paint, a large bottle of glycerin, a roll of duct tape and a can of insecticide with a high-powered spray nozzle, the kind house painters use to exterminate nests of bees and wasps without getting too close. The nozzle fires a stiff beam of poison about ten or fifteen feet.

I got home in the late morning. There were no goons in sight. I went inside, cut paper bags, taped them together with duct tape and covered all the windows with three layers of the brown paper. I ran the tape around the edges to prevent any light from entering.

I then mixed the orange paint and the glycerin in a washtub and lifted it into the bathtub. When I'd finished there were still no goons in sight, so I slipped away and spent the day in Paterson walking along the Passaic and drinking in a tavern called the Italian Sports Club. It was the same place I drank that morning before the preliminary hearing on the assault charges. The same men were in there playing the game with painted wooden cards.

At about four o'clock I went to Angleton and waited until John Oswald got home from the office. I was behind the hedge, not twenty feet away when he got out of the car.

"Oswald," I called from behind the hedge.

He stopped and turned around. "Who's that?"

I kept hidden and called, *"Nghe dây,* Major. Say *chu hoi.* Call off your goons."

He ran for the house.

I went back to Newark, sat in Kelly's and had some Dickel.

At about eight I headed home through an alley. From a block away I peeked out and saw the same car turn the corner and pull over down the block from my place. I backtracked a few blocks, crossed the street, went down an alley to the back of Susan's shop and broke in.

I watched from the window of the shop as one of the men went up the stairs to my place. In ten minutes he returned to the car with a stack of papers in his hand—my journal. They sat in the car smoking and reading the journal.

I went down a few blocks, crossed the street and worked my way to the back of my building, then climbed up the fire escape and through the window to my apartment, being careful to tape the brown paper back to the window frame.

I stripped naked and shaved my head. I then stirred the paint and glycerin mixture, stood in the washtub and covered my entire body, even my eyelids, lips and the insides of my ears. The glycerin would keep the paint from drying so I could wash it off when the deed was done.

I peeled back the corner of the paper window cover on the front window, switched the lamp on, waited a few minutes, then taped the cover back to the window frame.

I heard the goons at the front door downstairs. They climbed the stairs together and knocked. I called for them to come in, then moved quickly to the wall so I would be hidden behind the door when it opened.

When both were inside I slammed the door shut, bolted both locks, walked casually to the table, picked up the lamp, removed the shade and smashed the light bulb against the table. It was pitch dark. I moved quickly and silently to a corner of the room, became still and turned off the brain signals. I smiled thinking about the expressions on the goons' faces as they watched the orange creature cross the room full of the junk constructions I'd made—the bolts, buckles, chains, hooks, washers, covered with foil or painted or left rusty, hanging from door frames, light fixtures, hooks in the ceiling, cluttering the table, window sills, shelves, radiator—so much detail in the creature's sanctum that nothing could be discerned.

With the light gone the goons were silent for a moment. I knew they didn't know what to do in the dark. And my bones weren't even there to be broken—I was gone, diffused in the dark.

"Find the lock," the one closest to me said.

"What the fuck is this?" the other one said.

Their voices gave me a fix. I moved closer.

"He's just some goddamn nut," the near one said. "Find the lock!"

As he moved clumsily toward the door I pictured him in the dark with his arms outstretched, groping for the door. I skirted the near man, moved in on the other, calculating the distance by sound and smell and the lizard sensory discs activated in my temples. When I was close enough to smell his nervous sweat I kicked to his ribs. He grunted loudly, fell to the floor, cursed and moaned. I moved silently to the far corner, stilled myself, then moved in on the other man from behind. I could plainly hear his heavy breathing. I had him pinpointed when I heard the man I'd kicked climbing to his feet, broadcasting his position.

I struck the man near me. It felt like I caught him on the back near the shoulder blade. I dropped quickly to a squat. He turned and fired what sounded like a .22 pistol. The flash illuminated him for a split second. I came up into his guts with a hard blow. He stumbled back, and I kept after him until I sensed his position, then kicked for the heart. He went down hard. I moved quickly for the other man, who was groping at the bolts on the door.

I mauled him as he stumbled backward, blow after blow, homing in on my target as though I could see in the dark.

Then, as I turned to go back at the other man, I *could* see him—a luminescent outline—though there was no light in the room. I couldn't see my own fists, yet I saw the man glow like a VC river craft through an electronic Starlight Scope. He was crouched down like a panicked animal, his eyes straining to cut through the blackness all around him. I walked up and kicked him in the face.

When I switched on the light, both men were curled up in a foetal position. They were marked with blotches of orange paint. Where the paint marked their faces it was mingling with blood. They both stared at me wide-eyed and frightened.

"Agent Orange is here," I said. "No fucking joke either. Not funny, right?"

The handgun was on the floor by the door. I tossed it out the back window. They had no other weapon. I went to the bathroom to touch up the paint where it had been rubbed off in the fight. The paint was settling enough to not smudge. I was a weird sight in the mirror—bald and glistening and empty in the eyes. I felt like a microscopic germ, a bacterium, a translucent orange worm—the burning corpse stared back at me, smoldering, dizzy. I knew my system was under stress from paint clogging my pores. I would have to act quickly.

I demanded the car keys from the men on the floor, and one produced them rather painfully. I took the high-powered insecticide in hand, walked across the street naked and orange and sped off on my way to Angleton.

Willie Sykes was standing on the corner by Kelly's with his mouth open, trying to confirm what he thought he saw under the glow of the streetlights. I'll never forget the look on his face when I passed. "Gotta tryout with the Cubs!" I yelled from the car.

The journal was jammed in the glove box. I stopped by a warehouse that was burned in the riots and stashed the journal there. There was a cop parked around the corner from the mayor's house. Oswald must have gotten nervous after my visit.

I made my way through five back yards, getting giddy and lightheaded as I went. I felt like when I used to paint my face green in the Jungle of Darkness, up to my knees in water, my feet in sucking mud, wrestling with the dense jungle to avoid daisy chains of grenades on the trails. I felt like I'd changed camouflage color to suit the environment—green for the jungles, orange for suburban Jersey. I think it made sense at the time, though I remember laughing out loud as I crossed Oswald's back lawn, peed at the foot of the chaise lounge and knocked at the door.

As he opened the door his mouth dropped, and I filled it with a blast of insecticide. He choked severely, unable to breathe, and stumbled backwards. As soon as he regained his breath I blasted him again. The power of the spray was devastating at that close range.

"Exterminator," I called, announcing myself. "Here to extinguish maggots, purge lice, ticks and bloodsuckers, eliminate cockroaches and terminate petty crooked politicians and vermin of all kinds."

Oswald covered his face and backed into the kitchen.

A man ran at me from another room with a fireplace poker raised over his head. I disarmed him, dropping the insecticide. When I went for the can to give him a blast, he got to his feet more quickly than I expected—probably limber from playing tennis at the country club—and ran out of the house. I realized my reflexes were arrested. I turned and blasted Oswald again.

"What the hell do you want?" he choked. "I have money in the safe. There's over four thousand dollars in cash."

"Neither money nor good sour mash whiskey will deter me from my mission," I said, "but if you have some George Dickel in the house I might have just a taste in a tumbler."

With the mention of George Dickel he tried to focus his eyes on me through the flood of tears. I was spaced-out by then, experiencing some kind of precognition, hearing my words before I spoke them. I knew what Oswald would say before he spoke, or my perception was distorted enough by the paint to cause this illusion. I heard him say, "The liquor cabinet's in the dining room under the jade urn," but after I'd dragged him into the dining room I could find no jade urn. As he struggled to his feet I blasted him twice and he ran to the liquor cabinet and opened it. I blasted him again, and he crawled away.

"No Dickel!" I said, sweeping the bottles onto the floor. "A man of your resources!"

He wiped his eyes on his shirt and squinted at me. "Who are you? What do you want from me?" The whites of his eyes had turned bright red. He kept spitting in the carpet.

"I'm Leroy," I said. "Remember Leroy? Only now instead of black I'm orange. What I want from you is some George Dickel. Is that a lot to ask?" I blasted him again.

He covered his mouth and spit and coughed. "I know who you are —you're the same goddamn barbarian who . . ."

"Shut the fuck up, you asshole." I held my finger on the trigger and gave him a long blast. "I told you to call off your goons, didn't I?" I was getting delirious, following him with the spray as he crawled around covering his face with his hand. "I am the by-product of the manufacture of you," I yelled. It sounded like someone else had yelled it. I looked around the room to see if someone else was there. No one. I squatted next to Oswald and aimed the insecticide at his face. "Now be still and listen, Major. *Nghe dậy.* Quick quiz before the law arrives and I have to disappear. First question."

Oswald rubbed his eyes, propped himself on his elbow. He was going to try to reason with naked orange Dr. Excitement—or at least stall.

"I'll give you a question that's right up your alley," I said. "I've done my homework on you. Here goes. Now this is purely economics, Major, so don't get all defensive about the goddamn war again. Listen hard. After we spent one hundred and forty thousand dollars for every North Vietnamese soldier killed with B-52 bombing of the Ho Chi Minh Trail —this is 1967, Major—that's one soldier for every three hundred, seven-hundred-pound bombs—what did strategists do to improve the kill ratio? Tic, tic, tic, tic . . ."

"Electronic warfare," Oswald said.

"You have all the answers, don't you, Major Mayor? You understand it all. Well I don't—*tôi không hiểu.*"

I moved the insecticide closer to his face. "Now, Major, give me an example of electronic warfare."

"The sensors developed for the McNamara Line," he said.

"Right again—the People Sniffers. Good, Major. I'm glad you brought this up. I *love* the People Sniffers. I love gadgets. My room is full of gadgets. This is a great example. We pump millions into the Jason Group Think Tank to devise gadgets like People Sniffers, which cost a few million more to manufacture and install on the bellies of choppers. Now, next question. How did People Sniffers work and what was the result? I *love* this."

"They could detect the presence of people from the ammonia in their waste," he said, coughing, eyes pressed closed.

"They sniffed enemy shit and piss, right, Major?"

"Yes."

"And what was the result?"

"They weren't very effective, though they did increase the kill ratio somewhat."

"Wrong." I let him have a good blast. "Now, what was the result? Answer: The B-52s dropped their seven-hundred-pound bombs on anything that shit and pissed, including animals and civilians. So I guess you're half right—the kill ratio did increase. I take back half of that last blast. But this isn't the good stuff. This next question is the good stuff. This is when I started looking at myself differently in the mirror. What did Uncle Ho do to counteract the People Sniffers? You have five seconds."

Oswald coughed and spit, his head turned away from me.

"Well, what?" I said. "Tell me, Major. This is the good part."

He tried to say something through the gagging.

I aimed the insecticide at his mouth. *"Ban da noi gi?"*

He dropped his head, his forehead on the floor. I told him to sit up, and he brought his head up again.

"Buffalo piss, you asshole," I said. "Bags of water buffalo piss hung in unused parts of the trail network. Uncle Ho made a gadget to attract bombs. That's what was bombed along the Ho Trail. Buffalo piss, Major. Don't you love that? This is our mightiest conventional weapon! The B-52 can drop a hundred bombs in thirty seconds, cutting a swath a mile long and a quarter-mile wide! That's quite a gadget Ho made. That's when I first wanted to learn to make gadgets."

He wagged his head from side to side as he spit on the carpet. He shrugged his shoulders and wagged his head. "What the hell do you want from me?"

He was feeling his officer's bravado, and it made me want to vomit. I blasted him, then felt something at my back—a light or a wind or something looking at me. My head was swimming from the paint. The room wavered like a heat mirage on the highway, and I drove toward it. A policeman stood in a doorway with a pistol drawn. I steered away from him and blasted Oswald. "Incoming!" I yelled, then a sharp pain above my ear. I dropped to my knees, my muddled head suddenly clear from the rush of adrenalin caused by the blow.

The cop was about to handcuff me when I put him on the floor, pulled his arms behind him and handcuffed him. Another cop appeared in the doorway with a shotgun trained on me. I put my hands behind my head. *"Chu hoi, chu hoi,"* I yelled.

He came toward me with handcuffs.

"Chât dôc," I said. "It's only fair to warn you—just getting close to me is enough to endanger your life, just breathing my stink. Look at Oswald there, and I never even touched him."

He looked at the other cop on the floor, keeping the shotgun pointed at my chest. He put the cuffs back on his belt and told me to walk to the car. He stayed a few feet behind, assuring me that he'd blow my legs off if I ran. He locked me in the back seat and got on the radio. The radio squawked, and we drove off.

"You're too close to me," I said, spreading my hands on the wire mesh behind his head. "I warned you. *Chất độc, chất độc.*"

He kept checking me in the rearview. I caught his eyes every time he did, spreading my hands behind his head and wagging my tongue as my mind reeled and hallucinated.

We approached an intersection where two highways crossed. I studied the area for a clue, but as hard as I tried I couldn't figure out where I was—not the town, not the highways, not the state. I couldn't have said what continent I was on. I was completely dislodged, disoriented, suffocating in limbo.

During the entire duration of the red light I couldn't place myself. It became a pleasant and liberating feeling. I held to the wire mesh and drifted with it, running at the mouth in Vietnamese.

We'd just turned left when a driver in the oncoming traffic changed lanes abruptly to get into his left turn lane and sideswiped a car evidently in his blind spot. It looked like slow motion. I extended my hand toward the car that was hit. "Incoming!" I yelled in the cop's ear, and the car that was hit jumped the dividing island. It was all dreamlike. "Incoming!" I yelled again, and the car hit us head on.

Both left side doors were sprung, so I got out. The cop was semiconscious. His forehead was covered with blood. I pulled him out of the car, got in the driver's seat and drove away.

I drove aimlessly for I don't know how long until I recognized Broadway in downtown Paterson. I got out and started knocking on doors, asking people if I could use their bathtub to wash the paint off. They were all blacks and Puerto Ricans. I told them I was suffocating, but no one let me in.

A crowd formed on the sidewalk behind me. They were all laughing and calling to others on the next block. People were hanging out of their windows.

"Are you from TV?" one boy asked.

"Yes," I said, "I'm Agent Orange. Take me to your bathtub." I laughed.

"The dude wants a bathtub," the boy yelled, and the crowd, which was steadily growing, hooted and laughed.

I climbed some stairs to try again for a bathtub. "No VC," I said. "No VC."

"Go away!" a voice yelled from behind the door.

"I need to wash," I said. "I'm dying. No TV. No TV."

"You ain't washin' in my tub!" the voice came back. "Go away, you nut!"

People were lining the stairs. They ran in front of me just out of reach. "You black or white?" one said. I staggered down the steps. Boys were dancing in front of me, taunting me, then darting away. I reached for one and almost fell. "Watch out, you little fucker," I said. "I'll explode. *Chât dôc.*"

Stopped cars were blocking the street. I stood in the middle of Broadway, looked around me at the mob and above me at the people in their windows. I cupped my hands around my mouth and screamed, "*Nghe dây.* I am demanding that I be dealt with now!"

The crowd howled.

"You want some statistics?" I yelled. "You want some dead black statistics?" I pointed at them, swinging my arm around as I turned in a circle. "*Chieu boi!*" I pointed at the people in their windows. "*Chieu boi!*"

I got back in the cop car and drove off. I drove a few blocks. I didn't know what to do. I couldn't judge distances, so I pulled over. I dropped my head back on the seat, and there above me I saw the rotating time and temperature sign on the Alexander Hamilton Savings and Loan Association.

The clock was at 9:20. It turned around. The thermometer read seventy-two degrees. It turned again, and the time was still 9:20. The temperature still seventy-two degrees.

I closed my eyes. The smell of paint was mingling and confused with my dizziness. I nearly passed out, popped my eyes open willfully, and it was still 9:20, seventy-two degrees.

I watched the thing rotate for what seemed like ten minutes, concentrating on the time and temperature to remain conscious. The entire time the clock was at 9:20 and the temperature remained at seventy-two. The car engine was smoking and clanking. People were gathering outside the car. I drove off.

After a few blocks the car stalled while moving. I coasted down the hill by Falls View hot dog stand, through the red light at the bottom of the hill and into the parking lot overlooking the Great Falls. There were sirens blaring in the distance. I coasted up to the marble pedestal and stopped. Alexander Hamilton, in his foppish duds and his aristocratic pose, stood above me, proudly surveying the river below.

"I will wash in the river," I said aloud. My eyes went black for a few seconds. It was a short climb down a rocky cliff to a fairly calm section of the pool at the bottom of the falls. I felt like I could make the climb if I concentrated hard.

Then I realized my fingers were wrapped around the mesh of a steel fence. Ten feet high. Strands of barbed wire angled toward me at the top.

I fixed my eyes on the water swirling below and started to climb. My arms were weak, and the steel wire hurt my bare feet. My arms would not pull. I fell to the concrete and got up and prepared to try again.

I heard conversations from TV shows I'd watched as a kid, curled on the sofa wrapped in blankets and fever. I heard the radio communications of ships at sea. I slipped through the fence and saw my orange body behind me gripping the wire mesh. I knew then that I wasn't just going to die, but go clear out of my mind first. I was on the fringe, about to mainline that river of hallucination.

I looked down at the Passaic again. The spotlights illuminated the turbulent foam, and the foam settled into a smooth black ribbon that slid off toward Newark and the Atlantic. I wanted to ride the river away and, like a vector of the seven plagues, contact the host organism at Newark Bay.

Near the bottom of the cliff I saw the concrete sluice where the drainpipe surfaced. I remembered standing on the sluice when I'd followed the pipe from the underground chamber across from Minardi's bakery to the river.

I'll wash in the river then disappear into the pipe and stay beneath Paterson, live on rats and rainwater and return, in reverse, back through the birth canal, from the river to the rain.

I struggled to the top where the barbed wire extended over my head and clung there until I couldn't hold on any longer, then struggled back down the fence, falling the last few feet.

I staggered to the statue of Alexander Hamilton and, on the pedestal, before his boots, I rolled over on my back. I saw the Buddhist monk fall forward in flames. I saw one bright star in the sky and held it. Then only blackness, the odor of paint, an orange wave of unconsciousness washing over me. I fought until there was no reason to fight, until I slipped into the odor of paint. I saw a light in the blackness, glittering distantly, then rushing at me. At first backlit and silhouetted, then, in detail, I saw, close enough to touch, a child, naked, holding a box turtle and glowing pink with the sacredness of life. I reached for the child, for my own face.

The first time I came to my senses, besides moments of confused dementia here and there, I was watching TV with the black shrink. Dallas was getting murdered, and Landry was pissed. A man sat next to me and handed me two pills—I swallowed them.

The defense couldn't contain the traps. The Viking backs were getting through the hole and breaking to the outside for five to seven yards a carry.

"The dumb Texas crackers oughta pull that outside linebacker in," the black shrink said—"they're trappin' the muthafuckas to death."

I watched the game for a while, but within twenty minutes I was just staring vacantly at the tube, fixed idiotically on the movement of dots.

15

THAT'S THE TRUTH ABOUT WHAT HAPPENED WITH OSWALD and his goons. I'm relieved to get it all down. I've been falling behind while I've been here, though I have been scrawling a few apocryphal entries with my big dull pencil, all designed for a specific purpose. I have a lot to get down before I leave.

John Oswald, mayor of Angleton, is missing. That's very funny. It appears that he blew town in a severe hurry either last night or this morning. According to the news there is no apparent motive yet. If they asked me I could tell them the whole story.

When I saw the piece on the news this evening I laughed like a demon. He liquidated as many assets and securities as he could, put together all his ready cash, packed his bags and left, according to the news. I wish the black shrink were here now. I wonder if he saw the news. I'm tempted to call him at home to jive him a bit, but maybe I should leave him alone. He's been depressed since our last session. That big ass has lost its bounce.

I wonder where Oswald fled to. Maybe it'll do him some good. Anyone carrying around that much paranoia needs a change. I guess Judy was right about him being obsessively afraid that the FBI was on to him.

I'll explain how his departure came to pass. It's a mild night for the end of December—clear and crisp. I'm in the mood to sit by this window and catch up on events, even if it takes all night. And I want to leave some more pages of lies specifically for the white shrink to "analyze" and publish in some professional journal or his fucking book. I'll give him a ruse of truth, too. Ever since he read some of this stuff —the pages I leaked out—he's been trying harder than ever to get his paws on more.

I intend to send this entire stack of new entries to Willie Sykes with instructions to put them together with the other notebooks stashed in the burned-out warehouse.

The black shrink, whose care I'm under, couldn't have cared less about what I write with my big dull pencil, so, when suddenly one day he expressed an interest in seeing my writings, I knew the white shrink had put him up to it. That was a sad day, and I saw the sadness in the black shrink's face. The dignity had left him.

There's been a trust growing between the black shrink and me, or, at least, the black shrink thought so, and the white shrink routinely seeks to exploit that trust. Actually, I still like the black shrink a lot. It wasn't really his fault—somehow it wasn't his decision. I think it was decided for him a long time ago, somewhere deep in the bowels of the machine. But it was a sad day, knowing what was happening and watching the black shrink be misused like that, though I guess it's all been entertaining.

I had a few givens to start with before I began mixing the chemicals that made Oswald disappear:

I knew the white shrink was in touch with Oswald periodically. I knew that because I asked the white shrink. I saw him in the main office one afternoon and said, "Are you ever in touch with John Oswald, the mayor who they say I tried to snuff with bug spray?"

The slimeball just ignored me.

Most people would want to be associated with Oswald because he's a powerful figure in state politics, which means it can be assumed that he has mob connections, which, oddly enough, in Jersey, is a feather in one's cap, if not an ace in the hole. People feel like they need an ace in the hole in Jersey, or an acquaintance with one. The white shrink is no exception; still, he kept his mouth shut. But inside, behind his pasty face that I wanted to push in for him, he couldn't deny knowing Oswald even if he was supposed to deny it.

"Hey, slimeball," I said, "I'm talking to you."

He tried to pass me to leave the office, but I grabbed his arm.

"Are you in touch with Mayor Oswald of Angleton?" I repeated.

My two attendants grabbed both of my arms from behind, which didn't break my grip on the white shrink's upper arm. For an instant I considered stomping the three of them just for exercise—after all, wasn't I a nut, a violent nut? It would have been the least I could have done to fulfill their expectations.

"Give him a message for me, will you?" I said, letting him go before the attendants got heavy.

He started back toward the inner offices, rubbing his arm.

"It's about the film," I said, "his wife's debut."

He stopped, continued to rub his arm and studied my face. "What about it?" he said.

I just laughed, and the attendant's hauled me toward the door. The white shrink followed us into the hall, but I just laughed like a nut, allowing the attendants to cart me away, knowing that Oswald and the white shrink had gotten together to trade slime.

I also knew Oswald had a private investigator trying to find out some details about my past. God help him. Between my efforts and the work of Navy intell and the CIA, not much is left back there—lies surrounding the mumbo-jumbo of a few citations for meritorious action, the official acknowledgment of a re-up application, a trumped-up missing in action report, some medical reports, a large gap in the tapes, the grid of a secret and sketchy map of a place that officially never existed, an out-of-focus photo of a youth in a new crewcut faded beyond recognition from sunlight.

I knew Oswald had a private eye on me because Willie Sykes came to visit me and told me he was questioned by a private eye. He told me Susan was questioned too.

Willie also told me the private eye asked him if he'd been questioned by a man named Freneau and what kind of official Freneau identified himself as, so I knew Oswald knew Freneau was visiting me at the institution, and I knew Oswald didn't know who Freneau was.

I knew Oswald had been suspicious about my true identity since I spoke to him about Vietnam in the diner that day. I could assume from Oswald's interest in me and his general paranoia that he was apprehensive about something—that he had something to hide. The crazed and delirious Agent Orange had turned too much attention toward him. The incident had made the local papers, and I imagine there was some speculation, at least on Oswald's part, about the significance of the bug spray.

This was enough information to begin the alchemy.

The police investigation that followed my arrest revealed, through scrutiny of my military records, which I'm sure have been adjusted, that I was in Nam. I'd told Oswald that night in the diner that I was a draft dodger. I imagine the gaps in my records, evident upon close perusal, made Oswald more than a little curious. I'm sure there are some gaps in his own records if he was a pilot high in the ranks of the secret war brigade. Because I know something about the chain of command and the procedure to authorize the dispatch of sorties in Laos and the general strategies there, I'm sure Oswald was wondering if the gaps in our records would coincide if superimposed over a map of Southeast Asia. That could make a man nervous, especially an officer and a gentleman. So much secrecy produces victims and breeds paranoia. Ghosts from either side could be tracking him. Men were sacrificed for the sake of intell cover—intell that reported mostly disinformation anyway. The military brass was disinformed by the CIA for security reasons, and the brass in turn disinformed their subordinate officers. There were lots of rumors. You could stab a buddy in the back, literally and figuratively, and not even know it until later.

So with John Oswald all I had to do was lay the bait. I figured he'd accumulated enough guilt from activities both in-country and in Jersey that just feeding him rope was sufficient.

I leaked some of my bogus journal entries through the white shrink to Oswald. It was just drivel to keep him guessing if I really was running a few quarts low or if I just wanted people to think I was nuts to maintain a cover for the operation. I wanted him to suspect a scheme—a plot against him.

I wrote about the nuances of the Bouncing Ball Therapy, about how to detain a pursuing vampire by scattering poppy seeds, about dropping insecticide bombs on Angleton, about playing third for the Chicago Cubs. I wrote some verbal gaps—alluring little non-clues. I created empty craters that could draw a man into them. I listed botanical categorizations and descriptions of plants that grew on the institution grounds and of plants, like the rosary pea, that were native to Southeast Asia. I laced the written word with poisonous berries, interfaces between the sacred and the profane, lunatic wuzu and surgical logic that found its way into Oswald's hands.

As a result I assume Oswald was convinced that someone was investigating him, though he couldn't have figured out who it was or what the investigator hoped to reveal because, in fact, no one was investigating him. It was just me stirring the concoction. It was just so convenient, having the white shrink at my disposal to initiate the liaison and set Oswald's guilt in gear.

It was unfortunate that the black shrink had to suffer in the process, but that kind of thing might be built into the circuitry by now.

What follows, for example, is a brief excerpt that I buried in a lot of drivel, lies and tedious entries typical of any journal:

> Met with Freneau today. He's very concerned about my man Oswald. He keeps asking questions: Why did I select Oswald to abuse? Do I know anything about Oswald's business affairs? Have I ever had any dealings with the mob? Did I know Oswald in Nam? What was the significance of the bug spray?
>
> It seems like this guy Freneau is more interested in Oswald than in me, which leads me to believe he is not really with the State Psychiatric Commission.

> *I'll remain here a while longer. Everybody thinks I'm nuts, of course, which provides me with opportunities to experiment with peoples' reactions, experiments that could come in handy later in this line of work.*
>
> *I'm working on a formula that I expect will change the very nature of reality to suit me more. It proves its own infallibility by systematically discrediting everything that might bring it into question. Quite ingenious and certainly in keeping with the prescribed order of things. Details later upon consummation.*
>
> *I wonder how Freneau found out about my meetings with Lt. Col. Swinburne in Newark. Someone besides me is interested in Oswald.*

Freneau's visits, of course, had nothing to do with Oswald. In fact, he never once mentioned Oswald. And Lieutenant Colonel Swinburne is an entirely imaginary piece of the bait.

Freneau told the authorities at the institution that he was with the Navy, and he told me he was with the State Psychiatric Commission, and he had credentials from both, but I'd bet anything he's a Company man—100 proof.

Actually, I can't be sure, but it makes sense that they'd send an agent on a routine check of a possible security risk evidently gone bonkers—a potentially dangerous leak that could spill into the environment for public consumption.

I can't believe they even bother anymore. Entire books have been written about the so-called secret wars, even if they do exclude the particulars. It's public knowledge that the CIA started the Gulf of Tonkin incident. Who cares anymore who was assassinated, who was blown to pieces by mistake, who was sacrificed to protect what lie, how many lives were lost in the timing of a US presidential campaign?

I almost broke up laughing when Freneau, during his first visit to the institution, casually asked, off the record, in his best fake psychiatrist's voice, if, during my tours of Nam, I'd visited any other countries—like I was on a vacation. "Laos, Burma, Cambodia?" he asked. "No," I said, and that put him at ease a little. Then we were both lying, and communication improved. "I was a soldier," I said, "doing a soldier's job."

I played along with Freneau. I just answered his questions and played it straight—kind of straight—up until yesterday, anyway, when I slipped out of here with Freneau on my tail. It was pretty funny. He didn't seem to care all that much. I think this is all routine for him. But Oswald was developing terminal indigestion as he watched from his reserved table at Riccardi's. That was his last public appearance in Angleton.

The black shrink and I were developing a good working relationship. I went along with him out of curiosity, a fellowship that I felt and the pure enjoyment of play-acting at times and being nakedly honest at times, mixing the elements of each into an intricate system of psychic tunnels that he would crawl into as duty called.

We bounced a handball back and forth across his office during our sessions. He'd hold it for a while, then I'd hold it for a while, as if it was significant to the discussion who was holding the ball, when, of course, none of it meant anything. It was something to do. He had to do something. It was his job to do something, and we both enjoyed the game.

Then one week when the weather was unseasonably mild he brought a hardball and two gloves, and we burned the pill at each other for most of the afternoon. The black shrink was definitely one hot-shit athlete when he was younger—I could tell.

"You've played some ball," I said when we stopped for a drink of orange juice.

"Nothing too serious," he said.

He had a big ass, and with sweat pants on I could see it was as hard as two watermelons. We went to the kitchen for the o.j. where he jived with the women of color who worked there. He drank almost a quart of o.j., popped one cupcake, and we strode back to the green.

The women in the kitchen liked him a lot; it was obvious. They flirted with him, and he flirted back. He was no doctor of psychiatry looking down his well-fed snout from the heights of arcane knowledge and mystifying class ascension. He was, rather, a big jovial and frumpy sort with a healthy lasciviousness toward younger women.

"I'm gonna burn some in, chief, if that's okay," he said. "You look like you can handle it."

"Knock yourself out," I said.

"I feel like burning some in," he said loudly as he jogged away from me.

"I'll burn some back at you," I called.

"Burn 'em back," he yelled over his shoulder.

He warmed up his arm for a while longer, throwing increasingly harder. Then he yelled, "Here it comes," caught my throw on a forward skip-step and winged one at me. He threw from about where short center field would be. He had an arm like a pro. The ball took off as it approached and sliced slightly upward, still gaining. I stepped into it and burned one back at him. I had a fair arm myself. An excitement passed between us, that boyish kind of thrill.

"Nice arm!" he yelled. "Nice goddamn arm!"

He burned one back and drilled me chest high. The son-of-a-bitch could throw.

We continued like that, pegging runners trying to score on the hard liners to center. The stands were going wild.

Then we threw some flies—towering drives to deep left-center—making lots of backhanded stabs looking over the shoulder. I tipped my hat to the bleachers. What silly heroes!

The feeling came back to me that you get when you know where the ball is going before it hits the bat, and you get that incredible jump on the ball. You could run down a high fly at the left field line all the way from center on days when you had that jump. Then one day I brought a pint of Dickel to our session. It was the Number Twelve, ninety proof, white label stuff. Willie had slipped it in under his coat.

The black shrink and I sat across the room from each other and bounced a rubber ball between us, sipping the sour mash and talking. This was talk therapy the way it was meant to be. I was entertained by the fact that such a thing could go on in a state institution. The black shrink was making more sense to me all the time. He really liked being tucked away in a cloister out of the mainstream, talking about whatever came up, trying to be of some help to people. I was not reveling in what I had to do to him.

"Now I know where you got your pseudonym for the psychiatrist caper," the black shrink said, "but I'd like to know where you got this bottle. I'm not a hard-ass, but you can't make a habit of this."

"Freneau brought it," I said.

"Freneau? You mean that dude from the State Psychiatric Commission?" He wrinkled his brow and poured us each a shot in a paper cup, then held the bottle up to read the label.

"That ain't no shrink," I said. "That's hundred-proof CIA."

"Is that right? CIA, huh?"

I bounced the ball to him. He snagged it out of the air and pointed his finger at me.

"I think you're wrong this time, chief," he said.

"I don't think so. He wants to see if I'll mention anything I'm not supposed to mention—see if information is safe with a lunatic. It's routine, man. I've been expecting them. It's almost funny at this point. I mean, who gives a shit anymore?"

"And he brought you that bottle? Is that what you want me to believe?"

"Nice of him, huh?"

"I don't know how to read you, man. Are you jiving with me again?"

"How can you be so black and not know jive when you hear it? I'm telling you the truth—it was Freneau."

"You can't have that bottle in the ward. I can't let you."

"I'm putting it in your care. You keep it here. Help yourself."

He bounced the ball to me. "I'm telling you the truth, chief," he said. "Freneau is no CIA man. He told us who he is."

"Careful what you call the truth. You think he's gonna walk right up and say, 'Hello, I'm with the CIA'?"

"Why wouldn't he?" He caught the ball and held it.

"Because that's not how they do it in the movies," I said.

"Those dudes aren't really into all that intrigue bullshit."

"That's right," I said. "You're right. They're too seasoned and worldly and superior and all-knowing for that."

"Look," he said, "you better not say I told you, goddamn it, but the dude's with the Navy. I saw the credentials. And, like you said, chief, it's just routine. You've got nothing to worry about, and that's the only reason I'm telling you. I don't want you thinking the CIA is following you around. That's all you need right now. Is that what you're thinking?"

"What difference does it make who's following me around? And the Navy wouldn't bother with this shit. And you think you're telling me the truth again." I sipped the whiskey. "This dude is hundred-proof CIA."

"You think so, huh, chief?"

"I can smell it."

"Okay, so the CIA is investigating you. What do they want to know?"

"They want to know if my brain is leaking and, if so, what the estimated damage of the spillage is. They want to know if I should be eliminated before I tell someone I assassinated Betty Crocker and made it look like the VC did it."

"So, did you play it straight with him? Or did you jive his ass off?"

"About Betty Crocker, you mean?"

"Yeah, chief, about Betty Crocker."

"I played it straight. You know me."

"Look," he said, "the guy's a shrink. I saw his credentials. And he's with the Navy, man. He's from the psych ward at the VA hospital. They're thinking about moving you. I'm telling you. I checked on his credentials."

"Oh. Well, that leaves little doubt."

"Even if he was CIA—I mean, what's the heavy trip? What can they do? They're gonna snuff you for shooting some mayor with bug spray?"

"I told you—it's the Betty Crocker rap."

"Are you really concerned about this? Are you really worried? Because if I determine it's hindering your progress I can keep Freneau's ass out of here."

"No, I'm not concerned. You think I'm having paranoid delusions about the CIA, so, therefore, you assume I must be bordering on hysteria —or, rather, *concerned,* as you put it. I'm simply telling you I'm being investigated routinely by the CIA because I pulled some weirdness dressed in orange paint, and . . ."

"Undressed," he said. "Undressed in orange paint."

"And they just can't understand shit like that in the Company. I'm not *concerned* about it. It's a blessing in disguise, really. It's all grist for the mill, herbs for the potion, metals for the alchemy. You are, too."

The black shrink sipped his whiskey, got out of the chair and sat on his desk, indicating a change of subject.

"I think at some point soon," he said, "we should talk more about what you did in Vietnam. Because I can't evaluate any of this rap about the CIA without more information—I mean, just for my own sake, man. Sometimes I feel like I'm just groping in the dark here. You jive my ass off one minute, then you seem like you're being straight with me the next, and I understand that you like to do that, and that's okay, but I'm feeling like I need some more foundation in that Vietnam experience. You dig? But that's later, okay. I want you to think about helping me with that. Right now I get the feeling you've been thinking about getting out of this place soon. You seem to have a habit of vanishing and reappearing. You thinking about that, chief? There's legal and illegal ways to do that, you know. I'd like you to do it the legal way. Not that I give a shit about what's legal and what isn't. But I care about what could happen to you."

"How about you?" I said. "You thinking about getting out of here?"

"I think we can get out of here, chief."

"I don't know. I need to be here for a while. I need to come down. And I wouldn't want to face any criminal charges. I guess I should get a lawyer and find out what's going on. I don't trust Oswald."

"I thought that was all over. Isn't *this* your sentence? You just have to contend with me and the staff here, and you're not doing badly that way. You didn't really hurt anyone except those two monkeys, and they were in your home trying to put a hurt on you. It's almost understandable what you did."

"Really?"

"Well, everything but the orange paint."

"You don't like the orange paint? I thought it was a nice touch."

"It's excessive," he said. "It scares people."

"It scares you, you mean, because you think too seriously about it. *People* don't mind it. It's just Hollywood. It's a chuckle in the morning paper. They pass it to the person next to them. That person chuckles. They sip their coffee, and they feel friendly, like life's okay for a moment. Orange Man Steals Cop Car. It's great. There's probably a gang of Puerto Ricans, all naked and painted orange, terrorizing Whitey in downtown Paterson every night. People need to run around naked. How could you pull off a serious mugging with no clothes on? I don't trust Oswald, though. He's a vindictive son-of-a-bitch. He could get me into court. I have to get him out of the picture. And really, how about you —you thinking about getting out of here?"

"Yeah, chief, I think about that." He bounced the ball to me.

"To what? Private practice?"

"I don't know, man. Maybe. I can't figure out why I've stayed in Jersey so long. Roots maybe."

"It's the water," I said.

"The ocean?"

"No, the drinking water. It makes you sleepy and forgetful. You forget you want to leave and you just go to sleep."

"I deserve better than this," he said. "I should go to some chic beach scene someplace where a man can enjoy his work more. Nice joint on the beach somewhere. Resident psychiatrist at Club Med, man. Hobnob with the other half instead of a bunch of poverty-stricken loonies in the care of the state. Maybe some loonies with money would be a nice change. Some of these dudes with corporate stress or some shit. Some of these luxury ailments, you know."

"Maybe you could be resident shrink with the Miami Dolphins." I bounced the ball.

"Yeah, right," he said with a chuckle. "You think they have their own shrink?"

"They must. You should think about private practice, though. Institutions just institutionalize you."

"You think I should, huh?" He bounced the ball.

"Sure. Why not?" I bounced it back.

"How'd you like it?" he asked.

"It was okay, really," I said.

"You had a good time, did you?"

"I had a good time."

"I heard a little about it."

"I bet you did," I said. "I'll tell you what. How 'bout this? I'll sub for you here for a while—"

"Yeah?" he said, reaching over to pour some whiskey in my cup.

—"and you can try a private practice," I said. "The white shrink and I can hold down the fort. If it doesn't work out, you can have your job back, and I'll move on to surgery or something."

"It's a good plan, really, chief." He laughed a particularly Negroid laugh. "I appreciate the offer. The white shrink would love it, man."

"The white shrink would check into the ward where he belongs," I said. "Whatta ya think? Wanna try it? Does it sound okay?"

"It's cool, chief. Everything's copacetic."

Just then the white shrink came in on cue. He looked at the bottle, then ignored it. I filled our paper cups.

"Excuse me, Doctor," he said.

"No problem, Doctor," I said. "We're having a little toast to my birthday. Will you join us?"

He ignored me and explained his intrusion to the black shrink. He had to borrow a file.

"No problem," the black shrink said. "We were just . . ."

"Knock next time," I said. "Don't you realize we could have had all the grotesque cartoon characters from my dreams and hallucinations out here on the rug?"

"We were just having a shooter for the man's birthday," the black shrink said. "It's my prescription administered under my care."

"Am I questioning anything?" the white shrink said.

"We can't lie to the white shrink," I said. "It's not my birthday. Actually, we're celebrating my induction to the staff here. I'm a colleague now. Give me a kiss."

The black shrink shook his head and smiled.

"Now I can help you analyze the irrational yet telling scrawlings of patients," I said. "We'll edit a book together. I'll be your Deep Throat in the nether world."

"You might as well be on the staff here," the white shrink said, closing the file drawer.

"What can we call the book?" I asked him. "Have a snort with us, and we'll think about it."

He left the room and closed the door behind him.

"Cheery fucker," I said.

"Can't take a joke," the black shrink said and tilted his cup. "Happy birthday."

"He's an asshole," I said. "Enough to make you depressed."

"You think so, huh?"

"Don't you? Let's be honest now, Doctor."

"I shouldn't discuss personal feelings toward my colleagues. It's not professional, chief. It just wouldn't be cool. Especially where an asshole is concerned."

"I guess you're right again."

"What are we supposed to be talking about today?" he asked. "Where did we leave off?"

"I was surrounded by daylight, and I didn't like it one bit. It was ominous."

"Yes, you were going to court."

"I was due in court at ten in the morning, and, as I've told you, it was that night, after the hearing, that I was caught in the woman's house by her brother. I left Paterson right after that and disappeared into Newark to go straight—kind of straight."

"That's right," he said, "and you changed your name again. I'm trying to get all these names straight."

"Well, I didn't even have a name at that point. The opium had erased it. Dr. George Dickel had been consumed by the darkness. I was being devoured name by name. I had to hole up for a while in Newark. I had to come down. Be reserved. Practice my invisibility."

"Now, what was the hearing about? What happened in court?"

"I told you about it already."

"I want the details, and I've been confused about the chronology of these events. Tell me again."

"You like stories, don't you?"

"Yes," he said. "Yes, I do."

"Once upon a time I was disturbed—mostly by having to come clean with my true identity because of the hearing. It was a bit of a trauma, Doc, but it was either that or leave town and have the local police and God knows who else on my ass. It would have been too self-incriminating, and I wasn't guilty of the charges against me. It really was self-defense, so I decided to stay and ride it out. But I left town anyway right after that, because of being caught at Ellen's, like I said. That was the first time the Company paid me a visit."

"What company?"

"*Thee* Company. The CIA. You remember—paranoid delusions."

"So you've talked to them before?"

"The Company man showed up with my lawyer. They both just appeared at my door one day."

"Maybe we'd better talk more about what you did for the Navy. What's with these CIA dudes always on your ass?"

"It's privileged information, as my lawyer told the judge. I'm not at liberty to discuss it, as they say in the movies."

"Oh, that's right. We're going to go through this again. The authorized dead end." He sipped the whiskey. "You know what's said between doctor and patient is kept confidential."

"Are you telling me the *truth* again, Doc?"

"It's the truth."

I poured us each some whiskey and remained silent.

"So," he said, "the CIA showed up with your lawyer. Why?"

"The Company man was very casual," I said. "He said he was impressed with my military record and wanted to help where he could. He never said he was with the CIA, but he reeked of it—hundred proof. He just said he was sent to help. He was so slippery. I remember I wanted to disarm him while his eyes were blinking just for kicks—pluck the nine-millimeter from under his arm and hand it to him and say, 'No, thanks, I don't need your help.' But I was a little scared at the time. I needed all the help I could get. I didn't like the idea of being who I was on my birth certificate. My cover was blown. I was out in the daylight with the enemy all around me. I was very shaky in public from a year of opium. It bummed me out. And I knew I hurt a couple of those dudes at the bar pretty badly."

"That's the homemade opium you happened to find growing along somebody's sidewalk. I find this a little hard to believe. Opium growing in Paterson? And, of course, that was several pseudonyms ago."

"What's with you and the pseudonyms, Doc? I've wanted to cover up ever since I got out of the Navy. I don't really want to know that dude. Being exposed at the hearing made me want to cover up more than ever. Having no name was better than having several fake names, but I wanted to be even further removed—invisible or something—so I worked on being invisible. I practiced by stealing food in small markets in Newark. I'd steal a few oranges or some cheese, walk up and stand in front of the counter for a minute, go back and steal some tuna fish, walk up again, and nobody would say anything, so I'd steal something else and leave, stay in my apartment for a week becoming more and more invisible, walk out on the street, and no one would see me. I was getting it down. I had to consciously make myself visible in order to hitch a ride to the shore. Then I met this guy Willie who insisted that I could be seen. It made me nervous for a while, but I couldn't shake the guy. I'd do something to discourage him, but he'd be right back the next day with two tea bags and some stale bread to put in my toaster."

"So you had to have a name then—with Willie you did, anyway."

"It seemed like the appropriate thing to do, you know. Suddenly I had a name, and then, little by little, I had to invent a little history. Next thing I knew I was almost a person. Though Willie never bugged me too much about my history. But eventually he got me involved in this . . ."

"So what name did you use then, with Willie?"

"Actually, I used my real name for some reason with Willie. That's how I wound up in the country club here with all you loonies in the care of the state."

"A few weeks ago," the black shrink said pensively, "when I referred to your pseudonyms as a.k.a.s, why were you so offended? I mean, it's standard jargon—a.k.a. this, a.k.a. that."

"Oh, wow, Doc, I think you're on to something heavy now. I think it has something to do with my mother's tits. Maybe it's my Caesarean birth."

"Don't bust my balls, man. Just let me do my job. Have another drink. You're a ball buster."

"Well, how the fuck do I know? I probably just needed to be offended by something. It's offensive just being here. You're basically offensive—sticking your goddamn probe into my flesh. And besides, it's a criminal tag. I was never *also known as* anything, and I don't like to think of myself as a criminal."

"Well, it's the first thing you've been so sensitive about," he said. "I'm just following your lead. You did impersonate a doctor. You made off with a cop car. You entered a man's bedroom and scared the piss out of him dressed as a vampire. That's criminal behavior."

"I entered a *woman's* bedroom. The man happened to be in the way."

"Well, what do you think of yourself as, if not a criminal?"

"I don't think of myself as anything . . . a monkey, maybe, a scholar of Swinburne, for sure, a toxic waste dump . . . I don't know . . . I don't understand—*tôi không hiêũ*—but I'm not a criminal or an a.k.a."

"A few minutes ago you told me that you don't want to know that dude who was in the Navy in Vietnam. Was that dude a criminal? Is that why you don't want to know him? Was he an evil fucker?"

"You should listen more closely. I said *at the time of that hearing* I didn't want to know him. He's not a criminal. He's a muthafucka, Doc. That's often used in black slang for not necessarily one who fucks their mother but for . . . well . . . how can I explain it to you. I'm not sure it translates to you bourgeois professional types."

"I grew up in Newark, chief. And you're evading the issue."

"I didn't want to know the dude because I didn't know how to show him the respect or the compassion he deserved. I crossed the street when I saw him coming. I'm no criminal a.k.a. psychopath a.k.a. deranged vet a.k.a. delayed stress syndrome a.k.a. case study number 317666 a.k.a. the white shrink's new publication credit a.k.a. the man running from himself—none of this bullshit or that bullshit—no B movie hero or villain. It's bound to be confusing—what I am—so don't zero in on no easy outs, Doc. I'll tell you one thing I am, and that's a highly skilled, highly trained bastard. I learned my trade in the U.S. Navy. I'm too highly trained to be an a.k.a. I've been dispatched, man. I'm the attaché of the attaché. The cadre of the monkey army. Are you kidding? I'm Agent Orange come home to be dealt with. Did you think we were going to get away with that shit? Did you think I would just go away and feel bad for myself? No way. I'm back. I was just laying low to recuperate. Out of the slime he rises, from the world of the dead he returns, without a clue he pushes onward, donning his sheerest slip he dances provocatively in the mirror—innocent of reason he eats the finest peaches in the sacred orchard . . ."

"Okay, okay then, let's deal with you. Back to the courtroom. So why were you in court and out in the daylight like that—all vulnerable like that?"

"It was legitimately self-defense. In fact, I actually tried to avoid the bastards. I remember that because it was against my better judgment to avoid them. I wanted to throw hands after their first comment. But I was trying to keep a low profile in Paterson, and I didn't want any trouble. Then these four crybabies couldn't take a fucking joke and went to the D.A. because I tore them up so badly in front of their friends at the VFW bar. It was pitiful. Ordinarily, I don't think the D.A. would have touched it, not in court, anyway, but two of the dudes got hurt pretty badly, and I think one of them knew somebody who could throw some weight around the city, and the D.A. was a little weirded-out when he saw the details of the medical reports."

"What was the charge?"

"Assault. He thought I got a little excessive. I guess you're supposed to respond equally—tit for tat. If someone slaps you with their hanky you're supposed to tap them with your glove. Except one of them picked up a beer bottle, but nobody saw that but me, and there were four of them, and I just did what I know how to do." I filled our cups again. "It never went to trial, though. My lawyer was slick. He appeared as if by magic with a D.C. address and a thousand-dollar suit on his back."

"I didn't even know they made thousand-dollar suits, man," the black shrink said. "So you made out all right?"

"I walked. I just played it straight with the judge—kind of straight. There were a lot of questions central to the D.A.'s approach that I couldn't answer for security reasons, especially with the Company man in the peanut gallery."

"You weren't at liberty to discuss it, right?"

"That's right."

"You weren't at liberty to discuss a bar fight? This is where I got lost last time we discussed this."

"This is where you assumed I have routine paranoid delusions."

"Well, it doesn't make a lot of sense, chief."

"I was not at liberty to discuss my *training,* not the bar fight. Try to keep up here, will ya?"

"What training was this?"

"The training I'm not at liberty to discuss."

"And this is what saved your ass in court. They couldn't nail you for assault because of this lack of liberty."

"Well, it was the quickest way out."

"Maybe it would have been better if you had gone the long way."

"That was my gut feeling at the time."

"This is the same lack of liberty that's blocking us right now, I think."

"I just don't have much interest in talking about this."

"How badly did you hurt these dudes at the bar?"

"Eyeball, vertebrae, knee joint, upper arm, teeth, noses, ribs . . ." I shrugged. "I'm not proud of it. You asked. They were fat and brittle and drunk and stupid. I could hardly touch them without hurting them. It was pathetic. I hurt them as badly as you would have hurt them in the same situation."

"I doubt that."

"Right, you would have turned your big black cheeks to them."

"Think back—seriously, man—did it necessitate that extreme violence? Could you have handled it any other way? You know, that's how you chose to deal with Oswald too. Not to mention his wife."

"Ex-wife."

"Do you ever think about that?"

"I suppose I could have dealt with it differently. I could have killed the fuckheads—I could have eaten their livers and disappeared, kept them out of Buddha heaven. What am I, Gandhi? What am I, Jesus fucking Christ almighty? Martin Luther Dead Martyr? I never had no nonviolent civil-disobedience instructor. I was taught how to survive, and that's what I'm doing. I'm ugly, man—very ugly. You just don't want to believe that. And I doubt if there are any scars on your other cheek, having made it from the ghetto to the burbs."

"We're trying to have a discussion here, remember, and we're not discussing me. We're discussing your tendency to deal with your problems through violence."

"O-o-o-o-o-h, is *that* what we're discussing? Seems a little panoramic. Can we narrow the focus?"

"You could try a little harder to offer something, instead of copping out. We're trying to understand, not argue. And I never lived in the ghetto—at least we never thought of it as a ghetto. My dad was a conductor on the Penn Central. He had benefits. We did okay. And I don't live in the suburbs. I have a nice old house with fruit trees on a country road. I renovated it myself."

"I was speaking figuratively."

"You were speaking bullshit, chief. I didn't eat people's livers to get where I am. Can we get beyond this? And you're right—I don't believe you're ugly. Let's talk about the Navy."

"I'm not interested in the Navy."

"What did you do in the Navy?"

"I learned a trade, just like the guy on the billboards."

"And what trade was that?"

"I can't remember—I was debriefed."

"Any combat vet is faced with the problem of bringing back to a civilized culture what he . . ."

"This is not a civilized culture."

"I tossed that issue around too many times in too many universities. The fact is—"

"The fact is fuck you, fat ass!" I screamed, yanking the desk lamp from the wall socket and smashing it off the wall.

The black shrink never moved. I sat down again.

"Does this mean more electroshock?" I said.

"Let's talk about the bar fight some more," he said.

"The sons-of-bitches were fucking with me. That's all. Like I didn't belong in the VFW bar. When it became obvious I wasn't going to be fucked with, they didn't know how to back off for their own good. They hadn't learned retreat, not like the VC had. Too much bravado as long as they were in a group, hulking together like so many pounds of chuck steaks, fucking with a stranger because I didn't fit into their ideas of the way people should think. So they thought they'd bend me to fit, but I explained—I explained with undeniable clarity—that I wouldn't be bent, not an inch of bend left in me. So the barkeep called the police. They just kind of sprawled there on the sidewalk, either unable to get up or not too excited about getting up. They just moaned like crybabies until the cops got there, and the cops took us away. The next thing I know, there I was, outside in the daylight, forced to own up to my real identity, feeling very anxious and aching to cover up again. And don't tell me you don't know the kind of honky assholes I'm talking about. I suppose you breezed through Newark with no chips on your shoulder, right? You didn't mind at all being a nigger in Korea. You never beat up on Whitey. You never realized it's all wrong from the inside out."

"We're not discussing me," he said, "but if we were I would disagree with all this bullshit. Everything is not wrong from the inside out."

"Yes," I said, "and that's true too—it's not."

"It seems that way sometimes, yes. It depends on what you do with this gift of life we have."

"You're nuts, Doc. We *should* discuss you for a while."

"You don't even believe what you're saying. Why haven't you offed yourself like so many of your brothers from Nam? I'm not ignorant of your problems. Twenty percent of all suicides in VA hospitals are vets from Nam, and only nine percent of the people in VA hospitals are Nam vets. Seventy thousand combat vets from Nam are in prison. The divorce rate among combat vets is double that of the rest of their generation, and the suicide rate is twenty-three to thirty-three percent higher than that of non-vets. I've done my homework, chief. But beyond the statistics, I know you've been through an experience that most of us can't even imagine—just by being there—just by being so close to death and dying. And I know that combat, especially that kind, can cut you loose from everything that roots you—everything. And I also know, and I think you know it too, that enough of you have become victims. You have to learn to respect yourselves and pioneer alternatives. Not that vets need to be made into heros, but what many people who questioned our involvement in the war did was change their opinions of vets from some kind of villains who murdered people in an unjust war to pathetic victims of abuse who deserve sympathy. I don't think either of these opinions help the vet. Then there are many less-sensitive opinions too. Few people are willing to deal directly with the fact that we sacrificed almost fifty-eight thousand American lives—not to mention post-war suicides, not to mention Vietnamese lives—and screwed up an entire culture over there—not to mention what we did to our own culture. We don't know how to deal with that. And we don't know how to deal with you people. You remind us of something we're trying to forget, something that doesn't make us feel very good about ourselves, and we'd just as soon not talk about it, thank you."

"This is boring. Tell me something I haven't heard a hundred times."

"You could make it less boring." The black shrink drained his cup and pointed his finger at me. "You didn't make that conscious decision to stay alive—to not off yourself like so many—because you think everything is wrong from the inside out, like you just said. Now why don't you come clean with me so we can get somewhere? I ain't jivin' with you—I ain't no Company man. I'm a human goddamn being who never would have busted his dumb ass through a hundred years of university eating ham hocks and beans on the GI Bill if I didn't think there was some hope for the sane and insane both inside and outside these fences. And I have a feeling, lodged in that darkness of yours is the same kind of hope, so come clean with me, man. Whether you want to or not—or whether you do or not—you can trust me. You like to play me for a fool—someone else you can abuse. I don't really give a fuck if this ends happily or not—whether we get along with each other or what. I'm gonna speak my mind about how you've been living, judging from what you've told me, before you go off and shit on someone else."

"Forget it," I said, and I meant it. "Save it."

"You're bright enough to know I'm being straight with you—you know you can trust me. I'm gonna say what's on my mind, and you're gonna listen. What you do with it is your business."

"Trust you? Goddamn. Why should I trust you? I trusted you with my journal entries—I gave them to you because you asked to see them—and you passed them on to the white shrink, who gave them to Oswald, who would like to keep me locked up forever. What kind of trust-building is that? Now go ahead—speak your mind, boy. I'm sure this is going to be a turning point in my sickness."

"Shit, man." He extended both his hands toward me. "I didn't want to do that." All substance had fallen out of his face—it was as expressionless as dead meat. "I'm real sorry about that, chief. The bastard pulled rank on me. I'm real sorry."

"No problem. It's not your fault. But forgive me if I take your wise advice and refuse to treat victims with sympathy."

"How the hell did you find out?"

"I found out because Oswald's private eye asked a friend of mine—this guy, Willie, in Newark—if he knew anything about Lieutenant Colonel Swinburne. There is no Lieutenant Colonel Swinburne, Doc. The only way Oswald's private eye could have known about Lieutenant Colonel Swinburne as if Oswald read my journal entries, and the only way Oswald could have read my journal entries is if the white shrink gave them to him, and the only way the white shrink could have gotten his claws on them . . ."

"Fuck, man. I don't feel good about this."

"I don't either."

"I knew it was fucked-up when I did it." He exhaled heavily. "The bastard convinced me that it was important to his research, and that it would be in confidence. He's doing this book on delayed stress syndrome. He pressured me, is what he did. He's the senior here."

"The boss man."

"I'm really sorry. Listen, chief, I'll . . ."

"I'm sorry too, Doc—I really am. It's no problem. I'm leaving soon anyway. You weren't going to make any difference in my psyche."

"Listen. We'll get the white shrink in here and we'll talk about this. We'll straighten it out and we'll come to some . . ."

"Talk, talk, fucking talk." I picked the desk lamp up off the floor and put it on the desk. "It will never be straightened out."

16

So the black shrink is bummed out. Maybe he'll get the hell out of this place.

And Oswald left town in a hurry. I'm happy to get him out of the picture.

The weather is so mild, the night so clear that I think I'll split this place tonight while it's dark rather than wait until tomorrow. But first I'll explain about Oswald's parting.

Yesterday, after our meeting, as Freneau walked to the parking lot for his car I slipped through the shoddy security and out to the highway. I stood in plain sight, trying to catch a ride. Freneau saw me and backed his car behind the hedge that borders the driveway. He waited until I got a ride, then followed me, through a succession of rides, all the way to Angleton.

I knew that every Wednesday John Oswald ate lunch at Riccardi's Italian restaurant with business associates, city officials, the mob, lawyers, all of the above—who knows? Who cares? It didn't matter who they were.

Of course, Freneau followed me into the restaurant, taking a seat at the bar in the adjoining room where he could discreetly keep an eye on me while I sat in the dining room.

I ordered a bowl of minestrone.

Oswald nearly choked on his fettucine Alfredo when he saw me.

I wasn't counting on Oswald recognizing Freneau. The private eye must have been on the ball with his 007 camera.

I wasn't counting on anything, really. I was playing it by ear. When Oswald kept craning his neck to see Freneau and finally went to the bar so he could get a better look at him, I knew the cards were turning in my favor.

Oswald couldn't have known what was happening, but I'm sure he knew it was happening to *him*.

I had no plan. I simply knew I had to confront Oswald to begin the alchemy. I could feel the metals changing to gold as I slurped my soup.

I was wondering if Oswald's private eye had been able to trace Freneau to his source. I'm sure it would have been difficult, but the difficulty itself would tell Oswald something about this man who'd been meeting with me at the institution.

When I finished my soup I ordered a Dickel and let it all stew a bit.

Then I walked to the bar and sat down next to Freneau. I wanted to see Oswald's face tying itself in knots, but I never looked at him. Freneau did a second-rate fake of an astonished look.

"What the hell are you doing out?" he said after a phony speechless moment.

"Calm down, Freneau," I said. "The fact is I lured you here all the way from the institution. I need to talk to you in private. Do you have a cigarette?"

He handed me a Merit. "What are you doing out of the institution? I'll have to report this," he said.

"That's funny," I said. "I didn't expect an agent to be smoking Merits. What, no Gaulois, no Gitanes?"

"What are you talking about—agent?" he said, prolonging the look of consternation too long.

"You're a bad actor, Freneau. I know you're a Company man."

"What do you mean—company man?"

"CIA, Doctor Freud. On a routine investigation."

"I'm not with the CIA. I'm with the . . ."

"Yes, I know—you told me—the New Jersey State Psychiatric Commission. Or is it Navy VA hospital administrator? I'm going to send a report to the chief on you, Freneau. You're a shoddy agent. Did they bring you out of retirement for this?"

"I must call the institution." He put the pack of smokes in his shirt pocket.

"You're carrying a weapon, aren't you?" I said. "I pride myself in my ability to detect shoulder holsters. What would a shrink be doing with a nine-millimeter? Pretty shoddy. Hard to break that hardware habit, isn't it?"

"I'm a doctor. What would I be doing with a weapon?"

"That's a popular question," I said. "Let me see, Doctor. What do you think about Jung's idea of the bush soul?"

"I'm not here to take quizzes, and Jung is not exactly discussed in circles of practicing psychiatrists. Jung is for students, poets and occultists. I haven't read Jung in twenty-five years."

"That was good," I said. "Now, how about the use of lithium for manic depression? What do you think about that?"

"We're having some positive results. Is this what you wanted to talk to me privately about? About lithium?"

"Yes. I mean no. I mean yes. I mean no. Gosh, Doc, I'm too depressed to know, and there's this dark-haired boy on my shoulder trying to confuse me."

"I'm going to have to call the institution. Are you going to cooperate, or will I have to call the police? I'm trying to be decent with you."

"I just wanted a bowl of Riccardi's minestrone," I said. "I'm on my way back as soon as I have another drink. I sure wish you were packing some Gaulois."

I leaned slightly toward him as I spoke, blocking my mouth with my hand. I could almost feel Oswald coming apart.

"I'd be willing to drive you back," Freneau said. "I think we should be going."

"That would be great," I said. "I'd appreciate that. I have some writing to do."

As we left I noticed one of the men at Oswald's table get up and go to his car. Oswald no doubt told him to follow us. I stopped to buy a paper at a machine next to a phone booth outside the restaurant. Freneau was trying to coax me along. I was like a child dragging my feet.

I spread the paper in front of my face and peeked over it blatantly at Oswald's man. He was sitting in his car ignoring me. I separated the first three or four sheets of the paper, folded them closed, tore a big semicircular hole at the fold, opened the pages and watched Oswald's man through the hole.

"Come on," Freneau urged. He was trying to be decent.

I walked toward Freneau with the paper covering my face, still watching Oswald's man in his car.

"Let's go," Freneau said. "What the hell are you doing?"

He finally got me into the car, and we pulled away.

"Do you believe this flunky is following us?" I said as we left the parking lot.

Freneau looked in the rearview.

"I bet it's the mob," I said.

"Why would it be the mob?" Freneau asked.

"Oswald," I said. "The mayor who they said I tried to terminate with bug spray. Ever use bug spray, Freneau? Pretty funny, huh? Oswald probably thinks you're with the FBI. He has to be wondering why you've been meeting with me. Haven't you noticed Oswald's private eye tailing you? He has photos of you. He spoke to Willie right after you did. Everybody's on to you, Freneau. You're walking around with your pants down, and you're into some heavy bullshit here. The Company shouldn't have sent a retired agent. The mob has millions tied up in Oswald."

"I told you I'm not with the CIA," he said, "and I'm not with the FBI either."

"Maybe that's the CIA behind us then. I know they must be around. They have to be checking up on me. I'm one of their honor students. I can spell Vientiane backwards. Woops. I shouldn't have said that. I'm leaking that dangerous spillage again. I should be more careful. It would be too easy to eliminate me now that I'm officially nuts and obviously self-destructive. My disappearance would be too easy to cover up. But then maybe I could terminate you first. I'm very skilled, you know. They must have told you that. Much more skilled than you. How many people have you snuffed, Freneau? I mean directly. How many? Huh?"

"I think you'd better calm yourself." Freneau was showing some frayed edges, dividing his uneasy concern between the car in the rearview and me.

"You're right, Doc," I said. "I'd better calm myself, or else the electric . . . or the happy needle . . . or the termination of a good soldier. But then maybe the mob will snuff us both. That would be expeditious. Suppose we discovered, for example, the details of a toxic-waste-dumping business worth millions? Would that be reason to snuff us? Oswald is a confused man right now. Why did we allow him to see us together? We must have known he eats lunch at Riccardi's every Wednesday. Did we want to be followed? No—cheap trick. Who are we? Who are you? Why am I out of the institution and meeting you at Riccardi's? I could pluck that nine-millimeter Browning out of its holster before you could hit the brake, Freneau. Extremely shoddy. But I'll tell you straight. I'm not crazy, and I'm not a security risk. Tell your people that. I've buried the dead in my stomach, or something like that, as someone once said when referring to something. And the corpses are trying to assassinate me from the inside, but I won't be had that easily. I think it was Swinburne who said that about burying the dead in his stomach." I laughed.

Everything was funny. Oswald's man behind us was funny. Oswald had been very funny. The cars driving past were funny, and especially the people in the cars were funny. Freneau was especially funny, trying to maintain his professional cool, and doing well enough, whatever he was.

"I'm just being funny," I said. "I'll tell you the truth, Freneau. I don't know anything about Swinburne. It might have been Rimbaud. 'I am a beast . . . I bury the dead in my belly.' Or was it Euripides? I can't remember any of that stuff. Once I was a decent student of literature —before I was kidnapped. I knew everything about Old Ez, Willie the Shake, Papa Hem, Greg Samsa, Blind Boy Grunt. . . . But that was a previous lifetime. Now I don't know anything. I don't understand what I'm supposed to be doing here. Maybe you could tell me."

"Just calm yourself," Freneau said.

"I'm calm," I said. "I really am."

"Well just remain calm. You do want to get out of the institution, don't you? I'm here to evaluate your progress, you know. Just stay calm and we'll work something out."

"I am out of the institution," I said. "And why don't you cut through this bullshit? Who the fuck are you to evaluate me? You know, you guys don't have to cover your asses anymore. You could tell the truth and create as much deception. And you don't have to sacrifice lives. It's obsolete. We've evolved out of that. We're on the edge of a new kind of understanding, and you guys are dragging your feet. I mean, really, Freneau, what's the last domino?"

Anyway, I went on bullshitting and telling lies and bragging and complaining like that all the way back to the institution.

Oswald must have left town that night or early the next morning. There was a story on the news a week or so later. There's no telling who's sniffing up his trail by now—the FBI because of illegal dumping, the CIA for the same reason they keep tabs on me, creditors because that's what they do, goons hired by chemical companies with too much at stake, the phantom of his guilt that when only slightly pricked bleeds profusely . . .

17

NOBODY'S ON MY ASS, PROBABLY BECAUSE MY ASS JUST SITS here, at the brink of suburbia. That's the genius of Susan's plan. I'm sure anyone who was looking for me has found me. Maybe they think the electroshock has corrected my condition for now. I don't understand how a person can walk out of a mental institution and not be hunted down, hog tied and hauled back. Maybe some intimidating authorized jerk in an expensive suit intervened in my behalf: leave him alone—we'll keep an eye on him. Maybe the state lackeys couldn't track me this deep into New Jersey. I just sit here and watch TV. Nobody bothers me. It's been about three months, and I haven't seen a single snoop or goon or spook—just fellow suburbanites shoving their snow blowers around and coming and going in their cars. Oh yes, the Buddhist monk has returned —suddenly, just a few days ago. Other than that—nobody.

After Oswald disappeared I planned to leave the institution and ride Amtrak to D.C.—for lack of any other direction. I figured I'd find a place there, work on fixing my throat somehow, become invisible, lay in wait for bigger game and continue deeper into the jungle toward the corpse that won't stop burning. But I hadn't a clue about this corpse— I couldn't figure out how to begin looking for it. I'm sure it was the electroshock that extinguished the corpse, dismembered it and mailed the pieces to the four corners of my brain. Oh well, I thought—I'll pick up some bagels and peanut butter, some brewer's yeast, some cosmic herb tea and begin working some kind of wuzu on my throat and take it from there. It seemed a little sketchy. I wasn't in the groove for any bagels or wuzu, though I knew I would have to do something soon. It all seemed so distant, absurd, unbelievable. I wasn't even sure what had really happened. Maybe the white spot had remained in my throat all along and I had myself believing it was gone. Maybe the electroshock brought it back. Maybe it came back of its own will. Maybe it's cancer and maybe it isn't. I can't tell.

It was the first time Susan had come to the institution. She told me she hadn't come sooner because she wasn't sure I wanted to see her. Plus I'm sure she must have thought I was a total whacko launched on the final burnout.

"Willie told me you're crazy," she said, "but he said that's okay and I should come to see you anyway, so here I am."

I told her I was glad to see her, and I was.

"Good," she said, "because I have it figured out."

I was happy somebody did.

"The best place for a degenerate like you to hide is in the burbs," she told me.

It was a good point, I thought.

"My folks have a place in Bricktown," she said. "City people move there to get away from each other. It's a horrible place to live. It'll be great. My folks share this condo in Florida till June, so we can have the Bricktown house for the entire winter. It won't cost us a cent."

What the hell—I'm flexible, I can adjust—I have nothing better to do. That's what I was saying to myself in the mirror, after one thing had led to another, the winter had passed in Bricktown, spring was upon us and I was there in the mirror, dressing for my wedding, spraying my hair black and applying the makeup—it's the truth.

Susan's parents had arrived the day before. They were at that moment, as I worked the blackface makeup into the backs of my hands, chatting with the Justice of the Peace in the back yard, waiting for Susan and me to emerge from the house and be married. Susan's older sister, brother-in-law and the kid had arrived that morning. They were all out there waiting. I looked them over as I pulled back the curtain to catch the light in the hand mirror to apply the pink lipstick lightly, subtly, on the innermost fringe of the lips. They looked like they would be a nice bunch of in-laws. I hoped they had a sense of humor.

Susan and I had made plans to go to Colorado on a honeymoon, then return to Newark to set up the shoe repair shop. We would live like church mice and be happy. I hadn't been to Colorado in a long time

—that was reason enough to go through with the ceremony. After the dormant winter Dr. Excitement's heart was stretching and yawning as he carefully covered all exposed skin with a thick black layer, following the inner contours of his ears with his index finger and dipping slightly into the nasal openings to eradicate the pinkness there. He slipped on the black wraparound sunglasses and tilted the springish straw-brimmed hat to a rakish angle. In the mirror he watched his black fingers, tipped with pink nail polish, unwrap the big Nicaraguan cigar.

I'd told Susan she was too ugly to kiss good-bye, but actually I'd grown to trust her. Lots of people get married—why not me? Things are getting stranger by the day. And now the Buddhist monk returns, I pick up this journal again, the white spot begins to wane a little—could this be Boy Excitement stirring in my loins, or Girl Excitement, or is it lust, or is it love, or is it spring, or is it another sad whimper of what could be if . . . ? Fuck if I know.

Susan and I stay home a lot. We do a lot of cooking and reading. We drive the pickup to the malls. We have the cable and we watch. I haven't bothered to write in this journal until now—nothing has happened. But the coming of spring has changed things. And now the Buddhist monk, burning again, at the brink of suburbia.

On the first day of spring the exterminator showed up at the door. "We've been contracted to do it every year," he said. "But we don't have termites," I said. "An ounce of prevention," he said, "is worth . . ." "Forget it," I said. "I have to do my job," he said. "I'll break both your legs," I said. Susan's parents called the next day.

I got on the extension. "Can't they come back and spray after we've gone," Susan asked them. "When are you going?" her father asked. That's when she told them about our marriage plans and asked if they could come up for the ceremony. "Married?" her father said. "That's wonderful!" said her mother. "I don't know this guy," said her father, "and he never asked me." "Mr. Jobenzi," I said, "I want to ask you something." "Jobenzi," he said, "where did you get this Jobenzi?" "Willie Sykes told me they used to call you that." "Willie Sykes?" "Yes." "You from Newark?" he asked. "Yes." "I wasn't sure any white people still lived in Newark," he said. Susan's mother asked how Willie was doing. Her father said, "You are white, aren't you?" "Oh, Joe," her mother said. "Does it make a difference?" Susan said. "Oh, Jesus," said Joe. "I want to ask you, Mr. Jobenzi," I said, "for your advice—you see, your daughter wants to marry me, and I was wondering if you have any ideas about how I can get out of this." Susan laughed. "Are you Catholic?" he asked. "Not any more," I said. "Well, that's one way," he said.

They told us the house had to be pumped full of poison every year and the guy would be back and we should let him do his job. The white spot on my throat, despite my new ritualistic remedy, had not gone away since it returned during the electroshock therapy, though it hadn't grown any larger either. The new TV ritual had it arrested, I think—kind of stupified. I wondered how a house full of poison would effect it. I had a notion it might help me snuff the cancer for good, but I was hesitant to take the chance and disturb the stability of the condition—these are touchy areas to enter without a proper sign.

The rebirth of nature and of her insects and other undesirables not welcome in the neighborhood—crabgrass, for example—touched off a mobilization of vigilantes that made Dr. Excitement's heart twitch in its cocoon. I began walking up and down every street of the neighborhood disguised as a suburbanite, scouting the tactics of the vigilantes. I watched them dust their roses and peonies and tulips. They sprayed the lilac and azalea bushes. I talked to a man who was setting poison in a burrow that had once been used by a mole. They covered their lawns with poison to kill things that shouldn't grow there. They dug it into their gardens to protect the root crops and dusted the vegetable sets with it. They sprayed it around during the first barbecues of the season to keep away mosquitos and flies. They sprayed it around in their screened-in porches to kill flies, bees, gnats, mosquitos, spiders, earwigs, caterpillars, fleas. . . . Men came in trucks to spray clouds of it into the trees for I don't know what reason. Then I saw this guy line his sidewalk with herbicide to keep the grass from growing over the neatly trimmed edge. At first repulsed by this spontaneous warfare, eventually I became intrigued by the energetic and cooperative participation in this massive group effort. I could really do without mosquitos. In fact, I've been sitting in the grass late at night after completing the TV ritual, and the mosquitos each night have ruined the peaceful afterglow. And so I began to wonder—if I use some kind of poison in the grass or spray it in the air around me or rub it on my skin, can I keep the pests away?

Then there was a toxic gas leak from a chemical plant in nearby Toms River and during the same week a report on NPR news about wood paneling and picnic tables that emit toxic gas for ten years or more from the insecticide they're treated with. A week later another news report told of a man who died when all his skin blistered and peeled off because he licked his golf ball before he teed off—evidently a reaction to one or more of the several poisons used to keep the green perfect. If a little taste could be this powerful, I couldn't help but wonder about the medicinal uses of poison, and I wasn't sure but I suspected there was a proper sign among this confluence of poison-related events.

As a result I stepped up the intensity of the TV ritual to take advantage of the apparent alignment of vernal forces and I began research into the variety of poisons available at local garden centers. I selected three poisons with three different active ingredients and dissolved them in water. I soaked a Q-tip cotton swab in the solution, reached into the back of my throat and dabbed the white spot several times. This practice has become a supplement to the TV ritual.

I haven't been able to get involved with any hocus-pocus or remedial diets—it seems demented, deranged, ridiculous—and there's no place to dig holes without ruining the lawn. Besides, why mess around with time-consuming rituals—we of little faith—when a little pesticide in the right place might do the trick overnight? I remembered the therapeutic qualities of traveling the Passaic River, easing into the gunky water and giving into the wide towing of the river, sweeping down toward the falls in the chemical bath. But the ease with which I gave myself to the Passaic is not with me now. Yet I must take some course of action.

After Susan goes to bed each night I stay up for a while with the TV. I sort through the program listing or spin through the forty channels until I find the right program. Often I pick a program the way a dabbler in gambling might pick a race horse. Sometimes it's old movies, sometimes late-night talk shows, sometimes HBO movies I've already seen three or four times, sometimes Spanish or Chinese stations, sometimes just the stagnant ID broadcast of the local cable channel. The ritual is simple enough—simple is best, I decided.

I put my mouth against the screen and allow the radiation and electromagnetic waves to bathe my throat. There is no mental process that goes along with this. It depends somewhat on the selection of the program and the specific area of the screen directly in front of my mouth. It's sometimes advantageous to follow a specific person around the screen with my open mouth. At times during the Chinese broadcast I put my mouth to the speaker to bombard my throat with the sounds of the language, then return to the screen and cover the mouth of the person who is speaking with my mouth. I move from person to person, following the dialogue. I turn the brightness knob up all the way for a generalized shotgun effect. I tweak the color knob to get the advantage of varying spectrum intensities. I don't have to get involved in any concentrated effort to twist the mind into some phony faith in contrived metaphysical healing. It's easy, instant, improved. This is the basic approach I've practiced all winter.

But when I sensed the vernal forces aligning and the vigilantes were diligently exterminating insects and weeds, I was moved to spin the channel selector round and round as rapidly as I could to pull all available electromagnetic impulses into the white spot, to overwhelm and terminally confuse the cells that still want my body for their destructive purposes. I have to do something. I can't even find any decent bagels around here.

It was the night before the wedding day. I was spinning the dial at a fantastic speed, holding my mouth wide and pressing my teeth against the glass, when I noticed Joe Bovenzi standing in the doorway watching me. It was hard to explain. It seems as though an integral part of these rituals is getting caught in the act. It's possible that the activation of a primary healing function depends on this—I don't know. If getting caught is what makes them work, its a small price to pay, since the discomfort falls mostly on the person who catches me. I, basically, don't give a fuck—a heck of an attitude, especially when it concerns my father-in-law-to-be, but when Dr. Excitement is working he can't afford to care. New research is always ridiculed—pioneers must maintain a degree of aloofness.

So, relieved as Susan's father was to confirm with his own eyes that I wasn't black, he was nonetheless noticeably ill at ease with my manner of TV viewing. He put his palms to his forehead and grimaced, walked to the glass slider and stared despairingly into the impenetrable confusion of house lights reflecting off the glass. I think then he must have wished that I had turned out to be merely black, for he must have sensed something even more engaging that would entangle his daughter and therefore himself during a time in his life when he wanted nothing more than to be untangled, disengaged and rewarded with retirement the way it's supposed to be. So I refrained from suggesting—though the notion strongly preoccupied me at the time—that if only I had a satellite dish I could surely defeat the cancer once and for all. I don't think he could have taken me seriously and I don't think he could have found it funny either—to expect him to do both was to expect too much. So I didn't tell him anything. I just sat back and watched TV.

After I was dressed and made up for the wedding, all I had to do was walk into the back yard where Susan's family was waiting. All I had to do was take Susan by the hand as she stepped out of the house, be still for a few minutes until it was done, accept heartfelt congratulations, eat from the homemade buffet, get acceptably loaded on champagne and live happily ever after, but as I checked out the wedding outfit I'd pieced together in a thrift shop that morning I knew there was no chance of it all going down that smoothly.

When I finished dressing I was the spitting image of Leroy, that suspicious character who'd made a point of running into me at Oswald's Halloween party so long ago. Leroy's costume was my inspiration. I could hear the throaty fake southside Chicago accent already rumbling in my larynx. Why Leroy had surfaced from the distant confusion of my past, I don't know. Why the Buddhist monk would reassemble himself just to burn himself again, I don't know. Why the membrane of my innermost ear seems to shimmy with a kind of samba that goes on in the lobe of the brain for the blurting out of uncontrolled sentences, I don't know. And I don't know why all the aphids on a rose petal pitched forward every seven seconds in unison. Does it all have something to do with the low-impact microwave antenna that has recently been installed nearby? Are the fillings in my teeth receiving something they shouldn't be—should I be suspicious of their dense absence in x-rays? I don't know.

Surely this family has a sense of humor, Leroy assured himself, adjusting his suspenders to bring the gray-and-black pinstriped pants up snug to the pillow that was tied around his waist beneath the white-on-white shirt. The fake paunch and the elevator shoes redistributed his weight and changed entirely his physical appearance. After all, Leroy thought, if *I* can find humor in this then why not they? Shit, baby—Leroy will make fast friends of his in-laws. He will get away with blowing cigar smoke in their faces because this will be associated with his knack for being utterly direct in his conversation, a trait that in time they will learn to admire. He will flirt openly with Gina, Susan's sister, which she will find flattering because she is too swiftly approaching forty. He will talk politics and sports, which he knows little about, with Mike, his new brother-in-law, and by smoking a lot of Mike's cigarettes, Leroy will make himself indebted to Mike, which will put Mike at ease, even when Leroy turns the discussion to the themes of anarchy in the work of Swinburne. He will not offer one iota of explanation about his costume to Joe Bovenzi—in that way he will not have to think about it himself. He will love the fact that Susan will not be offended by his behavior but will think it is *great.* Leroy thought that he might actually be able to love this woman, Susan, in sickness and in health. For Susan's sake, Leroy would be understanding of these white folks, almost gracious, almost sincere. He would sip whiskey and celebrate with exuberant spirit this union with his new family.

It wasn't going to happen that way as hard as Leroy tried—I knew that much. But I never would have guessed that Susan and I would wind up in the infamous Orchid Lounge that night.

The family's initial reaction to Leroy was somewhat confused. Even Susan didn't know it was me, not until I took her by the hand and led her out the door. From the distance I'm sure the family thought I was a real black man and I'm sure they would have been relieved to find out that I was some black friend of mine who showed up at the last minute, and in a sense I was just that.

When Susan and Leroy stepped through the slider and into the yard, she burst into laughter, stamped her feet, held her side and cried real tears—Susan has a sense of humor. While the family waited anxiously to be let in on the joke, Susan controlled her laughter, tightened her mouth into a thin smile and prepared to go through with the ceremony. Leroy played it deadpan all the way.

Joe Bovenzi stepped forward with his mouth open. Susan motioned him back to his place. We were positioned in front of the Justice, who was not sure what to do except start the show, and so that's what he did. Susan's father mumbled something to his wife. The Justice paused to look at them, then continued with the routine. We hadn't even gotten to the last call for protests or the part when Susan's father gives her away when old Joe Bovenzi piped up. "No, sir," he said, which seemed more like a spastic impulse than a comment on anything. "No, sir," he repeated, affirming the propriety of his spasm. "Not on your life."

I guess it was my life he was talking about—or Leroy's, rather.

"Joe, don't," his wife urged.

"Never you mind *don't*," he said. "This'll be a normal wedding here for my daughter or it won't be a wedding at all. I won't have this, Maureen," he said to his wife.

Maureen knew when to give him the floor.

Susan sighed heavily. "Shit."

"Let's just eat the food then," Leroy said in his hoarse Negroid voice.

Joe stomped off toward the house. He couldn't take a joke.

Maureen came over to embrace Susan.

"It's okay, Mom," Susan said, "it's okay."

"He takes it seriously," Maureen said to me.

"Of course," I said understandingly. I almost felt remorse for a second, but it wasn't going to be that clear-cut for me. It wasn't confusion I was feeling, though it could have passed for confusion. It felt more like an airy perch at the opposite end of the spectrum, like I was looking back at confusion, from nowhere. I almost laughed, only to encourage a sense of humor in the gathering. I wanted to allow something to be funny, but how would I know when to stop laughing? At the garter toss? And then, where to begin again? On cue? During the commercial? And where does this laughter, even one laugh, come from? From too much food? From business as usual? I just shrugged at Maureen.

Susan held me at the elbow. "Poor Daddy. He can't handle it."

"I'm sure you meant it as a joke," Maureen said to me, "but Joe wanted a church wedding and all. He's been upset. Susan is his . . ." She sighed heavily too.

"I'll go talk to him," I said, but *my* voice, coming from behind Leroy, sounded ridiculous to me. I didn't like the oscillation. I fired up the cigar to help smoke-screen any ambivalence, gathered the necessary gravel into my throat and bopped toward the house. Leroy found Joe at the kitchen sink.

"Hey, Joe, man," Leroy said.

Joe just looked out the window.

"Jobenzi, I don't think things are so serious—I mean, things are serious enough without adding unnecessary gravity. Let's lighten up, have a cigar." I held a cigar out to him. "It's Nicaraguan—the good stuff. Let's have a whiskey."

"I don't think this is a laughing matter," Joe said, refusing to look at Leroy, "and I don't think it will be funny after cigars and whiskey." He tried then to look at Leroy but he couldn't.

"Are you kidding?" Leroy questioned. "We could make it very funny —trust me. Anyway, we could try. We have all day, lots of whiskey, four cigars . . ."

"*You* have all day. I'm leaving."

"Ah, Joe, come on—let's get drunk and talk loud."

"What you do is your business. I'm done with it. That's the way I feel. What Susan does is her business."

He was more emotional than Leroy had expected. Must be the Italian blood, Leroy thought.

"You make a mockery of this holy sacrament," Joe continued, "and I'm supposed to . . . You can't even get married in the church! Out here in the shitty yard like a couple of . . . For what reason? Never mind, mister. Don't involve me in any of what you do. I'm done with it. I'm done with trying to understand Susan's . . . behavior. I've bent over backwards trying to . . ."

Susan stepped in through the slider in the dining room.

Joe put his hands in his pockets. Now *he* was sighing.

"Daddy," Susan said, "we don't mean to—"

"Listen, hon," he interrupted, "you do what you have to do—you have my blessing—but I've had it with this. This whole thing has been a heartbreak for me." He presented his open palm to Leroy, pointed to his little finger and said, "One, you don't have a job." Then, grabbing his ring finger, "You're living in my house." Pointing to his middle finger, "You have no skills." Index finger to index finger, "You don't even have a family to be here with you at your wedding." Holding his thumb, "You don't have a church." Holding his whole hand like a ham steak, "You don't really care if you get married or not." Pointing to the center of his left palm, "You have no pride in yourself." Two palms up, "Or anything else!" Both palms rising to his forehead.

How could I argue?"

"You want to take my daughter and give nothing in return. And you say this isn't *serious!* And I don't understand *this!*" He gestured at

Leroy's outfit. "And you have some *strange* habits with the TV at night." He bowed his head after that one.

There was a small heavy silence.

"What do you mean by that?" Susan asked. She looked from him to Leroy.

"I won't have anything to do with this marriage," he said finally.

Leroy liked the guy. He thought Joe would make a good father-in-law. Maybe Joe could get Dr. Excitement in with the mob, Leroy thought.

"I can appreciate how you feel," Leroy said, "but that doesn't say much for your sense of humor . . ." The last note of the sentence lilted upward, indicating more to come, and Leroy hesitated as if to think about what was to follow, but he didn't think about it at all. Instead the lobe for the blurting-out of uncontrolled sentences took over—"And it doesn't make you any less of a racist."

"A racist!" Joe shook his head as if to clear it. "This guy thinks he's really a shine!" He walked around the kitchen holding his head.

"Well," Leroy said, "it's white enough in this neighborhood to make a guy think he's black even if he isn't."

Joe walked to the table in the dining room and poured himself a drink. "A racist, he says! Good Lord in Heaven! Me! Joe Bovenzi! A racist! I fixed their shoes! I smelled the sweat of their feet all day! I shared the gin mills and parks with them! I sat next to them in church! Call me a racist! If it wasn't for Tony Imperiale I would have *lived* next to them!"

Leroy followed Joe to the table and poured himself a drink.

Maureen came in, took one look at Joe and walked him into the living room.

"He thinks he's a shine!" he said to Maureen.

Then the rest of the family came in and had a drink. After a while we got into the food. Leroy ate in the kitchen and Joe ate in the living room. It was when Leroy realized that he didn't have to chew either the quiche Lorraine or the manicotti before he swallowed that he decided to go to the Orchid Lounge. He hadn't even thought about the Orchid Lounge in over fifteen years.

"Where're you going?" Susan asked.

"Asbury Park."

"Why?"

"To think this over," he said, lying.

"I'll go with you."

"Love to have you," telling the truth.

She found the keys to the pickup, kissed her mom and dad and told them they'd talk later, took Leroy by the arm, walked him to the pickup, jumped into the driver's seat and they headed for Route 34. "You look great," she said.

Springwood Ave was as black as it always was, even blacker. It was Saturday night, and everybody was out on the street corners. The Orchid Lounge was jumping.

"Let's have a drink, Susan."

"You're kidding," Susan said. "You're kidding, right?"

"No," Leroy said. "Let's go in."

"I don't want to."

"I've *always* wanted to—ever since I used to come to Springwood Ave to go shoplifting for the latest styles."

"It's intruding. It's asking for trouble. It's intimidation. It's too scary. I don't even want to be driving on this street. If I had known you would . . ."

"I'm going into the Orchid Lounge and have a George Dickel."

"You're not."

"I am."

The men standing around the front door followed Leroy and his white friend into the bar. The news of their arrival traveled through the place in seconds. There were two unoccupied stools, but a man was seated between them.

"Would you mind moving over one so we can sit together?" Leroy asked the man.

The man stared for a moment, looked at the barkeep, who had paralleled Leroy and Susan along the bar, then got up and seated himself on the next stool.

"Thanks," Leroy said.

Susan thanked him too.

A crowd has a way of selecting people to deal with extraordinary events—responsibility is delegated with a minimum of talk. The delegation of four approached Leroy and Susan. Body size must have something to do with this selection process.

Dr. Excitement thought there might be trouble, but he couldn't tell for sure. The way he had it figured, the four men had every right to knock him on his ass, but he knew that wouldn't be easy. On the other hand, Leroy felt he had every right to be there in that public bar—in fact, it seemed vaguely like a sense of mission he was feeling, a spiritual trial that had to be confronted before he could progress any further on his vision quest, though he wasn't aware of the pursuit of any vision. Maybe Dr. Excitement is just plain crazy, Leroy thought.

He felt considerably less crazy on the way home from the Orchid Lounge that night, if that's any indication that he was more crazy as he sat there hoping words would come out of his mouth that would initiate a congenial conversation with the delegation of four, so they could all have a drink or two and laugh about everything at once and mean it, not thinking at all about when to stop or start this laughter.

"Leroy escaped from Marlboro mental hospital," Susan told the four men and the barkeep and most of the people in the bar—the place had become that hushed.

"It's the truth," Leroy said.

One of the four lifted Leroy's hat and parted his dyed hair. "It's a honky awright," he announced.

A man across the room started laughing heartily. A few others followed with laughter. The four-man delegation just stared down like a Negroid Mount Rushmore. The guy in the middle had a fist like a ham, Leroy noticed as he wondered how he would protect himself and Susan from harm. He quickly decided to trust reflex behavior.

"Besides that," Susan said, "he's an asshole—he really is. We were supposed to get married today, and he showed up dressed like this." She offered Leroy up as proof of his own weirdness.

He must have been a fairly convincing illustration. Two of the four men looked at each other in disbelief. The other two stretched their necks forward as though a closer look might enable them to see through Leroy's wraparound shades.

"He came to your wedding dressed like *this?*" the man on the right flank asked.

"Swear to God," Susan said, but she didn't have to swear—she is all the time utterly believable for some reason. "Is he fucked-up or what?"

"Why are you marrying some nut from Marlboro?" the biggest one asked.

"He's okay if you get to know him," she said.

"Why'd they put him in Marlboro?" the same guy asked.

"Because he painted himself orange and decided to take a swim in the Passaic River. They were afraid he'd go over the falls so they went after him in a boat. But he climbed into a sewer pipe and showed up later in downtown Paterson causing a traffic jam. He was heading for the river again when he passed out."

"This is some weird shit, man," the right flank said.

"I agree," Susan said. "How do you think I feel sitting here? I tried to talk him out of coming in here. I didn't want any part of it. I thought it would be potentially offensive to you people."

"It's potentially bullshit," the guy on the left flank said. "That's what it is. Why do you hang out with this dude? Why'd you come in here with him if you didn't want to? You do everything he says?"

"I knew better," she said, "but I did it anyway."

That sounded familiar. Leroy laughed.

"I couldn't let him come in here alone," Susan said. "Look at the size of you guys."

A woman sitting at the bar piped up. "Because she loves her man," she said, "that's why. What's *he* got to say for himself?"

"I was dying of boredom," Leroy said, "and I didn't know it. We've been living in the burbs. It's hell. It fools you—you think you like it. Next thing I know I'll have car payments. Then a man will appear at the door and ask if I'm commuting yet. He'll set me up with a job sixty miles away. The vernal forces are aligned like they haven't been in years. I need to take advantage of this. It's important to me. It's the first sign I've seen. And I've always wanted to come in here. I used to steal clothes down at Fish's when I was in high school and walk past here all the time. I remembered there was always a lot of laughing going on in here."

"This guy ain't so crazy," the woman at the bar said, "or is he?"

"I'd buy you all a drink," Leroy announced, "but there're too many of you."

"So did you get married?" the barkeep asked.

"Nah," Leroy said, "the old man got emotional."

"I'll buy you both a drink for almost getting married," the barkeep said. "Then you be on your way before we get trouble in here. We can't afford no more trouble in here."

We both had a George Dickel. Susan started talking to the woman who'd piped up, almost yelling across the distance of five men at the bar. After a few minutes of that she walked over to the woman and they started yakking. When Susan starts yakking she can really yak. Leroy doesn't do poorly himself—he beat his gums with the brothers, telling mostly the truth, though they thought he was crazy and told him so, and that was what got Leroy laughing.

Five or six or seven or eight, maybe nine drinks later it was closing time. Goodbyes were said and Leroy and Susan climbed into the pickup and drove back to Bricktown. Joe and Maureen had taken the big bed. Gina and Mike and the kid were sacked out on the living room floor. Leroy and Susan stumbled into the spare bedroom, giggling and walking into things. They climbed into the single bed and called it a day.

I guess it was two days later. Susan's family had left. There had been no wedding. Susan and I were driving back from the supermarket. It was raining again. The traffic was vicious.

"Buckle up," Susan said.

I buckled the seat belt, folded my hands in my lap, watched the malls going by. I'd calmed down some. It was that morning I'd discovered that the white spot was a bit smaller. I was feeling like myself again, I think —less preoccupied with the TV ritual, less convinced of the confluence of vernal forces, teetering on the brink of regret over what Leroy had done, scheming to make a quick piece of change so I could send Joe and Maureen the price of the plane fare they'd spent getting here and back to the condo.

"What's the matter?" Susan asked. "You're so quiet."

"Nothing." I didn't want to go back to the house, though I could think of no other place to go. "I'm confused."

Susan was silent for the duration of the red light. As she drove forward on the green she said, "Want to take a walk on the beach? It's such a lovely day."

"Okay."

"Let's drop off the groceries and get some rain gear."

By the time we got home we didn't feel like driving anymore. It was raining harder. We made dinner and ate. We hadn't spoken much. Susan had tried to get a conversation going, but it was no use. After dinner I tried to read but I couldn't. I just sat in the chair doing nothing.

After an hour of that Susan said there was a movie on TV and asked if I would watch it with her, make fun of it and scream at the commercials. I'd just seen something move in the dark of the yard. I went to the slider and cupped my hands to the glass to see out.

Susan asked again if I wanted to watch the movie with her. I told her I did. She switched the TV on and turned the channel selector. I saw the flames take shape in the yard—they were reaching upward, bright yellow and velvety—then the Buddhist monk in a saffron robe seated in the flames.

"This is it," Susan said.

The monk fell forward, the darkness shimmering around him.

From the corner of my eye I saw Susan turn her head from the TV to watch me exit through the slider.

I stood where the monk had been, looked up at the sky. Escaped headlights up there. One star veiled behind the overcast. I sat cross-legged in the grass. At my right knee, in the dim light from the windows, the serrated leaves of a young dandelion, *taraxacum officinale*.

Susan stood behind me and put both hands on my head. "Let's get out of here," she said, "tomorrow."

Secretly in the dark there I took the dandelion into myself, preserved it in rages in the dura mater, as I take it into this journal now.

I rubbed the wooden bowl with bruised garlic, tossed the tender leaves with vinaigrette, took them into my blood, down past *dent-de-lion*, past Medieval Latin *dens leonis*, "lion's tooth". I took the plant into the blood beyond the naming of things, and there I buried it in the dirt with ten glasses of water.

A few blocks away—maybe a few miles—there must be a person who doesn't give a rat's ass about the perfection of lawns. A renter, maybe, with no vested interest in the lawn—maybe a freeloader like me, living off the excess, serving as a bad example. *That* person will never get anywhere.

And the dandelions that thrive in this person's yard will go to seed without much work. A little girl wanders into the yard, picks the seeded dandelion, blows the sails free with ease. Next spring a lurid yellow beauty begins to spread like weeds, small flames of defiance in the neighbor's lawn, little Monkey leaves with lion's teeth, weeds of imagining, affirmative germs, wild flowers, uncultivated tough and tender things, so much depending on their stubbornness.